The Duchess of Chocolate

Rare Confectionery Book One

SYDNEY JANE BAILY

cat whisker press
Massachusetts

First Paperback Edition
ISBN 978-1-938732-32-4

Published by **cat whisker press**
Imprint of JAMES-YORK PRESS

Cover: Wicked Smart Designs
In conjunction with Philip Ré
Book Design: Cat Whisker Studio
Editor: EDH Professionals

Dedicated to all those who have a passion for chocolate.
(And to those who don't, I can only say, I'm sorry!)

OTHER WORKS
by
SYDNEY JANE BAILY

The RAKES ON THE RUN Series

Last Dance in London
Pursued in Paris
Banished to Brighton
Gretna Green by Sunset

The RARE CONFECTIONERY Series

The Duchess of Chocolate
The Toffee Heiress
My Lady Marzipan

The DEFIANT HEARTS Series

An Improper Situation
An Irresistible Temptation
An Inescapable Attraction
An Inconceivable Deception
An Intriguing Proposition
An Impassioned Redemption

The BEASTLY LORDS Series

Lord Despair
Lord Anguish
Lord Vile
Lord Darkness
Lord Misery
Lord Wrath
Eleanor

PRESENTING LADY GUS

A Georgian-Era Novella

ACKNOWLEDGMENTS

I am beyond grateful to strangers who answered my pesky emails regarding chocolate. First, John O'Keefe, who has been in the chocolate business for 40 years working for the greats, including Nestlé and Cargill. He kindly obtained and sent to me a large sample of Broc chocolate, the closest current recipe to Daniel Peter and Henri Nestlé's original 19th-century milk chocolate. John has shared so much of his knowledge with me, making this a far better book.

Secondly, big thanks go to Tim Hamilton, who works for the Black Country Living Museum in Dudley, England. This 26-acre, open-air museum offers a glimpse into 300 years of history, and Tim had valuable information on early sweet shops and the practices of confectioners in the 1870s.

Lastly, I sent a message in my halting French to Vevey, Switzerland, and I heard back from Albert Pfiffner, who handles the historic archives for Nestlé. He promptly answered my last-minute question about the availability of bulk chocolate in Victorian London from the historic Swiss Cailler chocolate factory.

To all these experts, again, I offer my deepest thanks.

CHAPTER ONE

London, 1877

The female whom Henry sought was practically prancing along New Bond Street, dressed in a plum-colored gown and a stylish hat upon her head with the identifying sapphire blue feather he'd been told to look for. He liked her on sight. If she'd been a dour, gray-clad woman, he might have questioned her ability to create the sweet magic of which he'd heard.

Henry tapped upon the ceiling of the carriage, and his driver pulled over. Leaning out the window, he called her name with a slight query to his voice although he had no doubt it was she.

"Miss Rare-Foure?"

He waited for her to turn and respond. After all, he didn't want to be accused of accosting the wrong female. Actually, he didn't want to be accused of accosting any female when it came right down to it. He hoped after they'd spoken, she wouldn't be accusing him of anything except a pleasant arrangement.

He smirked to himself. In any case, no one accused a duke of being indecorous. He could say that with all the smug certainty in the world for it was true.

The woman in the plum-hued dress stopped, barely able to hold her own against the tide of passersby, and stared directly at him—mahogany-colored eyes in creamy skin, dark hair escaping from under her feathered hat, and a hesitant, questioning expression.

Since she was carrying parcels restricting her movements, she couldn't even raise a hand to swipe the tendril of hair that crossed her face as she turned.

"Who wishes to know?"

With that saucy statement, she seemed to acknowledge her identity, and then her gaze darted over the coat of arms on his carriage, and he watched her eyes widen.

Not awaiting his footman, he popped open the door and stepped out.

"*I do.*" Henry offered her a shallow bow, a greeting she tried to return in the form of a deep curtsey befitting his status, but she could hardly manage with her packages.

She ought to have a servant assisting her, he thought, a little irked that she was juggling so many items.

Before the chocolate-maker could drop any of them, he reached out and took the bag perched atop a box that she held with both hands.

"Oh," she gave a little yelp of surprise, and then said, "Much obliged, my lord."

He started slightly. No one had called him anything other than "Your Grace" since his father passed away, transforming Henry into the Duke of Pelham.

"Will you enter my carriage for a private *tête-a-tête*? I mean, with your maid, obviously." He looked past her for any such person.

"Oh," she said again in a slightly different tone, her rich brown eyes looking directly into his. "That's redundant, my lord."

"I beg your pardon?" *What was the woman on about?*

"A *tête-a-tête* is, by nature, a private discussion, and thus, there is no need—"

"I take your point," he said, not keen on being corrected by her. "I must tell you, I do not have a chaperone inside," he admitted, gesturing to his carriage. "Do you have a companion with you?"

"No," she said, glancing past him to where his coachman and footman awaited. "Nevertheless, I shall enter your carriage for two reasons. One, you are a well-known gentleman with a long-standing, spotless reputation, and two, because your coat of arms is plain to see, so obviously you cannot be engaged in anything remotely nefarious. We shall, of course, leave the shades up and the windows down. Agreed?"

"Yes, naturally." He watched her take a breath. She was a whirlwind, but hopefully not a chatterbox. He didn't have all day.

"And if you can drop me at Rare Confectionery after our discussion," she added, "I will greatly appreciate it, as that is my destination."

"I can get you there in a jiffy. In fact, I just came from your shop," he admitted, handing her bag to the footman, before relieving her of the rest of her parcels, which he also dispatched, so he could assist her personally into his spacious coach.

"That's how I knew what you were wearing and where to find you," he said to the backside of her pleated bustle.

"Very clever of you, my lord," she said, as he clambered up behind her and closed the door.

Tidily done, he thought.

"My purchases?" she added, glancing out the window.

"John will hold them safely until we arrive at your destination."

She nodded, folded her gloved hands—also plum-colored—in her lap and waited.

As the carriage got under way, maneuvering around the other carriages and the blasted omnibuses that were a blight upon the streets, he took her measure, and two words came to mind, *intelligent* and *capable*, simply by her manner and the interested look upon her face.

He also thought another word, *beautiful*, but that was not important to him, so he dismissed it.

Henry knew her reputation as a chocolate-maker—more than that, as a veritable artist of chocolate, a Michelangelo of the cacao bean, as it were.

"I have heard what you are doing in your little shop. I've been told you have a magical way of making chocolate confectionery so delicious, one cannot help but consume it, eyes closed, raving over the quality, under an enchantment of ecstasy. Very impressive."

Her high cheekbones blushed with a pretty shade of rose. "Thank you, my lord. Have *you* tasted my confectionery?"

"Sadly, no, not yet. But I hope to remedy that soon. It is the reason I wish to speak with you. For you see, Miss Rare-Foure, I am in need of a wife."

AMITY SHUT HER MOUTH so quickly, her teeth clacked together. She was sure they made a loud sound, but that might have been only in her head. In any case, her ears were filled with the beat of her own thumping heart.

A wife, she thought. *The Duke of Pelham was speaking to her about needing a wife!*

"Are you indeed?" she asked when she could finally make a calm and sensible response. Inside, she was screaming *a duke, a duke, a duke!*

Good lord! She was riding in a ducal carriage with not just any duke, either—*although any duke was impressive enough*—but *the* Duke of Pelham, famous for his massive fortune, his lovely London home on St. James's Place, his good looks, which were in evidence that very moment, and his comely smile, which she had yet to see, among other things.

Actually, she didn't know anything else about him except that he had a sister who was recently married and, thus, also in the papers. *What did he like for breakfast? Did he like to read? Was he kind or cruel, of good humor or ill-tempered?* None of that was mentioned in the gossip rags she enjoyed with her morning cup of hot chocolate.

The duke's carriage was regally plush. The soft and smooth leather seat was firm beneath her, promising a comfortable ride even for a long journey. The "shades" she'd mentioned keeping open turned out to be curtains of a thick brocade, shot through with gold thread. And the interior smelled heavenly of some enticing manly *eau de toilette.*

With her nose being nearly as good as her palate, Amity tried to pick out all the individual scents—orris and bergamot, cedarwood, musk, sandalwood and more, even something floral, perhaps jasmine. Whatever it was, the duke's rich fragrance seemed to wrap her in elegant cashmere and tanned leather, making her want to close her eyes and dream of something special upon the horizon. And to desire it!

Oh dear, her thoughts were flitting wildly. They occasionally received dignitaries and titled people in the shop, and thus she and her sisters had learned a little bit about keeping one's head and maintaining a calm, professional behavior when nobility suddenly appeared. More often than not, however, their servants came in.

She certainly had not anticipated the praise regarding her chocolate creations would engender a marriage proposal from a duke. Besides, she had a suitor—if only she could recall his name or his face at that instant.

"And when I cast my net over London, one lady came to mind," the duke continued, his gaze unwavering.

One lady came to mind? Amity echoed silently. *Herself!* And he sounded serious.

"Because you love chocolate?" she asked. *Why else would he choose her?*

He chuckled, and the sound made her shiver. *How strange.* She usually only had that exciting response when tasting a new strain of cacao bean or creating a brand-new chocolate sweet.

"I am not utterly enamored with it, no," he said. "I have drunk my fair share like everyone else, but sometimes, it is oily, even slimy, or has a disagreeable aftertaste."

Poor man! Amity shook her head. No one should suffer with inferior chocolate. The world had been made a better place, as far as she was concerned, when Dutch processed cocoa had been brought to England.

"Possibly, you have been drinking impure cocoa, my lord, with animal fat and potato flour. I assure you there is nothing more pleasant and delicious than a cup of Cadbury's Cocoa Essence."

"What I have eaten has been no better," he protested. "Rather grainy, in fact. A little bitter and coarse."

"Fry's Chocolat Delicious à Manger," she muttered, thinking of that company's early solid chocolate bar. "Quite unpleasant by today's standards," she added. Chocolate had come so far since then. Apparently, the duke had not yet enjoyed the best.

He nodded. "I understand *you* can change my mind. I believe you can work wonders with your confectionery and make anyone say yes to anything—that's what I was told. That's what I'm counting on."

Lately, she had been receiving rave reviews from all quarters, and even the palace had ordered a pound of her cleverly crafted chocolate squares, some infused with orange and some with raspberry liqueur.

Reaching for her reticule, which dangled from her wrist, Amity set it on her lap and opened the drawstring closure. Drawing out a very small, slightly crumpled paper bag, she held it out for him.

"Go ahead, my lord. Try a piece."

He stared at the white sack with "Rare Confectionery" stamped upon it in blue ink. "You carry chocolate with you?"

"Almost always. Forgive the appearance. They might be a little squashed, but children seem to know who I am wherever I go around Mayfair, and they expect me to have something for them to sample, the same way they get to have a taste in the shop."

He opened the top of the sack and peered inside.

"There should be three or four left, my lord. Assorted, so I cannot guarantee which flavor, but that's half the fun, don't you think?"

Glancing at her briefly, he looked again into the bag. "It is rather amusing," he agreed, sounding surprised.

For her part, she loved nothing more than eating chocolate, except for making it, which she did almost daily in the back room of their lovely shop with her sisters nearby and her mother often at the counter.

"If you don't care for these, and I don't have a confection to your liking in our shop, then I can create one," she insisted.

For the duke, her new husband, she would create a special line. The *Pelham*, smooth and creamy, with a hint of—

"It seems we are thinking in a likeminded way, Miss Rare-Foure. I do want a specially created confection. You see, I wish to be married in the not-too-distant future. Everything else is going well in my life, so it's time. What do you say, Miss Rare-Foure? Will you help me with my marital goal? Please say yes."

He was leaning forward so earnestly, making her heart beat a quick tattoo in her chest.

"My lord!" she exclaimed.

"Yes?" he queried.

"No, I meant the other . . . that is . . . ." She paused and pointed skyward. "Merely an expression, you know. Good lord, dear lord, oh, my lord!"

"Ah, yes, I see," he agreed, looking at her as if she were a little touched in the head.

Amity needed to get this discussion back onto the marriage path before the duke opened the carriage door and sent her flying along with her confectionery supplies. Because while it was unusual amongst her class to be proposed to by a man she didn't know, it was far more commonplace in the nobility. Perhaps to him, this abruptness was entirely normal. Moreover, he seemed, at first, second, and third glance and after a few minutes of discussion, to be someone extremely likable. His tone wasn't nasally, nor was it harsh. His manner was friendly and agreeable. His brown hair was thick and a little wavy. And his eyes—a vivid shade of green—were clear, not red with lack of sleep or too much drink. Beyond that, he was a duke!

On the other hand, it was highly unlikely she could continue as a chocolatier if she were to become a duchess.

And just like that, her fantasy melted away. Nothing was more important to her than being with her family at Rare Confectionery and making chocolate.

"How long would it take?" he asked, breaking into her see-sawing thoughts.

Amity frowned. Many in the upper class were engaged for a year to prove there had not been a compromising indiscretion causing a rush to the altar. It also allowed the couple time to become familiar before marriage, since they usually didn't know one another at the time of engagement any more than she knew the duke. In this case, a year or a day made no matter.

"I'm sorry, my lord. I cannot do it." Dreaming of marrying him was a silly notion, yet it had been impossible not to muse upon his exciting request. After all, he was a larger-than-life duke.

"Are you so very busy at your shop? Can you not create something for me in a fortnight? I am having a large party in two weeks, and I want it revealed then."

An engagement revealed in two weeks? Suddenly, Amity had an inkling she'd got the wrong end of the walking stick.

The duke nodded, looking satisfied. "I would be happy to come to your shop and assist by way of sampling or telling you my thoughts on the perfect confection."

He wanted to come to her shop?

"I want something original, never hitherto tasted," he continued. "And in two weeks, we shall reveal the chocolate at my party and entice the lady in question."

She was beginning to realize she had made a rather large and erroneous assumption. Not usually considered a ninny, Amity had to put the blame on being swept into a carriage and "seemingly" propositioned by a duke. There could be no other explanation for allowing her fanciful thoughts to run away with her.

"Yes," Amity changed her answer, thinking of the great benefit a duke's patronage would mean for her family's store. "I have time to create a chocolate for you. Go ahead and taste, my lord," she insisted, reminding him he still held the bag of chocolates.

Watching him take one out at random, Amity had never hoped a customer enjoyed her confection more than at that moment. His eyes remained locked on her gaze as he popped the entire square in. She liked that, how he jumped right in.

"Not a nibble or a bite," she murmured.

He closed his eyes. She knew the chocolate was melting quickly upon his tongue, allowing all its sweet and subtle flavor to release.

"Mm," he said, rather like a low moan that made her shiver.

In quick succession, he ate the rest. She counted three more. Each time, as soon as the confection was in his mouth, he closed his eyes and savored the taste. Like a true connoisseur. The way her mother did with wine she particularly liked or her father with his favorite cigar.

When the duke finished, he opened his eyes and grinned at her. *Ah, there was that famous smile, just as handsome as she'd heard. With dimples to boot!*

She shook her head, cleared it, and recalled her professional demeanor as a chocolatier. "What do you wish, my lord? Chocolates in the shape of swans is rather romantic? Perhaps chocolates with sweet cream centers or with exotic nuts? Or maybe heart-shaped chocolates to woo your lady with her sweet tooth?"

As he nodded at her suggestions, any remaining tendrils of fantasy dissipated from Amity's brain.

"Perhaps not shaped like a heart," he said. "That seems too obvious. She does like sweet things, however."

"Hopefully, your lady still has teeth in her head," Amity added, taking the empty bag from his fingers and crumpling it before stuffing it back into her reticule. "Although at the rate our fellow countrymen and women are consuming sugar, it's a wonder any of us have anything but gaps in our gums and toothaches in the remaining teeth we have left."

He frowned. "Miss Rare-Foure, you started out making my mouth water and ended by making me feel a little sickened. Do you really think sugar is ruining our nation's teeth?"

She shrugged slightly. "When it was used by only the very wealthy, from the late sixteen hundreds—to make those lovely sculptural table displays, for instance—right up until a few decades ago, diseases of the teeth seemed to be worse in the nobility and the royalty, including blackened teeth, abscesses, and loss of choppers altogether. Find a farmer eating his meat and potatoes, and I'll show you a man with more good teeth than King Louis of France."

The duke stared at her, then blinked.

"And how about now?" he asked. "I'm almost afraid to ask."

"Now, twenty years since the prices plummeted and everyone started eating more sugar—over thirty-five pounds per person in a year—don't you think you see more toothless people than when you were a child?" She doubted he could disagree.

"I . . . I . . . ," the duke trailed off.

Amity bit her lip. She *was* a ninny! Since he wasn't around the masses, he would hardly be seeing more or fewer toothless people.

"Smile for me," he commanded unexpectedly.

She couldn't help rolling her eyes. He might be nobility, but she wasn't a horse he was determining whether to buy. Nevertheless, since it was all in good fun, she gave him a broad smile.

"Perfect white teeth," he pronounced. "Yet you must spend a great deal of time tasting your creations. Do you brush daily?"

"Of course. And I have a highly effective tooth powder recipe with peppermint oil." She leaned forward. "Come closer."

Looking startled but intrigued, the duke did as she suggested.

"Hah," she huffed her breath directly upon him. "Well?"

"Fresh and minty, I must say."

She sat back with a delicate lift of her shoulder. "What did I tell you?" Then, before she thought, Amity added, "Smile for me, my lord."

She might have gone too far, but luckily, the duke didn't look affronted. Instead, he produced an attractive grin that showed not only his dimples but his straight teeth—and a whole set of them, too. Amity decided not to point out he had a small piece of almond stuck between two of them from one of her chocolates. If he did brush daily, he would discover it soon enough.

"Satisfied?" he asked, his attractive green eyes locked on hers, causing her stomach to twinge oddly.

She nodded.

"I won't breathe in your face if you don't mind," he said, "but I can assure you I use the finest tooth powders."

"I have no doubt, my lord."

He looked as if he was going to say one thing but changed his mind and said another. "How do you know so much about sugar?"

"My father made his fortune in the sugar market, my lord."

"I see. Is that why your family got into the confectionery business?"

"Yes, my lord. My mother started Rare Confectionery when she and my father first were married."

"You come from enterprising stock, it seems. And thus, back to business, Miss Rare-Foure. I believe we have an agreement, yes? Before a fortnight is out, you will create a chocolate delicacy specifically for my party, and we shall name it for the woman I hope to marry."

Why hadn't he said that in the first place? She hadn't given him the chance, she supposed—instead jumping to an unfortunate assumption that had sent her on an emotional ride along with the carriage ride. Good thing she did have a suitor in the back pot, as it were. Jeremy Cole was definitely the name she had momentarily forgotten, and his affable expression swam in front of her eyes framed by sandy brown hair. A perfectly good man.

"The name, my lord?"

"Lady Madeleine—"

"Brayson," she guessed.

"Yes. How remarkable!"

"No, not really." Amity ought to have known instantly without going on her outrageous journey of delusion. "Everyone who lives within a stone's throw of Mayfair has heard how Lady Madeleine has taken the Season and the *bon ton* by storm. Why wouldn't you want her?"

If rumors were true, she was the most beautiful creature to grace London's ballrooms in a donkey's age. Amity had never seen her, but not because her family didn't have the money for a ball. In truth, she didn't care for the whole debutante and match-making notion of a Season. It seemed passé and a little degrading.

The carriage came to a halt, and she realized they must be in front of her own shop.

"I hate to tell you this, my lord, but there is already a famous sweet treat named *the Madeleine*, some call it a small cake, some a soft biscuit. Anyway, it's a cakelike treat baked in a dainty shell-shaped mold. Everyone in the bakery or patisserie world has heard of them already."

He made a face of dissatisfaction, while remaining as handsome-looking as ever. She hated to disappoint him.

"Perhaps her last name, my lord. We could call it a *Brayson*."

"Not as pretty sounding as a *Madeleine*," he protested.

She shrugged. "The *Maddie*, perhaps?"

He winced slightly. "I shall think on it, and we shall name it later."

Nodding to the waiting footman who peered discreetly through the coach window, the duke waited while the man opened the door, let down the steps, and assisted her onto the pavement.

Keenly aware when the duke alighted directly behind her, Amity turned to face her new patron.

"John will help you inside with your packages," the duke insisted as his footman gathered her belongings from the storage box. "I shan't go inside your shop again as I created a bit of mayhem last time."

Amity groaned inside her head, imagining how her mother and sisters might have behaved.

"Good day, my lord. I will not let you down." *A ridiculous thing to say*, she chided herself, as she curtsied. She wasn't a diplomat stopping a foreign war. Merely a chocolatier developing a confection for an over-indulgent man to give to the beautiful woman on whom he'd set his sights.

Undoubtedly, her creation would win over the fair Lady Madeleine to any proposal the Duke of Pelham made during the party or after.

Even more assuredly, Lady Madeleine did not need chocolate to persuade her to marry the duke.

"Good day, Miss Rare-Foure. A pleasure to meet you."

Turning away, she sighed at such handsomeness and went inside with the duke's footman trailing behind. And, as expected, all hell broke loose.

CHAPTER TWO

Like King Louis XV, who prepared his own hot chocolate in the kitchens of his private apartments in the palace, Amity was considered by her family to be the greatest lover of this creamy, delicious beverage. No matter the season, no matter the weather, she started her day like a French royal with a cup of steaming, milky, liquid chocolate. Close at hand, her slender white and gold chocolate pot was perched delicately on three feet upon the table.

Depending on her mood, she added aromatic vanilla beans to the boiling milk, ground cloves, or cinnamon. It was often enough to keep her fueled like a workhorse until the early afternoon.

Sometimes, when in a hurry, she used Cadbury's pure Cocoa Essence, which she found superior to any of the other cocoas that were on the market. Apparently, the Duke of Pelham had not been so fortunate as to discover it. In any case, above all, she preferred her own homemade concoction of shaved Swiss chocolate and milk.

After yesterday's excitement, the next morning, Amity thought she might need a dash of vanilla bean and some extra sugar—and risk the tooth decay!

As soon as she had stepped from the duke's coach into her family's shop the previous afternoon, she'd been assailed.

"Amity, you'll never guess who stopped in," her mother crowed to her from behind the counter, her usual place, with a clean apron pinned over her day gown. "Fine-looking as the new day and tall and eyes a shade of—"

"Mother!" This from Beatrice, the next younger of Amity's two sisters, for they were a family blessed by females, which was a joke among them for her father had said he couldn't believe he'd had another blessing and then another.

Beatrice, with the sole blue eyes in the family, was looking past Amity to the footman wearing the ducal livery.

"Do not interrupt," their mother said.

"Mother," Beatrice tried again, wanting to stop her from saying anything more embarrassing until after the footman left.

"*Ooohhhh,*" squealed Charlotte, the baby of the family at seventeen and who'd just come in from the back room carrying a tray of newly sculpted marzipan. "Has the dishy, dashing duke returned? Or only his servant?"

Amity sighed. She could picture the pandemonium she had missed when the Duke of Pelham, himself, had stepped into Rare Confectionery earlier in search of her. Her father's tempering nature, so useful at home, had been absent as he always left the running of the shop entirely in the capable hands of his wife and daughters.

After requesting the footman place her packages on the nearest counter, Amity had sent him on his way with a sack of four chocolates for his trouble. She couldn't help watching through the glass door as he climbed aboard the coach that whisked her duke away.

Her duke! Lady Madeleine's duke actually. But for a few moments . . . .

Amity sighed, still thinking about it the following morning. In the sunny dining room of their home on Baker Street, with its cheerful yellow and cream wallpaper, everything was perfect. She sipped her chocolate, enjoying the peace and quiet—

Charlotte gamboled in, somehow being noisy even when saying nothing. The "saying nothing" didn't last long.

"Wasn't yesterday exciting?" Amity's youngest sister went to the sideboard and gathered her breakfast onto a plate, helping herself to tea, coddled eggs, and toast.

Amity knew to what—and to *whom*—she referred. "It was," she agreed.

"When he came in," her sister continued as she took a seat, "my eyes about popped from my head, and you should have seen us all curtseying so low, my chin was practically between my breasts."

And Charlotte had an ample bosom in which her chin could nestle, Amity thought ruefully, while her own was what she considered merely adequate.

The day before, after the duke's footman left, they'd all started talking at the same time, and then a customer had entered and another and another. Soon, the workday had finished, and everyone scattered to their various interests or concerns. Their mother went to her ladies' gardening society meeting that spent more time tipping sherry than discussing blooms.

Charlotte accompanied a friend to an oil painting class although none of them could imagine why since she didn't seem to have an ounce of talent for it. She hadn't produced a finished work in two months, and they were all starting to think she had her eye on the friend's older brother, rather than on the canvas at hand.

And Beatrice had attended a literary salon at Lady Turbity's townhouse as she did twice a week without fail.

Amity spent the evening in the kitchen playing with various recipes, imagining what would represent the perfect *Brayson* chocolate. Everything had come out unpleasant and even bitter. When she'd gone to bed, she'd dreamt of the Duke of Pelham wading through a thick chocolate river to get to her, only to have Lady Madeleine scoop him up on a silver spoon right before he reached her.

Amity eyed her sister, who was enthusiastically buttering her toast in between sentences.

"I hope you all didn't behave too vulgarly when the duke entered," Amity said, idly stirring the molinet, the long whisk resting through a small opening in the hinged finial of her chocolate pot. Swishing the molinet kept her chocolate from settling or separating, ensuring the second cup was as well-blended as the first. And she very much enjoyed a second cup.

"No, of course not. Well, maybe a little," Charlotte grinned, her sweetly bowed lips curving upward. "But when he asked for the talented chocolatier whose reputation was spreading throughout London, we were disappointed to say you weren't there."

"Never mind. You described me to him, and he found me. It was a little shocking." Amity smiled at her sister. "I rode in *his* coach."

Charlotte whistled with excitement, a nasty habit no one could break her of. "Tell me everything, particularly what he wanted with you. Will you become the Duchess of Chocolate?"

It was so close to her own misinterpretation of the duke's proposition that Amity swallowed her hot beverage down the wrong way and began to cough.

"Don't be silly," she managed when she could breathe. Grabbing the napkin off her lap, she wiped her mouth. "The duke wants me to create a special chocolate treat for the female he has set his cap on."

"A man doesn't set his cap," Beatrice's voice preceded her into the room. Taller than either her older or younger sister, the middle Rare-Foure sister had a regal air as she came unhurriedly into the dining room, helped herself to breakfast, and took a seat. "A man sets his *sights* upon a woman. A woman sets her *cap,* but she sets it *at,* not *for,* a man."

Amity glanced at Charlotte, and they rolled their eyes.

"Very well, Professor Bea," Amity said. "The Duke of Pelham has set his sights upon one Lady Mad—"

"Madeleine Brayson? Again?" exclaimed Charlotte. "Well, that's crabbed the morning."

The three sisters laughed, and Beatrice agreed, "Simply open today's newspaper and look at the society pages. I'm certain there will be plenty more news of Lady Madeleine dazzling the *bon ton,* enough to keep you in an ill humor all day. She is everywhere it seems, and on everyone's tongue."

"And soon, our sweets shall be on her tongue, too." Amity wanted her creation to exceed the duke's wildest expectations.

Beatrice cocked her head and considered. "A chocolate bonbon to win a lady? Good idea on the duke's part. How will he present it to her?"

"At his home during a party," Amity told them, trying not to feel a little let down. "In a fortnight."

"Get invitations for all of us," Charlotte said. "What's wrong with that?" she exclaimed when her sisters stared at her. "Don't you think, as the chocolatier making the magic happen, you should be there to witness what your creation does at the very moment it is unveiled?"

Amity wasn't at all sure she wanted to do that, except for the mildest curiosity to see the stunning Lady Madeleine in person. *What about her could put this woman above all others?* Her face, figure, or personality? Why should she be praised more than Charlotte with her sweet temper and curvy figure, or Beatrice with her grace and intelligence, or herself, with her . . . her uncanny ability to blend the perfect chocolate treat?

Amity drained her cup.

"Even if Amity were to go," Beatrice began, "which, in truth, I think she should, why should you and I go?" she asked.

Charlotte shrugged. "To see inside the duke's home, of course. I hear it is beyond luxurious."

"Yes, I know that, but why would he invite us for such a purpose, two single women of modest means who've never had a Season or been introduced to society?" Beatrice asked, her voice growing softer with each rather sad word. "Besides, we would surely outshine the woman he means to make his duchess," she finished, winking at Amity.

They all laughed again. The Rare-Foure sisters had no illusions about their status. Their father was a second son of a French baron. They were raised as he had been, with gentility and privilege, yet they were untitled and didn't have the inheritance to snag a nobleman.

On the other hand, what they did have was a marvelous sweet shop on New Bond Street, nestled amongst the most luxurious stores in London. And they were having a truly wonderful life.

Amity rose to her feet, eager to get to her work area in the back of the shop and replenish any chocolates which they'd sold out of. With that accomplished, she would try her hand, or rather, try her palate, at creating the *Brayson*.

HENRY WAS AT SIXES and sevens. While he wanted to continue to court Madeleine, he didn't want to let on his intent to ask her to marry him. He feared she would guess if he spent too much time with her between now and the party. She already knew she was the guest of honor, and that he'd invited her parents and brother, as well.

In point of fact, she probably already knew he was going to make a public proposal since she'd first protested the attendance of her parents with a frown upon her breathtaking face, and the words, "Whyever for? They can be such wet blankets who might lie upon our glittering flames of fun and extinguish them."

His mouth had opened, and he hadn't known what to say. They were riding in Hyde Park along Rotten Row with her professional chaperone an appropriate distance behind. At first, he'd thought she was speaking in jest for it seemed a chilly, albeit poetic, thing to say about one's parents.

After a pause, he'd said, "I think it would be appropriate to have them there. They will undoubtedly enjoy the evening and all its events. I know you will want them there, too."

Lady Madeleine had looked wide-eyed at him, then a knowing smile had turned her face into that of a serene goddess. She'd acquiesced at once.

Today, he intended to drop in at Rare Confectionery and see what the chocolatier had come up with overnight. He supposed it was a bit premature, but he had ideas, and before Miss Rare-Foure got too far along in her creation, he thought she might like to hear about them.

After all, who knew Madeleine better than he? Many people, in fact.

He laughed at his own joke. From the balls and dinner parties they'd attended, he knew she liked extremely sweet things, whether her tea or her sponge cake or even her lemonade. He also knew she liked to dance, the polka more than the waltz. And he knew she had a number of strong dislikes and an opinion on practically everything.

Unlike many women, she had not kept her thoughts to herself, even upon their first meeting. He supposed he should admire a female who didn't hide her opinions behind her fan or the façade of polite indifference.

Occasionally, however, he wished she would retreat behind the façade if only for a few minutes. One didn't need to proclaim about everything and often in a negative fashion. Still, he hoped it was an active mind that made her so . . . assertive.

Henry left his home on St. James's Place, got out of his coach precisely where Old Bond Street met New Bond Street, and took a deep breath of air. He coughed—for London was a tad smoky at the best of times. And he loved it anyway, while thoroughly appreciating a couple months, twice a year, at his country estate in Kent. There, he could take in the delightfully refreshing sea air. Why, he could practically see Calais from his third-floor chamber!

The confectionery door had an attached bell that tinkled in a pretty fashion as he entered, exactly as it had done the day before. He hoped today he didn't have to chase the chocolatier down the street.

As he strode in, the aroma of chocolate swirled around him. After tasting Miss Rare-Foure's confections in his carriage, he now knew how delectable chocolate could be, and the rich, decadent scent caused his tongue to twitch. Soon, he knew he would be enjoying the taste again.

His gaze swept the bright, tidy shop where everything was either white or the brilliant blue of the Rare Confectionery stamp that was on the tins and bags. To his left was a glass display case of shelves filled with paper-lined trays of sweets, and behind it was space for those who worked there. In front of him was another glass case of confectionery, and to his right, anchored to the wall was shelf upon shelf of attractive tins of various sizes. He assumed these all contained selected chocolates and toffee should one wish to purchase more than a small sackful.

Connected to the end of the first glass case was a marble counter at which one of the young women he'd encountered the day before was presently stationed. By a familial resemblance, Henry assumed she was related to the chocolatier, most likely a sister.

Looking up with a smile upon her face, her eyes widened with recognition. When she took a deep breath, drawing his gaze to her expansive bosom, he thought she was going to shriek. Happily, she released the breath and seemed to regain her sensibilities.

"My Grace," she began, and her face turned red as a freshly boiled beet. "I mean *Your* Grace, my lord."

"Just one of the two will do," he said, approaching the counter. "Are you also a Miss Rare-Foure?"

She gaped at him. "I am." Then, in the space of a second, she disappeared from view.

Startled, Henry waited, but she did not reappear. He coughed to clear his throat, hoping to conjure her return. It didn't work. *Had she fainted at the notion of his presence in the shop?*

He peered over the top of counter. Down, on the other side, the young woman was curtseying deeply, and where her apron fell forward, she gave him an excellent view of the generous upper swell of her breasts and the enticing dark valley between.

"Please," he said, trying to avert his eyes and failing, "would you stand?"

"Yes, Your Grace." And she did.

"Is your sister here?" he asked.

"Which one?"

"The chocolate maker," he clarified, thinking that would have been obvious.

"Oh, yes. She is, and hard at work, too. I believe she has been working on the special chocolate for your party. By the way, don't you think my sister should attend the party?"

He hadn't actually given it a thought. Now that he did, he supposed, it would be a good idea. He would pay well for the confections, and it would add the right gravitas to the occasion to have Miss Rare-Foure present them on a silver tray.

"I believe, miss, you are quite correct."

The young woman smiled, which was very becoming. Neither too toothy, nor gummy. She behaved precisely as a sweet sister should.

Until she rounded her full lips and let loose a shrill whistling sound.

He took a startled step back unable to stop himself. *What on earth?*

Directly after, the curtain that was draped across an opening toward the rear of the shop parted swiftly, and the chocolatier appeared.

"Charlotte, why did you—?" Then she spied him and halted. By the look upon her face, she was embarrassed for her sister.

"My lord," she said, offering a curtsey, not nearly as deep as her sister's, nor with the same accompanying view. "I apologize. My sister has quite the way of expressing her delight."

"That is no matter," Henry explained. As long as he didn't have to encounter her delight *very* often, he didn't mind in the least.

"His Grace is here to invite you to his party," her sister blurted.

That was a blatant lie, but he decided to go along with it. "Yes, I was remiss in not extending an invitation to you when last we spoke. Obviously, it is *your* creation and *you* should present it to Lady Madeleine."

Strangely, Miss Rare-Foure didn't look thrilled.

"Honestly, my lord, I would not like to steal the limelight, as they say, from you. Not that I could. After all, who am I?" She gave an unsettled laugh. "Only please consider, it is your special night to propose and, after you've settled the account, the chocolates will be yours to present. I would be in the way at best."

Her sister was staring at her as if she'd grown a third eye, and he understood why. Not many people would turn down a direct invitation to a party at his home.

"Not at all," Henry told the chocolatier, determined now to carry through with the scene he was envisioning. After dinner, all guests would go from his dining room to the ballroom where musicians would play a short concert. Possibly a pianist. A violinist, too. He couldn't recall precisely what his mother said was the plan for the music, but she had arranged for something splendid. Of that, he had no doubt.

And afterward, as the last strains of the music died down, Miss Rare-Foure, dressed perhaps with an apron as she wore now—though cleaner, of course—would enter the room. He couldn't ask her to kneel in front of Lady Madeleine, but he could ask her to silently hold out the tray with one perfect chocolate upon it while more servants—not her loud, whistling sister—would enter behind her with more trays filled with the treats for the other guests.

"No one must taste one yet," he would declare to much anticipation. At such time, he would propose to Madeleine and say something about how if she could declare the chocolate to be terrible, then she could turn him down.

No, that wasn't right. In any case, he had nearly a fortnight to plan exactly what he would say.

Nevertheless, Miss Rare-Foure simply must be there to present. He had made up his mind.

"I insist you come," he told her in his most authoritative voice.

She took a breath, her nostrils seemed to open a little larger and her mouth took on a look of mutinous distaste. He thought she was going to tell him no, something that hardly ever happened—in fact, it had never happened—since he'd received the title upon his father's tragic demise. Even before that, as a marquess, he had rarely encountered resistance to any of his plans.

"And you probably would want the rest of our family there, too," the larger bosomed Miss Rare-Foure added from behind the counter.

"No," he said at the same time as the chocolatier. They looked at each other, her gaze locking with his.

"That is," Miss Rare-Foure explained, turning to her sister, "I believe his lordship said it was a modest dinner party for his close friends and family."

"I'm afraid your sister is correct," Henry said, hoping to soften the blow as the young lady looked quite crestfallen.

"It wouldn't do to have too many Rare-Foure ladies hanging about. My other guests would be outshone by your charm and beauty."

The young lady behind the counter nodded, as if accepting such a circumstance might be true. "I suppose you are right. Hopefully, my sister won't be too much of a distraction, pretty as she is. All in all, everyone's eyes should be upon Lady Madeleine on such a special night."

Henry had to hide his smile. As if any woman could really take the attention away from Madeleine. It was laughable! Turning his gaze back to the chocolatier, with a smudge of brown upon her cheek, she seemed to read his thoughts as if he'd said them out loud.

What's more, she didn't look as if she appreciated what he was thinking. Her glance turned withering, as she brushed her hands upon her apron, leaving cocoa prints in two trails. Then she put her hands on her hips.

"Precisely, why are you here, Lord Pelham?"

CHAPTER THREE

Amity wished her question to the Duke of Pelham had come out sounding a little more cordial. Something about this arrangement was making her feel snappish, or as Charlotte had said that morning, crabbed! And that *something* was undoubtedly Lady Madeleine. She might be a perfectly sociable person, intelligent and witty, but all anyone ever talked about was her incredibly lovely appearance.

Amity rearranged her expression until she offered the Duke of Pelham a friendly smile. She had best change her sentiment regarding his ladylove, or she would never be able to create a delicious chocolate treat. And her reputation was on the line, along with that of Rare Confectionery.

"I came to give you my input as to Lady Madeleine's likes," the duke said, "so you don't add a flavor of which I already know she would disapprove."

Amity nodded. "How prudent of you, my lord." She glanced at Charlotte who was hanging on every word, looking like an eager puppy. Their mother was not coming in today, and Beatrice was coming in later to make her famed treacle toffee, which they sold by the pan full.

"Please come into the back with me, and I'll show you some of the choices we have at our disposal. I shall take notes on the lady's preferences."

She noticed out of the corner of her eye as Charlotte's expression altered to one of surprise. Amity didn't usually have customers in the back room, nor did she particularly like people watching her as she blended and created. However, this was a special circumstance.

He nodded. "I would be honored to see where you make your confections."

Charlotte's brows rose. Amity ignored her.

"This way, my lord." She raised the curtain, holding it aside as she stepped through to the back, the familiar thickly sweet, delicious aroma of chocolate immediately relaxing her. It was exceedingly strange to have the Duke of Pelham at her back, and then she looked at the room through his eyes.

Oh, dear! "It's a little messy," Amity admitted, seeing her early-morning endeavors by the light of the window in the back, which overlooked the small alley.

Upon the cooktop, there was her *bain-marie*, with a pot of chocolate being kept at the perfect melted temperature. She'd left spoons, a whisk, and a bowl of grated orange peel on the copper counter beside the cooker.

Opposite, on the other side of the small room, blocks of Swiss Cailler's and French Menier's plain chocolate sat upon her marble workspace, the surface she used for cooling melted chocolate and blending it with her wide scraper. Small bottles of fruit essences and an open can of Borden's condensed milk also vied for space.

On the shelf above the marble, oils of peppermint, cinnamon, and orange were lined up in vials. And next to a bowl of soft chocolate fondant, which she was blending with other flavors, she had a few Fry's bars.

In bins and on the shelves were her molds and presses, small jars of walnuts and almonds, a grinder, and heavy pots. Knives were laid out on a wooden cutting board atop the marble, along with candied ginger in a glass jar.

"Well!" he exclaimed, his gaze taking it all in. "It seems as much like a chemist's space as that of a chocolatier, although it smells better than any other shop I've ever entered."

"As you may be aware, my lord, all chocolate in England, particularly drinking chocolate, started out being manufactured in chemist shops for medicinal purposes, just as it was in the past for Marie Antoinette and as far back as the Mayan's bitter brew of ground cacao beans."

"How interesting," he said, sounding sincere. "There is more to this than I could have imagined." He had already tugged off the glove on his right hand and started to reach out to—*oh no!*—put a finger toward her pure fondant, and she scrambled to pull the bowl out of his reach.

"Please, my lord, you mustn't contaminate the chocolate."

"Sorry," he muttered, stepping away from the table.

Amity crossed the room to a desk under the window and picked up her tablet of paper for taking notes. She'd already written a few things on it from her ideas the night before. All under the heading "Lady Mad," underlined with an exclamation point. She clutched it to her, turned so he couldn't read anything, and grabbed for a pencil.

"Would you like to tell me some of *your* ideas?" she asked. After that, he could go away and she could get to work. She certainly couldn't get anything done with his larger-than-life ducal presence crowding the back room.

Besides, with him there, she found it difficult not to be distracted by his dark, wavy hair, perfect for running one's fingers through. Or gaze into his green, intelligent eyes. *An unusual shade*, she thought.

And then there was his mouth, which presently was speaking.

"... thus, no raisins, if you please."

She shook her head to clear it. "No raisins."

For some reason, the duke noticed the Fry's. "What do you do with those?"

What a silly question! "Eat them, of course."

He barked out a laugh. "In Rare Confectionery, you eat Fry's Cream Sticks?" He grinned at her, and her stomach did that strange twinging again as it had in the carriage. *Most disturbing.* Her stomach never twinged when Jeremy smiled, but Jeremy didn't have the duke's devastating dimples.

She shrugged. "I spend all day tasting and dipping and heating and creating. Sometimes, I want to eat a confection someone else has made. They are not competitors. Or rather, we are not competition for them. If you want a packaged bar of plain chocolate or a sweet, white minty cream stick—and who wouldn't?—then you should grab a Fry's. They are superb. Would you care for one?"

"Frankly, I'd rather taste something you've made."

"You shall, but back to my notes." Glancing down, Amity realized she had written nothing so far. She penciled in "no raisins."

"What flavors does Lady Madeleine enjoy?"

"Roast pork and pheasant, potatoes, sponge cake, oysters."

She pursed her lips. *Was he making fun of her?*

"None of those will go with chocolate, except the cake, my lord."

"Perhaps chocolate would go beautifully with a potato, Miss Rare-Foure. Or perhaps on a green bean or over peas. And how would it be on a crispy piece of pork?"

Her stomach turned over again, this time with a sick feeling as if she might lose her last cup of hot chocolate all over his shiny boots. Then he cocked his head, eyes sparkling, and she knew he was only speaking in jest.

"I'm sorry, my lord, but I will not be a party to such monstrosities. If you wish to eat chocolate on your pork, you may melt a Fry's or Cadbury's chocolate bar upon it and dig in."

The duke shrugged, not minding her saucebox mouth, but he did look a little doubtful.

"I cannot see how you will make anything special if you use similar recipes and ingredients."

Amity knew her jaw had tightened when her teeth squeaked together. The difference between one of her chocolates with a hint of raspberry essence compared to a raspberry-flavored Fry's Cream Stick were like night and day.

"How can one horse be any better than another when they all have a mane, a tail, and four legs?" she asked.

"That's different," the duke protested. "Some are bred for speed, some for strength. And some simply have a special spirit for being a great horse."

"Exactly." She opened a cupboard at the back of the room and drew out a medium-sized tray followed by another one, both of which she placed on the marble surface in front of the duke. He examined the chocolates in various shapes and sizes.

"This one," she said, pointing to a small, flat disc of pale chocolate about the size of a shilling in which she'd added the merest hint of cinnamon. "This one is for speed."

He looked up at her with questioning eyes.

"Go on," she encouraged him. "You may pick it up and pop it into your mouth."

The duke did as directed, and she watched him take it with clean fingers and equally clean nails. She scrunched her own hands into her apron, knowing she had chocolate under her nails as well as on her fingers.

He barely hesitated to examine the coin-sized sweet before slipping it between his lips. Personally, she would have eyed it, sniffed it, and probably licked it once or twice ahead of actually eating it. Only if she were alone, though, and tasting something for the first time.

His eyes widened, and he smiled. "It melted on my tongue so quickly. It was a burst of flavor, and then it was gone."

"As I said, that one is made for speed." She looked over the tray and pointed to a thicker chocolate containing walnuts and her sister's treacle toffee chips. "Try this one. Be careful, give it time on your tongue. And for heaven's sake, don't crunch it too quickly or you're liable to crack a tooth."

"I didn't know there was danger of injury involved," the duke said with a teasing tone before picking up the larger piece of confectionery and putting it into his mouth.

And what an attractive mouth it was, she thought.

"Mm," he murmured around the chunky chocolate in his mouth. *"Mm, mm."*

Meanwhile, she turned around to pour him a glass of water from the pitcher she kept for cleaning her palate.

He took it from her but hesitated. "I hate to wash away the flavors in my mouth. That was astonishingly good."

She enjoyed his compliment down to her toes. Then he sipped the water and set the glass down.

"That chocolate, if you follow our analogy, was bred for strength. It didn't melt quickly on your tongue. It allowed you to work for it, chewy and crunchy. It's one of our bestsellers. Some people eat a couple as a snack between meals. You'll find it gives you a boost of energy, a veritable zing to your step."

"Miss Rare-Foure, I don't see how you can cap that climax, but I have a feeling the thoroughbred with spirit awaits me."

"Indubitably," she said. Instead of the cupboard, she turned to the shelf where a glass dome sat upon another plate of confection. "These are best at room temperature, but not any warmer, nor, for that matter, any colder."

Lifting the glass, Amity let him look at eight round balls, dusted with the finest pure cocoa powder. He eyed them and looked at her.

"These are soft and buttery, guaranteed to make your fingers dirty, I'm afraid."

"I know they shall be worth it," he said. Without any further hesitation, he picked one up and popped it between his lips. After an instant, he closed his eyes, and she could look at him unobserved.

An interesting face with well-shaped, tidy eyebrows and dark hair falling over his brow, a nose that had clearly never been broken, and that mouth! Lips dusted with cocoa over a strong chin without a hint of stubble. *Naturally!* He probably had a team of servants who took care of every aspect of his body.

At the thought of his body, she swallowed at the same time as he did. Then his eyes snapped open.

"Good God!" He licked his lips, drawing his tongue over the cocoa powder until they were clean. "That was . . . utterly fabulous. It had spirit to spare. It was . . . what was it exactly?"

"A secret recipe, but basically melted chocolate, cream, and a hint of—"

"Orange?" he guessed.

"Orange liqueur."

He raised his eyebrows. "It's perfect."

"Perhaps it will do for Lady Madeleine?" she suggested.

"Do you already sell them in your shop?" he asked.

"Quite a few, my lord."

"Unfortunately, it will not do. It must be original, created for her."

She sighed. "Perhaps something similar in texture and shape, creamy, soft, with a different flavor than orange?" Amity needed some hint of an idea to work from. Otherwise, she could go in too many directions. "No one else makes these soft chocolate balls in London."

"Yes, I very much like the feel in my mouth. And the way it is firm but soft. It's rich, decadent even. I want another one, but I know with one too many, I might feel ill."

"True. As with most sweets, one should know the fine line over which if you step, you go from tasting something delicious to sickly unpleasant. You could have another of any of these, however, without risk."

He smiled again. "I shall choose another of these with spirit," and he picked up one more cocoa-dusted ball.

Soon, she had a short list of some fruits and nuts which Lady Madeleine liked. They chatted about native blackberries and elderberries, both of them preferring these fruits as wine rather than coated in chocolate. Yet Amity failed to convince him chocolate-drenched wild currants were delicious.

"The tart little berry is a sharp surprise on the tongue when surrounded by sweetness. So, they're best with a highly sweetened chocolate and not plain chocolate."

"Tart little berries," he repeated. "You make it sound intriguing, and I hope you will offer me a sample in the future."

"As soon as I have some, my lord, then my berries will be yours."

What had she just said? It sounded terribly coquettish, and she was positive her cheeks were flaming.

"I have taken up so much of your time. I should be leaving."

Had she scared him off with her ridiculous words? Apparently not, for even though the duke had said he was leaving, he hadn't moved toward the curtained doorway.

Amity did, in fact, have a lot of chocolates to make for the shop and for other customers. She should get started, but she could hardly ask a duke to move along.

Instead, she smiled at him. "That's quite all right, my lord. Rare Confectionery appreciates your patronage. And after your party, we shall have many new customers. We are in your debt."

HENRY CONSIDERED THE YOUNG woman who stood before him in the cocoa-stained apron. He liked her tremendously so far. She had an easy manner and a lopsided smile when it appeared, as it had a moment earlier. He also liked it when she spoke of tarts and berries, but that was merely him being a devil. And childish, to boot.

"On the contrary," he said. "If all goes well, I shall be eternally grateful." *Because she would have helped him to obtain Lady Madeleine, the prize of London.*

"My wife and I will have your chocolates at our wedding celebration." *Would it be appropriate to invite Miss Rare-Foure to that as well?* He didn't know if she would be willing to serve chocolates to his guests or if she would be an honored guest herself.

Regardless, he should be thinking of Madeleine on his wedding day, not this wonderfully gifted chocolatier.

"I shall make presents of them to my wife for the rest of our lives," he added. *Christ, that sounded like a long time.*

"Of course," she said a little frostily, and he could tell the mood had changed.

"I will come to your shop and pick out the chocolates myself," he added.

She offered him a tepid smile, and he realized he'd spoken like a pompous twaddler, as if his very presence would be a gift.

She was tapping her foot now, impatient to get rid of him. *Him!* A duke with whom everyone desired to spend time. But Miss Rare-Foure had work to do.

"I shall leave you to it and come back tomorrow."

Her eyes widened. "Whatever for, my lord? Don't you trust me?"

He did! Her ability was obvious with the few samples he'd had. But he wanted to be a part of this creation. He'd never done anything like it before.

"I do, but since this is such a personal gift, I would like to oversee it. Will that be a problem?"

She frowned but could hardly refuse him.

"Perhaps tomorrow, you could show me the various types of chocolate. I know I tasted more than one today. I am certain I can discover more of what Lady Madeleine likes and report back to you."

Now, her perfect dark brown brows rose up along her smooth forehead.

"You shall be like a Detective Sergeant in the Metropolitan Police, my lord."

Was she mocking him? He didn't much mind because her smile was back. Her right cheek rose higher as her pretty pink lips upturned in a sweetly crooked manner.

He should not be noticing her lips. Or her smile.

Then an irksome thought floated through his head—he had no idea what Madeleine's smile looked like. In any case, he knew it wasn't the least bit lopsided, nor did it alter the perfect symmetry of her exquisite face. If it did, he would have noticed.

"Well done. I shall be on my way. I am meeting a friend at White's." He didn't know why he'd told Miss Rare-Foure that, either. She was going to continue working—albeit at one of the best tasks imaginable—while he was going to sip coffee. She probably thought him a topper, for sure.

Giving her a shallow bow, waiting while she curtsied in return, he added, "I will see you tomorrow."

Because he *wanted* to. Because he could. Because he was a damned duke, and she'd better appreciate his custom.

Not that he would say any of that out loud.

CHAPTER FOUR

When Henry left his club on St. James's Street, he was still marveling at how the remainder of chocolate flavor in his mouth had somehow made the rich brew in his first cup of coffee taste even better. Maybe everything was better with chocolate. Maybe Miss Rare-Foure was incorrect and chocolate could cover pork or pheasant or even a lowly brussels sprout. Perhaps together, they would invent something entirely new.

Not that she needed his help. He'd been raving about her chocolates to his two chums, Charles Jeffcoat and Daniel Waverly. They'd laughed at his exuberance and asked if it was really the chocolatier herself who had him in such a state of excitement.

He'd rolled his eyes, but in truth, he couldn't get Miss Rare-Foure out of his mind. What's more, he had to keep reminding himself it didn't matter about her strangely attractive smile or her inviting, brown eyes. It was her creations that mattered to him. That third chocolate had been sublime. Firm but melty, creamy with the perfect bitterness from the outer dusting of cocoa powder.

If she had invented it right then, it would have been the perfect gift for Madeleine, the *Brayson* as he'd come to think of it, even though that name made him think of donkeys.

Did his soon-to-be-fiancée have a middle name? Perhaps it would be the perfect name for a sweet. To that end, and to determine her favorite flavors, he decided to spend time with her that very day. Sitting in his carriage, however, Henry realized he hadn't the foggiest notion where she might be. He knew where each of his friends were, which of them were at the Palace of Westminster attending Parliament or at a shooting party in the country and who were at their clubs or remaining abed at that late hour.

Nevertheless, of Madeleine, or most ladies for that matter, he had no idea. They didn't have clubs, at least not the kind he went to. What's more, he had no idea who her friends were. When they had first met at a ball, she was surrounded by other men, whom he scattered with a wave of his gloved hand. He monopolized her time and couldn't recall her speaking with any other women who might be her friends.

When he picked her up at her home on Tremont Street for a dinner party, she had come down the stairs and her parents had not put in an appearance, nor a sibling. Apparently, since he was a duke, they didn't need to know any more about him.

In his carriage, with her chaperone seated by the window, they'd spoken of the weather, and she'd asked him about his country estate. He'd asked her about her father's. Then they'd arrived at a party at Lord and Lady Lindsey's townhouse, and conversation had been more general among the group. After two more balls and another dinner party, Henry grasped the fact he didn't know too much more about her except for her opinions on certain other people, on unmanageable horses, and on the very best color for a drawing room. Dove grey.

He did know he wanted her to grace his life. She was exquisitely lovely and had a very pleasing tone to her voice, even when espousing on what she did not care for. She was a superb dancer, too. He'd had to share her with other dance partners, but by the third ball, it was coming to be recognized by others that she was his. She was the superior lady in the present Season's crop, and he was the most eligible bachelor, so naturally, he should have her. Even if he'd still been a marquess and his father very much alive, Henry figured he would have trumped all other suitors.

From a little digging, not only of his own but by his own mother and his friends, he'd discovered Lady Madeleine's parents, Lord and Lady Brayson, traced their lineage back to the Normans, had holdings in Yorkshire and Wales, and owned outright their townhouse on Tremont Street with no bank loan. They had the fairest daughter in the land, and a son, David, heir to his father's earldom, who'd attended Eton and wanted to become Prime Minister. No one at White's could figure out what his qualifications were for dreaming of such a lofty position, but that was neither here nor there.

Nonetheless, all that told him little about the lady herself. Today, he was determined to delve a little more deeply into her nature than her enjoyment of champagne over red wine and prunes over dates. Not that her preference in chocolate was any deeper, but it was time he asked her how she liked children and dogs, for he fancied a few of each. He liked London, but also spending time in Kent. *Was she willing to leave the city for a month or two each year?*

And it was time to kiss her. Past time, in fact. He had tried once and received Madeleine's cheek for his effort. Either she would not kiss ahead of a formal engagement or he'd been woefully premature in the attempt. He suddenly had the terrifying thought she was one of those females who would want to wait until marriage to exchange even a simple kiss.

That wouldn't do. Determining such a thing was more important even than finding out her chocolate preference. He ordered his driver to take him promptly to the Brayson home. He was risking much by showing up uninvited, but he couldn't think how else to find her.

Thirty minutes later, he was seated in Lord Brayson's drawing room. Alone. He'd been waiting for ten of those minutes, seated on a stiff, gold-brocade sofa. The butler had not been specific about whether the earl or his countess was home, but the man had said Lady Madeleine was accepting visitors.

So, there Henry waited, unused to being left to cool his heels.

At last, she entered, followed by her personal maid, and all doubts, if he'd had any, evaporated at the sight of her. *How could any woman be so lovely?* Blonde hair, both piled high and in ringlets hanging down, sapphire-colored eyes, pink-tinted lips, and pale skin without cocoa smears—*why did that pop into his head?*

Madeleine wore a blue silk gown with silver underskirt, looking how he imagined Aphrodite might have appeared. He jumped up at her arrival. She paused to offer a splendidly graceful curtsey before holding out her hands to him.

"Your Grace," she said as he took hold of them. Long graceful fingers, perfect for playing the harp or pianoforte, both of which he knew she did, and not a speck of chocolate anywhere upon them, nor under her nails. *Cool-to-the-touch hands that were clearly meant to be those of a duchess,* he reminded himself.

"How are you?" he asked, as her maid went to the far end of the room and took a seat.

"I am well. To what do I owe this wonderful surprise?"

A nicer greeting than Miss Rare-Foure had given him earlier, to be sure, when the chocolatier practically demanded he state his intent as if he were bothering her.

"I simply wanted to see you and speak with you. That is, if you're not too busy."

"Never too busy for you. Later today, I am going to tea at Marlborough House. I've been assured the Princess of Wales will be there, and perhaps the Prince himself. I have spent the morning deciding what to wear."

How could she question her perfection? "The dress you've chosen is precisely right."

In a flash, that statement earned him a withering glare.

"This?" she asked disparagingly. "This is my day gown for seeing you and other visitors. I would never wear this to Marlborough House!"

He didn't know what to say. In some way, she had insulted him as being less important than her tea gathering, even if it was with royalty. On the other hand, he supposed it meant she was comfortable enough with him she wasn't worried about looking her best.

"In any case, dear lady, I cannot imagine you looking any better than you do right now."

Her smile returned, and it was a flawlessly symmetrical smile. *How perfect!* And yet, he wasn't sure it lit her eyes, not the way Miss Rare-Foure's crooked smile made her soft brown eyes sparkle.

Rich brown eyes made him think of delicious chocolate, reminding him of his mission. However, asking Madeleine about her taste in confectionery suddenly seemed as though it would be inappropriate. Better to start with the banalities.

"Will you sit?"

Henry waited for her to take a seat, then sat opposite, realizing at once they were too far apart. Except for the single time in his carriage, when her chaperone had run back indoors for Madeleine's forgotten dance slippers and he'd attempted a hurried kiss—and was rebuffed—he hadn't found an opportunity to be alone with her or even close. The lady seemed always to have a wall of propriety encircling her. Some might say she had the air of frigidity, but he appreciated a little reserve in his woman. *A little.*

He neither wanted her to be an ice princess, nor a lightskirt, just something pleasurably in the middle.

Thinking he should test the waters and see her receptiveness, he suddenly stood and moved around the low table between them, taking a seat beside her on the sofa. She didn't flinch or cringe, but she did seem to hold her breath and look askance.

"Am I making you uncomfortable?" he asked.

"I trust you, Your Grace. It's only that I wouldn't want any hint of scandal."

"I don't believe our sharing a sofa could cause one." He guessed that kissing was out of the question, even if the maid weren't there.

"Also, I wouldn't want you to think ill of me. If I sat close to you, what would stop me sitting close to another man?"

He frowned. Hopefully her regard for him, some affection in her heart, perhaps, would stop her. Since that was a thought he couldn't say aloud, he nodded in agreement.

"I trust you keep your distance from anyone of the opposite sex, except when dancing," he added. Henry tried to remember if she'd allowed him to hold her closely when they'd waltzed but seemed to recall she'd kept space between them even then.

How would he know what she did for the sake of appearances, and what was because she didn't have an interest in him at all?

For the first time, he wondered if his proposal might be turned down. Then quickly dismissed the shadowy uncertainty. He was a duke, and a young one, at that. He had all his hair and teeth. *What more could she want?*

Not a vain man, Henry had every logical reason to believe he was more than adequate to win her, even without the chocolate gift, which was planned more as a lark than a serious offering. While she had a high level of beauty, he wasn't a bridge troll. Nor would he mind when someday, his dark hair turned gray at the temples and his face became lined with the joys and sorrows of life.

Be that as it may, currently, they would make a well-matched couple.

"Lady Madeleine, do you have another name? Besides your family name, I mean."

Frowning, which, if possible, made her look even more beautiful, she said, "I do. Why?"

"Merely curious." He had no way of knowing if she even knew his given name, nor had she ever asked him much about himself, but he assumed that would come later.

"Elizabeth, for our virgin queen of centuries past," she said proudly.

They could hardly name the chocolate after Queen Elizabeth, as it would entirely overshadow Madeleine. He would have to settle on the *Brayson*. Still, he could ask his other questions.

"Do you like to stay in Town all the year round?" he asked her. "Or are you amenable to country living, too?"

She blinked. "I suppose I have not given it much thought, Your Grace. I have no doubt your estate in Kent would make any inconvenience of leaving Town worthwhile."

So, she was thinking of blending their lives. That was a good sign.

"I prefer carriages," she continued, "to riding horses, as you know."

Did he?

"And I am not fond of too much thin air. I think the thicker air of London has more substance. I also don't care for farm animals, but I imagine if you have flocks, I won't need to go near them. Their smell can be so offensive, don't you think?"

Unlike the stench of London's Thames? He considered how often he saw people running around with a scented handkerchief under their nose.

He was still trying to work out what she thought was "thin air" when she added, "I also don't care for carriage travel as much as by train. I assume your estate is on one of the rail lines?"

As usual, he had learned more about what she didn't like. *Carriages over horses, but trains over carriages.*

"There is a station not too far, that's true. My flocks, as you call them, are all downwind. The air is not too thin as my estate is close to the sea. I think the salt thickens it?" He knew that had come out as a question, but he wondered if she would agree.

She nodded, and thus, heartened, he added, "I believe you will find the air to be perfectly satisfactory."

That statement left him feeling a little foolish. Inwardly, he sighed. Again, she had told him more about her dislikes than her likes, and he'd been reduced to insignificant babble. He must try harder.

"What are your feelings on children?"

Lady Madeleine gasped and put her hand to her chest. "That question might be considered brazen," she protested.

Might it? Henry couldn't see how. Unless her mind had flown directly from the existence of children to the creating of them. *Interesting!* Perhaps a passionate nature lay buried— *deeply buried*—beneath the surface of her genteel and cool exterior.

"However," she continued, "since I believe we are heading toward an understanding, I shall answer." Madeleine stared straight ahead instead of looking at him. "I am prepared to provide an heir and two extras, just in case of tragedy. And I shall require a wet-nurse as well as a nanny."

That seemed reasonable, if rather businesslike, for a woman talking about her own offspring, ones he hoped she would love with all the warmth she could muster.

For his part, he would take his children to Rare Confectionery where he would let them purchase whatever they liked. He might even ask the more endowed Rare-Foure sister how she made that piercing whistle. He imagined it would come in handy for calling his children if they were in another part of the house or summoning a dog, for that matter.

"And your feeling on dogs?" He might as well ask his future wife now.

Her head whipped around, and her eyes finally blazed with passion.

"I cannot abide them. Smelly, yappy things, always scratching or yawning or relieving themselves. My father had one for a short while, and after two weeks I made him get rid of it."

"Ah, well then. Perhaps a cat?"

She shook her head and launched into further vitriol about shedding and clawing and vomiting. She'd *allowed* her mother to keep a cat for three whole weeks once!

He decided not to ask about the more unusual pets he'd encountered in some of England's finest houses, such as squirrels, owls, or monkeys. His children would have to grow up without the fun of a four-legged friend, except for their horses.

Suddenly, he had a terrible thought. "Lady Madeleine, do you like the taste of chocolate?"

She gave him her perfect smile again. "Of course, Your Grace. One would have to be uncivilized not to."

"I refer not to the regular drinking kind," he clarified. "I am speaking of the solid chocolate, such as a Cadbury Fancy Box or even a Fry's Cream Stick. Have you had one?"

"I have. The sweetness of the cream stick is a treat."

Internally, he heaved a sigh of relief. His plan remained a good one. And he would tell Miss Rare-Foure, the sweeter the better.

"Chocolate is the very opposite of an orange, don't you think?" she added.

He frowned. "I'm not sure I take your meaning."

She lifted a delicate shoulder. "I mean that I like sweet chocolate almost as much as I dislike a bitter orange."

He nodded even though he recalled the third, orange-infused creamy chocolate with great fondness. What's more, never in his life had he considered the sweet fruit to be bitter, but apparently, Lady Madeleine did.

AMITY HAD JUST FINISHED pouring boiled, nutmeg-infused cream into a bowl of chocolate pieces when her mother called to her through the curtain.

"I can see the Duke of Pelham's carriage has pulled up. And there he is. He's coming in. Again." Mrs. Felicity Rare-Foure had a sing-song tone of approval. She liked her store being patronized by the finest ranks.

Amity heard the tinkling of the shop's bell and pulled off her apron to look more presentable while immediately wishing she didn't care a fig if he thought her so or not.

By the time she stepped through the curtain, her mother was already speaking with the duke. The sight of him gave her the same thrill as a new shipment of Chocolats au Lait Gala Peter, a ready-made milk chocolate drink from Monsieur Peter's factory in Switzerland. Anticipation tingled through her.

"Here she is, my lord," her mother said.

Amity stepped forward and curtsied. "I did not expect to see you again so soon."

"I said I would return," he reminded her, looking like the perfect gentleman in a charcoal gray morning suit. His ascot was meticulously tied.

In truth, she'd assumed he would find something else to occupy his time between yesterday and today.

"And there is nothing more important than getting this right," he added.

Ah, yes. When a man was on a mission to win the heart of a lady, it trumped all other interests.

"I understand, my lord," she said. "I haven't as yet had a chance to make anything new. I had an order to fill for the palace."

"Indeed! How exciting. I have definitely chosen the right chocolatier," he said, making her cheeks warm with his praise. "I have information that may help in your artistry," he said. Pausing, he looked past her toward the curtain.

Did he actually want to return to her workroom? *What a strange man!* She couldn't imagine another duke in all the world who wanted to spend time in the back of a confectionery.

"Very well, my lord." She glanced at her mother, knowing she might already be concocting fanciful notions in her head. Seeing the duke return to their shop, Felicity Rare-Foure was as likely to tell her husband that an aristocratic wedding was imminent.

"We're going to work on the chocolate surprise for his lordship's special *lady*," she reminded her mother, hoping to knock any silly ideas out of her head.

"Of course you are."

Rolling her eyes as she turned so the duke wouldn't see her, Amity led him through the curtain. She grabbed her recently discarded apron and pinned it at the top before tying it around her waist.

"Would you care for an apron, my lord?"

"Not if my life depended upon it," he said, then grinned.

Did angels start singing? Amity had to look away to stop herself from blushing, so strong was her attraction to him and his dimples.

"Do not blame me if you walk out of here with chocolate stains," she said, reaching for her notebook. "If you get too close to me or to my worktable, you are bound to get soiled."

To her amazement, he stepped closer, reaching his arms around her. She gasped, feeling the heat of him along the front of her.

Staring down into her eyes, he said, "That's a risk I'm more than willing to take."

CHAPTER FIVE

Amity was about to close her eyes and tilt her head upward for a kiss, when he snatched a chocolate off the marble counter beside her and backed up.

Popping it between his lips, he closed his eyes and savored it.

That gave her time to regain her balance and her senses. The Duke of Pelham wanted to offer his hand to the most beautiful woman in London. He was hardly going to swoon at the feet of a shopkeeper's daughter. Or sneak a kiss, for that matter.

"That was delicious," he said when he looked at her again.

"That was what went to the Palace," she told him. "When Her Majesty isn't eating parboiled bone marrow on toast, she enjoys chocolate-smothered treacle squares."

"I bet you learn quite a bit about your customers."

"Those of us with an interest in serving the queen, and especially in getting the royal stamp of approval, tend to make it our business to find out her likes and dislikes."

"The queen's cooks pour a good cup of gossip-water, do they?" the duke asked.

"For the right amount of chocolate, yes, they do."

"I hope, Miss Rare-Foure, you are not going to gossip about my likes and dislikes."

She blinked. "Absolutely not, my lord. In plain truth, I know very little about them."

He raised a perfect eyebrow.

"And even if I did," she added, "I would not babble about you. You are a customer. I will not disclose anything about Lady Madeleine, either."

"Isn't the queen a customer?" he asked. Amity could see by the smile playing about his lips he was teasing her.

"The queen is a different kettle of fish entirely."

"I suppose she is. She also might not like to know she had ever been described as a 'kettle of fish.'"

"I suppose not. If you keep my counsel when next you see the queen, then I shall keep yours."

"We work very well together," he said, glancing over to the marble top again to see what else he could taste.

Amity couldn't help but laugh. "We haven't done much work thus far, my lord. You've simply started eating my chocolates." She followed his glance, saw her heated cream melting the chocolate, and grabbed for her whisk.

"I must finish this, my lord. That is, if you can wait."

"Yes, of course. If you don't mind, I'll watch."

Trying to pretend he wasn't there, she beat the concoction over and over until it was shiny, smooth, and completely blended.

"You have a strong arm," he commented into the silence.

"Not as strong as a baker," she remarked, thinking of stories her mother told of Grandfather Rare with biceps like tree limbs from kneading dough.

He laughed. "I suppose not. What is it you're beating so mercilessly?"

"Two parts chocolate to one part heated cream," Amity explained.

He fell silent again while she gave the chocolate a few more stirs before putting the bowl into the cold box, a wooden structure with ice in hidden trays above and below. Sandwiched in the large space between the ice trays were metal shelves where she kept butter, cream, milk and now the bowl of chocolate. Another bowl was already in there cooling quickly.

"It needs to set for at least an hour while it becomes like paste, or a very thick custard. I use it to make the squishy center for the orange-flavored chocolate you liked. Some chocolate-makers abroad are calling it *fondant*, and thus, so am I. Regardless, it gives us plenty of time to talk about the confection for Lady Madeleine."

"I know you said you hadn't a chance to create anything, but that's good because I have new information."

"Really?"

"Yes, I visited with Lady Madeleine yesterday."

How superb! He had gone from seeing her with cocoa on her hands and face, her stained apron in place over her unadorned work dress, to the sparkling Lady Madeleine.

"I discovered she definitely doesn't like orange, but she does like chocolate, the sweeter the better. That helps, doesn't it?"

"Very much so, my lord." She wiped her hands on a cloth. "Would you like to sample more of the confections I have already made, and we can go from there?"

His eyes lit up, and she knew the duke was well and truly ensnared by the magic of chocolate. For a man who'd said he didn't care overly much for it, it hadn't taken long after he'd tried her well-crafted confectionery.

"One moment." She dashed into the front of the shop, avoided her mother who was helping customers, snagged a tasting plate, and helped herself to two milk chocolates with different flavored centers and two plain ones.

When she returned, he had her cold box open, letting all the chill out.

"Close it," she ordered before she could stop herself. When he startled and looked over his shoulder, she added, "Please, my lord."

He did so at once, then turned, appearing chagrinned. "My apologies, Miss Rare-Foure. I should have known better. I was too curious."

"I shouldn't have snapped at you. That's more like my sister."

"Is she the one I met yesterday?"

"No, you met our youngest, Miss Charlotte, and she's hardly ever snappy. Never mind, let's see if we cannot crack this nut."

She held out the plate to him. "I shall let you taste and figure them out for yourself."

He considered. "Are any of them citrus fruits?"

"Yes, one with candied lemon." She pointed to it.

"Since she doesn't care for orange, we should probably skip lemon, too." With that statement, he picked it up and ate it, making her smile and shake her head.

"What?" he asked innocently. "We don't want it to go to waste."

"It wouldn't have, my lord. I would have returned it to the case where it would probably have sold by the end of the day." As she spoke, she heard the bell tinkle and what sounded like two pairs of shoes.

He actually blushed slightly. "Sorry. I knew it would be good."

"That's quite all right. I will be charging you a fortune for the chocolates for your party."

"Will you?" he asked and gave her a broad grin. "I like a woman with good business sense, especially a forthright one. You might as well tell me when I am going to be fleeced."

"I beg your pardon! You shall not be fleeced. My chocolates are worth every farthing, I assure you."

"I already owe you a few guineas, at least," he quipped.

"At least," she agreed. "Have you heard of the Mayan people, my lord?"

He nodded. "I had a thorough education, I promise you, and the dons succeeded in knocking some geography and knowledge of ancient civilizations into my thick head."

Amity ignored his slightly offended tone. She was learning dukes could be prickly when their superiority was questioned.

"Wonderful. Then you may already know how the Mayan people used cacao beans for money, so in essence, we are exchanging one form of currency for another."

"That is an amusing way of looking at it," he agreed.

They were close, their heads bowed over the tray, exchanging banter. She liked this man far too much, especially when he smiled at her.

"Do you think Lady Madeleine will enjoy the ginger?"

"If it is sweet. May I?"

She nodded and pointed to the correct one.

He ate it. "Oh, that is good. We must keep that flavor in the horserace."

"Try the raspberry, my lord," and she indicated which one.

He swallowed, tilted his head, and frowned.

"Didn't you like it?" Amity couldn't believe it.

"Oh, I did. Very much, but I've never tasted anything quite like it. The chocolate was sweeter and . . . ," he trailed, looking for the word.

"It's called milk chocolate," she said. "I think I am the only chocolatier in London, maybe in all of Britain, who has it. I get it from Switzerland, from the factory of Mr. Peter's in Vevey. He is still perfecting it, trying to make it last longer on the shelf, as milk tends to sour. But these sell so quickly, I don't worry."

"Milk chocolate," the duke mused. "May I?" He pointed to the other lighter confection.

"Yes. That one has a figgy center."

He ate it. "Strange how the chocolate is sweeter, but the fig wasn't as sweet as the lemon, which I would have expected to be sour."

"It was not a fig, but *figgy*. I used a prune base. A figgy center could also be dates or raisins, for example. And the lemon is candied and, thus, sweeter."

He nodded, soaking in the information. "I liked the figgy one too, by the way, especially the milk chocolate."

She reminded him, "You've liked them all."

He smiled. "It's true. I have."

She set the plate down and wrote in her notebook to avoid orange and lemon but perhaps include ginger or raspberries. Then she scrawled "no figgy" as it seemed dull in comparison to the other fruit flavors.

"Do you find this terribly tedious?" he asked suddenly.

"Oh, no. I love my work."

He persisted, "Do you ever grow tired of tasting chocolate?"

"Again, no. I love my work." She couldn't imagine a day when she tasted chocolate and felt anything less than delight.

Nodding at her answer, he asked. "Did you always know you would do this?"

"Yes," she confessed. "I had a good palate for it, my father says, from early on. When my sisters would cram any sweet into their mouths, even those awful boiled colored balls which we all now detest for their poor quality, I would be more discerning."

Keeping her face blank, she asked him, "What about you? Did you always know you would be a duke?"

He blinked, opened his mouth, got the joke an instant later, and then laughed uproariously.

Amity felt a wave of warmth trickle through her at having amused this man. It gave her genuine pleasure to make him happy.

"Water, please," he said when his last chuckle died away.

She poured him a glass, which he drank down quickly, probably thirsty from so much chocolate. He set it down and wiped the back of his mouth on his hand, looking entirely at home in her work room.

She straightened. She mustn't allow herself to get too comfortable with him. This wasn't a real friendship, and their association would undoubtedly end entirely in less than a fortnight.

"I suppose we should concentrate on the texture of the third chocolate from yesterday. You thought that had the most spirit, and for your purpose of winning the Lady Madeleine, I think we need one with spirit, don't you?"

He was staring at her and simply nodded in agreement.

Feeling a little ruffled at his scrutiny, she continued, "That one was plain chocolate with orange liqueur. The *Brayson* will be plain because we don't want to risk the milk chocolate and not orange flavored. I can create some samples with the other flavors we've discussed. Do you think you—or rather, *she*—would like a filled center, such as a piece of candied ginger, or shall I keep the same creamy smoothness in the middle and add a flavored syrup or oil?"

"Creamy smoothness," he said, staring at her.

Amity was certain his gaze dropped to her mouth when he spoke, and a frisson of excitement sizzled down her spine.

"I shall work on a few later, perhaps with ginger juice or essence of pear which might do nicely—"

"Why not now?" he asked.

"With you standing here?" The thought unsettled her. "Won't that be a terrible waste of your time?"

The duke shook his head. "If I am not in the way, I would very much like to stay." He looked around. "I'll sit on that stool, and if you need me to taste something, I shall."

A strange request, but she could hardly turn down a duke. Nor did she want to, for she enjoyed his company tremendously. If he stared at her and made her nervous, however, she would have to send him on his way.

Instead, he told her stories of the *haut ton* that kept her laughing for the next hour, and in between, she showed him how she melted solid chocolate in her *bain-marie*. He stood close and watched while she explained how chocolate was too delicate to come in contact directly with the bottom of a flame-fired pot, hence the pot-inside-a-pan-of-water method. She even let him stir, unable to keep from smiling at him since he looked like a child helping in the kitchen for the first time.

With a start, she realized it probably was his first time over a stove. *Sweet Mary!* She had put a duke to work over a cooktop.

"You really should let me pin an apron on you," she offered again.

He sent her a scornful glance, then asked, "Is it done, do you think? May I taste it?"

"It will taste exactly as before it melted, except it will be hot. So, the answer is no. There will be plenty for you to taste in a minute. Now, pour two-thirds onto the marble."

"Directly onto it?"

"Yes, I cleaned it while you were stirring. Go ahead. Pour it in a big circle, a puddle. Don't worry, it won't flow off the marble. It will start to cool at once."

As he'd been told, he poured until she told him to stop. However, when he nearly put the hot pot down on her Italian marble, she shrieked.

"No!" She grabbed his wrist to restrain him. Their gazes locked. "I mean, please, my lord, set it on the trivet. We shall need it again soon." She released him, not quite able to believe she'd laid hands upon a duke's arm. It felt like any other man's, firm and strong. *Like Jeremy's,* she reminded herself. *The man she would eventually marry.*

The duke did as she instructed, and then she let him pull up the stool to the counter.

"Don't *you* wish to sit?" he asked, hovering over the merrily painted blue stool Beatrice liked to use when making toffee. "I cannot sit if you do not."

His gentlemanly manners prevented him breaching the rules of gallantry.

"I prefer to stand when I work," Amity told him. "I can easily reach everything I need and move quickly about the room." She frowned. "Perhaps we can agree to leave the standards of decorum at the curtain," she said, gesturing toward the rich blue hanging that separated them from the rest of the world.

"What happens in here," he suggested, "can be an exception to the rigid behaviors of so-called proper society."

She nodded. "In here, we shall behave as comfortable friends. Agreed?"

He barely hesitated. "Agreed," he said, taking a seat on Beatrice's stool, which squeaked slightly.

Amity hoped the duke wouldn't end up on his backside upon the floor.

"Now, we shall temper the chocolate."

HENRY COULDN'T REMEMBER WHEN he'd enjoyed himself more. He watched her wield two differently shaped tools, one with a long narrow blade, one with a shorter, wider one, yet neither were sharp. She scraped the chocolate from the marble over and over, flipped it, then spread it upon the marble again.

When she seemed satisfied, she held the pot with the scant remaining chocolate at the edge and scraped all the cooled, thicker mixture into it. She stirred this until she'd created a delightfully, glossy blend.

"Tempering crystallizes the cocoa butter in the chocolate. I'm doing that first by warming it to the right temperature, then with movement. The cocoa butter in tempered chocolate is transformed into a stable form."

"Meaning?" he asked, leaning forward to look into the pot.

"I've guaranteed that when it cools, which is in a matter of minutes, the chocolate will hold shape, break with a satisfying snap, and have a beautiful shininess."

"Now what?" he asked, realizing he was speaking softly as if watching a play.

She bit her lower lip. "This will harden in about three to five minutes, so we must roll our balls and dip them in."

"We?" he asked, but he washed his hands at the sink and let her put him to work.

Using the now firm chocolate fondant from the cold box, which had become like a creamy paste as she'd told him it would, they rolled it into balls with their palms. Next, they quickly dipped each ball directly into the tempered chocolate with their fingers and set them on trays lined with wax paper.

He hadn't been in such a mess since he was a small boy. Frankly, he loved it.

"I should have made the balls first ahead of tempering the chocolate," Miss Rare-Foure said, working silently and quickly, making two or three balls for each one of his.

"Why didn't you?"

She barely spared him a glance. "I was distracted," she muttered, stirring the tempered chocolate to keep it fluid until they'd finished.

By him? He kept working until they'd used up all the soft chocolate but still had some of the tempered. He wanted to drink it before it hardened. He watched her give it another few vigorous stirs and reach for a tray of hardened treacle toffee. To his amazement, she poured the remaining chocolate on top and put the tray in the cold box.

"There," she said with satisfaction. "Done and dusted, as they say, and nothing wasted. And now for the *Brayson*." Retrieving a smaller bowl of chocolate fondant from the cold box, she it on the marble. "Let's blend a few and see if you like any."

When Miss Rare-Foure wasn't silently concentrating as she dropped minute amounts of essence into small spoonfuls of chocolate or stirred in a ground spice, she was nibbling or handing a spoon over for him to try, waiting with a curious expression for his opinion.

"If I am doing a whole tray, as we just did, I add whatever I'm blending into the chocolate at an earlier stage, as I did before you came today. Here, try one of the balls you made."

Henry picked one up, amazed at how hard the tempered chocolate had become, like a shell around the rich fondant middle. He took a bite.

"It's like magic. When did you put in the nutmeg?"

She smiled at him, and he felt his insides do a jig. "Nutmeg was in the boiling cream I poured over the chocolate pieces when we first started. You have a good palate, my lord."

Her words pleased him more than nearly any compliment he'd ever had. She tried chocolate with a little rosewater, wrapped some of the gooey chocolate fondant around a piece of chopped date, and even added turmeric and cardamom to another. He liked the way she occasionally puffed out her cheeks when she was thinking.

She seemed to find him amusing, too, which gave him a happy feeling, especially when they could laugh together. Miss Rare-Foure laughed abruptly and without shielding her mouth the way many females did, as if they thought it a sin to show true merriment

"And to think," she commented at one point, "for me, it all started with my reading that jolly children's primer. You know the one, Mrs. Lovechild's? 'The Bees' story sent me on a quest for honey in our kitchen, and our cook at the time kept it with the sugar and tins of cocoa. Naturally, I started experimenting. There was also the story about the boys working together. 'The Hedge Hog,' wasn't it?"

She smiled at the memory, and he easily recalled the stories she mentioned from the same book in his childhood nursery.

"I bullied my sisters—quite the opposite lesson of the primer," she added, "into deciding to work in our mother's shop, each of us doing something different to help out. Beatrice—she's my next younger sister—hit me over the head with Mrs. Lovechild's primer one afternoon when she was tired of preachy, moral lessons. I think it was the last time I saw that book."

She was enchanting. Before he knew it, the time had come for him to leave as he had a late-afternoon appointment with his mother at their bank. He couldn't let down the Dowager Duchess of Pelham, not since stepping into the role of duke and running their estates. For two years, he'd tried to make things as easy as possible for his grieving mother.

"I believe we've developed a few promising new chocolates, which I will try in the shop over the next few weeks, but I think you didn't love any one of them enough for your lady friend."

Miss Rare-Foure was his lady friend. That irrational thought whipped through his head. At least, he believed they had formed a friendship of sorts despite him being a customer. He didn't foresee a time, even after he became engaged to Madeleine, when he wouldn't want to drop by and visit with the chocolatier. It would be different, of course, when he remained in the front of the shop, coming in simply to buy a tin of chocolates.

"I am grateful you allowed me to come in the back and watch you work."

"You were most helpful," she said. She was leaning on the marble counter and rubbing her back. His fingers prickled, and he wanted to reach out and rub the sore muscles for her.

"Was I? Truthfully?" he asked, staring at how her hands kneaded just above the flair of her hips.

"Well," she began as she straightened, turned to him, and made a wry face.

He couldn't help laughing when she teased him, and it felt good to do so freely. Most people were entirely too proper around him, as if the moment he became a duke, he also became stuffy and would be offended by people acting too familiarly around him.

"The shop seems to do a steady business," he said, "from the sound of the bell and all the noise."

"It does. We are fortunate."

"Skill," he corrected, as he stood, making their bodies suddenly too close. She blushed either from his compliment or his proximity, he couldn't tell, and then she walked toward the curtain.

Impulsively, he put his hand out to stop her pulling it aside.

"After we leave this space, we shall have to follow the rules again." He said it lightly, like another jest.

She nodded. "Ah, yes, society's rules of propriety and chivalry, and whether you can even sit when I do not."

He looked down at her and she gazed up at him, and Henry would swear until his dying day that a special bond or affinity had passed between them in that instant. Her eyes widened and her lips parted, as she gasped ever so softly. Undoubtedly, the chocolatier had seen something in his eyes and noticed his own expression of surprise.

Henry knew he had better step through the curtain right away. She was entirely too fetching, with her lovely mahogany-colored eyes and her sweet upturned mouth. He was ready to take her in his arms. In fact, he longed to feel her against him and to claim her lips under his.

Sweeping the curtain aside, he said, "I hope to see you tomorrow although I may have other engagements that keep me away. I very much enjoyed your company."

"Thank you, my lord. As I enjoyed yours." She preceded him through the opening, and he followed her out into the shop.

"How did you two get on?" her mother asked. "Did you create magic for Lady Madeleine?"

"We're unquestionably getting closer," Miss Rare-Foure told her mother.

Henry looked at her sharply. *Did she mean that as a message to him?* He could almost believe it was a *double-entendre*, for he definitely felt closer to this woman than he had a few days earlier.

If at all possible, he would be there again the next day.

CHAPTER SIX

After Lord Pelham left the shop, and no other customers had entered, her mother gave her a pointed look.

"What is it?" Amity asked her. "You look nettled."

"You mustn't let him go back there with the curtain closed. If we'd had a shop full of people when you came out with your face all pink-cheeked and smiling and his lordship saying he'd enjoyed your company, only imagine!"

"But he's a duke," Amity protested, wrinkling her nose, "in the workroom of a chocolate shop."

"Exactly. For what reason could anyone imagine the Duke of Pelham would be back there except to spend time with you."

Amity closed her mouth on the protest she'd been about to make. Her mother was correct. The appearance was decidedly improper.

"If we'd had some other member of the nobility in here, they would have recognized him and tongues would have wagged. Soon, all of London would be wondering what you were offering in that back room."

"Mother!"

"Amity, don't be naïve. I hate to say it, but the duke might actually be hoping for something along those lines. And the ruin would be all on your side, not his. He would be considered blameless while you would be labeled a trollop."

She felt the blood drain from her head. "I didn't think clearly." Right then, she was very glad she had a caring mother.

"Sometimes I think you forget how lovely you are."

At that, she shrugged. "I take your warning to heart, and it won't happen again, but do recall I am making a special chocolate for him to give to Lady Madeleine on the night he intends to propose. You have read the glowing reports of her beauty. Why would the duke want to dally with me when his sights are set on her?"

Her mother rolled her eyes and shook her head. "Amity, Amity, Amity. I know you're my eldest daughter, but sometimes, I vow, Beatrice seems ancient in comparison to you."

They left it at that, and Amity returned to the back of the shop, a room that now smelt of the duke's maleness and . . . she sniffed . . . the lingering scent of his *eau de toilette*. Strange, when he was next to her, she'd been focused on the chocolate and other flavors, and hadn't noticed his fragrance.

Now, reentering the small space, she breathed in the complex aroma of whatever luxurious men's perfume he'd been wearing, just as when she'd first climbed into his coach. The lush, spicy floral scent was couched on a bed of sandalwood, cedar, and clean, soapy musk. Amity decided the duke smelled like heaven. *Masculine heaven!*

Sitting upon the stool he'd vacated, she considered the look he'd given her directly before they'd left the room. She *was* naïve, as her mother said. And of course she was inexperienced, except for a few kisses with Jeremy, which had been pleasant to be sure. Even so, she knew she'd seen something in the duke's expression and glistening in his eyes—regard, even admiration . . . or, perhaps, attraction.

She could admit to herself she, at least, had felt a sizzle of desire.

Her body wanted to be close to the Duke of Pelham.

Her and every other woman in London, no doubt!

She shook her head at her foolish fancy, and then she got back to work.

THE NEXT DAY, DESPITE telling herself not to, Amity kept her ears pricked for the bell, and was disappointed each time she realized it was a *regular* customer answering Charlotte's greeting.

Her mind was only half on what she was doing. That was clear when she scalded a batch of chocolate, something she hadn't done since she was ten years old.

"Stop it!" she muttered, as she made a tray of chocolates shaped like fish that were going to a dinner party the next evening. Sadly, they ended up looking more like sausages, and she knew she would have to remake them. To her continued distress, her elegant swans came out like long-necked chickens.

The duke had said he might not be able to come. Nor should she be hoping he would. He was a distraction. Worse, after just a few encounters, she was becoming attached, which was beyond asinine.

Amity removed her apron, tidied and readied herself to go on her errands. She'd had her eye on a new mold, shaped like a walnut, which would hold a decent amount of chocolate and a large piece of nut in the center. Rare Confectionery would have to charge more for those chocolates because of the size, but the shape would make them popular in the autumn and during the Christmas season.

With her favorite plum-colored cloak on and her hat pinned in place, she opened the door and ran directly into the Duke of Pelham.

"I'm too late," he said, reaching an arm out to steady her.

"Good day, my lord." Amity looked up into his handsome face and felt regret. Even if he'd come earlier, she wouldn't have allowed him into the back room as she had done the previous time. Not after her mother's rebuke.

"Have you finished your artistry for the day, Miss Rare-Foure?"

When someone tried to push past them to get into the shop, he moved aside and drew her with him. How strange to have his hands on her arm as if they were a couple. However, because they were on the public street, Amity wiggled her arm until he released it.

"No, my lord. I'm off to purchase a few supplies and stretch my legs."

He looked up and down the pavement, then back at her. "May I accompany you?"

"*Um* . . . why?" She bit her lip as soon as she'd spoken, hoping she didn't sound terribly rude.

He chuckled. "Why, indeed? I am at sixes and sevens, I suppose. I finished up some business this morning as quickly as I could and intended to spend time with you. Figuring out the chocolate," he added quickly. "Thus, I have time to spare and no plans."

She could hardly turn him down even though she had no chaperone with her, and never did for her quick errands in the neighborhood. After all, what could be safer than London's most exclusive shopping district? Still, her mother might not approve.

Amity lifted her chin. She was not a child, and the duke posed absolutely no threat.

"I suppose it would be all right?" Her words had come out as a nervous question.

His smile died. "I don't wish to impose myself upon you."

"Oh no, my lord, I am very pleased to see you." *Gracious, that sounded too eager.* "It is the possible impropriety of the two of us together that concerns me."

"I believe in broad daylight, given our two stellar reputations, no one could find fault with us walking beside one another and going into a shop or two. Why, I could be your chaperone," he suggested. "Think of me as your maid or footman."

She laughed and gestured for them to begin walking as they were creating more of a scene by huddling against the front window of Rare Confectionery.

"Since you look nothing like either of our maids and we do not have a footman, I shall simply think of you as my friend."

"Perfect," he said in his rich voice, like warm chocolate to her ears.

Shaking her head at the ridiculous and rather disgusting idea of chocolate poured into her ears, she knew she'd best stop all her whimsical thoughts.

"My errands are not too exciting," she warned him.

"It is no matter. I confess to enjoying your company."

Her steps briefly faltered. When he said something such as that, those whimsical thoughts came rushing back.

"Where are we off to?" he asked. "And do we need my driver?"

"No, everything today is within walking distance. Most of our bulk supplies are delivered. Occasionally, I go into the East End—"

"I beg your pardon?" he asked, sounding concerned.

"Never alone and never after dark, I assure you. But the cacao bean warehouses are on St Katherine's Dock, near the tea. Sometimes I've had the good fortune to be told of a new type of bean. Obviously not new to those who grow it." She chuckled at the arrogance of Europeans thinking they'd discovered anything new when the tree had been cultivated for centuries. "But new to us. Anyway, it's a treat to be one of the first in Britain to sniff the beans or even chew one."

"You chew them whole?"

"Yes, my lord. Bitter but I enjoy them anyway. Sometimes raw, sometimes roasted."

He nodded and said nothing to that. He must think her an undeniably odd woman. After another few feet, he asked, "Do you make your own chocolate?"

She wished she could say yes. "No, but that's because I could not do it as well."

His footsteps faltered slightly at her side, and she turned to him. "I'm surprised," he confessed.

"It is more complex to make quality, smooth chocolate than you can imagine. The beans are roasted and the shells removed to reveal the nibs, and then, as with coffee, they must be finely ground. The result is a cocoa paste, which is pressed to draw out the cocoa butter, the slimy part you mentioned when too much is left in your cocoa powder."

"So, the paste is solid chocolate?" he asked, sounding interested.

"Well, it is," she said, as they passed store windows, slowly making their way through the multitude of pedestrians. "However, it isn't very pleasant to eat. To make an edible chocolate bar, you need to add back in more cocoa butter and, of course, sugar. And you must blend this for ages to make it smooth and delicious. Our store buys readymade blocks of chocolate, mostly from Switzerland and France, because it is superior to what I could create."

In fact, Rare Confectionery had a wonderful relationship with the chocolate manufacturers who supplied their shop. When Amity renounced having a Season, her family had spent the money saved for ballgowns and party tickets on travel. Her first destination had been to Vevey, Switzerland, where she'd learned secrets from Monsieur Peter, the man who invented milk chocolate and now sold it to her by the block. Everyone adored its creamy sweetness.

Afterward, her family had spent time with her father's parents in France. Amity visited the famed Debauve and Gallais chocolate shop on the 30 Rue des Saints-Pères in Paris where it had already existed for sixty years. She'd come home with the so-called *pistoles* or chocolate "coins" created by the French royal chemist, Monsieur Debauve, for Marie Antoinette to stave off her headaches..

Another highlight had been her tour of the Menier chocolate factory in Noisiel, perched directly upon the Marne River so water wheels could power it.

"The ornate iron-and-brick factory, itself, looks like a confectionery treat," Amity told him, recalling how charmed she'd been by its facade. "I came home with their popular version of drinking chocolate for my own consumption, and it was superb. Menier recently opened a factory here in London at Shoreditch. Most convenient, my lord."

Amity hoped she wasn't boring him, but she loved sharing what she knew about the best thing in the world. "We could not be more fortunate than to live at this time," she declared.

"Because of the chocolate?" he asked, a teasing tone to his voice.

"Exactly," she agreed. "Today, I intend to purchase some molds from the tinsmith's finished goods shop on Cork Street. Do you know it? We also get our tins for gift-giving there."

A strange expression came over the duke's face. "I confess I do not know of any tinsmith on any street anywhere. Do you think less of me?"

She burst out laughing. When she recovered, she said, "I expect you also don't know the best place to purchase the purest sugar or the creamiest butter."

"Both appear as if by magic on my dining table as needed." Then he snapped his fingers. "I do know where to buy the best brandy."

"And cigars, too, I'd warrant," Amity guessed.

"Certainly," he agreed. "And most definitely coffee beans. Although usually I send my footman to purchase all of these items."

"As you should. Thus, we both have our areas of interest, do we not?"

"We do," he said amiably, holding her gaze for a long moment.

She directed his steps down Clifford Street and, after a short block, they turned onto Cork Street. The second shop window from the corner glittered with tin molds.

When they entered, she appreciated how he immediately had an interest in his surroundings.

"They have every shape and size," he marveled.

"There are molds for soap, candles, sweets, and even if you wish to get fancy with your blancmange or aspic."

He hesitated and stared at her.

"I mean your cook, my lord. Not you," she amended hastily in case she'd offended him.

"No, it wasn't that which gave me pause. Just the notion of *fancy* aspic. I've never cared for jellied anything. I much prefer my chocolate in a decorative shape than my aspic." He shuddered.

"Agreed. Today, I want to buy twelve walnut molds, and if you see something you would like for Lady Madeleine, we can decide against the fondant chocolate center, which must be hand-rolled into a ball, and I will make molded chocolates instead."

"Very well. I shall look, but if I find something, I will buy it," he insisted, "not you."

She wasn't going to argue with him, since he probably wouldn't allow her to use it again after creating the original *Brayson* chocolate.

When he chose a flower-shaped mold for his lady, she explained she needed a tray of at least a dozen into which she could pour tempered chocolate.

"See this," she said, showing him a tray of rabbits hinged to bring the front and back sides together and create a fully formed rabbit. "But your molds should be flat on the bottom, so no hinge."

She watched the duke wander around again, exclaiming over the cleverness of one after the other, until he found a tray of flowers he thought suitable.

When he picked up a well-crafted stag, he went quiet. Amity crossed the store to his side.

"Do you like it?" she asked.

"It reminds me of my father," he said softly. "He had a painting of a stag like this in his study, which is now my own. It makes me think of when we went hunting together."

The duke had a wistful tone to his voice, and Amity decided to return and purchase an entire tray of stag molds. When she finished Lady Madeleine's chocolate, she would craft him a special stag-shaped confection.

"Where next?" he asked when they had finished making their purchases.

Thus, she found herself accompanied by an escort from the highest echelon of British nobility while she purchased yards of blue ribbon her mother wanted to tie around the tops of their white Rare Confectionery bags. The strangeness wore off quickly, and they chatted like friends, pointing out items in the shop windows. Amity had the feeling he didn't window shop often or shop at all very much. Nevertheless, the duke seemed to enjoy himself.

"It's the chocolate lady," came a young voice at her elbow. She didn't always recognize her youngest patrons, but they absolutely recognized her.

Reaching into her reticule, she drew out a paper sack. Today, she had balls of chocolate fondant with a small marzipan center hidden inside. Handing one to the boy, who thanked her and ran off, she looked up to see the duke staring hard at the sack, like a dog would at a bone.

Laughing, she offered him one.

"Oh," he exclaimed after devouring it. "That's very good."

"That's Miss Charlotte's marzipan," she told him, "elevating the humble chocolate into something else entirely."

"I believe that's the delicious chocolate elevating the humble marzipan," he quipped.

"Dear God! Don't let my sister ever hear you say that."

"No, I wouldn't dream of it." Then suddenly, he froze.

"Pelham!" exclaimed a well-dressed man who came to a stop in front of them.

"Waverly," the duke returned with less enthusiasm, sounding strangely cautious.

They shook hands while the other man's glance came to rest on Amity, a questioning look upon his face.

"Miss Rare-Foure," the duke said, "This is the Viscount Waverly."

She curtsied.

"Waverly, this is Miss Rare-Foure, whose family owns Rare Confectionery."

The viscount inclined his head to her. "I believe you mentioned her before," he remarked, his eyes dancing with merriment, raising Amity's curiosity.

The Duke of Pelham had mentioned her to his friend?

"Yet you failed to give an accurate account of her loveliness," Lord Waverly added.

Even knowing the man was being a shameless flatterer, Amity felt her cheeks warm.

"Waverly," the duke warned, "don't try your charm upon Miss Rare-Foure. She has a better head on her shoulder than to fall for your nonsense."

Did he really think effusive words about her appearance to be nonsense?

"Careful, Pelham," the viscount said. "By the frown upon her face, you may have insulted Miss Rare-Foure. There is nothing nonsensical about her beauty."

Hating how this man had read her expression so easily, she suddenly spoke up. "If you gentlemen will excuse me, I must get back to my shop. I have work to do this afternoon."

"Let me walk you back," the duke offered.

"No, thank you. As I said, I have work to do, and I cannot be entertaining you at the same time." It sounded unkind, but she was suddenly feeling crabby. "I am not a lady of leisure, you understand."

The duke's eyes widened, and his friend coughed behind his glove, which she suspected was to hide his laughter. The other meaning for the term struck her a second later—as the very trollop her mother had spoken of.

"Good day, my lords." With her cheeks flaming scarlet, she snatched her packages from the duke's hands, curtsied to them both, and hurried away. Thankfully, he didn't come after her.

HENRY TURNED BACK TO HIS friend who was openly laughing now Miss Rare-Foure had dashed off in a state of mortification. That hadn't gone well.

"Why do I think that was all your fault?" Henry asked. "And stop your insipid braying, dammit."

"I say, she's a feisty thing, isn't she?" Daniel Waverly noted. "Putting you in your place about keeping her from her work and making mention of the offensive class of lightskirts. Lady of leisure, indeed." He began to chuckle again.

"She didn't intend to," Henry said, feeling irritated. "Anyway, what did you mean with your flattery and telling her I'd spoken of her to you. You embarrassed her."

"You should have joined in and praised her. Every woman in London is touchy about her looks since Lady Madeleine made her debut. But I daresay I would enjoy the sweetness of your chocolatier, plus the benefits."

"Are you trying to make me defend her honor and punch your beak?"

Waverly shook his head. "I meant only the benefit of an unlimited supply of quality chocolate. I've had the pleasure of a sweet from Rare Confectionery. I don't know what you thought I meant, but I believe you are getting caught up in the romantic notion of being with a shopkeeper's daughter."

They had started walking in the opposite direction to which the chocolatier had dashed off.

"She is *not* a shopkeeper's daughter. Well, I suppose technically she is, but she's much more than that," Henry insisted. "She's a chemist and an artist and a chef—all for confectionery. Moreover, she's very smart and amusing. In short, she's good company."

"You didn't defend yourself against my claim you are thinking romantically about her."

Henry should have dissuaded him of that at once. "Because it's too preposterous to dignify with a remark."

"Of course," his friend said.

Henry rolled his eyes. Waverly would say anything to get him to step aside from his pursuit of Lady Madeleine. On the first night she'd appeared in a ballroom, it was Waverly who had pointed her out and wondered aloud who the beautiful creature could be.

When Waverly found out she was an earl's daughter, he'd liked her even more. Yet Henry outranked him and, thus, would triumph, in all likelihood, if there had been any competition among suitors. There hadn't been. They'd all stepped aside to allow his pursuit, and he'd become the sole wooer, as it were.

He sighed. It seemed a little mercenary when he considered it. He believed he had spent more time talking to Miss Rare-Foure than he had to Lady Madeleine. He would have to remedy that in the near future.

"So, Pelham," came Waverly's amused voice, "are you truly only sampling Rare chocolate, or do you intend to sample the chocolatier as well?"

CHAPTER SEVEN

Henry couldn't very well clobber Waverly in the middle of Bond Street although he was sorely tempted. Instead, he kept walking and thought the best defense of Miss Rare-Foure's reputation was to pretend his friend must be joking.

"Amusing, Waverly. My sights, as you are well aware, are set firmly upon Lady Madeleine. Are you hoping to push me aside and derail my suit with ridiculous innuendo to clear the field for your own pursuit of Brayson's daughter?"

Waverly laughed. "Maybe. But Miss Rare-Foure is certainly pretty enough for a tumble."

Outrage and an unexpectedly strong desire to protect her arose in Henry.

"She is pretty enough and also decent and smart enough to warrant a husband who cherishes her. Taking a tumble with a shopkeeper's daughter is rather last decade, don't you think, Waverly?"

His friend shrugged. "I suppose. Look at Lord Langley marrying that nobody from America instead of merely bedding her."

"A nobody with a fortune," Henry pointed out, glad they were back to idle chatter about other people and not Miss Rare-Foure. In truth, he'd already spent too much time thinking about her, and didn't need to spend more time going over her virtues with his friends.

He had planned his marital path, and it was a beneficial one to both parties. He would get a beautiful wife with a good-sized dowry who was raised to make a fine hostess. Privately, he hoped Madeleine would be as interesting and friendly, as smart and joyful, and as pleasant to be around as Miss Rare-Foure. He had no reason to believe that when they got to know each other that wouldn't be the case.

"Where are we going?" Waverly asked.

"Haven't the foggiest," Henry told him, and they laughed. "Are you attending the dinner party at Lady Peabody's tonight?"

"Absolutely not. They tried to partner me with a last-season debutante, Miss Someone or Other. Honestly, it doesn't matter. Once you arrive with Lady Madeleine, no one will look at any other female."

"Hm," Henry said, for he was thinking how nice it would be to escort Miss Rare-Foure somewhere special. He wanted to know what she thought about everything, including the food and the other guests. He wanted to take her to Gunter's, a fashionable eatery in Mayfair on Berkeley Square, and taste ices and sorbets with her.

Would she like the saffron mousse or the maple cream ice?

"Are you listening to me, Pelham?"

"No," he said truthfully. Feeling guilty that his focus wasn't solely on Madeleine, nor had it been for far too many days, he had half a mind to go back to the confectionery and buy her a little gift. On second thought, he decided against doing so. Henry wanted his gift of chocolate to be a complete surprise, and the party was now just over a week away.

"I think I'm going to buy Lady Madeleine a token, something feminine and lacy."

"Like drawers or a shift?" Waverly asked, a wicked expression on his face.

"Why not? I shall walk up to her with her parents in the room and gift her a pair of Belgian-lace drawers. That should go over well."

They laughed again and passed in front of a haberdashery. "I suppose a handkerchief," Henry said, and turned into the shop, not caring if Waverly followed.

"Enjoy your shopping," Waverly called after him and continued along the street.

AMITY HAD ON HER favorite plum-colored evening gown. Luckily, it matched her favorite plum-colored day gown perfectly so she could wear the matching mantle. Her mother had insisted she dress the part even though she was not a guest for tonight's party but only delivering the chocolates.

"Through the front door," Felicity Rare-Foure insisted. "We are *not* servants. Lord Peabody should have sent someone round to collect the chocolates. Whatever happens, you are not to go behind to the mews and knock at the back door like a laundress or milkman."

"Yes, Mother." And she sent Delia, their maid-of-all work, an apologetic look in case she was offended by the general denigration of servants. The middle-aged woman, however, shrugged, seemingly unbothered, and handed over Amity's gloves.

Because of her youngest sister's keen interest on the homes and habits of the wealthy, Amity took Charlotte along for company, dressed equally well in a rose-colored gown.

"Please remain calm," Amity begged her sister as their carriage pulled up in front of a townhouse on Charles Street, off the west side of the fashionable Berkeley Square.

Nevertheless, fizzing with excitement as if they were actually going to be honored guests and seated at the dining table, Charlotte whistled her happiness. Amity gasped.

"For heaven's sake, don't do that no matter how excited you become, no matter who you see, or how nice anyone is to you. Do you understand me?"

"Yes," her sister said, her brown eyes sparkling.

Amity grabbed her arm as Charlotte darted ahead toward the front door.

"I mean it," she reiterated. "Behave or I shall tell Mother you cannot go out in civilized society. No upcoming Guy Fawkes party, either. No bonfire with your friends."

Charlotte slowed her step and sighed. "Very well. Thank you for letting me come."

At that, Amity smiled. She'd known how much pleasure her youngest sister would get from seeing inside the luxurious townhouse, even if no farther inside than the foyer.

The door opened ahead of their knocking since the butler was undoubtedly stationed at the entrance to admit guests. This would be absurdly early, however, as their mother had said the party didn't start for another hour.

By the sound of the many voices coming from the drawing room, their mother had been blatantly mistaken. Amity hoped the chocolates were intended for *after* dinner, as it seemed guests were already having drinks.

The butler tried to take their mantles, but Amity dissuaded him.

"We are not staying. We brought the chocolates ordered by Lady Peabody," she whispered, not wanting any of the guests to overhear. "If you could direct us toward the kitchen," she added.

"Mother would not want us going to the kitchen," Charlotte said, her voice a little too loud, then she turned to the butler. "We are *not* servants, you see." She sounded exactly like their mother.

Amity wanted to shush her sister before she offended the man. But Charlotte gave him a large smile and continued.

"Not that there is anything wrong with being a servant, you understand. Especially not a butler. You have an entire house to oversee. My sister, here, she oversees the making of all our chocolates. She is like the butler of Rare Confectionery. That's the name of our shop."

The butler sighed as if listening to a young lady prattle on was beyond his duties.

"Would you like to take the chocolates?" Amity asked him, "or perhaps you could fetch the housekeeper?"

Before he could respond, a booming voice called out to them from the open drawing room door.

"Young ladies! Pretty young ladies! Come here at once. The party has begun."

Amity was almost positive this was Lord Peabody, for she'd heard his voice in the outer room of the shop when he stopped in with Lady Peabody to order the chocolates.

"My lord," she said and curtsied. Looking sideways, she realized Charlotte was frozen, and quickly tugged on her sister's black velvet mantle until she, too, bobbed low.

After his lordship nodded in return, they rose.

"You must be the St. Germain sisters. Naughty, naughty, you are late. Your dinner partners await you in the parlor. Gerald, take their cloaks."

Again, the butler stepped toward them, and again, Amity fended him off.

"Excuse me, Lord Peabody, but we are not the St. Germain sisters, nor are we guests."

"They are from Rare Confectionery," came another voice. This time Lady Peabody crossed the foyer. She slipped her hand through her husband's arm. "I wondered where you'd got to, my love," she said, looking fondly at the older gentleman. "Now I understand, for you are drawn to a lovely face the way a bee goes to a flower, and here we have two lovely *young* women."

Lord Peabody laughed. "You know I only look, my love."

Amity exchanged a glance with Charlotte.

"My lady," she began again, "we have the chocolates you ordered. There must have been a misunderstanding, for we were told your party wouldn't start for another hour. We never would have barged in if we'd known it had already started."

"But then we wouldn't have our delicious chocolates, would we?" Lady Peabody asked, entirely unconcerned by their late arrival.

At the chiming of the doorbell, their butler moved quickly from their small group to the door, returning with a note which he handed to his lordship.

"What does it say?" Lady Peabody asked.

"No St. Germain sisters, my love. One has a headache and the other thinks she may get one at any moment. They send their regrets."

A look of annoyance crossed Lady Peabody's face. "What a nuisance! In my day, if one had a megrim, one simply bore it bravely and carried on, especially if one had a commitment."

Then she stared at Amity and Charlotte. "Gerald, take their mantles. We mustn't keep our other guests waiting."

Charlotte giggled nervously, but Amity clutched her mantle with her free hand while her other still held the sack containing three large tins of chocolates.

"My lady, what can you mean?" she asked.

"Miss Rare-Foure, you are a respectable young woman, dressed appropriately for the evening, as is your sister. Are either of you engaged?"

"No, my lady, but—"

"I consider you both to be heaven sent. I have two single gentlemen in my drawing room expecting to have dinner partners. And now they shall."

"Oh, no," Amity began, "that hardly seems—"

"Please, dear sister," Charlotte entreated her, "we have been invited. We mustn't be rude to our host and hostess, and I am not going to whistle, I promise. Mother would want us to help out Lady Peabody, don't you think?"

Amity eyed her sister, who'd suddenly matured into a reasonable person.

"Yes, please," Lord Peabody said, with a note of teasing that made his wife dig her elbow into his side.

"Very well," Amity said, finally giving the butler her mantle as Charlotte had already done. "In that case, I thank you for allowing us to be part of your evening. The chocolates," she reminded them, removing the tins from the sack, which she also gave to their butler.

"Take them, my love," Lady Peabody ordered her husband. "Oh, such pretty containers. We shall put them on the sideboard for after dinner. The chocolates will go so well with port or sherry. Did you manage to make them look like elephants?"

Lady Peabody didn't wait for a response as she and her husband led them into the drawing room. Amity felt a little lightheaded. Despite her comportment in the foyer, Charlotte was given to rather silly behavior at times. Furthermore, she, herself, was equally inexperienced in the ways of a fancy party with—

Lord Pelham! Her eyes found him as soon as she entered the room and their hosts stepped to the side.

"We have a lovely surprise," Lady Peabody told those gathered, and Amity knew her cheeks were the color of raspberries. She and Charlotte could hardly be a lovely or a welcome surprise for anyone, especially the crème de la crème of London society.

What would the duke think, seeing two shopgirls where they obviously did not belong?

"Very lovely," Lord Peabody added, earning another dig in the side from his wife.

Lady Peabody continued, "We have lost two guests while almost instantly gaining two others in their stead. Our hosting reputation has maintained its perfect rate of partnering."

The other guests raised their glasses, some laughed at Lady Peabody's little quip, and others said, "Bravo."

To Amity's amazement, Charlotte stepped past her as if she belonged and took a glass of wine from a servant whose sole job seemed to be to stand perfectly motionless with a tray of filled wine glasses. Then naturally, her sister went toward the only person she recognized.

"Your Grace, so good to see you again."

Amity's eyes widened at Charlotte's aplomb. Snagging a glass for herself, hoping it gave her a little of her sister's courage, she took a healthy sip and followed her.

"A delightful surprise," the duke said, a smile playing about his lips. She sensed he understood her discomfort. And a pleasant thought struck her. *Was he one of the single gentlemen Lady Peabody had spoken of?* He seemed to be alone.

As if they were at a play and a cue had just been given, a hush went through the room at the same time as Lord Peabody said, "There you are, dear girl. Did you get lost finding the water-closet?"

Less romantic words were never spoken, Amity was positive, at least not to this lady. In had walked a radiant young woman with the fairest of complexions and the lightest blonde hair she'd ever seen. She wore pale blue silk that seemed to catch the lamplight and shine a halo around her.

The lady—for by her manner and dress she was titled—allowed her gaze to sweep the room, perhaps making certain every eye was upon her, as assuredly they were. Then, at last, her glance landed on Amity, revealing a pair of luminous blue eyes. And all at once, she knew who it was—Lady Madeleine Brayson.

The newspaper descriptions hadn't lied. She was stunning, like a doll crafted from porcelain and bestowed with the prettiest coloring imaginable.

Lady Madeleine's glance passed over her to Charlotte, hovered briefly, and settled on Lord Pelham. At that point, her face broke out in a spectacular smile, and even Amity gasped softly at her beauty.

"An angel," Charlotte murmured beside her.

Amity looked at Lord Pelham to see he was utterly entranced, staring at the woman he intended to make his wife as she approached. *Who could blame him?*

When she got close enough, the duke made introductions. While polite, Lady Madeleine was disinterested at best. Thankfully, Lady Peabody came over to play the hostess.

"Let me introduce you to your dinner companions." With that, she led Amity and Charlotte away from the lady and her besotted duke.

On the other side of the room were two young men, brown hair and sandy-colored hair respectively, well-dressed, who nodded politely as they approached.

"Lord Greenley, this is Miss Rare-Foure." The paler haired man looked blandly toward Amity and nodded after she curtsied.

"And this is also Miss Rare-Foure," Lady Peabody added. She looked at Charlotte who was grinning broadly. "This is Lord Ridley. I shall leave you ladies in their care. Now that you have rescued my seating arrangement, I must tell Cook we are ready."

Their hostess left them with the strangers, and Amity plastered on her best shopgirl face, both congenial and accommodating. They chatted about nothing, which was a relief, until Lord Ridley asked about their family name.

Amity was unsure about the correct etiquette. *Would they be offended to learn they had been saddled with shopkeepers' daughters?* Whoever the St. Germain sisters were, they undoubtedly did not earn their keep selling wares on New Bond Street.

Before Charlotte could answer with something embarrassingly honest, Amity said, "Our father is of the Foure barony in France." No need to say he wasn't in line for the title of baron. "Our mother is from the very old English Rare family." Mostly a long line of bakers, but there was no need to mention that, either.

Their family had always flirted with the upper echelon, so to speak, being occasionally welcomed into their company, as they were tonight, whilst staying firmly rooted in the middle class. They had nothing to be ashamed of.

So why was Amity couching her family's status in omissions and half-truths?

"Fascinating," Lord Ridley said, sounding not the least bit fascinated and looking past her toward the rest of the guests.

Lord Greenley, for his part, did nothing but stare down her sister's dress from his superior height. It was the inevitable course of things, Amity supposed.

Feeling protective, she endeavored to get his attention away from Charlotte's ample bosom.

"You are related to the Greenleys on Hyde Park Street, are you not?" They'd had an order months earlier for a large quantity of chocolate from the Greenley household. Payment hadn't been forthcoming without two notices of account going out.

"Indeed," Lord Greenley said. She guessed he recalled the incident for he asked, "Are you related to the owners of Rare Confectionery on Bond Street?"

"Yes," Charlotte piped up, eager to chime in and speak with the two eligible men. "Our father owns it."

Lord Ridley's attention returned to their little group. "Your family *owns* a confectioner's shop?"

"My sister is our chocolatier," Charlotte said and gestured to her, as if there was any question to whom she referred. "Amity is very talented. She slaves away for hours in the back room and comes out with the most delectable creations."

The gazes of both the wealthy, titled gentlemen turned to her, examining her as if she were another species, and Amity wanted to sink beneath the richly carpeted floor and hide.

84

CHAPTER EIGHT

Oblivious to their reactions, Charlotte continued, "We brought some chocolates with us. Obviously, we didn't bring them willy-nilly. Lady Peabody ordered them, and my clever sister created them. Thus, you shall taste our confections after dinner."

Amity was happy her sister was proud of her. Nonetheless, at that moment, she would rather Charlotte had not referred to her as *slaving in a back room*. She might as well be dressed in her chocolate-smeared apron with her hair under a kerchief.

"Fascinating," said Lord Ridley again, sounding even less impressed. Clearly, he wanted to be partnered with anyone else in the group than the lowly Rare-Foure shopgirls.

"I can hardly wait to taste *your* chocolate," Lord Greenley said to Charlotte, arching the sculpted brow over one eye and winking the other.

Charlotte shrugged slightly, missing any innuendo, and Amity wanted to slap his face.

Thankfully, Lady Peabody announced dinner. As Amity turned, she found Lord Pelham staring directly at her even while he was taking Lady Madeleine's arm.

He smiled, and she smiled back, glad he was there. He might not truly be her friend, and he was evidently smitten with his beautiful lady, yet they had shared a few pleasant interactions. She couldn't help but consider him an ally among London's elite. Hopefully, he would be seated close by at dinner.

Even though it had seemed as if Lady Peabody had presented her to Lord Greenley, that man took Charlotte's arm, forcing Lord Ridley, with his palpable air of ennui, to take Amity's.

Their host and hostess went first, followed by Lady Madeleine and the Duke of Pelham, indubitably the most important guests in the room, and everyone else made their way after.

The dining room was decorated with lavish reds and golds, both in the wallpaper and the fabrics, mirroring the current craze for everything oriental. The long table was festooned with a pretty lace cloth, barely visible under the array of candlesticks, plates, flowered centerpieces, multiple forks, spoons, and knives at every place setting, each containing a massive plate with a smaller plate and a bowl on top, along with glasses of every size and shape.

How many courses and how long this meal would go on for, Amity could hardly imagine. The guests milled about, looking for their names on small white cards.

"Look," Charlotte exclaimed, "we have place cards. How clever for Lady Peabody to make them up for us after we arrived."

Despite *Foure* being spelled incorrectly, Amity agreed it was kind of their hostess. When seated, she found herself directly across the table from Lord Pelham. She doubted they would be able to converse, however, what with the forest of vases full of roses and candelabra between them. There was even a whole pineapple displayed, which reminded her of the chocolates she'd brought. Apparently, Lady Peabody liked to show off her wealth, and pineapple was her luxury of choice.

Sending her a companionable look, the duke shrugged, and she smiled again. Then Lady Madeleine took his attention and the dinner began.

After removing her gloves and placing them in her lap, Charlotte leaned across her dining companion, Lord Greenley, and tapped Amity on the hand.

"No bags of meat tonight," Charlotte whispered, loudly enough for the man to hear. It didn't matter though. Amity could tell Lord Greenley was using only one of his five senses, given his good view down her sister's décolletage.

All Amity could do was smile slightly. Certainly, at the Peabodys' table, there would not be any sausages to which her sister so crudely referred. Rather, their hostess announced each new course in French with much rolling of her *R*'s. Luckily, with French grandparents and a good education, Amity knew what she was eating. From the turtle and spring-time potage to the filet of sole, oysters and breaded whiting during the fish course, through the chicken and roast beef, the lamb cutlets and breaded quail, the roasted figs and asparagus, the meal went on and on.

Amity realized by the *relevés* course during which the main meat was served that she ought to take the smallest bite of each dish or she would never make it to the *entremets sucré*. And she did so love fancy desserts. It would be a shame to be too full.

Shooting a glance at Charlotte, she set her fork down and hoped her sister followed suit. She also peeked across the table. The duke happened to look up from his *poulets a la régence*.

With the smallest lift of his brow, Lord Pelham asked her how she was doing. With a returning lift of her shoulder, she indicated she was fine. It was the best exchange she'd had during the meal so far. In another minute, Lord Ridley finally attempted to show an interest by questioning where her father went to school, Eton or Harrow, and from what part of England the Rare family hailed.

After her answers seemed to dissatisfy him, he looked to his right for someone else with whom to converse. Thus, Amity sat unspeaking for an entire course, feeling shunned and a little sorry for herself.

With Lord Ridley's shoulder firmly toward her, she knew her only hope to escape her isolation was to engage Lord Greenley in conversation. She almost wished her gown's neckline were lower cut. Yet with half the meal still to come, and while Charlotte was conversing with the gentleman to her far left, Amity would make a valiant attempt to gain the attention of the man who sat silently to her left.

"My lord."

He turned slowly, his glance dropping to her bosom and the lace at her décolletage that obscured his view. When his gaze rose to her face, he gave her a wan smile, nothing like that of Lord Pelham, but at least he seemed to recall common courtesy and spoke.

"How are you enjoying the meal?" he asked.

"Very much," she returned. "And yourself?"

"It's better than some, not as good as others. In a word, it will do."

"Goodness, my lord, your palate must be extremely persnickety not to find this to be a sumptuous repast. I cannot find fault with a single dish."

He sniffed, twisted his mouth in an expression of mild distaste, and deigned to look so impossibly arrogant, Amity laughed out loud.

Absolutely unexpected, the laughter burst from her before she could stop herself. To her horror, it seemed to cause an immediate cessation of all noise in the room except for the clattering of a fork dropped carelessly onto a plate.

Turning toward the sound, Amity realized it had come from Charlotte, who was now staring at her with large, alarmed eyes.

Oh dear! Oh dear! Oh dear!

Amity's mouth went bone dry. Reaching quickly for her wine, she proceeded to knock it over, making their hostess exclaim while some ladies tittered at her clumsiness. One of the servers rushed forward to mop it up, remove the glass, and replace it with a full one—all within about thirty seconds.

The longest thirty seconds of Amity's life—with the other diners staying completely silent. She could only be eternally grateful the wine had been white.

"Doesn't anyone laugh at a dinner party anymore?" Lord Pelham suddenly asked. Amity looked at him with gratitude, and he winked at her. "I, for one, am delighted at the happy sound and am ready to laugh along with the lovely young miss."

"Perhaps if we knew what had caused the outburst of good humor," said Lady Peabody, without any malice, sounding as if she genuinely wished to be in on the joke.

Drats and double drats! Amity could hardly say it was Lord Greenley's sourpuss expression that had engendered her involuntary laughter. In fact, by the look on his face, he knew she had been laughing at him, and he didn't look the least bit pleased.

Reaching slowly this time, Amity picked up her wine glass, aware of every eye trained upon her. She took a small sip of chardonnay, careful not to gulp or to cough. At last, she spoke.

"I was thinking of a jest I read in the newspaper the other day," she lied. Fending off anyone asking her what it was, she looked directly at Lord Pelham. "I'm sure all of you have read it already. Perhaps someone else has an amusing story or a joke to tell."

That sounded like the utterance of a half-wit, but it was the best Amity could do, along with sending the duke a beseeching look, which unfortunately, Lady Madeleine also caught, making her raise a delicately perfect eyebrow.

"I shall think of one," he said, "if *you* come up with the next one, either a story or a joke."

The infernal man! She had nearly succeeded in getting all the attention off herself, and then he had to say that.

The tension in the room relaxed, however, as the duke launched into a story about his own boating misfortune the previous summer, involving a lost oar and a leaky hull. It was self-deprecating and amusing, and soon, everyone was laughing along with him.

Meanwhile, Amity considered what she would say. Her sisters always thought her a good storyteller. But doing so in private was far easier than being on display in the Peabodys' dining room.

Her stomach tensed as the duke's gaze landed upon her once again. He tilted his wine glass in her direction. *Your turn,* he seemed to say.

As the attention of the other guests returned to her, she breathed deeply, pretended they were all simply eager customers, and launched into a story about a confectioner in Switzerland whose very large vat of melted chocolate broke on the table in front of him.

"Making him the first chocolate-covered chocolatier," she concluded.

It was a success. And when they were all laughing again at the image of the man covered in a warm, brown sticky mess, Lady Peabody asked, "Is there anyone else who wishes to tell us a humorous tale? I very much like this table game. But the rest of you must continue eating or we shall fall dreadfully behind. Then Cook will start sending courses out stacked atop one another to punish us for lagging. Besides, we have the most delicious chocolates awaiting us in the drawing room."

Amity looked at Charlotte, who had turned pink-cheeked with pleasure. They were mingling well with the *haut ton.* Undoubtedly, her youngest sister couldn't wait to tell Beatrice, who still held a little resentment from being snubbed in their own shop not long ago. She had tried to converse with a lady only to be told by the servant that her mistress didn't speak directly with shopgirls. Beatrice had loudly told the lady she didn't sell sweets to anyone whose head was so large.

The servant had almost laughed, which would probably have caused her termination. The insulted lady had patted her hair as if to confirm her head size was normal, before gliding out of the shop without a word.

"Good riddance," Beatrice had said, also loudly. "I do wish we could have slipped the maid a piece of chocolate. Can you imagine being in servitude to such a pompous creature?"

Lords Ridley and Greenley would have applauded that haughty lady, Amity thought. What's more, some of the people in the room might have acted in precisely the same manner, turning up their noses at Beatrice.

Sighing softly, Amity wished she didn't feel as if she and Charlotte were play-acting. Despite being well-spoken and wearing pretty gowns, they didn't truly fit in. Worse, she was on edge for fear of making a terrible mistake, especially in front of the duke, and looking a fool.

Half listening to the other stories being told—of misplaced servants, mishaps with gowns, the convenience of steam trains—she ate a forkful of the *meringue à la Chantilly* and one of the *beignet* with bananas. *How would any of the guests have room for chocolates?* Regardless, she was more than ready to go home and wished she knew the etiquette of who was allowed to leave when and in what order.

Suddenly, she realized Charlotte was speaking. As long as she didn't whistle, Amity supposed her sister was harmless, until she heard her own name mentioned. Wanting to throw the contents of her wine glass atop her sister's head, anything to stop her talking, Amity was helpless to do aught but sit as the tale unfolded of her and a horse, ending with her knocked off by a low branch.

Amity supposed it wasn't the worst thing that had ever happened to her. She glanced at the duke, who wore an amused expression though not unkind. Unfortunately, beside him, Lady Madeleine looked both disapproving and almost pitying. Among these horsemen and horsewomen who spent their leisure time trotting their mounts up and down Rotten Row, she probably seemed like the most uncouth female. At least it wasn't the ice-skating story—

"Once, all three of us were ice skating," Charlotte began anew.

"Dear sister," Amity interrupted, "it's not polite to monopolize the conversation." She glared at her, causing Charlotte to firmly close her mouth.

Certain she heard the duke chuckle, when Amity glanced at him, he was the picture of innocence, blinking back at her.

"Are we finished?" Lord Peabody asked, pushing back his chair and circling the table so he could draw out his wife's chair. As others began to stand, their host and hostess led them from the room.

Amity thought Lord Ridley might have forgotten her entirely, but at the last moment, he pulled out her chair. She didn't put her gloves back on, as she noticed other women weren't, either. She supposed the threat of chocolates soiling one's gloves was enough of a deterrent.

Clutching them in her right hand, she rested her other on Lord Ridley's forearm.

"Nearly over," he muttered though Amity wasn't at all sure whether he was speaking to her or to himself.

"Thank God," she whispered back, in case he was, in fact, conversing with her.

With that, he gave her his first genuine smile of the evening and escorted her back to the drawing room. No one was eager to take a seat after the long hours of dining, so the women all found a place to stand, which wasn't difficult in the spacious room. Lord Peabody, meanwhile, took the men somewhere else for brandy and cigars.

Amity sighed, pondering how much more there was to the interminable evening. She sidled toward Charlotte, who rather than looking bored, was drinking it all in with a great deal of joy. With the identical expression of bliss as when she ate a piece of Turkish lokum, her sister appeared eager for whatever came next.

"Sherry, port, or madeira?" came the question from their hostess, and then, as if by magic, the servants arrived with trays of all three.

Amity would trade them all for a nice cup of well-made chocolate with a splash of brandy in it, knowing it would scandalize every lady in there if she requested it. Deciding on port while noticing Lady Madeleine had madeira, Amity wondered if the chocolates would wait for the men's return or—

"Would you like to do the honors?" Lady Peabody asked, and it took an instant for Amity to notice she was addressing her.

Oh! Her mother would not be thrilled to see her eldest daughter serving chocolates at the party. Apparently, Charlotte thought not either, for she shook her head.

"By chance, my lady, do you have a platter," Amity asked her, "preferably chinaware, not silver, on which your cook could arrange them?"

"Certainly," Lady Peabody agreed, and she rang the bell. "Are they all the same?" she asked Amity.

"They are exactly as ordered," she said. "Half milk chocolate, half plain—all in the particular shape you requested with the sliver of candied pineapple on top." She'd had to spend most of the profit buying the wretched prickly fruit, not to mention the trouble she'd had tracking one down on short notice.

"Wait till you see," Lady Peabody said to the other ladies even though Amity couldn't imagine why their hostess would think the shape so amusing.

When her maid entered, Lady Peabody gestured to the tins and gave her instructions. In a very short time, the girl returned with two large porcelain plates, the lighter chocolates on one, the darker on the other.

"Elephants!" Lady Madeleine was the first to remark. "So clever."

Amity looked to Charlotte who blinked back at her. Neither had a clue why the elephant-shaped chocolates were considered "clever," but all the ladies murmured their agreement, and Lady Peabody beamed.

"Surely, it's the taste you will enjoy most," Amity said.

Some of the ladies laughed, and Amity closed her mouth, determined not to put her foot in it again that night. Instead, she sipped her port, took one of the milk chocolate elephants for the sheer comfort the taste provided, and hoped the men would return soon so the evening could draw to a close.

After about twenty minutes—with endless vapid talk of dress styles, the best new fragrances, or the perfect color silk for each shade of hair—the men rejoined them. Amity's gaze instinctively sought out the duke, who seemed to be looking at her, too, until she realized she was standing in the way of his view of Lady Madeleine.

Quickly, stepping aside, she searched for Charlotte and found her conversing with another female and appearing perfectly at ease. Even Lords Greenley and Ridley were keeping company on the other side of the room. Amity ended up standing alone by a potted palm, relieved to take a second glass of port as the servant came past.

She watched from her vantage point as the male guests ate their share of her chocolates, confident this party would result in future customers.

Hoping the evening was nearly at its end, she prayed Lady Peabody would not announce the onset of parlor games. Amity highly doubted it. These people seemed far too stuffy to play *The Minister's Cat* or *Snap-dragon*.

While finishing her port, Amity allowed herself to bask in the accolades heaped upon her chocolates, although every single partygoer she overheard congratulated Lady Peabody and the "witty shape." Except for one.

When the duke suddenly appeared beside her, she startled.

"The chocolates are delicious," he praised, "and you created a perfect elephant. I take it they are from a tin mold."

"They are, and yet I have no idea why the design is amusing everyone," she confessed.

"Truly?" he asked, and she stood up a little straighter, feeling out of place again.

"I don't believe it was because our hostess is simply fond of them," she surmised.

"No," the duke said. "It's a jab at the queen. Some don't like her declaring herself the Indian Empress. Just the same, there's not a man here who wouldn't lay down his life for Victoria."

And not a lady there who wouldn't give her eye teeth to become an empress, herself, Amity thought. *Elephants, indeed!*

When the duke finally escorted Lady Madeleine out the door, he did it with nary a backward glance. Even with her feelings hurt, Amity couldn't blame him. They must all seem so dull in comparison to his lady friend.

At last, the rest of them were free to make their hasty goodbyes and disappear into the smoky, foggy London night.

HENRY THOUGHT HE OUGHT to be flogged. For most of the party, instead of being devoted to the woman he intended to marry, he had been watching another. Not as shamelessly as Greenley had ogled the younger Miss Rare-Foure's breasts, but still, he'd done a great deal of staring. It was strange and wonderful to see the chocolatier out of her shop and in the midst of *his* world. Indisputably, she'd had one or two *faux pas* but finished the night having charmed their hosts and the other guests with her story and her chocolates.

Amity had caught him looking at her more than once.

Thoughts of her in the rich plum silk that complimented her dark hair and clung to her body had accompanied him to bed in the wee hours of the morning when he'd finally made it home.

Awakening to the mid-morning sun, his first notion was to go see her. Amidst the confectionery, he could relax and chat with her, enjoy her company, and dream of—

No, no, no, he admonished himself. His dreams must be about the most beautiful, coveted woman in London, perhaps in all the world. Lady Madeleine had expressed her liking for the chocolates, and because Lady Peabody had fastened upon the exact idea of presenting a tray of them at *her* party, it in no way invalidated his own upcoming surprise. After all, *his* chocolates would be extra special. Amity would see to that.

To that end, he had every right, almost a duty, to return to the confectionery and discuss his party with the chocolatier. He only hoped Lady Madeleine hadn't noticed his wandering attention. He could hardly explain it to her since he couldn't explain it to himself.

Jumping out of bed, Henry asked his valet to fetch him a cup of coffee and looked forward to going to Bond Street. Two hours later, he strolled into Rare Confectionery, feeling right at home. Waving to Charlotte and happy that the elder Mrs. Rare-Foure was not in evidence since he had an inkling he was being slightly improper, he parted the curtain to the back room.

There was *his* chocolatier—in the arms of another man.

CHAPTER NINE

Henry froze as the couple before him broke hastily apart.

Miss Rare-Foure's cheeks turned scarlet, and her chocolate-smeared apron was creased from being held against the man's body.

Wanting to tear the stranger limb from limb, luckily, Henry's civility restrained him from doing anything rash. Miss Rare-Foure's mouth was parted in surprise—or perhaps because she had been about to let herself be kissed—and since the young man was staring as if shocked out of his boots, Henry spoke first.

"My apology for barging in." He didn't say *his sincere apology* because he didn't feel sincere at all. "I assumed you would be working on your chocolate creations, not . . . that is, I shall return at another time."

"No, please, my lord," Miss Rare-Foure said, finding her voice and taking a step in his direction. "Let me introduce you to my . . . my friend. This is Mr. Cole. He has recently returned from a trip to Scotland. Mr. Cole is a lawyer."

She smiled, looking between him and the detestable lawyer, then added, "This is His Grace, the Duke of Pelham."

The lawyer paled and stuck out his hand, bowing at the same time. It was most unfortunate and awkward. Henry nodded, yanked off his right glove, and took the man's hand, despite feeling an instant aversion at having to look at the top of his head.

In that moment, he wanted to whisk Miss Rare-Foure away to his own townhouse and let her make her chocolates in his kitchen. And when she wasn't making confections, he would dress her in the finest gowns and show her off all over Mayfair.

What could this lawyer offer her?

The man raised his head, and Henry let go of his hand.

"A pleasure to meet you, my lord," the man said. "Amity told me about the special chocolate she is making for you."

Amity? Henry realized he hadn't even known her given name. He thought of her as many things—including *his chocolatier*—but her name suited her perfectly. He loved everything about it, except for having to hear it from this other man's lips.

What did it matter this lawyer erroneously called Henry "my lord" instead of "Your Grace," just as the rest of the Rare-Foures did? Mr. Cole might not have all the social niceties, but he apparently had her fond regard.

Was the man soon to be her fiancé?

"I didn't break a confidence lightly, my lord," Miss Rare-Foure promised him. "Mr. Cole doesn't know for whom we are making the chocolates, nor would he speak of this to anyone."

Henry appreciated her assurance. "I trust you," he said and meant it. But he didn't trust this oily lawyer, who was probably going to spend his life in the dreaded Court of Chancery and become whey-faced, bald, and trembling. He couldn't imagine his lovely chocolatier, so full of creativity and life, living in some pokey little house far outside the city where they could afford to eke out an existence, where she might have to give birth to his brats.

Why was he feeling so damnably hostile toward Mr. Cole?

It couldn't be because the man had been touching her. *Could it?*

Yes, it could!

"Solicitor or barrister?" Henry asked curtly.

"Solicitor, my lord." Mr. Cole said it without the least embarrassment, even though he'd taken the lowlier path with less prestige, money, and influence. *What a short-sighted dunce!*

Henry knew he was close to saying something entirely inappropriate so he had best be away.

"I shall return tomorrow," he announced, not wanting to be in the small space with these two lovebirds.

"Oh no, my lord. Please stay. Mr. Cole was about to leave," she said. "I am more than happy to discuss your chocolate creation at present. Perhaps you had some insights after last night."

"Last night?" asked the lawyer.

Last night, Henry whined the words in his head. *What a nosey bloke!*

"Miss Rare-Foure and I attended the same dinner party," Henry told the man, not hiding the triumph from his voice.

"Really?" The lawyer turned to her. "When you said you were out for dinner, I didn't imagine you were at a grand party with a duke." Then the man smiled. "Good for you. I hope you enjoyed yourself. You work too much."

Mr. Cole was being a tad too gracious. He probably didn't mean a word of it. He was in all likelihood burning with jealousy at the notion.

"I'll see you later," he added, and Miss Rare-Foure nodded.

And to Henry's intense displeasure, this . . . this . . . lawyer reached out and squeezed Miss Rare-Foure's shoulder. *The nerve!* Naturally, Mr. Cole wasn't jealous—he was going to see her again later.

"If you get a chance to go by Berry Brothers on St James's Street, would you bring that Spanish wine my mother likes?" Miss Rare-Foure asked him. "We shall celebrate your return."

"I will make it my duty to get the wine," the man assured her. "A pleasure to meet you, my lord." With a bow in Henry's direction, the earnest fellow departed.

Lucky chap! He would be dining with her family and was intimate enough to know Mrs. Rare-Foure's favorite wine.

Henry suddenly felt foolish for thinking that he and the chocolatier had any type of friendship at all. And considering his own evening ahead, he even felt a little lonely. All the more reason for him to secure the hand of Lady Madeleine and take her as his wife. The sooner, the better.

During the party, they'd had a few pleasant discussions. Notwithstanding, he couldn't remember anything too meaningful, something about her touring the zoological gardens or finding a hedgehog in a garden or some such story.

He hadn't really been listening. He'd been too entranced with the woman across from him who now stood waiting for him to speak. His obsession—for plainly that was what it was—had to stop.

"Have you made any progress?" he asked her a little sharply.

Instead of being annoyed, she offered him her sweet, lopsided smile. "Yes, this morning, I used the flower molds to create something new. See if you can tell what I added?"

"But they're dusty," Henry pointed out, when she presented him with the tray.

She laughed, and there it was, the silvery sound he hadn't heard in too long. Hours, in fact, which felt like years.

"I dusted them with cocoa powder. Try one."

Taking off his other glove, he shoved them both into his coat pocket. Then he chose one of the chocolates, letting the bitter cocoa powder blend with the melting plain chocolate.

"I am tasting something a little like mild perfume, but very pleasant." He realized what it was as soon as he swallowed. "Gin!"

"Very good!" Miss Rare-Foure clapped her hands. "What do you think?"

"I'm not sure." He hated to disappoint her, but it seemed terribly risky. "I don't know how the lady feels about gin." He didn't know how Madeleine felt about a lot of things.

The chocolatier puffed out her cheeks and expelled her breath with a sound of exasperation. He thought it the most charming thing he'd ever seen, especially when the soft curl at her temple blew up then fell back.

"Your lady is a tough nut to crack." She set the tray down again.

I want you *to be my lady.* That terribly scandalous thought flittered across his brain and disappeared before he even realized it. But even after it was gone, he stared at her and realized it might be true.

"Mr. Cole is your intended?" he blurted out.

She widened her eyes and quickly dropped her gaze. "He will be, in due course." Her tone was soft, and she seemed to be speaking to the floor.

"Yet you are not formally engaged?" he pried, wondering why he was asking. "What is causing the delay?"

At this impertinent question, her glance lifted and locked with his. "Do you wish to discuss chocolate or the personal details of my life? If the former, you may stay. If the latter, then I must ask you to leave."

He grinned at her properly affronted tone.

"Very well. Chocolate, it is. Although, if you ask me, your Mr. Cole is a muttonhead for waiting."

AMITY SIGHED. "IT ISN'T his fault. He wanted—" She snapped her mouth closed. "Oh, you almost tricked me."

"I did no such thing," the duke said innocently, but she could see by his expression he had tried to get her to speak more about Jeremy. They had known each other for nearly a year and a half, but she had been in no hurry to marry him. She'd gone with her father to Lincoln's Inn one day when he was speaking with his solicitor and had met the attractive Mr. Cole. He had since passed the bar and set up his practice. She thought he was hinting at a Christmas engagement, which would be . . . nice.

"Mr. Cole has nothing to do with you and your chocolate. And he is not a muttonhead."

"You are speaking far more comfortably to me here than you did last night."

Amity sighed. "What a fright that was!" she began.

When he looked surprised, she added, "I mean, we were there simply to drop off the tins. What if my sister and I hadn't been dressed appropriately?"

"Why were you properly dressed for the party?" he asked, idly plucking another gin sweet from the tray.

She would charge him extra for all the sampling. After spending an evening in the world he inhabited, she knew he wouldn't even notice if she doubled the price.

"My mother has her pride," Amity said, watching him swallow. "She didn't want her daughters showing up in work clothes."

The duke nodded. His next words surprised her. "You looked beautiful."

Their gazes caught, and she could not look away as warmth spread through her entire body. *The Duke of Pelham thought she had looked beautiful.* She could hardly credit it, especially when Lady Madeleine had been beside him.

"Both you and your sister," he amended slowly, but the way his intense gaze was fixed upon hers, she felt like the only woman in the world.

"Thank you." Her voice came out in a croak. She cleared her throat.

Before she could steer the discussion back to chocolate, however, he said, "I apologize on behalf of your dinner partners. You certainly got stuck with a couple of churls."

She couldn't help smiling. "They would not have been my first choice of companions." The man standing in front of her would have been. *No! Jeremy would have been. Of course!*

"Their conversational skills were practically absent, and Lord Ridley . . . ," she trailed off, realizing she was about to criticize one of the duke's peers. That could get her into rapid trouble.

"Ridley what?" he persisted. "I thought your main complaint would be with Greenley's roving eyes."

Amity couldn't help blushing, even though it was on Charlotte's behalf.

"I was lucky enough not to be under his scrutiny." *Lucky? Not to have a full enough bosom even for a lecherous lord?* She felt her cheeks grow even hotter. "I mean, at least I was nearly able to converse with him. Lord Ridley didn't even try, but merely gave me the shoulder."

"Lord Ridley is a fool who cannot see past the large silver spoon sticking out of his thin lips."

Amity couldn't help the chuckle. "I take it he is not one of your favorite people."

"Hardly. I have one sister, Penelope, and she thought herself smitten with that idiot until she overheard his mercenary reason for courting her."

"That's terrible." She was glad she and Jeremy were on identical footing class-wise and financially, for she knew his affection was genuine. "I hope your sister has recovered from being so ill-treated."

"Yes. It was a mild bump in her romantic vision of the world, and she has since happily married. I would like you to meet her. I shall bring her in another time. I think she would like you."

"And how does she like Lady Madeleine?" Amity asked before she could stop herself. After all, that was far more important than the duke's sister meeting her.

He looked surprised. "I . . . I don't know to tell you the truth." He frowned. "Have they even met?"

Amity shook her head at his puzzlement. "I'm sure I don't know. Don't you socialize in the same circles as your sister? Doesn't Lady Madeleine show an interest in your family?"

His frown became deeper, and he shrugged. "My sister and her husband do not frequent the events I do. As a single man, you see, I tend to be thrown in with the matchmakers, like Lady Peabody. As for Lady Madeleine, I don't believe she has met Penelope. We haven't spent too much time speaking about each other's families." He paused, then added slowly, "She has a mother—"

Amity snickered.

"—who had a cat once," he finished.

Amity couldn't help it. She started to laugh and couldn't stop. Tears came to her eyes. *She has a mother!* She doubled over with laughter. Fortunately, the duke joined in.

"Oh," she held her stomach. "I'm . . . sorry, my lord." She started laughing again. "It's only . . . do you suppose she has a father, too?"

They both laughed together at the inanity of his statement. It took a few minutes for her to regain her normal composure. When she finally reached for her notebook, they were still smirking at each other.

"Gin is questionable," she said aloud as she wrote the words, which started them chuckling again.

"Well, *I* like it," the duke said. "For that matter, I think brandy would be delicious inside your chocolates."

"Already have those on the shelf," Amity said, looking over her ingredients for inspiration. "The candied pineapple was very good last night, wasn't it? Did Lady Madeleine adore it?"

"Even if she did, you cannot use it," he reminded her, "since she's already had a Rare Confectionery with pineapple."

She considered a moment. "Shall I search for another exotic fruit?"

"As long as it's not—"

"Orange," she finished for him. "I know. I think we should narrow this down to what fruit Lady Madeleine likes."

"Narrow this down?" he asked. "I am a pest, and you are eager to get rid of me."

She shook her head. "Not at all, but we are running out of time. Cherries or apricots?"

He shrugged sheepishly, and looked so inviting, so attractive as he did, she felt tingly from looking at him.

"Peaches or . . . how about greengages?" she persisted.

He looked at her strangely. "I'm afraid I don't even know what that is."

"Truly?" She realized he was staring at her mouth as she spoke, making her quite self-conscious of her lips, which she licked nervously. "They're like plums except smaller."

The duke smiled and took a step closer. "Then why not simply ask me if she likes plums?"

"All right." Although suddenly barely breathe able to breathe, her mouth formed the words, "Peaches or plums?"

"I haven't the foggiest," he confessed. She couldn't step back as the marble tabletop was behind her, pressing into her backside.

"We are going to have to guess," she said. It was getting distinctly hot in the small space. "What is *your* preference for the perfect *Brayson*—candied cherry, plum, peach, or apricot? A candied apricot is quite heavenly."

"Are those my only choices?" he asked infuriatingly, his eyes appearing darker as he gazed at her.

How many choices did he need?

Nervously, she laughed again, but he stepped even closer, causing her to stop abruptly, her laughter ending in a hiccupping sound.

Slowly, unexpectedly, his arms went around her. She stilled before relaxing into the warmth of him and letting the tingling sensations overtake her.

The curtain was open, the way her mother had insisted. Customers might be in the shop. She hadn't been listening for the bell at all since he'd arrived.

"I like being with you," he whispered.

"I . . . I . . . ." She wanted to tell him how much she liked being with him, too, however inappropriate it might be.

Then he lowered his mouth to hers and claimed her lips.

CHAPTER TEN

The kiss probably lasted seven seconds, time enough for the duke's mouth to move sensually across hers, time enough for him to nibble on her lower lip before he drew back.

The kiss was a revelation. Amity was awfully glad the worktable was close behind to support her for she didn't have a bone left in her body, and her breath had been stolen from her lungs.

As she opened her eyes, she refilled her lungs with an unladylike gulp, breathing in that intoxicating fragrance he wore.

Briefly, she saw a look of tenderness and something else upon his handsome face—desire, if she understood the expression, undoubtedly mirroring her own. Her body was aflame with wanting more. Another kiss, a touch of his hand on her skin.

Heaven help her! She was soon to belong to Jeremy, and the duke belonged to Lady Madeleine.

Was he toying with her? Amity had heard of a titled gentleman ruining a maid in his employ. It was a clichéd tale, but it happened all the same. Nobility felt entitled to take what they wanted because no one ever told them they couldn't. Privileged lords preyed on the powerless—and even the not-so-powerless, such as Charlotte and how Lord Greenley behaved with open disrespect.

The duke backed away. He didn't apologize. In fact, he didn't say anything. He looked as confused as she felt. Nevertheless, he had determinedly cornered her and kissed her!

She was about to tell him to leave—or beg him to kiss her again!—when he nodded stiffly and walked out of the room. Hurrying forward and peering through the open curtain, Amity watched him go, without acknowledgment, straight past Charlotte who was behind the counter and past two customers deciding on what to buy.

He tugged open the shop door, his broad shoulders held rigidly as he strode out into the watery London sunshine.

Well!

HENRY HAD NEVER DALLIED with a woman in his life. He was no saint, of course. He'd not only kissed a few willing ladies in the gardens of Mayfair's best townhouses, but upon occasion, he went to the most expensive brothel in London and, for a long night of passion, spent more than some men earned in half a year. Once or twice, discreetly, he'd even taken a mistress for a month.

But that kiss! His behavior had been different than anything he'd ever done, grabbing the chocolatier and kissing her because she was within arm's reach and because he desperately wanted her.

He still wanted her. Now, he wanted more of her, but to what end besides slaking his own lust? For that was all it could be. He wanted to strip her down and see her stretched out upon his sheets with a blush of desire on her cheeks and her soft lips parted. He wanted to dust cocoa powder upon Amity's skin and taste her like a sweet confection.

Dammit! He was thinking of her now as Amity and not Miss Rare-Foure.

And if he did experience her delights—after seeing how her brown eyes and dark hair looked in the moonlight as well as in the morning sun following a night of lovemaking—then what?

He could hardly take her home to his mother and present her as his bride-to-be. *The Duchess of Chocolate?*

Troubled, he climbed into his carriage, belatedly realizing he hadn't told his coachman where to go.

Leaning his head out, he said, "To White's," before he slid the window back up.

His future rested securely and properly with the most desirable woman in London. It wasn't as if he were settling for anything but the best. Lady Madeleine was bred to be a duchess, to handle their dinner parties with aplomb, to manage household affairs, to entertain at his country estate, and to be a partner in his entire aristocratic life.

And she was beautiful, to boot. But then again, Amity was perfectly lovely and vibrant, funny and smart. *Why on God's earth did she have to be a shopkeeper's daughter?*

She was also spoken for. That lawyer was the natural choice for her—Mr. Cole and his affable manner and his ability to provide a modest life for her. She could probably continue to work in her shop if the lawyer married her, whereas if Henry claimed her, she would have to give up all such endeavors. A duchess could hardly go to New Bond Street and make chocolates in a back room to fill the shelves of a confectionery.

He thumped his knee with this fist. *Why was he still thinking of marrying Amity Rare-Foure?*

Henry needed Waverly and Jeffcoat to talk him out of this madness, and he needed to spend more time with

Madeleine. He ought to kiss the earl's daughter to expunge the memory of how perfect was the kiss with Amity. When he kissed the glorious Madeleine, stars would shoot across the night sky, the earth would shake, and he would drop to his knees with desire for her.

And if he didn't? Then heaven help him!

AMITY GAVE UP TRYING to do anything useful. She made sure Charlotte had ample stock of their best-selling items, added a tray of Beatrice's treacle toffee to the display case, and went for a walk.

Window shopping was a good way to purge any troubling thoughts from her head. Usually, she took pleasure in idly strolling along and looking at the pretty things London had to offer. Today, however, when she looked in Mayfair's luxurious shops, she saw the Duke of Pelham's world, and its vast difference from her own.

She could dress the part for an evening and hold her own at a dining table with English aristocrats. *Almost—except for the rude laughter and the wine spillage!* Be that as it may, those of his ilk lived a life she could not really comprehend, nor did she desire to.

Two ladies stepped out in front of her from a jeweler's store, their hands empty. Behind them came a maid carrying small parcels with the jeweler's stamp. No matter the size, those packages might hold unimaginable wealth of precious stones set in gold, and these ladies didn't even care enough to hold them!

Amity wandered along aimlessly behind them, not eavesdropping but unable to help from hearing their words. And that was only because the ladies spoke at a pitch meant for everyone around them to hear. They talked of fashion and pointed out things they liked in the next shop window, a haberdashery. They spoke of traveling abroad soon since everything on Bond Street, no matter how fine, was undeniably months behind what they would find in Paris or Milan. *What nonsense!*

As other women passed them, they spoke loudly about their rivals' clothing. They hardly seemed to notice the few fashionable men, wanting mostly to be certain they looked better than the other ladies. And if they didn't, then they had a harsh putdown for them.

"That Lady C is such an unfortunate dullard. What matter if her hair is lovely when she can barely read a clock?"

"Her figure is fine, but that dress color makes Lady T look positively sallow. Someone should tell her, poor thing."

These snide remarks were accompanied by lighthearted giggles.

And when they passed a gallery, suddenly, they were art critics. Meanwhile, the maid traipsed along behind in what was undoubtedly her best clothes, and yet her boots were so well-worn, Amity could see the girl's stocking through a hole in the right heel.

She glanced down at her own comfortable but stylish ankle boots and her rather fashionable day gown in gray and pink. She was firmly, irrevocably in a position betwixt the maid and the ladies. Just as the Duke of Pelham was firmly above them all.

But the kiss! It was as perfect as she'd ever imagined a kiss to be. It wasn't her first. She and Jeremy had managed to steal one here and there. His kisses were enjoyable. They made her happy. He smelled of familiar Pears soap and treated her with care. He was safe, never giving her a moment's anxiety.

Never making her truly tingle, either.

When the duke had kissed her, she hadn't thought about his station in life or her own. She had thoroughly enjoyed every second. He had smelled like a god and tasted of her own confectionery. At the instant their mouths fused, they were not from different worlds. Class had meant nothing where, normally, it meant everything. They had been—*dare she think it*—equals! For he'd enjoyed the kiss equally as much as she had. Of that, she had no doubt.

On the other hand, she was under no illusion the duke had rushed off to tell Lady Madeleine he no longer wished to escort her around town. This was the type of thing the upper classes did and quickly forgot. By tomorrow, he would never again think of their kiss, and soon, with the help of Amity's chocolates, he would be engaged to his lady.

On her part, she'd felt the pangs of guilt. After all, if she thought Jeremy was kissing another woman, she would end it with him at once. She gasped. *Was she supposed to release him from their tentative agreement because of her small indiscretion?*

When Amity finally strolled back into the shop, her youngest sister was impatiently drumming her fingers on the countertop.

"Thank goodness," Charlotte said, removing her apron. "I thought you would never return."

"Bea has arrived, hasn't she?"

Charlotte scrunched up her face. "You know how she is with customers. I couldn't leave her to make her toffee *and* come out here every time the bell rang. She would be annoyed with people for interrupting her, no matter they are the reason we do what we do."

"Thank you for staying," Amity told her. "Did you manage to get some of your own confections finished?"

That question made her youngest sister's face brighten. Unlike Amity and Beatrice who both preferred the back room while they worked, Charlotte was pleased to remain behind the counter crafting her marzipan creations. She chatted with their customers while she shaped the almond paste like a sculptor with clay. In fact, some lingered to watch her artistry as she used edible dyes to paint the marzipan shapes or create small faux fruits, using cloves for stems to make them look real.

Charlotte had already cleaned up her workspace consisting of a marble slab, a glass jar of freshly made marzipan, a bottle of almond oil, and her sack of powdered sugar to keep the almond paste from sticking to her hands and the surface. On the top shelf of the display case was a new row of adorable marzipan pigs with a blush of pink to their almond paste skin and dark eyes.

Amity looked closer to see Charlotte had fashioned tiny marzipan tails that lay coiled upon the pigs' rounded backsides.

"You have outdone yourself, sister. They are splendid."

"They taste even better than they look. The pink blush is a hint of cherry juice. I've sold four already in the past hour."

"Well, now you're free to go home. You might want to remind Father that Mr. Cole is coming to dinner."

Charlotte grimaced slightly, and a sliver of alarm sliced through Amity.

"Don't you like him?" *Had her sister seen some terrible flaw in Jeremy that Amity hadn't noticed?* Or perhaps, she knew about the kiss.

"Oh, I like him fine. Besides, it is *you* who must like him, tame as he is, not me. Anyway, it's not that." Charlotte sighed. "But after last night, when we were in the lap of luxury and refinement, it's hard to go home and sit in our dreary dining room and hear Father and your Mr. Cole discuss boring business or law cases, or a trip to Scotland." She finished with a roll of her pretty brown eyes.

Amity laughed. "If I'd known one night out would ruin you for our perfectly comfortable life, I would have taken Bea. And hearing about a journey can never be boring, can it? In any case, didn't you find last night's conversations a tad dull—except for the storytelling?"

"I suppose they were a little, but the man on my left, Lord Cameron, was nice. Far more pleasant than Lord Greenley with his bulging eyes."

"They were bulging in but one direction," Amity reminded her.

Charlotte shrugged. It wasn't her fault she had a figure most women would shave their heads for.

After retrieving her coat from the back room and saying goodbye to Beatrice, Charlotte hugged Amity and strolled out, taking a box of the pigs with her. "Six for tonight."

Amity peeked through the curtain to find Beatrice seated on her stool, her feet stretched out in front of her. She was wrapping toffee in paper squares and twisting the ends.

"Good afternoon," she greeted. "Shall I put on the kettle?"

"Yes, please," Beatrice replied. "What do you think about toffee with fruit in it?"

"Depends on the fruit, I suppose." She lit the stove and set the kettle full of water atop it. "I think anything citrus would be rather nasty, but I can imagine a sultana or even a blackcurrant."

Beatrice nodded in agreement, then yawned.

Amity crossed her arms and yawned, too. *The late night at the Peabodys' had taken its toll, but why did Bea look put out?*

"Are you getting bored of being the most revered treacle toffee maker in London?"

Beatrice laughed. "Am I that?"

"Of course you are! Your tins of toffee fly off the shelves."

"Even faster when we coat them with your chocolate."

"True." Amity scooped tea leaves into the pot and poured the boiling water over them. She would have preferred a cup of chocolate but decided to please Beatrice, who preferred tea. She was ever so grateful for the close relationships with her sisters, beyond pleased by how they each crafted confectionery that was wonderful alone and even better when combined.

"I'm trying a couple new items, too," Beatrice added. "I've coated some toffee in a caramel sauce, but so far, it isn't really working." She held out a plate for Amity to see where the warm caramel sauce had softened the hard toffee pieces and the whole thing lost its shape to become partly gooey, partly stiff blobs.

"*Hm,*" Amity said, picking up a piece, getting it stuck all over her fingers. When she stuck it in her mouth, however, she couldn't help but smile. "Delicious!" she said thickly, with her teeth nearly stuck together.

"Maybe if I lightly dip chunks of toffee, it might work, but I'm not sure I've gained anything with a slightly softer outer layer."

"You said you'd tried two things?" Amity took a tin of Cadbury's chocolate-covered biscuits from the shelf, perfect for dipping into her tea. She offered them to Beatrice, who took two.

"I'll share the other one when it's perfected. Meanwhile, I'll stir in a few blackcurrants in the next batch of toffee and see if it helps or hinders."

"Don't forget, Mr. Cole is coming for dinner."

Amazingly, Beatrice produced the identical grimace as Charlotte.

"Don't tell me you don't like him either."

"Either?" asked Beatrice, sipping her tea. "Why? Who doesn't like him?"

"Never you mind," Amity said. "I guess we all do, but Charlotte said the dining room discussion will be boring."

"Compared to your unexpected adventure last night, you mean?"

"Exactly. I told her she should not compare our dining room to Lord and Lady Peabody's. I firmly prefer our own. It is relaxing and comfortable, and no snout-noses in sight."

"Oh dear," Beatrice remarked. "Someone didn't enjoy her evening."

Amity shrugged. "I did, I suppose, once I got used to it and overcame my nervousness. Regardless, it seemed as if everyone were on display and needing to watch their step and their words. Except for the host and hostess, and Lord Pelham."

Beatrice cocked her head with interest. "*He* was there?"

"Yes, as was the sublime Lady Madeleine."

Her sister straightened and set down her teacup. "You saw her?"

"Yes." Amity tried to remain neutral despite having a feeling of distinct animosity toward the beautiful lady.

"Was she exactly as everyone says?" Beatrice asked.

"More so." Amity shrugged.

"Good lord. Why on earth would Charlotte want to spend an evening competing with the likes of that paragon of all things desirable?"

Amity sighed. "Fortunately for our younger sister, she has a couple of things men desire." They blinked at each other and started to giggle.

"Bless her heart," Beatrice said. "She doesn't realize how adorable she is, while being womanly at the same time."

"We're lucky she doesn't realize yet. If she demands a Season, Father will have to keep the suitors away with a cricket bat." Then she looked at Beatrice. "I'm rather set with Mr. Cole"—*except when she was kissing the Duke of Pelham*—"but what about you? You're as adorable *and* womanly as Charlotte. Plus, two years and somehow decades more mature. Have you got your eye on anyone?"

"No. Truthfully, sometimes I despair of having anything or anyone outside this shop."

Amity was stunned by her sister's admission. "What? That's ridiculous. Simply because I didn't want a Season, doesn't mean you can't have a coming out party and attend events. Shall we talk to Father tonight?"

"No, I don't want to bother. I would have to wait until next April for an appropriate time to coincide with the titled misses being presented to the queen." Beatrice shook her head of thick brown hair, a shade lighter than Amity's, and sighed mightily.

"Most of those girls aren't worrying over the cost of a Season. As soon as I was declared a shopkeeper's daughter, I would be ostracized anyway. And as you said, I'm about two years older than most, and four years older than many. Why, off the top of my head, I can think of at least four gentry brides who got married at age sixteen in the past few years. If we go by them, then I am firmly over-the-hill."

At this, Amity laughed. "You are nineteen and perfect. Your life is just starting. What's more, you are talented."

"As a toffee-maker? I might as well be a seamstress or a cobbler."

"Nonsense. Yet if you wish to learn the skill of patisserie, I think Mother would be thrilled. She's always on about the superior pastries in Paris."

Beatrice shrugged. "I don't think so. I've never had an interest in baking. You know I like making toffee, but it doesn't have the artistry of your chocolate creations or Charlotte's marzipan sculptures. I am in a rut, I suppose."

She sipped her tea again. "I think running a household and having a husband and children sounds rather heavenly compared to spending my days with treacle, sugar, and butter."

The shop bell tinkled, and Amity went out to sell half a pound of chocolates, two marzipan pigs, and another pound of toffee to a very joyful woman, who was grateful for complimentary samples for herself and her three young children.

She could see what Beatrice meant about having a family and had been lucky to find Jeremy quite by happenstance. Having his children would be fulfilling, but she intended to continue making chocolate after her marriage and even after motherhood. It was her passion, and she delighted in watching people enjoy her confections. *How could she help Beatrice find a good man?*

Wandering into the back room again, she realized her sister was cleaning up for the day.

"Do not worry," Beatrice said. "I'll see what comes. Tell me more about Lady Madeleine, while I scrub these pots."

"If I must. She had on a gown of the palest shade of blue—"

"Thus, cold and unappealing?" Beatrice asked mischievously.

"More like angelic and breathtaking. Her hair was styled as a golden crown of braids. She had extraordinarily blue eyes, the palest skin, and a lovely shade of pink to her lips."

"Artifice and make up," Beatrice interrupted.

Ignoring her, Amity added, "She had a soft voice. I didn't hear her speak too much, to tell you the truth, so I couldn't tell you if she was intelligent, but the Duke of Pelham hung upon her every word. As he should," she added quickly.

Beatrice arched a brow at her. "Why do you say that?"

Amity shrugged. "No reason."

But her middle sister was like a hound at the hunt. "Tell me. Something has happened. I can read it on your face. Come on, you're dying to."

It was true. She was desperate to tell someone, preferably her thoughtful sister, and get her opinion.

"All right, I'll tell you. The Duke of Pelham kissed me."

CHAPTER ELEVEN

As soon as Henry told Waverly, he regretted it. His friend promised discretion, but still, a woman's reputation was at stake as well as his own future happiness. Waverly raised a knowing eyebrow but looked sympathetic.

"You are not the first to be tempted by the charms of a warm and willing ordinary female. They are right there in our midst, after all, and so readily available, infinitely more so than our titled ladies who must keep their lips and legs firmly closed until after the wedding."

Henry frowned at his friend, sipped his brandy, and tried to discern any truth from his rambling palaver. He couldn't credit any advice that termed Amity as *ordinary*. Moreover, as with a titled lady, she had as much cause to keep her lips and legs closed. Why should any of them assume middle-class women mustn't guard their reputations as fiercely as Lady Madeleine or Henry's own sister?

"Balderdash," Henry said finally. "Miss Rare-Foure deserves the exact same courtesy as any titled lady, and she cannot be any freer with her person if she wishes to gain a husband. Besides, she already has a man in mind for that position."

"Then why did she let you kiss her?" Waverly began. "I'll tell you why. Because as with every single female around any man whom they think is eligible, your Miss Rare-Foure thought one kiss and you would be hooked like a trout upon her line. That is the sole reason ladies let us kiss them at balls and parties, no matter how secretly and hastily we must do it in a darkened corner of a damp, miserable garden."

Waverly sounded a little bitter. Henry wondered who'd soured his cream, but his friend wasn't finished espousing his theory.

"Even if she already has a suitor, as you say, your chocolate-maker didn't mind kissing a duke in hopes of snaring you into marrying her. They all want a similar thing, I tell you—a titled man as long as he has a good fortune to go along with it."

"So cynical," Henry observed. "The thing is, however, *she* didn't really kiss me. I surprised her with a hasty maneuver of which Wellington, himself, would have been proud."

Waverly nodded. "Did she draw away?"

"She couldn't. I had her pinned between me and her chocolate-covered countertop."

His friend lifted his glass in salute. "Well done. But afterward, did she cry foul, slap you, make a fuss, or in any way offer protest?"

Henry shook his head. "I left in great haste and gave her no opportunity. It was a swift forward foray followed by an even swifter retreat."

Waverly laughed. "Then, my friend, I don't know what to tell you. I suppose you will never know if you angered her and ruined your chances of having the best chocolates in London at your proposal party unless you return to the scene of your frontal assault. Either she'll make doe eyes at you and hope you are going to ask for her hand after your rash impudence, or she'll be faithful to her suitor and give you a tongue-lashing."

Henry thought more likely it would be the latter. He couldn't imagine Amity making doe eyes or using her feminine wiles to lure and trap him. Feeling ashamed, returning to Rare Confectionery seemed a bit embarrassing albeit necessary.

"I suppose I must go back and apologize."

"Exactly. But if she starts to scream about your attempt to ruin her, you must deny you ever kissed her at all. Elsewise, you might find yourself married to her and perhaps working in the shop." Waverly chuckled at his own words. "Wearing an apron," he added and laughed even harder.

Henry recalled how Amity had offered him one and felt a little disquieted at the notion. He finished his brandy. He had already sent a missive to Lady Madeleine's parents' townhouse. He intended to kiss her before the sun set on another day.

IT WAS NOT THE easiest dinner, what with Charlotte being morose because they weren't in one of Mayfair's finest townhouses and with Beatrice's wide-eyed expression of utter disbelief every time she looked at Amity. Their conversation over tea in the confectionery had been cut short by final customers before they'd closed up.

Still, her sister now knew of the unbelievable indiscretion with her sole question being, "Did you enjoy it?"

The more Amity looked at Jeremy across the dining room table, the more she thought she should confess.

She had done something she would have thought impossible if asked, an action entirely out of character. More than that, it was blatantly wrong and was causing her no end of painful emotions. She was no longer moral and upright, keeping herself pure for her beau. True, she hadn't invited the kiss, yet nor had she pushed the duke away or even protested. She recalled moving her mouth against his and feeling pleasure.

It was not the kiss itself but having enjoyed it so very much that most bothered her. Surely it meant she was depraved and not to be trusted. *What if another man tried to kiss her after she was married, and she not only let him but enjoyed it?*

After dinner, in the parlor, tormented by her thoughts, Amity suddenly rose to her feet causing all the chatter to cease. Even Delia, their maid, faltered mid-step while carrying in a tray with a decanter of port and six glasses that rattled until she resumed her duty and set them down on the low table between the sofas.

"Jeremy, may I have a word with you in private?" Amity barely glanced at her parents for permission since they had already welcomed him into their family and trusted them both to be respectful of each other and the bounds of propriety. They'd sat alone in the parlor on numerous occasions and even ridden by themselves once or twice in Jeremy's carriage.

"Perhaps we could step into my father's study," she suggested.

"Yes," Beatrice exclaimed, jumping to her feet, "but can you wait a few minutes?" she added, speaking to Jeremy. "I have something crucial to tell Amity about . . . about her chocolate."

Without waiting to hear how this statement went over, Beatrice grabbed Amity's arm and hauled her from the room.

As soon as they were on the other side of the closed parlor door, Amity whispered, "That sounded ridiculous!"

Beatrice whispered back, "What are you doing?"

Amity knew what she meant. "I am going to tell Mr. Cole the truth." They moved farther along the hallway so their voices wouldn't carry. "I cannot live with this horrid feeling of betrayal."

Beatrice rolled her eyes and, hands on hips, asked, "What outcome can you hope for? You will hurt Mr. Cole and possibly lose him. Do you want either of those things to occur?"

"No, of course not."

"Then don't tell him. It was a single kiss—"

"But I shall see the duke again when he comes to the store for his chocolates."

"Never mind about his blasted chocolates," Beatrice fumed. "I will take them to his home as soon as you've finished them. You should keep your distance in case—"

"In case he tries to kiss me again?"

"Just so."

"But I enjoyed it," Amity insisted.

"Well, who wouldn't? But does that mean you must throw away your future? Unlike me, you have a good, educated man who loves you, and he is easy on the eyes, too. Don't push Mr. Cole away by filling his head with doubts over your fidelity when nothing more will ever happen in that regard."

"That's precisely it," Amity said. "How can I be sure?"

Beatrice looked shocked. "What are you saying? I know you. You didn't intend this, nor, once engaged, would you ever let such a thing happen again."

Amity felt like crying. "I have kissed Mr. Cole before," she admitted.

"As expected," Beatrice said. "What ninny would commit to a lifetime with a man without kissing him? Ultimately, it might be so terrible, one never wishes to do it again."

Should Amity tell her what haunted her?

"The kiss with the duke was . . . more . . . it was somehow . . . . Oh dear! I cannot even say it, it sounds so terrible, so awful of me to compare them."

Beatrice put her arms around her, and Amity didn't have to tell her how much better it was, didn't have to put into words how the pleasure had flowed through her. Kissing Jeremy was *comfortable*. Now, it seemed as if it had been like kissing a family member, tame and unexciting in comparison to the duke's kiss.

And that thought made her wrench away from Beatrice's embrace. She didn't deserve comfort. She didn't deserve Jeremy. He would want the woman he kissed to feel bliss and pleasure. His affection warranted such a response and devotion.

"What shall I do?"

Beatrice wiped her thumbs over Amity's cheeks where a few stray tears had fallen.

"Kiss Mr. Cole. Again. Now," her sister advised. "Take him into Father's study and kiss him. Afterward, if you believe he will not suffice, you can let him go. But you must be certain, for you know you shall not get the duke, and another man may not come along who is any finer than Mr. Cole. Shall we be the Rare-Foure spinsters, me at nineteen and you at twenty?"

Amity had no words to respond to her wise younger sister. "I'll go to the study. Will you send him to me?"

Beatrice nodded. "I hope to be toasting you and Mr. Cole by the evening's end. And remember, you do not have to tell him. It will hurt him needlessly."

Nodding, Amity turned away and slipped into her father's study, her heart pounding with trepidation.

HENRY WAS SURPRISED HOW easily he had been able to snag a kiss with Amity whereas Lady Madeleine was like a slippery eel. She was impossible to catch alone and absolutely unwilling to let him within a foot of her when it was only the two of them, even with her maid seated discreetly close by.

He had called upon her without prior notice and even wangled a dinner invitation—for they could hardly refuse a duke showing up close to the dinner hour. He hoped to become more familiar with her and with her parents. The conversation as they dined, however, had been uninspiring at best. Her mother, an attractive woman, remained mostly silent while keeping a besotted smile on her face and looking at him as if *she* were the one he might marry.

Her father, Lord Brayson, was pleasant enough, if one liked a man intent on mentioning every possible achievement he'd ever had or every farthing of wealth he'd accrued. Henry wondered what was the point of the man's boasting when he could never hope to match the prestige of a duke, nor should he try.

Frankly, Henry found it a little vulgar.

Nonetheless, he could overlook both parents' flaws for Madeleine's sake. She was charming over the pottage and told a witty, albeit rehearsed story with the roast. It was after, when they were having port in the drawing room, that he realized how impersonal was every phrase she uttered. She could have been at any ball or party speaking to anyone, not to the man who might mean something special to her.

Henry decided to grab the bull . . . or, rather, the cow by . . . well, not by anything.

"Tell me about your childhood, Lady Madeleine. Did you spend most of your time in the country or in Town?"

Madeleine smiled and looked to her father to answer. Henry sighed and let the earl disclose the many fine acres they had at their country house and the number of horses. Yet when he started to give an account of his livestock, Henry interrupted.

"Livestock!" He laughed as if her father had meant it to be a joke. "Surely, your daughter and wife have no interest in our discussing your pigs." Henry certainly had not a damned ounce of interest, either. He wanted to ask

Madeleine if she'd been a lonely child, but there may have been siblings who'd passed away, and thus, he couldn't broach such a sensitive topic. Then he recalled she had mentioned a brother although without any particular affection.

For a moment, he couldn't think what he wanted to know about her despite having everything to learn. She remained, confoundedly, a stranger. Once more, he turned to her.

"Did you have a favorite book growing up, Lady Madeleine? Do you like to read?" He couldn't help but think of Amity's animated retelling of Mrs. Lovechild's primer, something practically every British child had in his or her nursery.

Madeleine's lovely face remained placid. She ignored the first question and answered the second.

"Currently, I enjoy a few magazines. I don't read the newspapers as there is entirely too much offensiveness and vulgarity, and stories of low people behaving badly."

"Too much," her mother murmured.

Henry couldn't help but notice Madeleine didn't ask him a question in return. That left him to forge ahead. He already knew of Madeleine's dislike of small tamed animals, as well as oranges, raisins, and now newspapers, but everything else was still a mystery.

Tapping his fingers upon his thigh, he realized all three Braysons were staring at him with polite half-smiles upon their faces.

"Have you traveled abroad much?" Henry had been to the Continent thrice, and there was much more he wished to see. He loved strolling the streets of Paris and discovering cafes with each Parisian trying to outdo the next with the perfect cup of coffee.

Lady Madeleine made a moue of dislike. "I cannot swim," she said.

"No," her mother murmured.

Henry was confounded. *What the deuce did swimming have to do with it?*

"There are ferries," he pointed out, not meaning to sound rude. *Was she under the impression she had to swim the English Channel?*

"I know there are ferries," Madeleine snapped, making her mother gasp in distress at her daughter's discourteous tone. The young lady took a breath and softened her expression. "Those boats are *on* the water, are they not, Your Grace? If something happened, I would sink below the channel."

"Sink," her mother echoed.

"If I had a bit more money," the earl said, "I would build you a bridge, dear girl, from Dover to Calais." That ridiculous statement was met with smiles from both the females as if it were a distinct possibility.

Henry supposed he could always travel alone when he so desired or with one of his chums.

"What about in Britain? Ireland is out of the question, what with the sea between us, but have you seen the sights of Scotland and Wales or, perhaps, the coast of Cornwall?"

She shook her head. "Are there any? Sights, I mean?" She gave a little chuckle and her parents joined in. "Is there anything greater than London and its outskirts, Your Grace?"

Her parents both murmured their approval of her response.

Henry supposed it was just as well she hadn't traveled all over as they could do so together on their honeymoon. Whereas he had been on hunting trips as far north as John O'Groats at the tip of Scotland and been sailing off the tip of Penzance on the south Cornish coast, there was much in between he hadn't seen and much he would like to share with her.

Until she added, "I have no wish to do so."

"No wish to see your homeland?" he asked, surprised and unable to keep the disapproval from his voice. In this age of easy train travel, it seemed a shame not to explore one's own country.

Her father, perhaps hearing Henry's tone, sat up straight, scooting to the edge of his chair. "While no one wishes to force our Madeleine to a watery death, I'm positive she would be honored to travel with her *husband* around the countryside, at least as far as that man's country estate, whomever he may be."

Lady Brayson smiled at this obvious ploy to get Henry to declare himself the man who would be her daughter's husband.

Madeleine pursed her lips, glaring at her father, then looked at Henry. "I would go to my husband's country estate, Your Grace, and glad to do so, but why experience the trouble of traveling farther afield when green grass is green grass everywhere?"

"True," her mother said, *sotto voce* again. Her mincing tone was starting to get on Henry's nerves.

Another few minutes passed. He was feeling a little desperate to engage in some type of meaningful discourse.

"Coffee," he blurted out. "Do you like it?" It might not be meaningful, but it was an important part of his daily routine.

Madeleine scrunched up her face, looking, if possible, even lovelier. "No. I think it too strong and terribly unpleasant. I don't even like its pungent aroma. It's so foreign, Your Grace. I prefer tea, or even hot water with lemon."

"Lemon," her mother agreed.

Henry decided against pointing out how very foreign the now-ubiquitous tea leaf was or even the once-exotic lemon. No need to borrow trouble. Besides, when married, he could go out to drink coffee whenever he wanted. He wouldn't need to expose his new wife to its dreadful pungency at home.

Still, he sat back wondering how anyone could not like the delicious smell of coffee. The sole thing that rivaled it was stepping into Rare Confectionery and enjoying a noseful of the rich, decadent chocolate bouquet.

Nodding, for want of something better to do, Henry finished his last mouthful of port. Bored out of his mind and suddenly wishing he was anywhere rather than trapped in the Braysons' drawing room, he realized he did not have to stay another instant. He was a duke, *dammit all*, and could come and go as he pleased without explaining himself to anyone. At least, he could until such time as Madeleine became his duchess and these people were his in-laws. Then, he supposed, he would have to take greater care with courtesy.

At present, though, he could escape at will. To that end, he stood abruptly, causing her father also to get hurriedly to his feet.

Offering them all a smile, hoping it wasn't a pained expression, Henry said, "I must take my leave now. Again, my apologies for having turned up uninvited and my gratitude for the splendid meal you provided me upon such short notice."

Madeleine slowly rose to her feet, and Henry crossed the distance to take her hand. Neither of them had on their gloves, and thus, he could feel her soft skin. Her fingers were quite cool, and he wondered if she needed to eat more. At least he could discern for himself she was *not* made of porcelain as he had started to think.

Her extraordinarily beautiful eyes—a chilly blue, if he were honest—stared into his, and, for the life of him, he couldn't fathom her thoughts. Yet her pretty lips curved up in a perfectly winsome smile.

Those flawless lips which he still hadn't managed to kiss!

"So good of you to come, Your Grace," Lady Madeleine said. "I hope to see you again soon."

Did she really? He would have sworn, after that evening, that she couldn't care less about anyone or anything, particularly not whether she would ever be in his company again.

As he got into his carriage, he knew he had better find a way to kiss her—and soon. What's more, it had better be spectacular in order to chase away any misgiving as to whether she was actually the woman for him.

When he leaned his head back against the squabs and let his eyelids shut, it was Amity's face which floated in his imagination. A sweet face and those deep brown eyes, so warm and welcoming. Naturally, his next thought was of the press of her soft lips against his. He sighed.

She had her Mr. Cole, he reminded himself, and he had his Lady Madeleine. Or, he would in a very few days.

He shook his head to try to make sense of his thoughts. For months, he'd had no doubt he wanted the earl's daughter to be his wife. Now, a single week of knowing the chocolatier had caused him to question himself. *Had she bewitched him with her chocolate?* He'd heard tell her creations were magical, but he'd expected to use their delicious enchantment on another, not become captivated under her spell.

Her spell. Amity Rare-Foure was a difficult woman to get out of one's mind. Should he try to kiss Madeleine again tomorrow, or should he go back to Rare Confectionery, beg Amity's forgiveness for his boorish behavior, and continue with the plan?

Both, he supposed.

CHAPTER TWELVE

The bell tinkled about half an hour ahead of locking the door. Amity had already cleaned up, Charlotte had left, and Beatrice was finishing trays of toffee in the back.

All day long, on pins and needles, Amity had expected the Duke of Pelham to return. He might have come the previous day when she'd stayed home, her emotions in upheaval following an unpleasant scene with Jeremy in her father's study. She'd needed a day of solitude in her room to recuperate and come to terms with her feelings. And she hadn't dared ask her sisters or her mother if the duke had stopped by in her absence.

Yet again, for the umpteenth time that day, at the familiar sound, Amity's stomach clenched, and she looked up from arranging marzipan roses in a tin to see their latest customer. Once more, her anxious anticipation was for naught.

Instead of the duke, in strolled Lady Madeleine, with her enviable, flawless complexion and her light blonde hair hanging in perfect coils from under a blue velvet hat. Her matching blue mantle and light blue eyes again reminded Amity of a doll. In fact, there was one of her exact likeness in a store window halfway down the street.

Amity had to admire the young lady's beauty and swallowed her envy at such effortless grace.

Greeting her with a slight curtsey, Amity said, "Good day, my lady."

The earl's daughter allowed her gaze to scan the store, taking in the glass cases and the confections inside them. At last, her glance landed on Amity without a hint of recognition and slid off her again to rest upon the chocolates.

For a moment, Amity wondered if the Duke of Pelham had sent her, perhaps to taste different flavors, but quickly dismissed the notion. His Grace seemed to cherish the notion of surprising Lady Madeleine with his grand gesture.

At least, he had—*before* their kiss. *Had their kiss changed his mind?* Perhaps he no longer intended to return to the confectionery.

"How may I help you?" Amity asked.

Lady Madeleine approached one of the display cases. Only then did Amity notice the maid who must have come in behind and who kept her gaze lowered.

"I tried some of this establishment's chocolates at a dinner party. Elephant-shaped chocolates with some exotic fruit atop each one. I liked the chocolate though not really the fruit. Maybe it was an orange."

Amity nodded. It dawned on her that Lady Madeleine truly did not remember her from the party, nor did she know she was the chocolatier. What was more appalling, the young woman's palate had not identified the candied pineapple. Lady Peabody would be most unhappy if she knew her expensive fruit had been mistaken for the far humbler orange.

"Would you like to try something? Perhaps a milk chocolate?"

"I'm sure I don't know," Lady Madeleine said, scanning the contents of the case. "Whatever is very sweet, I suppose, not bitter."

Amity grabbed her tiny silver tongs and put a small square of milk chocolate on a plate the size of a tea saucer. She didn't mind giving samples since her customers never failed to go on to buy sweets after tasting.

"We don't sell any bitter chocolate here, my lady." And Amity held out the offering.

Lady Madeleine looked at the plate, her eyes narrowed slightly. Slowly, she removed the glove from her right hand and picked up the small confection. She studied it before putting it between her lips and nibbling at it tentatively.

Why had the duke looked ever so attractive when tasting chocolate, while Lady Madeleine simply looked . . . feral?

In the next instant, the lady smiled, not directly at Amity, but staring into the far distance over Amity's shoulder, seemingly smiling to herself.

"May I give a piece to your maid?" Amity asked, noticing the girl's furtive glance around the shop, her gaze quickly returning to the swept and polished wooden floor.

That snapped Lady Madeleine's attention back to Amity and wiped the smile from her face.

"Absolutely not. How foolish! She would develop a taste for it, and what would be the point in that?"

Indeed! Amity thought. Undoubtedly, this lady would never gift her servants an ounce of pleasure. Of that, she was positive.

"More," Lady Madeleine commanded.

"How much would you like?" *Would the earl's daughter buy a few ounces or a pound?*

"Just another square," she insisted.

Apparently, the lady was still sampling. "Of the same chocolate?" Amity asked.

"Yes. Are you simple-minded?" Lady Madeleine snapped. "Give me another one."

Amity didn't care for her rude words or her tone of voice but placed another piece on the plate and held it out. Lady Madeleine put this piece in her mouth more quickly than the last.

"Very good," she declared.

"How much would you like to purchase?" Amity asked.

"Purchase?" Lady Madeleine repeated the word as if she didn't know it.

"Yes, purchase." *Now who was being simple-minded?* "To take home."

"Oh, that was plenty," Lady Madeleine said, waving her hand in a gesture of dismissal. "Obviously, I could eat more. I could probably eat every piece in the entire shop if they are all as nice as that, but then I would gain an obscene amount of weight."

"And if you ate all our confectionery, we would have nothing to sell and our store would close," Amity said, knowing her tone had taken on an unusually sharp edge.

Getting hold of herself and returning to her usual cheerful shopgirl's tone, she asked, "Are you certain you don't wish to buy anything for later? Perhaps to share with your family?"

Lady Madeleine's expression soured slightly. "Don't you think you shall benefit from my custom without this vulgar begging for me to grease your palm as well?"

"That will do," came Beatrice's voice from the other side of the curtain, sounding annoyed.

Before Amity could react, her sister emerged from the back, slipped through the opening between the counters, and halted within two feet of Lady Madeleine.

"Since no one on the other side of that door knows or cares you're here," Beatrice pointed out, "and since we have customers farther up the rank than the likes of you, including the queen, I don't see how having you eat our confections for free benefits our shop in any way. I would think someone such as yourself would have better manners than to take advantage of us."

Amity stared in horror over her sister's shoulder during this dressing down. Her outspokenness was the reason why they kept Beatrice in the back.

Lady Madeleine went a becoming shade of rose. Her beauty didn't dim in the slightest, no matter the hue of her skin.

"How dare you!" the earl's daughter retorted.

Amity groaned. That tepid response wasn't going to stop Beatrice in any way.

"*I* dare," Beatrice continued, "because this is 1877, *not* 1477. We are not serfs, and you are not our overlord. This is a business." She gestured around them. "If you are unfamiliar with the concept, we create a very fine product and we *sell* it. In return, people pay us. And my sister is too kind in giving out samples to greedy, thankless snout-noses such as yourself."

Amity gasped and slapped a hand over her own mouth. This could not be happening, not with this particular customer. If Lady Madeleine told the Duke of Pelham about her rude treatment at the hands of the shopgirls of Rare Confectionery, he might withdraw his order.

It was true that Lady Madeleine eating their sweets for free did not benefit them. However, having His Grace present a tray of their confectionery to his beloved and ask her to marry him, all while the finest flower of British society was in attendance, that would definitely increase their custom. And such a blessing should not be trifled with.

Unfortunately, Beatrice wasn't finished. "You," she said, pointing to the maid who had not said a word but whose gaze had lifted from the floor in stark astonishment as soon as the insults had started flying. "Would you like to taste something?"

The girl paled and looked to her mistress, who stared her down with the force of the Gorgon Medusa.

"No," squeaked the maid, shaking her head adamantly.

Beatrice sighed, looked at Amity and back at Lady Madeleine. Then she retreated toward the curtain with a shake of her head as if she had done her best and could do no more.

Parting the velvet, she muttered again, "My sister is too kind," before disappearing into the back.

Silence cloaked the store like funeral crape draped across a mirror, and Amity locked gazes with the fuming Lady Madeleine.

"I apologize for my sister," Amity began wishing her voice hadn't come out so tense and terrified.

"Don't apologize on my behalf," Beatrice called out from the other room, absolutely unbothered by the damage she had done.

"What is your name?" Lady Madeleine asked, icily.

"Miss Rare-Foure."

The lady raised an elegant eyebrow. "I see. You are not merely a shopgirl. Well, Miss Rare-Foure, I hope you have enjoyed your success here on Bond Street. If there is anything I can do to bring it to a swift end, make no mistake, I shall do so."

Turning on her heel, Lady Madeleine didn't wait for her maid to open the door. She yanked the handle so forcefully the bell tinkled wildly for many seconds after she strode out of the shop.

The maid turned wide eyes to Amity, and then, against all odds, she grinned and followed her mistress onto the pavement.

Amity wished she could have given the girl a chocolate. She also wished she could have stuffed a rag into Beatrice's mouth to stop her saying such awful things.

Parting the curtain, she found her middle sister seated on a stool stirring her famed warm treacle toffee, entirely unconcerned.

"Are you mad? Do you know what you've done?"

Beatrice shrugged. "I've sent an arrogant peahen packing and, I hope, put her in her place."

"No, you didn't put her in her place. You created an enemy among the *haut ton*, the highest echelon of our clientele. You may have destroyed us."

Beatrice hesitated but began stirring again. "Don't be melodramatic."

"That was not simply any arrogant peahen," Amity protested. "That was Lady Madeleine Brayson, darling of all London. The *crème de la crème* hang upon her every word. If she tells people at a salon or a party that Rare Confectionery is not to be patronized, they will listen. I know we have customers from all classes, but the majority of the income, the greatest spenders, if you will, come from a one-mile radius of Mayfair."

She paused for a breath, but couldn't help continuing her first harsh words aimed at Beatrice for years. "Do you realize over half the homes surrounding us are owned by titled nobility? About one hundred and twenty of them, in fact! And they are all enamored of that young woman you just insulted. In a word, sister, we may be sunk."

Beatrice remained silent for a long moment before muttering, "That's four words."

"Argh!" Amity yelled, then turned around and went straight for the chocolate in the display case, snatching one of the nutty, chewy "strength" chocolates Lord Pelham had so favored. She devoured it swiftly.

The duke! She would call upon him as soon as visiting hours began at eleven o'clock the next day. Unless Lady Madeleine were going to see him that very evening, Amity could hope to get to him first. She would beg him to persuade the lady to forgive her and Beatrice and not to ruin Rare Confectionery.

And she would take him more chocolates to try. She would stay up all night if she had to, crafting the very best confections she could think of for that peevish shrew the duke desired.

"All that external beauty is wasted on her," Beatrice called out. "Come taste this batch of toffee and see what you think? I added something special."

Amity rolled her eyes. She couldn't stay angry at her sister, who meant no harm but called a spade a spade—and to the devil with the consequences.

AT TEN MINUTES TO eleven the next morning, Amity stood upon the pavement in front of the Duke of Pelham's magnificently appointed mansion. Not a shrubbery was out of place. Located at the premier St. James's Place, the duke's home was intimidating. Next door was Spencer House, and she'd passed Devonshire House to get there. Everywhere were dukes and earls, it seemed. Amity couldn't believe she was going to breach the walls with a tin of chocolates as her battering ram.

To that end, she had a separate offering for whomever opened the door, probably a butler. As expected, a tall, stately fellow who looked to be as aristocratic as anyone he could possibly serve, peered down his nose at her, and then he glanced past her to Delia, their maid-of-all-work, whom she'd brought as a companion.

"I am here to see the Duke of Pelham," she began immediately, hoping all her words were coherent. "We must discuss the sweet surprise for his upcoming dinner party. My name is Miss Rare-Foure. Here is my card. And here, if you please, is a small gift of my chocolates."

She thrust into his hands one of their small sacks with a blue stamp of their store name.

The butler took it but looked at the bleached white paper sack as if it might smell bad or explode. Either way, he was not impressed.

"Do you have an appointment?" he asked.

Drats! The man already knew she had no appointment and no invitation, for any butler worth his salt would know the schedule of his household.

"No." She paused. "His lordship was at my shop recently and intended to go there again soon, perhaps even today. I am creating a brand-new chocolate confection for him. Thus, I am here to . . . to accelerate the process."

Handing the tin of chocolates behind her to Delia, Amity reached for the paper bag the butler continued to hold at arm's length. Opening it for him, she raised it under his long, aquiline nose. He sniffed. His face remained entirely expressionless. However, his eyes widened slightly. Then he blinked and looked down at the contents.

"Would you like to try one?" she asked. *Who could resist after catching the delicious aroma of chocolate?*

Slowly, he took the bag from her again and tipped it on its side. A chocolate square slid out onto his white-gloved palm. He scrunched the bag with the remaining chocolate into a hidden pocket in his livery and picked up the square, putting it into his mouth without preamble.

Amity watched his expression relax as he briefly closed his eyes. He swallowed before his lids snapped open again.

"This way, miss."

Stepping back, he allowed her entry, followed by her maid. Closing the door, he strode across the spacious foyer and up the stairs. Apparently, his lordship's parlor was on the second level.

Trying not to appear as a bumpkin, she glanced at the splendid décor, looking up surreptitiously at the enormous foyer chandelier. As her gloved hand slid along the polished handrail, her feet sank into the carpeted stairs. She couldn't help looking sideways to exchange a glance of awe with Delia.

Upon the landing, the butler turned into the first room on the left, an expansive parlor, with pale blush wallpaper and an oriental carpet. The various seats around the room were plush with cushions. It looked to be a very pleasant place to meet and chat.

Unfortunately, Amity's insides were quaking, and she feared throwing up on the luxurious carpet if this discussion didn't go well.

"Please wait here, miss. I will see if His Grace is available to meet with you."

"Thank you." She couldn't imagine she would be standing there, marveling at the grand fireplace, the massive painting above it, or the graceful statue in the corner if she hadn't bribed the help with chocolate.

Sometimes she wondered at the powerful intoxicant at her disposal. One certainly didn't get that response from a regular Fry's Cream Stick. She turned to their maid.

"I cannot believe we've managed to get this far."

"You are a skilled chocolatier, miss. There's no reason why the duke shouldn't fall at your feet with the very first taste."

That wasn't exactly what Amity was hoping for, but it bolstered her nevertheless. Delia was a kind soul in her middle years, who'd helped out the Rare-Foure family for a decade. After taking it all in, her maid handed her back the tin of chocolates and wandered down to the end of the room where she took a seat in a comfortable-looking winged chair. She waved at Amity before drawing a penny-dreadful from the pocket of her coat, slipping spectacles on her nose, and beginning to read.

After a very few minutes, the Duke of Pelham entered the room. Her stomach twinged at the sight of him, without a hat or gloves and in more informal clothing than she'd ever seen him wear. Even after her insides settled, her heartbeat continued to race. He was so very appealing, and her reaction still caused her a tremendous sensation of guilt. He was not hers to admire and never would be.

Amity lowered into a deep curtsey.

"Please don't do that. I do not deserve it," the duke said. "I came to your shop two days ago to speak with you, but you were not there." He ran a hand through his hair, and she realized his dishevelment wasn't simply because her visit was unexpected but because he was in some distress.

"I have been berating myself more strongly than you or your father—if it came to that—ever could. I behaved terribly."

She was surprised, for while floundering in her own guilt at having enjoyed his kiss, she'd nearly forgotten how ungentlemanly were his actions. It truly was his fault. Yet, in light of Lady Madeleine's threat, she could hardly spare a thought to anything else.

"What's more, Miss Rare-Foure," the duke added, "I know why you've come."

CHAPTER THIRTEEN

ad Lady Madeleine beaten her to the Duke of Pelham's elegant door? Amity had been prepared to confess her sister's rudeness, but perhaps there was no need.

"I don't think you can possibly know why I am here," she told him, then waited to see if he mentioned the earl's daughter.

"I expect you would like an apology and only out of your desire for discretion did you not ask your father to come demand one, which would be his due. I willingly tell you, Miss Rare-Foure, I am deeply sorry, and I hope you will forgive me."

She glanced at Delia, whose gaze remained fixed upon her magazine, knowing her maid would probably wonder what His Grace had been apologizing for. How Amity wished that had been the cause of her visit.

"I do forgive you, my lord," she assured him while wishing she could ask him why he'd done it and what the kiss had meant to him. Yet men and women did not have such a conversation, not when they didn't have a prior understanding.

Even when they did, such discussions were oft fraught with emotion and confusion. Amity had spent an entire day pondering her difficult encounter with Jeremy in her father's study the night of the duke's kiss. In the end, she'd taken Bea's advice and asked him to kiss her. Despite Jeremy doing so with enthusiasm, Amity had felt strangely indifferent. He'd sensed it, too. And with him already looking wounded, she'd decided against easing her own conscience by confessing to the duke's kiss and hurting her beau further. Instead, she'd suggested they take a little respite from their close association, which had hurt him anyway.

Shaking her head of these painful thoughts, Amity took a deep breath and plunged ahead.

"I did not come here for an apology, my lord. I came to offer one."

The duke looked stunned. "Dear Miss Rare-Foure, although your smile and your sweet nature beguiled me into my reckless behavior, you can hardly take the blame."

Oh dear! "No, I do not."

He smiled at her frankness, and her insides melted with . . . fondness for him.

"I wish it were only that," she confessed. Ever since the previous day's debacle with Lady Madeleine, Amity had imagined on the night of the duke's proposal, how his ladylove might knock the tray of chocolates aside rather than accept a Rare Confectionery. And worse, she would publicly denounce the shop in front of his well-heeled guests.

"You look perturbed," he said. "Will you take a seat and tell me what's troubling you and why you feel, however unnecessary, the need to apologize to me?"

Amity hoped to secure his help in smoothing things over with his soon-to-be fiancée. To that end, late the previous evening, she had attempted something new and stunning.

Sadly, her creativity in creating a *Brayson* had all but dried up after meeting the famed Lady Madeleine. *How could she honor such a difficult woman?*

Beatrice had stayed with her, but everything Amity had given her to try was met with an unimpressed shrug or an outright shudder. Nothing had made her sister smack her lips and ask for more. Then Amity had created one last chocolate.

"I brought a few more samples. I have a tin."

She held it out to him, feeling like a ninny. *I have a tin*— she rolled her eyes at her own inanity, but her anxiousness at how this conversation might end was getting the best of her.

"Very considerate of you, Miss Rare-Foure. Yes, I can see you have a tin."

Still, the duke didn't take it from her. Instead, he gestured for her to sit, and when she did, he sat across from her on the other sofa.

"My lord, it would be easier if you were to sit next to me. Unless you intend to open your mouth wide and let me toss the chocolates in from here." Now, she was simply being too familiar, some might say insolent. Her nerves were making her act strangely. She held her breath.

Thankfully, the duke grinned and changed seats so he was mere inches from her on the same sofa. They both looked over their shoulders at Delia, who continued to be engrossed in her reading.

"All right, Miss Rare-Foure, what have you brought for me? I must say, I was looking forward to visiting your shop again. You've converted me to the pleasures of the cacao bean, and the aroma that greets one entering your store is nearly as good as the taste."

Amity opened the tin. *It was almost entirely filled with lies!* Except for one, these were chocolates they already sold on their shelves, but which she hoped he had not as yet tasted. She knew they were delicious. And when he was satiated by her confectionery, she could broach the subject of the unfortunate incident.

Having arranged the chocolates on two layers separated by a thin tin plate. Amity lifted the plate out by its ingenious small handle and placed it on the table. Now, the duke could see all twelve chocolates.

"'Zounds! How could you have created so many so quickly? I cannot possibly eat all of them. Will you help me?"

He had a devilish light in his green eyes.

"If *I* eat them, that won't do any good," she said, unable to take her gaze from his. *Did he know how magnificent his eyes were?* "You must taste them, not me."

"Perhaps we could split some of them," he suggested.

He reached for the closest one, a rectangle about half an inch high and two inches long, and bit into it, leaving a little less than half clasped between his fingers. Closing his eyes, he chewed slowly and swallowed.

"It has a licorice flavor, yes?" he remarked. Before she could answer, he held out the rest of it to her.

Was he expecting her to eat it from his fingertips? Apparently so.

"Hurry," he said, "it's melting."

Leaning forward, she put her lips to the chocolate, trying to take it without actually touching her mouth to his fingers, and also without letting it fall on his pantleg or, worse, his sofa cushion.

When she managed that feat, she had to lick chocolate off her lower lip and noticed his gaze dart to her mouth. She was probably a mess.

"Yes," she said. "I mean, no, not really licorice. That's anise, which is very similar. Do you like it?"

He shrugged. "Not particularly. I don't like Pomfret cakes either, even if some people say licorice is good for the digestion."

Oh, dear! Not a good start.

"Why don't you choose the next one?" he suggested.

No one could resist the blend of plain and milk chocolate which she'd hardened with the sweet milk chocolate in a swirl design. It had no added flavors, but the two chocolates settling on the tongue simultaneously were a delight. At least, she thought so.

"You first," he said when she held it out to him.

After nibbling the edge of it, she held it out to him, hoping he would let her place it on his palm. He didn't. Next thing she knew, one of his hands had clasped her wrist, guiding her fingertips to his mouth.

Gracious! Her fingers were against the lips of the Duke of Pelham!

Her stomach decided to celebrate the strangely exciting sensation with a pleasant swoop.

"Mm," he said. "That one I like very much, but I thought we'd already decided on plain chocolate in the shape of a flower. That, however, has possibilities. Would you be able to do the milk swirl in the shape of an *M* or a *B?*"

Amity sat up straight for his suggestion was brilliant. *How easy!*

"Yes, and instead of creating a brand-new confection, I could make anything you like into the shape of her initial.

"No, no," he said, looking into the tin at the bottom layer. "That would be cheating."

The whole tin was cheating, so he might as well give up with tasting them. Except one. She searched until she found it. This was the last chocolate she had made the previous night and hadn't even tasted. Beatrice had declared herself unable to nibble another, and Amity had been too full or maybe too heartsick to eat it. Now, she feared it would be bland and perhaps overly sweet.

Handing a plain discus of chocolate to him, she said, "You first, my lord, and if you like it, I will make it flower-shaped."

Biting it in half, a strange expression came over his face as the flavors melted on his tongue. He frowned, and her spirits sank.

"It is different than anything I've ever had," he admitted.

Amity had a jolt of hope. That was a start, unless he meant different in a bad way.

He sniffed the remaining morsel. "The scents are floral and something warm, too."

"Do you like it?" she asked, and then she amended her words. "No, do you love it?"

"I do not love it."

Amity's confidence plummeted until he added, "But I don't have to. Lady Madeleine does. It is sweet enough and has something about it that does, in fact, make me think of her."

"Lavender," she whispered, for the young lady's fragrance had lingered in the shop after she'd left, a little too heavily for Amity's liking.

"Yes," he exclaimed, looking shocked. "That *is* her fragrance."

"There's something else," she added, wondering if he could guess.

"The chocolate is very sweet, which I know she will love, and there is something rich about it, beyond the floral."

"Do you wish to guess or shall I tell you?" she asked.

"Tell me," he commanded.

"Vanilla bean."

He stared at her. "Miss Rare-Foure, I think you are brilliant."

She couldn't help smiling as happiness infused her body. "Thank you, my lord."

"And do you like it? No, do you love it?" he asked, echoing her words.

She shrugged. "I haven't tasted it."

"What?" He evidently found that astonishing.

"I mean, I tasted it while blending, but I haven't since it cooled and hardened."

"Then you must." And he held out the remainder of the piece, right in front of her mouth.

Their gazes locked. "Don't you think you should eat the rest of it," she said, "in order to make sure."

"I will come to the shop again and try more of these, if you like. But I am quite sure." He nodded at the piece he held, urging her to eat it.

Parting her lips, she allowed him to place it on her tongue. A little too slowly, he withdrew his fingers. She closed her eyes to focus.

First, the unmistakable taste of pure chocolate followed by the burst of lavender-infused sweetness. *Very pleasing.* Lastly, the subtle woodsy, fruity vanilla became apparent as she swallowed.

"There is a little," he started to say, "upon your lower lip."

Her eyes flew open to see him bending closer, and she knew he was going to kiss her, if only to taste the chocolate again. *Of course!*

Delia coughed. Apparently, her maid was no longer buried in the slim pages of the penny-dreadful.

Lord Pelham drew back quickly. He had seemingly forgotten the existence of anyone else in the room.

He had the grace to look remorseful before he smiled and wiped her lip with his thumb. Astonishingly, he licked it, making her insides coil.

"Even in this small, sticky remnant, I can taste its perfection."

"Perfection?" Amity echoed.

"For Lady Madeleine, yes. You have done it, Miss Rare-Foure. She will love it! This shall be the *Brayson.*"

Then, all at once, Amity thought of the prior day's events and the spell of success was broken. She recalled why they were having their lovely meeting. Not so she could share sweets with this alluring man, but in order to make certain his proposal went as planned.

"It may all be for naught, my lord. I must confess, Lady Madeleine may not accept this gift if she knows it is from my shop."

"Why would you say that?" he asked, perusing the chocolates, seemingly intent on eating another.

"Because—and I'm terribly sorry to say this—we insulted her yesterday, or rather my sister did, but I may have started it."

"Started what?" he asked ahead of putting another sweet in his mouth and not looking in the least bit worried.

"A bit of a quarrel. In any case, no matter how it began, Lady Madeleine has threatened to ruin Rare Confectionery, and I am here to beseech you to help us."

CHAPTER FOURTEEN

Henry looked at the talented woman beside him, whose pretty mouth was speaking of trouble, making it no less kissable. A minute ago, he had given in to the temptation—the momentary madness—only to be halted by her maid.

Thank God! He realized the usefulness of a chaperone was to prevent stupidity.

All the same, he would do anything to help Amity. Under no circumstances would he allow her wonderful shop to be put out of business.

Not even at the hands of Lady Madeleine.

"As I said, I thought you had come to demand an apology, which I heartily give to you. But even worse, I thought you might be here to declare you would no longer be my chocolatier. That would have been far more difficult to deal with than whatever the situation is with Lady Madeleine," he told her. "Let me get us something to drink first, and after you can tell me everything. You would like tea, I suppose."

"Oh, please, my lord, don't go to any trouble."

"I assure you, unlike yourself, I'm not heading down into the kitchens to put on the kettle." Not that he didn't like that about her. There was something very attractive about a woman who could handle herself at the cookstove, which naturally, he never saw happen among his own class.

Getting up to ring the bell, he told her, "You have less than a minute before my butler will arrive to ask what we want."

"Mostly, I drink chocolate."

"Surely, not all day long," he said.

She shrugged, which he took to mean she actually did.

"I doubt we have the superior drinking chocolate you're used to."

She hesitated, then seemed to be making a confession. "If I don't have time to shave and melt chocolate into milk, I will use cocoa. And you are correct. I am quite fastidious about which one I drink. For instance, I won't drink anything like Iceland Moss." Amity shuddered in a fashion that made him want to laugh at her dire seriousness over cocoa, but he refrained out of good manners.

"Nor will I drink Pearl Cocoa," she continued. "It has arrowroot added to absorb some of the oil in the cocoa, which should have already been pressed out. I won't touch Rowntree's on principal. I have it on reliable authority that company used spies and subterfuge to learn secrets of the superior cocoa producers like Cadbury. Of course, there's Sloane's and Taylor's and a hundred other manufacturers of varying purity—"

"Miss Rare-Foure," he interrupted her.

Warming to her topic, she hardly seemed to notice, even though his butler had now arrived to determine their wishes.

"I have always preferred Cadbury's Cocoa Essence," she said, this time, addressing his butler as well, as if Mr. Giles was a fellow cocoa connoisseur. "It is very pure. Do you have that? Or Cacao Barry? It costs more as it is made in France from African beans. Though I suppose the additional cost would mean nothing to you, my lord." She bit her lower lip delightfully and then admitted, "I also enjoy a mug of saloop."

Henry grinned. "Strange you should say that. I know it's not at all remotely fashionable, but so do I. Or, at least, I did. When I was a boy, we had a cook who made it just so. She was very particular, as are you, when it came to her flavors. I haven't had it since I was in short pants. Truthfully, I don't even know what it was made from?"

"Orchid roots. I'll make you a cup sometime," Amity promised him. "I get a tin of the superior Turkish salep powder from the supplier of our best lokum, which some are starting to call *Lumps of Turkish Delight*."

He liked the notion she would do something special for him, separate from her business and nothing to do with Lady Madeleine. Solely for him.

"Thank you."

He stared at her, and she stared back, smiling. Something about his chocolatier made it difficult for him to catch his breath sometimes. If he didn't know better, he would say he was smitten.

"Coffee, Mr. Giles, for two," Henry told his butler.

Amity raised an eyebrow. "For some reason, despite my father's family being from France, my parents love tea beyond anything, and thus, coffee has never been a staple in our house."

"But you've had it?" It would be fun to introduce her to something new for a change, instead of the other way around.

"Yes, I have, at a party. It was . . . interesting."

"You didn't care for it?" Henry felt a little let down. "Oddly, a few times, after I left your shop, I went to White's, and the taste of chocolate still in my mouth combined exceptionally well with coffee."

"Truly?" She glanced at the chocolates in front of her. "I shall be most interested to sample your coffee."

At her willingness to try, his good humor returned and he sat again beside her. "Come to think of it, White's started as a hot chocolate emporium."

"Yes, indeed," she agreed. "Mrs. White's Chocolate House. There was also The Cocoa Tree, and Ozinda's, all here in St. James."

"Rather interesting how all the seventeenth-century chocolate houses gave way to eighteenth-century coffeehouses. At one time, there were literally thousands of coffeehouses in London. Now, they are reduced to a few gentlemen's clubs and the odd tea shop that deigns to serve a bitter, boiled brew when it serves coffee at all. In France, the coffeehouses are superior." He hoped he didn't sound like a pompous ass.

She seemed to take his condemnation of British coffee in stride. "It seems we both enjoy learning the history of our beverage choices," she said.

Henry chuckled. "I'm glad you will give coffee another try." He was startled to discover it mattered to him that she like it. "I suppose, while we wait for the coffee urn, you had best tell me what occurred with Lady Madeleine. I hope it was only a misunderstanding."

Amity lowered her head a little, puffed out her cheeks, and then blew out the air, which Henry found charming.

"I do not think I misunderstood Lady Madeleine when she said if there was anything she could do to bring Rare Confectionery to a swift end, she would do so."

Henry frowned. That sounded so passionately forceful for Madeleine, he could hardly credit the words. He'd never seen her worked up about much except her dislike of oranges and dogs. Nonetheless, he didn't doubt Amity was telling the truth.

When she took a deep breath and sighed, he realized he was staring at the intriguing upper swell of her fine bosom barely visible at the neckline of her gown.

Did her creamy skin tone continue over her entire body?

Worse, she caught him at his inappropriate scrutiny, for when he looked again at her face, she was staring directly at him.

He coughed. "That sounds so unlike the composed lady I know. Can you tell me more?"

Reluctantly, Amity gave him a summary of what her sister had said.

With difficulty, Henry refrained from laughing. "And your fearsome sister said all this because you gave Lady Madeleine a few samples. How would your sister treat me if she knew I sat here with twelve chocolates I haven't paid for?"

Amity blushed. "That's entirely different, my lord. I am trying to bribe you into rescuing our shop."

He couldn't help the laughter that bubbled up in him and burst out. It was especially nice when the chocolatier, herself, joined in.

"Frankly," she said, "that's the first time since I saw the back of Lady Madeleine leaving our shop that I have felt the least bit of levity."

"I understand your concern, but I don't see how Lady Madeleine can destroy your business."

Amity opened her mouth to tell him how when his butler entered with the coffee service. They paused their discussion until they were alone again. Or as alone as two people could be with an eavesdropping maid in the corner.

Before they went back to the unpleasantness of Lady Madeleine, though, Henry couldn't deny he was eager to learn whether Amity enjoyed his coffee. He always bought the finest beans and didn't let Cook boil the water for too long.

"I have a regular drip pot from France," he told her, "as well as a flip pot, but Cook doesn't like using it as much. She says it is too 'fiddly.' Do you know the kind I mean?"

His chocolatier shook her pretty head.

"It has three tin chambers hooked together into one so you can heat the water in the bottom one, and when it has barely boiled, you flip it over, like so." With his hands, he demonstrated. "Thus, the water goes through the coffee in the center chamber and down to the bottom. But, as I said, Cook prefers the usual drip one."

He poured coffee into both their cups. "I like it with a spoonful of sugar and a splash of milk. May I?"

"Yes, thank you," she said. "I'll try it however you like it."

Henry stirred it for her and handed her a cup and saucer. This coffee ritual felt intensely intimate as their fingers touched, and he was pleased to be sharing it with his chocolatier.

Amity looked at him over the rim as she took a sip, leaving him mesmerized by the shining depth of her brown eyes.

"I've been to Café Mange Mereds," he couldn't help boasting. "It is the oldest coffee house in Paris, and I think this is just as good right here in my home."

She closed her eyes and took another sip, still without saying anything.

He was practically holding his breath to hear her opinion. Finally, her eyelids fluttered open, and she sent him her lopsided smile, making his heart squeeze painfully.

"It is utterly delicious," she stated. "Not bitter or burnt like the coffee I've drunk, nor in the least gritty."

"Gritty?" He grimaced. "You must have had badly made coffee indeed."

She nodded. "Compared to this, it was swill. This is bright-tasting and smooth. It lacks any plant taste of tea, which some, like my parents, may not appreciate, but I find it refreshingly different. In a way, it reminds me of my beloved cup of chocolate. Perhaps with even more milk in this coffee, it would be the difference between plain chocolate and milk chocolate."

"There are coffeehouses that serve it with almost all milk," he explained, "and a very little strongly brewed coffee stirred in. Served that way, it is thicker and fills you up, like a meal."

"I would like to try that sometime."

Henry nearly said he would take her to Paris, because over there, women had much more freedom to join men in the bistros and cafes. He caught himself in time. When Madeleine was his wife, if he left her at home on this side of the Channel, he could hardly take Amity Rare-Foure as a traveling companion.

"The chocolate," she reminded him. "I imagine the plainer, the better." Delicately, she chose one and popped it in her mouth before taking her next sip.

Her eyes widened with joy. "Oh my. That is beyond delicious. The flavor is layered and complex." She picked up another chocolate and handed it to him.

"I'm afraid these all have some type of flavoring. This one has a little ground hazelnut. Personally, I don't like *gianduja* chocolate or the hat-shaped *gianduiotti* coming out of Turin. I find the hazelnut paste they add to be overwhelmingly strong and too earthy. Many like it, I suppose."

Henry knew he wore a dazed expression. He'd never heard of a *giand . . . giand . . .* whatever she'd said. "I know nothing about those hazelnut chocolates," he confessed.

"Maybe you shall taste the *gianduja* in Italy someday," she mused, wearing her own faraway look as if she were already strolling through Turin.

At once, he thought how nice it would be to have her by his side if he did so. A second later, she broke the spell of an impossible daydream by pointing to the chocolate she'd given him.

He ate it and sipped his coffee. "I adore it."

They grinned at each other, and he wished they could go on drinking coffee and eating chocolates all day.

"We haven't cured cholera, nor have we hitherto solved the problem of the downfall of Rare Confectionery. Yet I feel as if we have created something wonderful," he said.

She laughed. "I shall begin to tell our customers to set aside their teapots and enjoy our chocolates with a good cup of coffee instead."

"And I shall speak with my broker about buying more shares of coffee farms. But now, back to your concerns."

Amity nodded. "You must understand while we do advertise, much of our custom depends on the good word of people such as yourself. For example, if Lord and Lady Peabody had been unhappy with the confections I brought to their party and mentioned it to others, our orders would drop. And if the guests at the party hadn't enjoyed them, they would probably have told someone about the poor experience. Instead, we had four people after the Peabody's party come in and purchase goodly quantities. Five, if you count Lady Madeleine even though she was not there to buy."

"Just to sample," he said lightly.

"Please understand, my lord, I am happy to let people try our confections," she gestured to the ones spread out on his low table. "Because most go on to buy something."

"Except Lady Madeleine."

Amity lifted a delicate shoulder in a shrug. "Even if she had sampled and left, that would have been fine."

Henry felt a little ashamed on Lady Madeleine's behalf although he knew he should rightly take her side and tell Amity to better curb her sister's tongue. "I take it the lady said something."

"I do not wish to cause problems and see no reason to tell tales. I shall only say she acted every bit the earl's daughter that she is, and in doing so, my sister felt we were being slighted."

He nodded. "I will speak with her, and if I have to, I'll confess I have a surprise that involves your store. Hopefully, that will be enough to placate her."

"Why don't you give her the rest of these, too? She enjoyed what she had, and none of these have any—"

"Orange?"

"Precisely," she said.

"I will be seeing her later," Henry told her, realizing he wasn't looking forward to it. Compared to how much he laughed and enjoyed conversing with Amity, the contrast would probably not be in Madeleine's favor. "And I will do my best."

The chocolatier breathed a sigh of relief, making him smile again. Then she stood, which didn't make him quite so happy.

He rose quickly to his feet.

She curtsied and said, "Thank you, my lord."

He didn't want to embarrass her by pointing out it was incorrect to style him as "my lord" instead of "Your Grace." A part of him knew he ought to tell her, but there was no harm in the small error.

"I will let you get back to your day," she finished as she drew on her gloves.

"On the contrary, Miss Rare-Foure, you have made my day. I assure you." He almost bit his tongue at his own gushing tone. Waverly would be appalled. Amity blushed becomingly.

"And I thank you also, my lord, for introducing me to good coffee, and to our new collaboration."

"I may have to keep a steady supply of chocolates at the ready to eat with my coffee," he quipped as she moved toward the door.

Her maid rose and came to stand behind her mistress, and there was nothing left to say. He couldn't even tell her he would return to her shop since they'd decided upon the lavender and vanilla chocolate.

Unless . . .

"I will come by this week to discuss how many chocolates for my party. I want everything to be perfect for the proposal."

Miss Rare-Foure became all business. "Very good, my lord. I do want this to be perfect for your party. If I am not at the shop when you arrive, either my mother or my sisters are well able to take your order."

That startled him. He thought she would *want* to see him again, but perhaps he was being arrogant.

"I hope you will be there," Henry confessed.

She curtsied again, which nearly made him chuckle except she looked so somber. And beautiful. Then she was gone.

DESPITE BEING AWASH IN jealousy over the duke's parting words about wanting everything to be perfect for his proposal, Amity felt like whooping with joy when she and Delia were inside their carriage.

"I am certain he will help," she declared and slumped back against the seat.

"Of course he will," Delia said, settling beside her. "He's half in love with you already."

"What?" Amity sat up again.

"Simply because I sit a few yards away doesn't mean I can't see and hear plainly."

"You're supposed to try not to," Amity reminded her. "But tell me what you thought you saw."

"And heard," Delia added. "His Grace has a nice manner about him, but do you think he's that way with everyone? He's a duke. He is used to telling people what to do and having them do it quickly. I guarantee he doesn't usually apologize—not that I know what he was apologizing for, nor do I want to."

That was just as well because she had no intention of telling Delia about the kiss.

"Anyway, I think you're wrong," Amity protested. "I can't imagine him behaving any differently with anyone else.

I have never seen him act in an arrogant manner. When he was with me in the shop, he was very 'normal.'"

"He was with *you* in the shop. I think you're making my case like a barrister," Delia said. "And what about at the party you and Miss Charlotte went to? Didn't he act the part of a true peer of the realm when among the other hoity-toities?"

Amity recalled how he had been a little more distant at the Peabodys' home and how he left abruptly without looking aback at any of the guests, including her. "I suppose."

Delia was enjoying the discussion. "My dear girl, can you imagine the duke pouring someone's coffee like he's a servant? And stirring in their sugar and milk?" Her maid started to chuckle. "It was priceless. He even wiped the chocolate off your lip like your own personal napkin." She went off into guffaws of laughter.

"You did notice a lot," Amity said, leaning back. "Next time, I need to make sure you have more than one penny-dreadful to keep your attention."

"You and the duke were far more interesting."

"Delia!" Amity cried, but they both laughed anyway.

Whether the duke liked her more than was proper signified nothing for he had reminded her he wanted his proposal to Lady Madeleine to go as planned. The carriage rolled to a stop outside Rare Confectionery.

"I'll tell you something, Delia, His Grace had a brilliant idea about pairing coffee and chocolate. I wonder if Rare Confectionery should start selling cups of coffee. No, we don't have the space, nor the skill, but perhaps we could sell bags of ground beans or even—*Dear God in Heaven!*" she interrupted herself, looking out the window. "What is going on?"

CHAPTER FIFTEEN

Her driver opened the carriage door, and all Amity could see was a throng of people. On second look, she realized they were mostly women. And not actually a throng. Perhaps five ladies, all impeccably dressed, each with a maid and some with a footman, thus giving the appearance of more.

The very moment Amity recognized Lady Madeleine standing closest to the door of Rare Confectionery, the lady turned and saw her. A terrible but perfect smile broke over her lovely face, and Amity's heart sank.

"There she is," Lady Madeleine said, impeccably dressed in a cream-colored gown with gold trim. "The chocolate seller, herself."

"What is going on here?" Amity asked as the group of ladies grew quiet and turned to face her. In a very short time, she and Delia were surrounded.

"These ladies are my friends," Lady Madeleine said. "We are shopping, and I wanted to point out your shop to them."

"How kind of you," Amity said, hoping if she behaved civilly, Lady Madeleine might change her tune.

The ladies tittered and gave her pitying looks. Their maids stayed silent, cautiously observing everything their mistresses did.

"I told them how your chocolate made me sick," Lady Madeleine said loudly. Some passersby, trying to get through the crowd on the pavement, halted to listen. "I wanted to make certain they knew which store sold the rancid chocolate."

Amity shook her head. "We do not sell anything rancid. Moreover, you do not appear ill."

"Are you calling me a liar?" Lady Madeleine asked.

Some of the ladies huffed with indignation.

"Careful," Delia whispered in Amity's ear. She was right to warn her as London society had become litigious of late. Not only were the newspapers full of frivolous lawsuits, particularly for defamation, Jeremy had recently told them at dinner about the alarming speed with which one might find oneself brought before the bench.

But wasn't Rare Confectionery being defamed, too?

"You fell ill and now you have recovered?" Amity asked, maintaining her level nature.

"Yes, you simpleton. I told you she was a bit thick," Lady Madeleine said to her friends who all laughed again.

Amity ignored them all. She took a step toward the earl's daughter, who seemed to think this was an amusing game and not a risk to the livelihood of an entire family.

"How do you know it was the complimentary samples you had from my shop that made you sick? How do you know it wasn't what you had for lunch? Bad fish paste on your toast, perhaps?"

Stop talking, she counseled herself, but ignoring her own good counsel, Amity added, "Or an extra helping of broxy meat at supper!"

To a person, everyone around her gasped, even the servants. The idea that a lady would eat a cut of meat from an animal which had dropped dead was apparently as great an insult as Amity hoped it might be.

Lady Madeleine's face paled further if possible, and spots of angry color appeared high on her cheeks.

"Here it comes," Delia muttered.

"How dare you!" Lady Madeleine said predictably. "It *was* the chocolate, I tell you."

"Because you ate nothing else all day long except our fine confections that recently you proclaimed so delicious you could eat every piece in our store?" Amity had raised her voice, while her heart began to pound with indignation.

"Yes, I tell you." Lady Madeleine looked around at her insipid friends, who all glared at Amity.

She sighed. She should simply apologize, but she could see Charlotte peering out the left-hand window, her normally jolly face appearing worried. Lady Madeleine had caused distress to her sweet sister!

"Our confections are exceptional and fresh," Amity proclaimed. "Are you saying if I offer complimentary samples of delicious chocolates, some with candied fruit, some plain, some infused with liqueurs, I shall have no takers?"

"Exactly," Lady Madeleine spoke for her group. "Not a one of us shall darken your door ever again."

Amity looked around her at their faces. "Is that correct?"

The ladies' harsh stares faltered. One licked her lips. Another looked hesitantly at Lady Madeleine.

"None of you wish to sample a delectable slab of treacle toffee, some of it coated in rich chocolate? Or a sweet marzipan creation?"

"No, we don't," Lady Madeleine declared, while more than one of her friends glanced toward the window with something that looked like longing.

"Very well," Amity said. "I wish you all a pleasant day. Please know your custom shall be welcome when next you need fine confectionery. And to you, my lady," she stared at Lady Madeleine, "I suggest you keep a bottle of Paregoric at hand. Not only will it help with your extreme fretfulness, but also your loose bowels from your sour stomach."

After that insolent and somewhat repulsive statement, Amity bid Delia good day, as her maid would take the carriage back home to Baker Street. Then, quickly skirting the duke's ladylove, she reached the shop door.

At the very instant escape was at hand, and the door handle, too, she heard her mother's voice behind her.

"Amity, are you all right?"

Well, she *had* been, but her mother was occasionally as outspoken as Beatrice. If she didn't get the formidable Felicity Rare-Foure away from the confrontation, the situation could deteriorate.

"Everything is fine," Amity said. "Let us go inside, and I shall explain."

Unfortunately, Lady Madeleine wasn't yet satisfied. "Do you know who I am?" she demanded of Amity's mother.

"I do not," Mrs. Rare-Foure said. "But I believe you will find you are obstructing the other pedestrians of Bond Street. Would you all like to come in for a sample of our confectionery?"

Amity groaned. This would not end well.

"I am Lady Madeleine Brayson, and I shall never set foot in your awful shop again, nor speak with your doltish daughter."

Amity's mother reared back. If there was anything that set her to anger, it was an insult to her store or her daughters. The young lady had done both.

"Here we go," Delia muttered again, as she had not moved a step toward the carriage once her employer had arrived.

"I suppose the *appearance* of good-breeding," Mrs. Rare-Foure began, with a prolonged perusal of Lady Madeleine from her head to her toes and back again, "does not guarantee an ounce of good manners or good taste. Rare Confectionery has stood successfully here for many years and shall continue to do so for many more."

She glanced around her at the others who were hanging on her every word. "If you are of the same mind, like a herd of brainless sheep with this green girl as your shepherdess, then you may all move along for you are blocking our door, and we have many customers to serve."

"You will rue the day—" Lady Madeleine began.

"Oh, my dear young lady," interrupted Amity's mother, "I shall rue nothing where you are concerned. I can promise you that. Does your mother know you are walking the streets of Mayfair issuing threatening statements? Brayson, is it? The earl's daughter that all the society pages like to jabber on about?"

Lady Madeleine lifted her chin in acknowledgment.

"Hm," Mrs. Rare-Foure said, "I would have thought you to be prettier, but the papers have greatly exaggerated both your looks and your charm."

With that awfully rude statement, Amity's mother swept through the parting crowd like the queen herself and entered their shop. Even Amity stood back to let her pass.

Most of the onlookers had to take a moment to close their shocked mouths. Then, as the crowd dispersed, Amity waved farewell to Delia and followed her mother. A few others, who were not Lady Madeleine's friends, entered the shop behind her.

As Charlotte tended to the customers, Amity and her mother went into the back room. Instead of being upset, Felicity looked positively radiant when she turned to face her.

"That felt bloody good. What an awful piece of work that one is." Her mother stripped off her gloves and tossed them on the shelf where they kept them, along with hats, scarves, and extra hatpins.

Despite being worried things were somehow worse, Amity felt nothing but admiration. "You were splendid, Mother. But we may, indeed, rue the day we crossed paths with that particular lady."

"I cannot believe that colorless fish is the one all the papers have been raving over for weeks."

"Months, I believe," Amity said. "You do know she's the one for whom I've been crafting a unique chocolate, by request of the Duke of Pelham, don't you?"

"That had rather slipped my mind. In any case, I forbid you to do so."

"What? Mother, no!" Amity's heart started to pound again. *What would the duke think of her if she bowed out now?* That she was not dependable, maybe even cowardly.

"I've finished the new chocolate, and I've just been to see His Grace. He accepted my creation."

Her mother looked alarmed.

"Do not worry. I had Delia with me," Amity told her quickly. "I had to tell him we might have a little trouble with his lady friend, and he agreed to speak with her."

"A *little* trouble. How do these things happen as soon as I am out of the store? I should never go to visit friends or to a club."

"Beatrice happens," Amity murmured softly.

Her mother shook her head. "That girl—"

"Is exactly like you," Amity finished. "And we are all very glad of it. You two are the backbone of Rare Confectionery. And Charlotte is the heart."

"And what are you, dear one?" her mother asked, drawing closer, placing gentle hands on her daughter's shoulders. As they were the same height, they stood eye-to-eye.

"I am certain I do not know what I am," Amity began, lowering her gaze.

"You are the soul of our shop."

Startled, Amity felt tears spring to her eyes.

"What's more," her mother added, "I will not let you sell your soul by making anything with our name on it for that terrible creature."

Amity broke free of her mother's touch. "I gave the duke my word. I would hate to let him down."

At her mother's narrowed gaze, Amity blushed and looked away. Felicity Rare-Foure would know if her eldest daughter were hiding a secret *tendre* for a man with a single look into her eyes. Turning to the cupboard, she drew out a tray of *Braysons* and touched the tip of her finger to one of the smooth flowers.

"I know they're a smidgen too cool to taste properly," she told her mother, keeping her gaze averted, "but do so anyway."

Her mother took one and ate it, keeping it on her tongue briefly so the flavors could warm and become more discernable.

"The lavender and vanilla are a brilliant combination," Felicity said. "Does Lady Madeleine wear lavender?"

Amity nodded. Her mother nodded back.

"It does remind me of her, except it's too nice," Felicity declared. They grinned at each other.

"Since I have finished creating it, Mother, please let me sell them to the duke. These chocolates are commanding a hefty price. His party is not too many days away, and after, we shall be done with the both of them." Even though she didn't want to be done with the man who made her feel all sorts of interesting sensations.

"Regardless, I won't ever sell these in the store as they will always make me think of her."

Her mother gave her a hard stare. "So, the *Madeleine*—"

"The *Brayson*," Amity corrected.

"The *Brayson*," her mother repeated with distaste, "is for one night only?"

Amity sighed. "Unless the duke wants me to make them for his . . . his bride in the future."

"You don't sound as if that would please you."

"No," Amity admitted, "I guess it wouldn't delight me. Nevertheless, I will do so if it means Rare Confectionery remains in good standing with the uppermost layer of London's society."

Her mother rolled her eyes. "Don't be worried about that young woman—"

"That young *lady*, Mother, is an earl's daughter. You saw how she rounded up her . . . her pack of wolves."

This made Felicity laugh. "Hardly wolves."

Amity started to laugh too, recalling what her mother had said. "You called them sheep—to their faces."

"I did, didn't I?"

"I accused Lady Madeleine of eating broxy," Amity told her.

Her mother laughed harder. "No wonder she looked so put out."

"She told those ladies our confections had made her ill."

Her mother's good humor died at once. "That's a foul lie to spread."

"Which is why I hope the Duke of Pelham will rein her in like a willful horse that needs to be tamed."

Her mother nodded. "Still, with a lawyer almost in the family, we shall sue her for defamation if need be."

Not her mother, too! "So litigious," Amity protested. Besides, it was now somewhat in doubt as to whether Jeremy would be part of their family, but she kept that to herself. There had been enough drama in their lives for one day.

"You had best hope your duke convinces that sour puss to pull in her claws, or I shall speak to Mr. Cole about our rights. And I shall pen a letter to her parents.

Amity went to the stove and wordlessly poured milk into a pan.

"A cup of chocolate, Mother?"

"Of course, dear. What else?"

AS SOON AS LADY Madeleine and her chaperone climbed into his carriage, Henry smelled her lavender fragrance, and he thought of Amity and her chocolates.

That wasn't how it was supposed to work. He had it all cocked up and backward. Yet it was the truth. Chocolate, vanilla, orange, and coffee, they all made him think of Amity. Now, even Madeleine and her lavender scent brought Amity to mind, eating chocolates together, laughing in his drawing room.

He had better get the worst of the evening over.

Before he could broach the topic, however, Madeleine said, "Remember the chocolates we had at Lady Peabody's dinner party?"

It was as if she'd read his thoughts. "Why, yes. In fact, I was hoping to speak with you about Rare Confectionery."

She frowned. "How strange. I hope you are going to tell me that you think it is a most disagreeable shop run by the most irritating females. If you ever met them, you would agree."

"Met them? You do recall the eldest Miss Rare-Foure and one of her sisters were at the Peabodys' party, do you not?"

Madeleine looked perplexed. "Why on earth would a shopgirl be at a dinner party?"

He sighed. "Not a shopgirl. She is the chocolatier. She and her sister brought the chocolates and stayed as guests." He could not imagine how could she have forgotten the unforgettable Rare-Foure sisters.

She blushed slightly. "I suppose I had eyes only for you, Your Grace."

Henry chuckled slightly at her adept answer. "How kind of you to say." It was the first time she'd made an effort to single him out as if he meant anything to her. Apparently, his suit was making progress. That should fill him with gladness. *Why didn't it?*

"Beyond that," Madeleine added, "the mind plays tricks when things are where they are not supposed to be. If I saw a warthog dressed up and astride a horse on Rotten Row, I probably wouldn't think anything of it."

Was she comparing Amity to a warthog?

As he tried to form a response, she shook her head in dismay. "That seems terribly untoward, even shady, for our hosts to inflict such low-class women upon us as invited guests. I hesitate to go to another event at Lord and Lady Peabody's home. What next, sitting down at the table with the butcher or the lamp-lighter?"

He knew what the term *to bristle* meant but wasn't sure he'd ever truly experienced the sensation until then. Now, he felt himself bristling at her mean-spirited remarks.

"That's an unnecessary thing to say," he told her quietly. "And it is unbecoming of a gracious lady."

Her nostrils flared and her eyes widened at his rebuke, but then she lowered her gaze. After a long pause, she said, "I believe you are correct. It was wrong of me."

Henry didn't know her well enough to discern if she spoke from her heart or was telling him what she thought he wanted to hear. One thing was certain, if she were to be his duchess, he would instruct her to be kinder with those beneath her since nearly everyone in society would be.

He still hadn't told her what was on his mind, his guarantee to Amity.

"I would very much appreciate, as a personal favor to me, if you let your spat with Rare Confectionery disappear like morning mist."

She opened her mouth to protest, but he continued, "I very much enjoy their chocolates and will continue to patronize them. It would not do for me to support the shop while you shun it. That discord would reflect badly on at least one of us, don't you agree? Especially if we are to continue to grow closer."

Her answer might end their relationship that very evening.

CHAPTER SIXTEEN

Lady Madeleine paused before responding and even sent a sideways glance toward the chaperone, whose own gaze was fixed pointedly out the window.

"As long as I do not have to return to the shop—and I see no reason why I would—then I shall simply ignore its existence as well as the awful women who run it," Madeleine said quietly.

"Thank you." Henry was relieved for Amity. Also, he could continue in his pursuit of the earl's daughter. Although why that hinged on whether she tried to destroy a confectionery, he could not say. Nothing seemed straightforward anymore since meeting the chocolatier.

"I suppose I must confess," Madeleine continued, "since it seems important to you. I already spoke with one of the shopgirls, maybe from the party. I honestly cannot recall. I had words with her mother, too, because they both accosted me, if you must know, as I was passing by their shop. I said my piece to them, and I think they received my message."

Her message? "Was there a public scene?" Not only would such a spectacle be unbecoming a future duchess, the more public the quarrel, the worse for Rare Confectionery.

Madeleine sniffed. "Rather public, I'm afraid. All on their side, of course. Berating me on the pavement like common fishwives. What could I do?"

Henry didn't like to think of the formidable Rare-Foure women ganging up on Madeleine. She might be a little narrow-minded and even arrogant, but she was also a mild-mannered female, harmless despite her frivolous threat regarding the confectionery. After all, she'd merely been sampling a chocolate when Amity's sister lashed out at her. Now, it seemed she had innocently walked by the store and was set upon.

He felt his ire rise on her behalf. He had told Amity he would handle it, and she should have trusted him to do so, not taken matters into her own hands.

"I am sorry you had to go through that," he told Madeleine, hoping to make amends and to reset his focus upon the one female who should matter to him. "By the way, have I told you how exquisite you look tonight? Every night, actually."

She rewarded him with her perfect smile, and it shone from her eyes this time, too. They were finally growing used to one another and becoming more friendly. Tonight, they would enjoy the opera and perhaps—if the stars aligned— he would finally enjoy a kiss.

The chaperone shifted in her seat, and Henry realized all the stars in the world weren't going to make that happen. He might have to marry this female without ever tasting her lips.

WHEN THE SHOP BELL tinkled, the last person Amity expected to see was the Duke of Pelham striding in. She thought they would no longer be graced with His Grace, as it were, not since she'd created the *Brayson* to his satisfaction. Perhaps he wanted to try it again and be certain. However, since his party was in two nights, she could not imagine how she could start over and hoped he hadn't come to ask for any changes.

Charlotte had run out on an errand, and thus Amity was alone. She could not go into the back room with him—nor should that have been the first thought in her head. *What was wrong with her?*

"Good day, my lord. How are you?"

"Well, thank you, Miss Rare-Foure, and yourself?"

The formality was all wrong, but they were in public and, despite being alone, acting any other way was impossible.

"Are you here to try the *Brayson* again?" she asked.

"I should, now that you mention it" he agreed. "If you have one on hand."

"Yes, I do. I've made a few trays," she told him and disappeared behind the curtain to retrieve a single precious *Brayson.*

To her alarm, the duke followed her all the way to the cupboard on the back wall, making butterflies take flight in her stomach.

Wishing to return to the shop front as quickly as possible, Amity found the correct tray. She snatched up one chocolate with her bare hand and whirled around, nearly slapping the duke in the chest with it.

Startled by his closeness, and how his heavenly fragrance already tickled her nose, she dropped it.

"Rats!" she exclaimed at her clumsiness. She hated to waste anything so delightful as a chocolate.

Simultaneously, they bent to retrieve the wayward confection, their heads bumping together with a loud clunk, knocking the duke's hat off and making Amity grab her forehead.

"*Ow!*" she cried.

"So sorry," he said.

Rising, the duke handed her the confection, which she tossed toward the rubbish bin in the corner. Too late, he removed his white glove, now smeared with chocolate.

"Let us try again," Amity said, rubbing her temple. More slowly and with composure, she reached for the entire tray, turned with a steady hand, and let him select for himself with his bare fingers.

He ate it slowly, his gaze never leaving hers, making her pulse race.

Foolish woman! she scolded herself watching his throat as he swallowed, causing her to swallow as well.

He nodded. "Yes, after spending the evening with her last night, I can say it is the perfect *Brayson.*"

Amity felt as if he'd slapped her. She was starkly aware this was all about bringing the duke and Lady Madeleine together, and yet the image of them keeping company the way she and he had done—perhaps sharing coffee and laughing—wrenched at her heart. All the same, she knew he hadn't meant anything unkind by telling her.

"What did you do? Last evening, I mean?" She didn't know why she asked and fervently wished she could draw back her words.

"We went to the opera house. Have you been?"

"Of course," she said, a little too quickly, her tone snappish. Simply because she wasn't titled did not mean she wasn't cultured. "It is lovely in London, but I prefer the opera house in Paris." *Let him chew on that.*

"I do, as well," he declared, jovially. "I think it's marvelous you feel that way. I am British to the core, but some things are better on the Continent."

"Like coffee," she teased, trying to regain her good humor.

"Or chocolate?" he asked with a playful tone.

She narrowed her eyes. "Sometimes perhaps. But when you are in the square footage of Rare Confectionery, there is no confectionery to better it anywhere in the world. Of that, I am confident."

In fact, she had a surprise for him, something she'd worked on with almost instant success. But this was not the time to present her gift. She planned to do so by taking a tin discreetly to his home and leaving it with his butler for after the party.

He grinned, and something inside her fluttered with pleasure. "I agree," he said. "And I would not allow your store to be diminished in any way. That's why I came today. Partly, at any rate. To tell you I spoke with Lady Madeleine. I told her since I enjoy patronizing Rare Confectionery, I would appreciate her leaving it alone."

Amity caught her breath. Before she could thank him, he continued, "After all, a duke and a duchess cannot be at odds over a sweet shop."

How utterly correct of him. How sensible! He must keep up appearances. *So why did she want to throw the tray of chocolates at his head?*

"Thank you," she said, knowing she didn't sound particularly grateful.

"You are welcome. Nonetheless, I need to add that, on *your* side, all the Rare-Foures must leave Lady Madeleine alone, too."

Leave her alone? "I beg your pardon, my lord."

"What I mean is," he clarified, "it isn't fair, nor particularly productive, for you and your mother to speak disrespectfully to Lady Madeleine, and certainly not in public."

Amity's ears were buzzing, and a slow burning fury began to simmer. She had best get him out of the shop quickly for she was apt to say something entirely unbefitting polite discourse.

"I understand, my lord. Now, if you'll excuse me, I have work to do." She tried to get past him, but he blocked the exit. "You are keeping me from it."

"Your tone is churlish," he remarked, sounding surprised. "Can you possibly be angry with me?"

Breathe, she counseled herself. "Will you let me pass?"

"You *are* angry," he realized. "Is it because I asked you to treat the lady civilly?"

Amity practically growled, but clamped her mouth closed to prevent gnashing her teeth with irritation. Suddenly, his hands were upon her upper arms, and she looked up at him, falling into the depths of his green eyes.

"I did not mean to offend you, not for the world," he said, his expression sincere. "Did I get something wrong? Did you not have words with her in front of your shop?"

"Yes, but—"

"And did your mother not also give Lady Madeleine a tongue-thrashing out on the pavement?"

"Yes, she did. However—"

"Then no matter how it came about, the two of you were against one, and she could hardly defend herself in similar fashion unbecoming a lady."

Amity intended to tell him precisely how unbecoming his lady was, with her smirking friends around her like military support, when the shop bell tinkled. Turning her head, two customers, both women, had entered, and now they looked directly at her through the open curtain.

And at the duke! With his hands upon her!

Amity shrugged out of his touch and exited the back room.

"Good day, may I help you?"

The customers stared at her, eyes wide, mouths slightly open in shock, and Amity knew her cheeks were aflame, making it worse.

At the same time, the Duke of Pelham followed her, his hat, which he must have snatched up from the floor, was perched slightly askew on his head, and he wore but one glove.

Her expression of mortification undoubtedly matched those of the women, who now turned wordlessly and left.

"Sweet Mary," Amity murmured, rounding upon the Duke of Pelham. "Between you and your lady friend, you are ruining not solely the reputation of our shop but my own, as well. I must ask you to leave at once."

He looked shocked. "Are you throwing me out of your store?"

"I believe I am." Although the damage had already been done, Amity needed him to leave. *If her mother ever heard of this!* She could only hope the customers had been regular people, and not members of the sometimes-vicious *ton*, but she could not be sure.

"I suppose it is for the best," he agreed. "I must say, it is a strange experience to be thrown out." He chuckled. "It has never happened before."

Upon seeing her disapproving expression, he coughed. "Again, I apologize for that indiscretion, but once they had seen us, there was no point in my hiding in the back, was there?"

"No," she agreed. "Far too late for that."

"At least we weren't kissing again," he offered, a hint of jest in his tone.

"That is not the least bit funny." Humiliation soaked her from head to toe both at his nonchalance regarding her reputation and at his casual reference to their kiss as if it had been merely another in a series of indiscretions. Probably, it had been insignificant to him.

"All right, I'm going," he said. "But you will still come to the party and present the chocolates, won't you?"

"That would be the very last thing Lady Madeleine would wish—to see me in your home, gifting her my confectionery."

"Don't you want to bask in the success and give your trade card to my other guests? Won't it help Rare Confectionery tremendously? And I assure you, Lady Madeleine will be nothing but pleasant at the party. The entire event will be more meaningful if you, the chocolatier, are there."

Amity considered. He was right about their shop gaining more custom if she were on hand, letting everyone knew who'd produced the chocolates. However, he was probably sorely incorrect about Lady Madeleine. If there was to be trouble, Amity wanted a family member with her.

"I shall come if I may bring my sister, as she very much appreciates your world of luxury."

"And you do not?" He tilted his head and looked heartbreakingly handsome.

Flustered, she waved her hand dismissively, then realized that might appear rude.

"Naturally, anyone would enjoy it, but I do not covet such a lifestyle. I want only the one I already have."

It was true, she realized, as she said it. She would not give up working with her sisters and her mother, nor creating her chocolates, not even to trade places with Lady Madeleine.

Not even if she could have the duke himself!

He nodded. "Please, by all means, bring your sister, as long as she is not the one who caused this senseless feud in the first place."

"No, not Beatrice. I promise." Amity paused but had to tell him. "There is one more thing. I will *not* serve Lady Madeleine the chocolates, meaning I do not carry trays at parties."

"Understood. You will be an honored guest." He went to the door. "I shall enjoy seeing you again on Friday evening. Let us hope for success."

After he walked out of the shop, Amity had to ask herself if she honestly hoped for the duke's success in his pursuit of his ladylove. He seemed like a nice person, and the lady . . . did not!

Nevertheless, he was smitten with Lady Madeleine, and, to be fair, perhaps she showed a better side of herself to him. Who knew what had transpired the prior evening during their outing to the opera, or what passionate kisses they might have shared in the confines of his carriage or some secluded alcove at the theatre?

That was not Amity's business. Her sole interest in the duke should be in bringing the most perfect *Braysons* to the party.

"WHY CAN'T I GO?" Beatrice asked later that evening.

"Because you said mean things to Lady Madeleine, and this is to be her engagement party. Besides, I didn't think you cared for the society of the *beau monde*."

"I wouldn't mind seeing them and eating their food," Beatrice mused, while playing a hand of Gleek with Charlotte and their father.

Charlotte giggled, and in truth, Amity would prefer the calm strength of her middle sister by her side, but with Beatrice came the risk of her outspoken manner. In any case, it was out of her hands.

"The duke specifically said I could not bring you. But I must ask if I may borrow your best dress, as he has already seen mine at the Peabodys' party, and I cannot possibly wear it again so soon."

Beatrice nodded. "Of course you may. We'd better try it on you first thing in the morning and see if Delia needs to take a tuck in it anywhere. Plus, you shall have to wear higher heels than you normally do, or the skirt will drag at the back and trip you at the front."

"What about me?" Charlotte said. "I already wore my best dress, too."

Their mother had just entered the parlor. "You must wear your second-best dress and make do. We have all day tomorrow to add a little ribbon or a flounce if need be."

"Don't look sad," their father said, peering at his youngest daughter over his hand of cards. "We shall buy you new gowns by February if you want to be part of next year's Season."

Charlotte let them all know of her pleasure with a piercing whistle of joy.

"Why did you ever teach her to do such a thing?" their mother asked their father.

He shrugged sheepishly, then he looked at Beatrice. "A Season for you, too, if you want. Because Amity didn't want to enjoy the buffoonery of the ballrooms doesn't mean you can't partake in London's finest social events."

"I know, and I thank you," Beatrice said, and nothing more, keeping her future plans to herself.

Amity could not spare an ounce of worry for either sister at that moment. Her nerves were stretched thin at going to the duke's party, seeing Lady Madeleine again, and hoping there was no unpleasant scene. More than that, she didn't really want to witness the presentation of her chocolates when the duke made his grand proposal. It seemed something better done in private just in case.

Amity was being a ninny. Lady Madeleine would hardly say no to the Duke of Pelham, and thus he didn't risk public mortification. In fact, the greatest risk was that Amity would fall over wearing high heels and disgrace herself.

"Come along," her father enjoined, "let us all play whist. Where has your Mr. Cole got to these days? I feel as if I haven't seen that young man in ages."

CHAPTER SEVENTEEN

As his valet helped him dress, Henry knew he ought to feel some sort of nervousness. After all, that very night, he would get himself engaged. Be that as it may, he felt calm. It seemed like any other party, except for the excitement of the chocolatier coming to his home to mingle with his guests and his family.

He didn't doubt she would comport herself well although both her sisters seemed a little unpredictable. He only wished he had told Amity about her repeated *faux pas* in calling him "my lord." Hopefully, tonight, he would get a chance before she said it in front of his friends.

"Finished, Your Grace." His valet did a final brush down of the back of his evening jacket. "I cannot improve a hair on your head."

"Thank you." The man provided impeccable service, but sometimes, it was like having a nanny again. Henry wanted to rip off his ascot or ruffle up his own hair out of spite.

Ingrate! he berated himself. He must always recall how fortunate he was to have been born into his particular circumstances. Strange how Amity had mentioned not coveting his world when everyone he met, even those such as Lady Madeleine who already lived within it, seemed to want more—more money, more luxury, more power, more of whatever it was they liked about being titled and privileged.

Furthermore, he could not dismiss Amity as a silly chit who didn't know what was what. She did know something of the world. She had traveled abroad, been to the opera, and met with chocolatiers in Switzerland and France. Hers had not been a sheltered, narrow existence. And still, she said she preferred her own lifestyle to his.

He sighed as he walked downstairs and decided to have a pre-party drink with his mother, his sister, and her husband. He needed to stop thinking about Amity and focus on his bride-to-be. As soon as he saw Madeleine again, he was confident he would feel some sort of thrill that she would soon be his duchess.

AMITY WANTED TO SCREAM. Not for any reason except to let out the nervous emotion that had built up in her all day long. Yet she could hardly do so in the carriage on the way to the duke's home on St. James's Place with Charlotte chattering at her side.

"I think my dress looks fine, don't you? The velvet ribbon around my waist and the extra lace at my sleeves were the perfect adornments, don't you agree? And Mother was so kind to lend me her garnet and pearls."

Amity nodded. She wore her favorite cameo pendant and small diamond earbobs that went with everything. Distracted and anxious about the evening ahead, however, she had barely noticed what Beatrice had draped her in except that it seemed to fit. When she glanced down at her gown, she realized it was the same green as the duke's eyes, causing her to grip more tightly the handle of the bag containing the tins of chocolates.

"You look frightfully wooden," Charlotte remarked. "Come along, sis. They will all love the *Braysons*, and Lady Madeleine will accept the duke, and it shall be a wonderful night."

Feeling queasy, all Amity could do was nod again. As their carriage pulled up to the magnificent residence in which she had previously sat comfortably, drinking coffee with the duke, she took a deep, fortifying breath—or as deep as she could, given the constraints of her corset and fitted silk gown.

"You are right, of course. And you do look lovely, Charlotte. But, please, be discreet. And absolutely no whistling," she added.

Her sister made a face. "I told you already, I won't. But let us have fun, shall we?"

Glancing up at the edifice, every window was lit, and the mansion looked particularly welcoming. "Yes," Amity agreed.

Knowing the mellowing effect of a glass of wine, she hoped there was a full glass readily available. As they approached the door, it opened promptly, and they were greeted by the butler as well a footman and a maid. If Mr. Giles recalled her bribing him with a sack of sweets to gain entry, he made no sign of it. Their coats were taken swiftly by the footman, and Mr. Giles led the way across the foyer to the staircase.

"The chocolates," Amity protested, turning to the maid to give her instructions. However, more guests arrived behind her. Fortunately, another liveried servant appeared, seemingly from thin air, to take care of the newcomers. This was the extra special touch of a ducal party—one didn't even have to wait for one's coat to be taken.

"Please give these tins to whomever is serving the confectionery course," Amity told the harried maid. "There are four of them. The three that are identical are for His

Grace's party. The one that is smaller is for the duke alone, for *after* the party. Is that clear?"

"Yes, miss," said the maid, and she rushed down the hallway toward the kitchen. The butler escorted Amity, Charlotte, and the other two guest upstairs where the Pelhams awaited on the spacious landing.

The duke and the dowager duchess were first in a small receiving line. Amity had always thought he looked handsome, but tonight, he was strikingly so, and her mouth went dry. She would have given her eye teeth for there to have been a servant on the stairs handing out glasses of wine as she'd ascended.

"Here she is, Mother," the Duke of Pelham exclaimed. "The chocolatier, herself!"

Amity curtsied first to the dowager duchess who greeted her kindly.

"So glad you could come," the woman said with enthusiasm. "I have had your chocolates before, I confess, but I am looking forward to tonight's treat."

"Thank you, my lady."

Next, Amity curtsied to the duke, who bowed deeply and then ruined the formality by grinning boldly at her.

"You look well tonight, Miss Rare-Foure. Thank you again for coming."

"Thank you, my lord." As if her tongue and her brain were wrapped in wool, Amity could think of nothing else to say so she curtsied again and moved along, with Charlotte behind her.

A young woman with a strong family resemblance introduced herself as the duke's sister, Lady Penelope, and beside her was Lord Yardley, her husband.

Finally, Amity turned toward the drawing room in which she'd spent a pleasant few hours with the duke. Nothing looked or felt the same, and she was comforted to have Charlotte, overflowing with happiness, at her side.

Unfortunately, there was no escaping the nerve-wracking introductions in there, either. Standing by the fire was the guest of honor, Lady Madeleine, with a small group to her left hanging on her every word. The couple standing on her right, watching with great interest, was undoubtedly Lord and Lady Brayson, and the young man with his back to his sister, speaking to another young lady, must be her brother by the flaxen coloring of his hair.

Amity didn't recognize another soul until Lord Waverly suddenly appeared at her elbow.

"Miss Rare-Foure, isn't it?" he asked.

"Yes, my lord. And this is my sister, Miss Charlotte."

"A pleasure," he said, bowing slightly to each one. "May I get you ladies a drink, or at least flag down a servant?"

"Yes," Amity said, perhaps too quickly, "thank you. Whatever anyone else is drinking is fine."

"I believe there is wine or sherry." He gestured for a servant with a tray to come closer so Amity and Charlotte could help themselves.

"Your next stop is to pay tribute to the lady of the hour," Lord Waverly said, half in jest, but Amity supposed she did, indeed, have to go closer and hope for the best.

"Will you introduce us to the others as well, my lord, since we do not know anyone here, and his lordship is otherwise occupied?"

"His lordship?" Lord Waverly frowned. Then he smiled. "Oh, you mean the duke. Yes, he and his family will be coming in shortly. I think almost everyone has arrived as it is not going to be a huge gathering."

And then Amity found herself presented to Lady Madeleine as if the young lady was royalty. Undeniably, she looked like a princess in a gown of shimmering gold silk with copper-colored satin ribbon for trim and very little lace or showiness. She was both elegant and understated despite the vivid hue. Amity felt almost gawdy in her verdant gown even though she was perfectly in fashion with what others around her were wearing.

As usual, compared to Lady Madeleine, they were all outshone.

Amity wondered if the lady would recognize a rude "shopgirl" when out of the setting of the confectionery. In truth, Lady Madeleine barely glanced at her before her gaze flitted over to Charlotte standing close by. Perhaps the lady looked at each female briefly to see if anyone could match her beauty, and when she found they didn't, she dismissed them.

Yet when her glance returned to Amity's face, her eyes widened slightly and she startled, her alarm barely detectable except for the wine sloshing in her glass.

"This is Miss Rare-Foure," Lord Waverly said, oblivious to any undercurrents.

"Good evening, Lady Madeleine," Amity said, refraining from a curtsey but giving her a gracious nod. "May I introduce my sister, Miss Charlotte."

This was greeted by utter silence. *Oh dear!* Amity supposed it was better than an immediate command to throw them out as she'd feared might occur. She should have known the lady was too well bred to make a fuss, especially at the duke's home.

"Pelham invited them as special guests," Lord Waverly added into the thick quietness. "He has grown very fond of their confections."

"Yes, I've heard," Lady Madeleine returned, polite as could be. Her gaze slid past them to more guests coming up behind. The Earl of Brayson gave a tepid greeting, and the countess murmured something too quiet to catch, so Amity nodded again and turned away.

As she followed Lord Waverly, Amity was extremely glad Charlotte stayed with her instead of trying to engage the Braysons in a chat about the weather or the price of almonds.

"Dare I say, the fair lady looked positively rigid, like marble," Lord Waverly declared when they were a few steps away from the Brayson family. He gave a short bark of laughter. The man seemed always to be in good humor. He also apparently knew everyone, and easily introduced them to Lord This and Lady That as they went around the room.

Amity smiled and nodded, seeing Charlotte do likewise. They couldn't hope to remember any of these people's names. In fact, her fervent wish was that she and her sister were seated on either side of Lord Waverly, so they could use him as their anchor.

In another few minutes, the Duke of Pelham escorted the dowager duchess into the drawing room, followed by his sister and her husband. Amity noted how the duke made sure his mother, who seemed awfully young to be widowed, was seated in a comfortable chair before asking if everyone had a drink. When he was assured they did, his eyes scanned the room and briefly found hers causing a frisson of heat to spark through her.

"Let us toast to a pleasant evening," he said.

"Here, here," many agreed.

Her gaze unable to leave him, Amity was mesmerized by the duke's appeal as he moved from guest to guest, perfectly in his element, an exceptional host and a devoted son. With the wine flowing into her empty stomach, she even began to relax and think this evening might not be too terrible, until she watched him take his place next to the golden Lady Madeleine by the fireplace. One day soon, he would be her ardent husband.

Undeniably, they looked to be the perfect pair. The duke said something to his ladylove and she smiled radiantly, which caused him to smile in return. They probably had forgotten anyone else was even in the room. A moment later, however, when the duke looked up to bring someone else into the conversation, he caught Amity staring at him and gave her a welcoming nod.

She nodded back, feeling her cheeks warm at being noticed observing him as if he were a specimen at the zoological garden. Averting her gaze quickly, she was grateful when Lord Waverly asked her a question about another shop on Bond Street, and she could speak like a woman of business instead of an ill-mannered guest.

For a few minutes, all went well. She needn't even have worried about Charlotte, who'd managed to catch the eye of a handsome young man. The discussion coming from their quarter seemed perfectly pitched and appropriate.

And then suddenly, Amity felt *him* at her side. Hesitantly, she turned to find the duke had left the perfect flame of loveliness to attend the weak flickering of her own feeble light.

"Unlike Icarus, you have escaped unscathed." These words came from Lord Waverly, making the duke laugh.

Amity knew the story of the boy flying too close to the sun only to spiral to his death and wondered at the duke not taking offense. After all, it inferred Lady Madeleine was a dangerous and poorly conceived goal.

"My best friend always knows how to bring the situation into sharp perspective," the duke proclaimed. "Is this rogue bothering you, Miss Rare-Foure?"

"Not at all," she promised. "As I know no one else here, except my sister, I am grateful you had already introduced us."

The duke glanced past her to Charlotte. "It seems your sister has also found a friend of mine to enchant. Jeffcoat's his name. He is a good man, without the unfortunate vision issues of Greenley."

"That's good to know, my lord."

Lord Waverly and the duke seemed to cough in unison, and Amity hoped they weren't making fun of her for she could not imagine what she had done wrong.

"I hope you enjoy yourself this evening," the duke continued. "I have asked Waverly here to escort you in to dinner. I shall enlist Lord Jeffcoat to attend your sister." With a friendly nod, he was gone.

"Good man, Pelham," Lord Waverly said. "Not a less stuffy duke could one hope to find."

"The dowager seems to have lost her husband very young," Amity observed, thinking of the previous Duke of Pelham, who'd passed barely two years earlier.

"True," he said. "It was unexpected, to say the least. I believe it was pneumonia or pleurisy. Pelham barely made it home from the Continent to bid his beloved father a final farewell, and he found himself appointed as the new duke the very next day."

"How awful!" Amity proclaimed, glancing to where he was leaning over his mother speaking quietly.

Waverly continued, "I hope the dowager likes Lady Madeleine and vice versa, for Pelham will want to look after his mother always."

Amity considered the tableau for a moment. "Hopefully, Her Grace will not follow the queen's example and go into unending mourning. To be practical, the dowager duchess might have many years ahead of her."

"Agreed," Lord Waverly said as the butler called them to dinner.

As it turned out, Amity found herself at the duke's end of the table, with him at its head and her seated directly across from Lady Madeleine, who was already treating her to an expression of disapproval. Amity couldn't imagine why the seating had been arranged thusly, but it was going to be a long evening.

At least Lord Waverly was to her left. Her sister ended up on the other side of the table with Lord Jeffcoat between Charlotte and Lady Madeleine. All the rest of the guests stretched down the table, probably eighteen or so, including the duke's sister, with the dowager at the other end.

As the soup course was served, the duke thanked them all for coming, and the conversation died down for a few minutes while they began to eat. Amity was very careful when reaching for her wine glass, spying the duke watching her. When she glanced directly at him, he winked, which caused heat to flow down through her entire body.

Looking straight ahead again, she received a frosty glare from Lady Madeleine and vowed to keep her attention on her dinner partner to her left. Lord Waverly was an excellent companion, and the meal passed quickly although Amity guessed it must have been about two hours.

The duke spoke to Lady Madeleine through much of it while occasionally someone farther down the table called his name, causing a brief conversation to be called back and forth. And Lady Madeleine joined in when addressed, also looking perfectly attentive and relaxed as she spoke with the man on her right, Charlotte's dining companion.

Amity could not find fault with the duke's ladylove, much as she wanted to. Lady Madeleine was decidedly at home at his table, displaying all the right signs of conviviality. It seemed she would make a good duchess, after all.

As if she were any judge of such things!

As the courses progressed—with the Pelham's cook displaying a mastery of each dish—Amity noticed the duke became quieter, spending more time looking thoughtful. When they were served the *entremets sucré*, she thought he might even be starting to appear a little anxious.

Perhaps he was simply digesting his meal in silence, she thought. More likely, he was growing nervous at his public proposal.

Glancing at Charlotte as they viewed the multiple dessert dishes spread out in front of them with enough staff ready to give each guest a slice or a scoop of whatever they wished. *There was absolutely nothing chocolate,* Amity noted with satisfaction. Her confections would not have to compete with anything there. While she had no doubt any other chocolate served would have been inferior, it was preferable not to have the taste of it already on the guests' tongues.

As the dinner drew to a close, Amity gripped the napkin in her lap, prepared for the duke to order her confections be brought out. He would stand, most likely, and make his proposal at the table, possibly following an effusive speech as to the many delights of Lady Madeleine.

He merely rose from his seat and said, "Shall we move to a more comfortable setting? I hope the gentlemen here tonight will not be offended if I beg off a separation of the sexes for cigars and brandy. Perhaps we shall get to that later, but for now, I would like to keep our merry gathering together. Come this way."

Instead of returning to the drawing room, with Madeleine on his arm, he led them across the hall to the other side of the mansion where the doors now stood open to a ballroom. Musicians were already playing softly at one end, and the room was lit with at least a hundred candles. It was gorgeous and romantic.

Every woman entering sighed as Amity did. Charlotte came up beside her and took her hand.

"Only think how your chocolates will be featured."

Amity couldn't stop the small chuckle escaping her. "I believe it is not the *Brayson* confection that shall be featured but the lady herself."

"Still, it's rather exciting to have your chocolates here, almost like an art exhibit at a gallery."

Amity squeezed her sister's hand as they moved forward with the other guests. In the center of the room was a table draped in blush pink silk and lined with glasses of freshly poured champagne.

The duke waited until they had all gathered around, with his family and close friends nearest to the table and the rest pushing closer to get a look. Then he glanced over to the string quartet, and they stopped playing.

"I am so very glad to have you all here," he began, as the servants started distributing the champagne. "As most of you know, I have inherited the title sooner than I would have liked and am honored to walk in my father's footsteps, even if I cannot hope to fill his shoes."

"Well said," someone called out in support.

"I have reached a time in my life when I require a help-mate, someone to fill my home with her beauty and grace, and hopefully fill our nursery, too."

A few people laughed, while Lord and Lady Brayson appeared a little scandalized, perhaps at such a blatant reference to their daughter giving birth.

"Where are the chocolates?" Charlotte hissed in Amity's ear.

"Just wait."

Someone near them frowned at their talking during the duke's speech, and Amity squeezed her sister's hand again to silence her. He continued to praise Lady Madeleine's beauty while having very little else to say about her. Thus, the speech was rather short before he asked, "Does everyone have a glass?"

They all held up their champagne.

"Good. I plan to ask the lady a very important question in front of all of you tonight. But first, I thought it best to ply her with something as sweet as she is. Something so impossibly delicious, if I promise to provide them to her for a lifetime, she can hardly refuse my request."

Again, people laughed. By this time, the guests all realized they were there to witness an engagement. They also knew it was basically a grand stunt, for no woman on earth would deny the hand of a duke even if he proposed over a piece of overcooked mutton with a glass of water.

Suddenly, two servants entered, and those behind Amity parted to let them pass. Right between her and Charlotte went two maids carrying trays of chocolates, which they set upon the table now nearly devoid of champagne glasses. As they set the silver trays down, Amity wished she'd remembered in her nervousness upon arrival to suggest porcelain.

Standing on tiptoe, she looked at the confectionery, blinked, and looked again. Horror of horrors, she realized a terrible error had been made.

CHAPTER EIGHTEEN

Gasping, Amity drew the attention of those around her and even the duke a few feet away, who turned in her direction and gave her his familiar smile.

"What's the matter?" Charlotte asked softly.

"They've put out *all* the chocolates, including those meant for His Grace alone."

"I didn't know about—" her sister started, but the duke began speaking again.

"There she is." He gestured toward Amity and every head turned toward her. "The chocolatier, herself. If you haven't been introduced to her as yet, my friends, this is Miss Rare-Foure of Rare Confectionery on New Bond Street, and her sister, Miss Charlotte."

Amity's hands were clenched, wondering if she should speak up and tell the duke. How humiliating it would be, having to go in front of everyone and pick through the trays to separate the round cocoa-dusted balls she'd made for him from the flower-shaped *Braysons*. Regardless, the duke wouldn't want her to be at the table, next to Lady Madeleine.

This was *their* special moment, and Amity's presence would ruin it!

Meanwhile, her sister gave a little wave of acknowledgment, looking happy.

"I make marzipan confectionery," Charlotte told the crowd proudly before offering her sweet smile.

Someone nearby snickered. Amity's head whipped around to locate the offending person, outraged on her sister's behalf. Most of the people around them, however, murmured kind words or said nothing, waiting for the duke to continue.

Relinquishing her anger as she had other problems to worry about, Amity looked back at him, realizing he was waiting for a response from her.

"Thank you for the kind acknowledgment, my lord."

Someone snickered again, and Amity looked around, ready to wallop the rude guest over the head.

"You are most welcome, Miss Rare-Foure. Thank you for coming to share this occasion."

Instead of looking away, somehow, their gazes locked. Amity felt a tremor of realization rock through her—she loved this man. His devilish smile, his green eyes, his infectious laughter, his quick mind, his sensual kiss. She knew she would love the rest of him, too, if she had ever had the chance to know him better.

His expression changed subtly, and Amity wondered if anyone else noticed. His attractive mouth opened slightly as if he might say more.

Then into the long pause, Lady Madeleine asked, "Are we going to try them, Your Grace? Or let them melt away in the candlelight? Our guests are waiting."

Our guests? Already, the lady assumed she and the Duke of Pelham were a couple jointly hosting the party. It shouldn't bother Amity as that was the irrevocable outcome after tonight, but it made her thoroughly heartsick just the same.

HENRY TURNED TO THE ravishing lady beside him and felt . . . nothing. He hadn't managed to kiss Madeleine, and he no longer cared if he ever did. When he looked out over friends and family, he realized he felt more strongly for most of the people in the room than he did for the earl's daughter.

Particularly for Amity, whose glistening, chocolate-brown eyes seemed to capture him whenever he looked into their lively, intelligent depths.

Nevertheless, he had to be sensible. Madeleine was bred to be a duchess. Naturally, she looked the part in her golden gown, but—he glanced at Amity again—his chocolatier looked infinitely more enchanting in her green silk, like a fairy creature.

Or at least, for some reason, she was the only female in the room who did absolutely enchant him. *But could she truly be accepted as his duchess?*

Madeleine didn't make any *faux pas* when it came to addressing nobility, nor did she gasp loudly in public or spill her wine. Neither did she kiss passionately enough to make his hair curl—or at least, he hadn't discovered whether she did or not. What's more, he realized he no longer cared to find out. With Amity, he knew exactly how spectacular her kisses could be and how wonderful the woman who bestowed them.

"The chocolates," Madeleine said again, more insistently.

Henry blinked. Hardly a few seconds had passed, but it felt as if he'd stood there for hours, silently thinking of Amity and how unfavorably Madeleine compared to his chocolatier's humor, warmth, sense of adventure, and companionable nature.

Christ! Everyone, most of all Madeleine's parents and his own family, were expecting a proposal.

"The chocolates," he repeated, lamely. "Try one, my lady. They will . . . win you over, and . . . in fact, they are named for you."

"Are they?" Madeleine seemed genuinely delighted.

"Yes," he said, glancing at Amity again, whose hands were now clutched in those of her sister's. *Why did they have matching worried expressions?* Of one thing, he had no doubt at all—Madeleine would love the chocolates. Amity need not be concerned over that.

He watched Madeleine select one from the tray, for the first time noticing there were two kinds, the round fondant balls he loved and those in the flower shape he'd chosen. She picked up a round, cocoa-dusted ball.

Keeping her gaze locked on his, Madeleine bit the confection in half. He knew at that very instant how it was melting decadently upon her tongue, how next she would taste the burst of sweetness and lavender, followed by—

Her eyes bulged slightly as her mouth twisted. It was the first time he'd ever seen her look less than beautiful.

"Ugh!" she proclaimed loudly, looking as if she might spit it out. Instead, as if with great difficulty, grimacing all the while, she swallowed and reached hurriedly for her glass of champagne beside her. Knocking it over, she grabbed for another one and drank it down in two great gulps.

In horrified silence, people started to look at the chocolatier, who now wore a stricken expression.

"That was vile!" Madeleine said loudly and slammed the remainder of the confection onto the pink silk tablecloth, smearing it with chocolate.

Henry was beyond stunned. The word *vile* did not go with anything he had ever tasted from Rare Confectionery.

Amity pushed her way to the front of his guests.

"There has been a mistake, my lord—"

Before she could get any further in whatever she was going to say, Madeleine turned on her.

"The Duke of Pelham is not to be addressed as 'my lord,' you dunce. Do you not realize how every time you say 'my lord,' His Grace is laughing at you? We are *all* laughing. A duke is to be addressed as 'Your Grace' or even 'sir,' exactly as his mother—or his *wife*—is always 'Her Grace' or 'madam.' It is nearly inconceivable that you do not know this common courtesy. Those of us who are *meant* to be here," she gestured around her taking in his opulent ballroom, "we learned this when we could barely read or write."

Amity took a step back, looking as if each of Madeleine's words had been a slap across the face. Her mortified glance went from her assailant to him, and Henry felt his own face heat with embarrassment, as much for Madeleine's rudeness and lack of graciousness as for Amity's innocent mistake.

The fault was all his. He should have told her. In private, of course, not like this. In any case, Madeleine was wrong— he had never laughed at Amity over the error. In truth, he found it quite endearing, but that was no excuse for not telling her.

"I . . . I . . . ," Amity began, then stopped.

"Lady Madeleine," Henry reprimanded, "you have spoken impolitely to one of my guests."

He wished his chocolatier's eyes would flash with anger at him or Madeleine. Instead, without another word, she turned and fled the ballroom. It was the last thing he'd expected to happen.

Her sister started after her, but she paused and turned. "Rare Confectionery has never produced anything but the finest," she stated loudly and clearly. "It is you," she pointed at Madeleine, "who is *vile*, the way you brought your pack of she-wolves to our shop to harass us. You should be ashamed, but I suppose your type doesn't know the meaning of the word *shame*. Your palate must be as crude as your nature if you cannot discern delicious chocolate when you taste it."

Miss Charlotte glanced around her at the stunned guests as if daring even one to say anything. Greeted by horrified silence, she turned and looked directly at him. Henry held his breath, wondering if she would unleash her anger on him next. Instead, she gave him a few words of advice.

"You should be careful of that one," she said, gesturing with a flick of her thumb at Madeleine.

"How dare you!" This from both Madeleine and her parents simultaneously.

Miss Charlotte rolled her brown eyes and continued to address him. This time, however, she offered the same smile with which she always greeted her customers, including him.

"The dinner was wonderful, Your Grace." She curtsied. "Thank you for inviting us," she added as if the entire experience had been a pleasant one. With that, she departed the ballroom.

Bravo! he thought, wishing Amity had seen her sister's composure. Even more, he wished it had not been necessary in the first place.

"Thank goodness those two are gone," Madeleine said spitefully.

Meanwhile, her mother picked up another chocolate and bit into it.

"Why, it's delicious," she pronounced.

"What?" Madeleine declared, rounding upon the usually meek and wordless woman.

"Chocolate and lavender," Lady Brayson mused. "How delightful!"

"Let me taste," and she snatched the remainder from her mother's fingers, popping it between her lips.

"Well?" Henry asked her, wanting her to repair Amity's reputation as a chocolatier in front of everyone.

Madeleine lifted her shoulder in a practiced shrug before admitting, "Much nicer than the first, I will say that."

Henry looked down at the discarded chocolate morsel that had so displeased her, almost afraid to taste it. *What could possibly be wrong?* After a pause, he picked it up and ate it.

Closing his eyes at the flavors, he could hardly believe what Amity had done.

AS SOON AS AMITY reached home, she went to her room, ignoring her parents and Beatrice who were in the drawing room. Charlotte could fill them in on her humiliation and abject failure.

At the Duke of Pelham's house, she'd waited in the downstairs foyer for her sister to join her, having asked the footman to summon their carriage. It had been a short, tense ride home. She wasn't the type to cry, but unexpectedly had felt tears pricking her eyes.

Charlotte had been uncharacteristically quiet, sitting beside her and placing a supportive hand on her knee for the journey back to Baker Street. Amity hadn't asked what she'd said to the gathering, knowing her sister had said something. That was inevitable. Hopefully, nothing embarrassing, but Amity didn't see how she could be more disgraced than she already was. Nor could she imagine how the damage to Rare Confectionery could be any worse.

Would they have any customers at all come the morning?

Of course they would, she consoled herself. Perhaps not among the elite, but they had plenty of regulars who didn't know anything about the Duke of Pelham or Lady Madeleine, nor had ever encountered the *haut ton. Lucky them!*

In her room, Amity sat heavily upon her bed. *Why hadn't the duke told her the very first time she'd committed the error in his presence? Or even Lord Waverly, for that matter?* Instead, she had been schooled by the most snout-nosed lady in front of the least forgiving people she could imagine. And now she knew a duke was not a lord.

How confounding! Although she'd often said "His Grace" when referring to him, she had never used "Your Grace" when speaking with him as it sounded ridiculous to her ears. *What else had she got wrong?*

Someone, either at the Peabodys' dinner or at the duke's that evening, ought to have had the good manners to tell her privately to stop making the mistake. *Obviously not!* Thus, she'd been humiliated in front of the duke's friends and family. *And what did he think of her? Had he really been amused by her repeated error?*

Amity lay back upon her bed in the borrowed gown and stared at the canopy above. She needed to dismiss from her mind the events of the night. Ruminating on things which could not be changed did not do one any good. She must look to the future, specifically hers. As for the duke, assuredly, he would have smoothed things over with his lady, hopefully identified the correct chocolates, and proposed as planned. The guests would have returned to the festive practice of drinking champagne, and all would be well by morning.

In a day or so, the engagement would be announced in all the papers. It was an important occurrence when one of England's dukes was removed from the marriage market. And Amity would try to find it in her heart to wish them both well.

She groaned and closed her eyes. How foolish of her to imagine herself in love with him and how correct Madeleine had been—a shopgirl did not belong in the Duke of Pelham's world. It was fraught with mud puddles of unknown customs into which she could step at any moment. The people were not kind—except for the duke and his dowager mother and even Lord Waverly. Everyone else seemed spiteful.

Amity had no business mingling with the nobility. It was as ridiculous as thinking herself in love with a shooting star racing far and high and out of reach. What she felt for the duke was infatuation, obsession, fascination—definitely not love.

Now that a little time had passed since the duke's kiss, and with the certainty it would never happen again, she could think clearly about Jeremy. Determined to speak with him the next day, she hoped they could salvage their relationship. Over the course of the past year, she had been content with him and had been quite sure of how well they suited. Unsurprisingly, they had each expressed a growing affection for the other, and there was no reason to believe it would not continue. That was, if he could still entertain the notion of having her as his wife.

Eschewing Delia's help, Amity managed to get herself undressed, took her hair down—*a hundred pins seemed to have held it up!*—and climbed into bed, absolutely exhausted.

In the morning, however, her plans to visit with Jeremy were for naught. The Rare-Foures were off to the country. When she went down to breakfast, Amity discovered some of the household was already packing up while Armand Foure read a paper with his tea and eggs.

"We never go away and close the store at this time of year," she protested over her cup of chocolate. "What about all the inventory on the shelves?" she asked her father. Her mother was conspicuously absent.

"We shall dispose of some of it as a quick sale this morning and give the rest away. Don't worry."

Having her father tell her not to worry caused Amity to start worrying immediately. When Charlotte came in with Beatrice close behind, their glances flitted between her and their father.

"What is going on?" Amity asked her sisters. Each went to the sideboard to load up their plates.

"Um," Charlotte said, keeping her back to Amity.

Beatrice turned and smiled, but it looked more like a grimace. Amity's stomach clenched.

"Will someone please tell me why we are rushing to Coggeshall as if the hounds of Hell were after us?"

It was Beatrice who sat beside her and said, "The papers have not been kind to your and Charlotte's attendance at the duke's party last night. Our store was mentioned and something about Lady Madeleine nearly being taken ill by our confectionery."

Amity felt the tears return, and she blinked hard to keep them from falling. "I told the maid which tin was for the duke alone," she protested, trying to explain to her family whose livelihood she might have ruined. "But someone put them out, and, with exceptionally ill fortune, Lady Madeleine took one of those with flavors she did not appreciate."

Her father shrugged. "It is no matter. We need a respite. Don't you girls agree?"

At once, Charlotte and Beatrice said they did. Their kindness made it worse.

Amity sighed. "Father, isn't it a mistake to close up the shop as if we are running away or hiding from something? Isn't it like admitting guilt?"

"I don't believe so, and I don't want any of you to be harassed, so we shall take a short holiday in the country. Three weeks in Essex at the very least. Maybe you'll have time to read up on any new developments in chocolate."

"New developments in chocolate?" she asked with incredulity.

"I've heard rumblings, my girl," Armand Foure said. "The Swiss are working on a machine—shaped like a conch if you can believe it—that will make chocolate even smoother. Some were discussing it at the sugar traders meeting. I found a few articles mentioning the method, which I'll bring along for you to read, but they're in French."

Smoother chocolate? That was worth reading about, even if she had to struggle with the translation. On the other hand, it seemed cowardly not to face the customers of Mayfair.

"Where is Mother?"

"Tending the shop this morning. We shall leave when she returns."

"She is by herself?" Amity asked with alarm.

"As I said, I don't want you girls harassed. She has Delia with her, and they will set everything to right and put a notice on the door regarding our sojourn to the country. Don't fret, Amity. Let me and your mother handle this."

She finished her hot chocolate, which didn't soothe her for the first time in her life.

What a disaster! So much for gaining new custom amongst the wealthiest by creating a special confection for the duke. Instead, it seemed, they would have no customers at all.

"May I send word to Mr. Cole about our departure and where he can write to us if he wishes?"

"Certainly," her father said, and to his credit, he didn't look the least bothered about his offspring having driven them to close their store and flee London.

Standing, she went over to him and kissed his cheek, glancing at her sisters' subdued expressions and noting the crumpled newspapers in a pile beside her father's elbow. Apparently, he wasn't going to share them today. At least, not with her.

Heading for their study, she sat down to write to Jeremy, wishing she could have spoken to him instead. As she set pen to paper, an awful thought crossed her mind. *What if he'd already caught wind of the scandal—if it could be called such—and no longer wanted to be associated with her?*

After all, in his profession, he must be above reproach. The taint of having supposedly made the future Duchess of Pelham become ill might follow Amity beyond the fleeting notoriety of the sordid gossip rags. She might become known as the *poison purveyor of chocolates,* or some such ridiculous moniker.

Perhaps she should leave Jeremy alone.

In the end, Amity decided to let it be his decision whether to resume contact with her. She wrote to him of their departure to Coggeshall, an unremarkable town in the heart of Essex, with the open invitation to write to her or even to visit.

And then she began to pack her personal belongings.

HENRY DESCENDED FROM HIS carriage and bounded across the pavement, his fingers on the door handle before he saw the notice on the shop window. The door did not open as usual with the welcoming tinkle of the bell. Looking through the window, he saw no pretty Rare-Foure sisters inside to greet him.

Drawing back, he read the message written in a no-nonsense script and hanging by a blue ribbon facing outward, against the glass:

> *Thank you for your custom. We are going on a brief holiday. The remainder of our confections are for sale next door at Asprey's. Please excuse any inconvenience.*

Frowning, he felt a twist in his gut accompanying the suspicion this was not a planned trip. Moreover, the unexpected shop closing didn't bode well for the Rare-Foures' bank account. He reread the message and hurried next door to the jewelry store, not to buy the remaining chocolates but to find out if the clerk at Asprey's knew anything more.

CHAPTER NINETEEN

Coggeshall, Essex County

Amity snapped closed Miss Eliza Leslie's *Lady's New-Receipt Book*. She'd been reading the American woman's recipe for chocolate cake over and over without taking in a word of it. Despite it being a favorite of their cook's and indubitably filled with good sense, the book could not hold her attention.

It had been five days since the disaster at the duke's home, and still, Amity could vividly recall Lady Madeleine's harsh words and the duke's look of embarrassment and disappointment.

Standing, she left the sunny window seat and decided to take a walk outside. Luckily, the weather was holding fine after a rainy spell over the prior two days. The sunshine and a long walk would undoubtedly improve her mood.

Thus, five minutes later, draped in her lightweight plum-colored cloak, she was strolling toward the River Blackwater, keeping her mind clear of thoughts of the nobility and London as much as possible. The grouse were rustling in the long grasses. Her father was not a hunter, nor did anyone else use their land, so they had an abundance of birds on the property, as well as foxes and deer.

How different would her father's life be if he had sons? She'd once overheard him tell their mother how glad he was to have daughters for he recalled his own upbringing where he and his brothers were little terrors—loud, troublesome, and dirty.

She frowned now recalling his words. She and her sisters were not any of those things, except for Charlotte's occasional loud outbursts. Yet Amity's problems with the *bon ton* could be considered troublesome at the very least. And just like that, she was thinking about the entire mess again. *Rats!*

"Miss Rare-Foure," came a male voice, startling her out of her thoughts. Whirling around, she saw Jeremy walking swiftly toward her. Her heart lifted like a sparrow on a gentle breeze.

She'd had no response from him to her letter and thought perhaps he'd washed his hands of her. Instead, he greeted her warmly, doffed his hat and replaced it, and as naturally as if they'd never been apart, tucked her arm under his. They continued together along the path. He'd visited her family's country house once before and seemed quite at home, directing their steps toward the small bridge over one tiny tributary of the river that ran next to their land. The bridge led to a modest-sized island, and on it a small gazebo, a romantic setting that had been there since Amity was born.

"It was good of you to come," she said and meant it.

"I should have answered your letter sooner. I had some thinking to do."

Understandably so. Amity waited for his decision, knowing it was a good sign he had come all the way to Coggeshall.

Then he added, "Your name and the shop were in the papers for a few days."

"How bad was it?" she asked.

He glanced sideways. "Didn't *you* read them?"

She shook her head and stepped into the small structure in which a few birds had made their nests in the rafters. "Not a word. I lived it, remember?"

He didn't smile. "They were not kind, but it seems you were in direct opposition to the beloved Lady Madeleine Brayson."

"Soon to be the even more beloved Duchess of Pelham," Amity added.

"Maybe," Jeremy said, looking around, "but that wasn't mentioned." He rested a foot on the bench, and she stood on the other side of the gazebo, watching the river.

After a moment, he asked, "What are the plans for Rare Confectionery?"

The way he asked her sent a shock sizzling down her spine, and she whirled around. "What do you mean?"

"Will it reopen?"

"Why wouldn't it?" she demanded, trying to keep her voice calm, but the idea that their wonderful, beloved shop might close forever frightened her. "We are only here for another couple of weeks, and then we'll go back."

"I see."

She took a step toward him. "Jeremy, is there something else?"

"Mostly the papers talked about you, more than the confectionery. I cannot help but wonder if you were no longer the chocolatier, might it be better for your family and for Rare Confectionery. One of your sisters could make the chocolates, or perhaps your mother."

She gaped in dismay before closing her mouth so she wouldn't appear as a dying fish. He spoke as if anyone could do what she did. She could no more sculpt a marzipan pig than fly, nor could she keep the treacle toffee from burning or separating.

"Why would you say that?"

He shrugged. "I merely thought if you distanced yourself, and let people think of Rare Confectionery without you, any damage that has been done to the shop's reputation would fade."

How badly had the newspapers treated her? She almost wanted to peek. *Almost.*

"Don't look so stricken," Jeremy said, coming toward her. "There is more to life than the back room of that shop. Which brings me to the reason I came. When you told me a couple weeks ago of your doubts regarding our future, I was hurt. Particularly as we had kissed directly prior. I thought you might have been testing me."

She had very much wanted that kiss to be like the duke's. It hadn't been. Neither was it repulsive or even unpleasant. It simply wasn't the same.

"In retrospect, I have to say I admire you for being cautious," he continued. Then he took both her hands in his. "I hope you have had a chance to think more about whether we suit. I believe by your sending me that letter, you were inviting my return into your life. Was I correct?"

Amity nodded. That had been her intent. She needed to put aside any silly hopes she'd been nurturing over . . . anyone else. "Yes, if you are amenable to such. I *am* glad you came, Jeremy."

The familiar sight of him, so unexpected, had buoyed her spirits—at least, until he'd started talking of her not making chocolate.

He smiled at her words. *Would he kiss her again?*

"I have done a great deal of thinking as well," he added. "And my life is emptier without you. I think you will make an excellent solicitor's wife. Also, I believe you will be happy and fulfilled with the duties of being my wife and, hopefully someday, a mother whether or not you continue to make chocolates."

Amity didn't like the tack of his conversation. "I love making chocolate and spending my days with my mother and sisters."

He nodded. "I know you do, but when you become a wife, it's normal to pull away from your birth family and cleave to your husband. Besides, the fruits of your labor must no longer go to Rare Confectionery, but to our Cole assets, however they develop."

"I receive an allowance," she began.

"You would need to be properly paid if you remained at Rare Confectionery since that would be a drain on the time and energy you have for our union."

Amity could not imagine asking her parents to pay her to work in the shop, and she told him so.

"If you have determined being a chocolate-maker is the only way to be happy, when we have saved enough, you could open your own confectionery. Cole's Confectionery sounds good or Cole's Chocolates."

She smiled. He was trying to be helpful and accommodating, while wanting to be certain her loyalty would lie more with him and being a Cole than with being a Rare-Foure.

"I understand," she said. Jeremy liked her family, and in the end, he would come around to letting her remain the chocolatier of Rare Confectionery, and as the duties of wife and mother took more of her time, she would grow accustomed to her new life and make any necessary adjustments.

"It hardly seems real to even be discussing our future," she said, trying to keep at bay any unreasonable feelings of disappointment at her life being mapped out, with no surprises left except the actual living of it.

Or was she experiencing disappointment over something else?

"Unreal but exciting," Jeremy offered.

Amity nodded even though that was not the case precisely. At least not for her. A degree of anticipation, undeniably, but not excitement.

"I suppose that leaves one thing to say. Will you marry me?" he asked.

These were the words, which, fortunately, she had not dreaded hearing from him. Looking into his kind and understanding brown eyes, she felt peaceful.

"Yes, I will."

Jeremy lowered his mouth to hers and kissed her.

HENRY WAS HAUNTED BY the chocolatier's distraught face as she'd left his ballroom, knowing he was to blame for not having corrected her use of "my lord." It had simply not mattered to him what she called him. If they'd had more time together, they might have progressed to *Amity* and *Henry*.

He still hoped they would get that chance. Meanwhile, he had to get himself out of a sticky situation. His friends had known of his intent to publicly propose to Madeleine, as had his mother, and from what he learned at his ill-fated party, so had Lord and Lady Brayson, and even the lady, herself.

Foolishly, he'd thought it was all such a carefully planned surprise, one which would allow him to change his mind with no one the wiser. Instead, he was in the limelight, like an actor on the stage.

The first surprise of the evening had been the wrong chocolate, causing mayhem. The second had been when no proposal had been forthcoming. He hadn't been able to do it, not even when facing the bewildered expressions of his guests. When all he desired was to run after Amity—and cared more for her hurt feelings than for Madeleine's insistence the chocolate was poisoned—he knew he had to reevaluate his priorities.

"Never mind," he'd told the earl's daughter as she fumed and made a face of displeasure.

All the while, he was savoring the delicious chocolate Madeleine had found so abhorrent, knowing as soon as it melted on his tongue that Amity had made it for him.

"Drink some more champagne, and you'll feel better," he told her.

When they had discovered there were two types of chocolate on the trays, and Madeleine had been persuaded by her mother to try the real *Brayson*, she'd adored it.

"It was so clever," she praised him, "for you to incorporate my favorite scent into a confection."

He had reminded her it was Miss Rare-Foure's cleverness, but she'd turned away to eat another.

His guests valiantly tried to recover from the drama, and most ate the chocolates with pleasure. At least, they ate the *Braysons*. Before any more errors could occur, he had confiscated eleven chocolates he knew without question were his and his alone. Chocolates flavored with coffee and the slightest hint of orange—they had been positively divine.

Then Madeleine had turned her blue eyes upon him and waited. He hadn't even felt like wiping the crumb of chocolate from her lower lip. Instead, he'd turned to his guests.

"It was good of you all to come and enjoy the new confection invented for Lady Madeleine by the talented chocolatier Miss Rare-Foure of Rare Confectionery."

And after that lame statement, as subtle as a newspaper advertisement for men's garters—with everyone awaiting the grand event he'd mentioned—he had simply nodded, smiled, drunk another glass of champagne, and tried to avoid Waverly's all-too amused stare.

"You had a question, Your Grace," Madeleine insisted.

Henry had sighed. He was not going to be allowed to drop the matter so easily. *Very well, a question.* He had to come up with one on the spot.

"Naturally, I need to know whether you prefer the confection to be called the *Madeleine* or the *Brayson?*"

Madeleine's pleasant expression became one of disbelief and then displeasure, and with both a scowl and a thinning out of her lips, she looked less than beautiful for the second time that night. Her father's face mirrored his daughter's, and her mother looked beyond nonplussed.

What a mess!

The following day, after finding Rare Confectionery closed, Henry had returned home to a scathing letter from Lord Brayson, asking to know what he meant by playing with his daughter's affections. In fact, he'd demanded the Duke of Pelham appear at their home the following day and declare his intentions once and for all.

Rightly so, too. Normally, no one demanded a duke do anything, and Henry could have refused. However, if anyone else had treated a young lady in such a shoddy fashion, he would have been firmly on the side of the lady and her family.

On the other hand, he had gone into his pursuit of Lady Madeleine with the best of intentions and had never *played* with her affections, since neither he nor she had exchanged a single affectionate word that he could recall.

Finally, he went to the one person whose wisdom he trusted most in the world, who always had his best interest at heart—his mother. When he confessed to the dowager duchess his heart's greatest desire, she was helpful and brutally honest, as expected.

"You know the choice you've made will not be the smoothest, not for either one of you, but I can see on your face it will make you happy. I assume you believe it will make your young woman happy, too. If so, then nothing in this world should stand between you."

With his mother's support, Henry believed it was possible to make Amity his duchess. Still, he owed it to the Braysons to speak with them in person. He showed up at their home as requested and a curt encounter ensued in which Lady Madeleine finally showed more passion than during previous meetings. Henry knew it was due more to the loss of a future title than to the loss of him as her husband.

"I am mortified," Madeleine proclaimed.

"My daughter is not to be your duchess?" Lord Brayson fumed.

"Not a duchess," Lady Brayson murmured sadly.

"I offer my sincere apology," he said, speaking solely to Madeleine, "if our few encounters and discussions led you to believe otherwise."

She had glared and somehow squeezed out a single tear, looking lovely as she tried to portray sadness when, clearly, all she felt was anger. Finally, she raised a hand to her forehead and fled the room.

For the first time, Henry was extremely glad he had never managed to kiss her. At least, he had not taken advantage of the lady.

Meanwhile, he'd learned from Asprey's jewelry store that Amity and her family had gone on holiday to their country home in Coggeshall, and he'd been sorely tempted to follow immediately. Or rather, as soon as he figured out where such a place was. From a gentleman at White's with a passion for maps, Henry learned it was in Essex.

In any case, with indecision reigning supreme, he had cooled his heels for a week, until at White's, an exasperated Waverly said, "If you are serious, Pelham, I think you should go after her."

"How can I show up out of the blue?" Henry asked, swirling the brandy in his glass. Even the amber liquid, full of subtlety and complex flavors, reminded him of Amity.

Waverly had laughed. "If you are waiting for an invitation, you'll have a deuced long wait."

"No, of course not." What *did* he want? "I would hate to get there and find she despises me."

"Why on earth would she despise you?" Waverly asked, with a jovial slap of the polished table. "Miss Rare-Foure doesn't know you that well. On the other hand, I do, and even I don't despise you."

Henry rolled his eyes and drained the last of his drink.

"I say," Jeffcoat interrupted, resting his foot on his knee and leaning back comfortably, "you must really like this girl to be in such a twist. Can you be worried she'll refuse you?"

"The look upon her face when she left the party," Henry reminded him and shook his head. She had appeared to hate him.

Waverly nodded. "Partly my fault. I should have told her the correct form of address, but I thought the evening would end and she would slip back to her world, never having cause to address you publicly again. Nor any duke, for that matter. How could I know you intended her for your wife?"

"How could I know?" Henry asked. "The notion slipped up and grabbed me, and now I cannot think how I can live without her."

"Amazing. I wonder if love shall attack me in similar fashion. It sounds positively dreadful." Waverly pretended to shudder.

Henry couldn't help smiling. "It's not dreadful. It feels better than thinking I might tie myself to someone for the rest of my life for whom I could scrounge up nothing more than a lukewarm interest."

"Even with Lady Madeleine's astonishing looks, you prefer your chocolatier?"

Sadly, Madeleine had *only* her looks to interest Henry. Besides, even in that regard, Amity outshone the earl's daughter. Waverly must be blind not to have noticed. "Did you *see* her at my party?"

Waverly refilled his glass, then Jeffcoat's and Henry's. "Who? Which one?"

"Miss Rare-Foure, you dolt! She is the most perfect woman. At the party, she was like a sweet sprite in her green silk, her hair burnished and gleaming, looking so soft I itched to touch it. And her sincere eyes, earnest and lively. Why, I cannot wait to look into them again. And her sweet, supple lips, the perfect shape for kissing . . . ," he trailed off at his friend's expression.

Waverly's mouth had fallen open, then he coughed. "You must, as I said, go to her at once. No more grand gestures and intricate plans. You can see how those have failed."

Henry sighed. "I cannot say my plans failed, as they brought me to Rare Confectionery. But you're right, I should speak with her as soon as possible. I could send word to their country home and see if I get a reply."

Waverly was shaking his head, humming his disapproval of such a tepid tactic.

Henry shrugged. "Or I could pack a bag and leave first thing in the morning."

"Hear, hear." Jeffcoat said, raising his glass with Waverly joining in although Henry did not.

"Why do you still look doubtful?" Waverly demanded. "You are the bloody Duke of Pelham!"

"That is the problem. If Miss Rare-Foure becomes my duchess, all she can do with her life is represent me and my position with grace. That and promise not to engage in anything scandalous."

Waverly lifted an eyebrow. "And why is that a problem? Do you foresee her becoming scandalous? Go on, tell me the details."

Henry sent him a withering look. "She would have to give up anything to do with Rare Confectionery and restrict herself to charity work. The closest she could get to chocolates would be placing them in a food basket for the poor, if that is even done. I'm sure the destitute prefer hearty bread and meat."

"I suppose you had better give Miss Rare-Foure that choice, mustn't you?" Jeffcoat asked quietly.

Again, Waverly raised his glass of spirits. "You or chocolate? That is the question."

CHAPTER TWENTY

Amity didn't like the sudden change in her sisters ever since Jeremy had arrived. After she'd agreed to marry him, they had walked hand-in-hand back to her family's modest country house to tell everyone.

First, he'd been closeted with her father for a few minutes, and when they reappeared, Armand Foure was slapping Jeremy on the back, looking pleased, and her mother had smiled when she heard the news. However, Charlotte had appeared more hesitant, and Beatrice gave the barest nod of approval.

Later, upstairs in the large bedroom shared by her two younger sisters, Amity asked them, "What on earth has soured your milk?"

"What do you mean?" Charlotte asked, plainly stalling.

Forthright Beatrice shrugged casually. Apparently, she had something to say, but as it was probably harsh, she had decided to be uncharacteristically cautious.

"Bea," Amity pleaded.

"You said you'd kissed the Duke of Pelham."

"What?" Charlotte exclaimed. "How did I not know this?"

Amity glared at Beatrice. "Because it was not necessary. It was one kiss and that was it. What possible bearing can it have on my engagement to Mr. Cole?"

"When did it happen? And where?" Charlotte asked. "Did you like it? Did he ask you first? Did he taste good?" Then she gasped. "Did he force you?"

All this came out in such a rush, Amity could but shake her head. "Do you see what you've done?" she asked her middle sister.

"All good questions," Beatrice said. "Why don't you answer her before telling us why you've settled for Mr. Cole."

"Settled? That's unkind. Did you say that because he is a commoner and not a nobleman? Or because he doesn't have a fancy house in Mayfair?"

"Neither," Beatrice snapped. "I said it because your eyes don't light up the way they do when you mention the duke. Because you've kissed both men but only dream about one. Am I right?"

"Stop it," Amity said. "What is the point of wanting something I cannot have? Do you really suggest I become the spinster you joked about, rather than enjoy a full life with Mr. Cole? If that's the case, I don't think you love me as much as I love you."

Beatrice paled, looking shocked. "That's a terrible thing to say. I want you to be truly happy."

"I will be." Amity took Beatrice's hands. "Mr. Cole and I do suit one another, and he loves me." Then she paused. Jeremy had not actually said he did, but she assumed he wouldn't have asked her to marry him if he did not.

Releasing one of Beatrice's hands, Amity opened her other arm wide for Charlotte to step into the sisterly circle.

"I won't have to worry about what I call my husband or what his friends think of me or whether I am fit for their company."

Charlotte shook her head. "It was merely a terrible mistake," she began.

"That's just the thing," Amity protested. "The mistake wasn't so terrible, was it? Calling a man 'lord' instead of 'grace'? Yet Lady Madeleine carried on so, and in public, with one mean-spirited end in mind—to humiliate me although I couldn't possibly be any threat to her. She made it seem as if I had mortally wounded one of her own."

Beatrice made a sound of disgust. "I'm sorry I wasn't there to tell her off."

Amity chuckled. "I didn't see it, but I know our Charlotte did that quite well."

Their youngest sister beamed at them both. "I did," she confirmed.

"Think how difficult such a life would be for someone of our class to be thrust into it unprepared," Amity reminded them. "Not that I even had that option. It was not as if I had a choice between the Duke of Pelham or Mr. Cole."

They all nodded sagely. "Besides," Amity reminded them, "the duke is now officially engaged to the person most suited to him."

Still, she allowed herself a little wisp of *if-only* for the man who had completely charmed her—and stirred her emotions. Somewhat painfully, Henry Westbrook, Duke of Pelham had tugged at her heartstrings, even if he hadn't intended to do so.

"Most importantly, as a duchess, I would not be able to make chocolates anymore. And I simply must do this one thing for nothing else gives me more pleasure than being with the two of you and crafting confectionery." No need to mention how Jeremy had mentioned opening her own store, for she had no intention of doing so. "So please, stop your reticence and don't send my fiancé sideways glances. He will be family soon, and I will have a happy life."

Unfortunately, the very next day, over a lunch of cold pork, bread and butter, and large helpings of bubble and squeak, Jeremy suddenly took it upon himself to announce how Amity would, in all likelihood, give up making chocolate.

Her father frowned and sent her a searching look. *Bless his heart*, she thought. He wanted only to know if it were her decision. However, all traces of happiness vanished from her mother's and her sisters' countenances.

"Why on earth would Amity not *want* to make chocolate?" Felicity Rare-Foure demanded, looking not at her future son-in-law but at her eldest daughter.

"Well, Mother, of course I *want* to continue. Mr. Cole means that my wifely duties, and later my maternal ones, might occasionally get in the way."

"I have both, have I not?" her mother reminded her. "Nevertheless, I continued to run the store and make confectionery until you three were old enough to take over."

Amity frowned. That was true. *Why hadn't she thought of that?* She looked to Jeremy for an answer.

"With all due respect, Mrs. Rare-Foure," he began, "you were working for the good of *your* family, and once married, Miss Rare-Foure should work for the good of *ours*."

Amity's father coughed politely to break the tension as his wife began to sputter. Her sisters were no help, staring angrily at Mr. Cole. She should have spoken to her family first and warned them about his strong views.

"We will all be one family," her mother protested.

"Except she ought to enrich the Coles, not the Rare-Foures." He stated this as he reached for a slice of apple cobbler.

This made Armand Foure sit up. "I say, will she *need* to work? Do you foresee being in such circumstances?"

Jeremy had the grace to flush slightly. "No, sir. I am sure we shall live well on my income. All the same, if Amity wants to make chocolates to bring in extra money, I would expect her to make them under her new name."

Amity feared for her mother's health when she went quite red in the face.

"Now, see here," Felicity began, but Amity's father patted his wife's hand.

"Do not trouble yourself, my love. Perhaps an easier way would be to give Amity and her new husband a share in the shop."

Her mother didn't look the least bit thrilled, but she also did not dismiss the notion out of hand. And while Amity wasn't keen on the idea of her parents giving away ownership of Rare Confectionery, not even to her new husband, if her father arranged it so she could continue to work with her sisters, she wouldn't protest.

To her amazement, Jeremy shook his head. "That's very generous of you, but she would still be thought of as a Rare-Foure and not a Cole."

"Is that so terrible?" Amity asked, speaking for the first time, since it was *her* future they were discussing.

Jeremy stared at her, looking slightly wounded, and she reminded herself this was the man with whom she would spend her life, give over her well-being, and on her wedding day, she would agree to obey.

"I'm sorry," she said quickly. "When I am your wife, I do want to be Mrs. Cole first and foremost." But she was positive she could convince him to allow her to make chocolate at Rare Confectionery.

He beamed at her, and she remembered how amenable he had always been.

"All I'm saying," Jeremy continued, "is I think Amity should get used to her duties as a wife before she commits to continuing to go to the shop daily. She may find there are other things she prefers to do, for that matter, rather than make chocolates."

There was silence. Amity shook her head slightly. Jeremy did not understand their passion for confectionery, but he would learn.

"Above all, we want you to be happy," her mother said to her, and they exchanged a smile.

Amity decided to let her future husband know her thoughts right away. "I believe I shall only be happy if I continue to make confections with my family."

Jeremy looked thoughtful and nodded. "After a brief break while we become used to our married life, you must continue to make chocolate, for your happiness will be my continual goal for the remainder of our lives."

Bless his heart! She had known he would be a sweet and understanding husband.

"Perhaps the shop can be renamed," he suggested, "as Rare & Cole Confectionery."

"Mr. Cole!" Amity protested, thinking he was taking advantage of her parents' kindness, but to her amazement, her father smiled.

"This young man will go far, I warrant."

And with that statement, everyone's feathers were soothed, and they finished eating in a more jovial atmosphere.

THE RAIN WAS ENDLESS, and Henry was glad of a well-constructed carriage. Even so, the dampness seeped in. His coachman, despite an awning to keep him protected, also needed his India rubber-cloth rain slicker.

Having left the city early, it was mid-afternoon when he arrived at Coggeshall and was directed toward the hamlet where the Rare-Foures had a house. His horses pulled his coach onto a tidy piece of land by the River Blackwater where a two-story brick home rose up to greet him.

He had brought neither his footman nor his valet, deciding to rough it. Leaving his coachman with the vehicle until a groom or a stable boy appeared to handle the horses, Henry took it upon himself to hurry along the tended path to the front door. There was no bell, so he knocked. He waited, holding his black umbrella aloft and hoping they had coffee.

When no one came, though he could tell there were inhabitants by the smoke coming from two chimneys, he decided to walk around the other side and see if he had more luck at a side or back door.

After trudging along a grassy path turned mostly to mud, he found a back door and knocked. No one answered. *Enough of this dallying,* he thought. He was getting chilled and—*dammit*—he was the Duke of Pelham!

With that thought, after rattling the handle to give fair warning, Henry pushed the door open and stepped into a mudroom. Still, no one was visible. He set down his dripping brolly on the flagstones and his hat on a bench along with his overcoat. There was nothing he could do about his muddy boots except wipe them on the braided straw rug, which suited the purpose tremendously. In fact, other pairs of boots and shoes were lined up by the side of the door.

After a minute or two of trying to make them presentable, however, mud stubbornly continued to coat the soles and toes of his boots. Giving up, he sat on the bench beside his hat and removed his favorite Hessians.

Sufficiently presentable, Henry removed his gloves and jammed them in his overcoat pocket before heading farther into the house in his stockinged feet. He encountered the kitchen first where a cook shrieked slightly at his unexpected appearance.

"Is there a groom or stable boy?" he asked her. "My horses need tending, and perhaps my driver could come in for a cup of tea and a biscuit if such are on hand."

With large eyes, the cook nodded, dropped the spoon she was holding and dashed out of the room. Hopefully, she was going to relay his message and not go for a rifle to shoot him as an intruder.

He followed her down the hall, past an empty study on one side and a dining room on the other, until he heard the sound of people talking. Sure enough, from the drawing room, out rushed the Rare-Foures with the cook in their midst.

"Your Grace!" exclaimed Mrs. Rare-Foure, dropping into a curtsey.

"I am sorry to intrude," Henry told her. "I knocked, but no one heard me."

A man whom Henry had never met stepped forward with an outstretched hand, not the least perturbed at having a surprise visitor enter through the back of his house.

"By my wife's address, you must be the Duke of Pelham. I am Armand Foure. We tend to be rather a loud bunch, all talking over one another. I have no idea where our man is," he added, ostensibly referring to their butler, unbothered by his servant's dereliction of duty.

Henry shook Mr. Foure's hand but was already looking past him for his chocolatier.

Amity stood with her sisters, staring at him with wonder but *not* with anger as he'd feared after her treatment at his own home. She looked the same—except for wearing a surprised expression on her lovely face—and his heart started to thump with gladness to be near her again.

"I came," he said suddenly, looking directly at her, "to apologize to Miss Rare-Foure."

Her eyes widened, and in truth, he had amazed even himself. He hadn't realized he intended to say that, at least, not publicly. It wasn't something a duke normally had to do. Regardless, it had come forth naturally from him, as he had hated how hurt she'd seemed when last he'd seen her.

Her family parted and she stepped forward, curtsied, and looked up at him with her unwavering, deep-brown eyes. He loved those eyes. He loved the woman who looked out of them.

"You had no need to come all the way from Town, Your Grace."

Henry couldn't help wincing at her particular use of his title.

"But I greatly appreciate your apology, however unnecessary," Amity continued. "Will you come into our parlor and take tea?"

The small smile she offered might have been because of their shared dislike of tea.

"I will. Thank you." He looked at her father. "My driver is awaiting assistance. A groom or a stable boy, perhaps?"

"Oh, yes, yes," Mr. Foure said.

"I'll handle it," said another male voice, and for the first time, Henry realized the lawyer—Amity's *friend*—was present. He'd been lurking in the parlor doorway, just out of sight.

Christ! The man was there, in the bosom of the family's country seat. This might be a little trickier than Henry had anticipated. It was entirely possible Mr. Cole and Amity now had an understanding which she had previously denied.

The man bowed to Henry. "Good day, Your Grace," the lawyer said, his gaze lingering on Henry's stockinged feet, making him feel all but naked. Then Mr. Cole accompanied the cook toward the back of the house.

Henry's glance shot to Amity again. Her cheeks had pinkened, and he feared he was too late. Furthermore, the man had also called him "Your Grace." Thus, the lawyer, too, had been told of Amity's shameful treatment at the hands of Lady Madeleine. He was half-surprised the man hadn't called him out.

Henry followed Amity and her still-silent sisters into the parlor. *Did he have the right to march in there and offer for the chocolatier's hand?*

Her parents came in behind them. Someone had sent for tea—and slippers—because by the time they all settled into their seats on the two sofas and the winged chairs, a maid came in with the tea tray, and Mr. Cole returned a moment later, carrying a pair of tartan-covered, wool-lined slippers. He dropped these at Henry's feet.

"Your driver is in the kitchen having a little sustenance, Your Grace, and your horses are being cared for."

"Thank you." Thanking this man made him feel even guiltier for wanting to snatch Amity away from him. *What hope did Mr. Cole have of keeping hold of her when a duke wanted the same woman?* Henry knew the answer was no hope at all.

On the other hand, the lawyer was probably considered a handsome chap. He was tall, had a full head of hair, and no pox on his cheeks. It wouldn't be hard for Mr. Cole, as a professional, to find another woman to be his wife. Maybe even one of Amity's sisters would do.

He looked at Miss Charlotte, and their glances locked. He hoped she wasn't embarrassed by what she'd said at his party, for she'd done well to defend her sister like a lioness defending its cubs. Henry quite admired her for it. Happily, she appeared unaffected.

Henry offered her a friendly smile, which she quickly returned.

Yet when he looked at Miss Beatrice, he received a scowl. *The deuce!* If looks could kill, he'd be flat out on the floor with his body smoking from her scorching glare. Any man would do well to keep clear of that one.

Nevertheless, Henry sent her a friendly nod. She pursed her lips and turned away. *Well!* He snugged on the tartan monstrosities, feeling his toes curl at the ends. He would drink the blasted dishwater—or tea, as some professed it to be—and then he would attempt to get Amity alone long enough to put forth his hopes for their future together.

"It is unthinkable and also utterly splendid, Your Grace, that you came all this way to offer your apology," Mrs. Rare-Foure said cordially. "A simple note would have done, if even that was needed. From what I understand, it was not you, but Lady Madeleine who—"

"Mother," Amity interrupted her, and Henry was left to wonder how the woman would have characterized Madeleine's ill manners. "I'm sure His Grace doesn't wish to hear you speak ill of his fiancée."

Henry started, nearly spilling his tea. "Oh, Miss Rare-Foure, I assure you I am not engaged."

Instead of appearing pleased as he'd hoped, a myriad of emotions crossed her artless face, until finally her expression settled upon looking crestfallen.

"The blunder with the wrong chocolate ruined your proposal. How awful!" She twisted her hands with dismay. "I cannot credit that Lady Madeleine would let a little thing like that dissuade her from accepting your hand in marriage. I feel terribly responsible. It is *I* who should apologize to *you*. Did your lady ever manage to enjoy a *Brayson*?"

Dear woman! Henry thought. She blamed herself for him not being engaged. Actually, it *was* her fault, but for reasons she did not yet understand.

"The lady did taste the *Brayson*, after all," Henry said. "What's more, she loved it! You are to be commended. I, for one, think you should sell them in your shop."

"I thought they were the perfect creation for your lady," Mrs. Rare-Foure agreed, "but we shall not be selling *Braysons*."

"I never got to taste one," Mr. Foure complained.

"I did," Miss Charlotte said. "I liked them."

"I am not fond of lavender," Miss Beatrice said, giving Henry another hard look.

"Nor I," he confessed, hoping to gain her as an ally, but she sniffed and sipped her tea. "In any case, despite Miss Rare-Foure's fine confectionery, I am not engaged."

Not wanting to speak any more about it, he swiped a plain biscuit off the tray in front of him and took a bite.

"I suppose it is not out of place in this discussion," Mr. Cole began, "for me to share *our* news." The man glanced at Amity and said, "Miss Rare-Foure and I are engaged."

Henry swallowed too quickly and choked. Suddenly, he was coughing crumbs onto his pants, rattling his cup and saucer to the point of spilling his tea, and desperately trying to take a breath. When Mrs. Rare-Foure and Amity stood in concern, causing the other men to stand, as well, Henry held up his free hand. *What did the women intend to do, smack him on the back?*

Knowing his face was probably ruddy with exertion, and still unable to speak, he simply shook his head, waiting for everyone to be seated once more.

"My apologies," he croaked, at last, all eyes upon him, even as his own were watering. *How embarrassing!* Pulling a handkerchief out of his pocket, he wiped his mouth and brushed down his pantlegs. "I suppose I was overly hungry and wolfed that down like a . . . well, like a wolf."

Miss Charlotte laughed, which made everyone relax. For his part, he was stunned. *Amity was engaged!* And she was blushing profusely, looking as if her shoes were two sizes too small.

Sipping the tea more carefully, finding it not as bad a beverage as usual, he let it clear his throat and tried to speak again.

"When?" he asked, looking from Amity to her fiancé, belatedly realizing how curt his question sounded. He should have congratulated them immediately, but what kind of man did that before trying to steal the woman away?

"Two days ago," Mr. Cole said. *The blighter!* Reveling in having taken the only female Henry had ever cared for. It had taken him barely a couple weeks to realize that fact, whereas this lawyer had known her at least a year. Mr. Cole had dallied all these many months and then snatched her at the last minute. *Outrageous!*

Her parents seemed happy enough with the turn of events. Surely, they would be even happier with a duke for a son-in-law.

He needed to speak to her at once. Setting down his teacup, Henry looked at Amity "May I speak with you alone?"

CHAPTER TWENTY-ONE

Henry should have expected his words would be met with collective silence, followed by a ripple of disapproval that quickly ran through the parlor's occupants.

"What I meant to say was that I would like to speak to Miss Rare-Foure about the chocolates. About more chocolates. Other chocolates, that is. A sensitive matter."

"A sensitive *chocolate* matter?" Mrs. Rare-Foure asked, looking doubtful.

"Just so," Henry said, keeping a steady gaze on Amity's mother, trying not to look the least bit untrustworthy.

"Fine by me," said her father. "Amity's a woman of business, out in the world, not like when you were young," he added to his wife.

Obviously, the man had no sense of self-preservation for Mrs. Rare-Foure took all of her attention from Henry's inappropriate request and set it squarely upon her husband's ill-advised statement about her age.

"What can you mean, Mr. Foure?" she asked him. "When *I* was young?"

Henry thought he heard the man gulp before answering. "I meant, my love, that you were sheltered for longer. Unquestionably, you are *still* young." Mr. Foure gazed around him a little wildly, as if hoping for help. No one could offer any. He was a man in a rowboat with no oars, heading for the treacherous falls.

"Frankly, I wonder sometimes," Mr. Foure added, "how a woman of your tender years can have three grown daughters."

Mrs. Rare-Foure crossed her arms, glaring at him.

Henry watched it as a life lesson in how not to speak to a female and noticed Amity's new fiancé doing the same. When their heads turned away from the tragedy of Mr. Foure, Henry realized his lovely chocolatier was looking at Mr. Cole as if for permission. Thus, in the end, it was the lawyer who gave the approval that Henry sought.

Mr. Cole cleared his throat. "Rules, even societal ones, are a little more relaxed in the country, don't you all agree? If the duke wishes to discuss chocolate with Amity, I see no reason he should not. It's as if they were having a consultation in the back room of Rare Confectionery."

Amity glanced at Henry, her cheeks pink, and he had to look away, their kiss uppermost in his mind. If they both looked guilty, the jig would be up and over before it began. He also found it necessary to avoid looking at Amity's sisters. The one had an expression of a saucy minx and the other, the narrow-eyed scowl of a fox.

Henry rose to his feet slowly, casually, as if this was an entirely unimportant matter. He felt his heart pound with trepidation. Amity stood, too, and after another glance at Mr. Cole, she preceded Henry from the room. He didn't dare look back in case anyone spied the devil's horns growing from his head.

Where would she take him? Not outside, which would have been his preference if the rain was not continuing to fall heavily. Instead, they went along the passageway to the study he'd passed earlier. It would all come down to the next few minutes.

AMITY'S EMOTIONS WERE SHIFTING like a carriage on the hills of Scotland, going up and down so drastically, she was a bit disoriented. Upon seeing the duke unexpectedly in her own home, she had been well and truly shocked. That sentiment had been followed by so many others in the brief few minutes he'd been in their parlor, she could no longer identify what her prevailing thoughts were.

Except curiosity. She was dying to know why he and Lady Madeleine were not engaged and what he wanted to speak with her about. She knew only it had nothing to do with a *sensitive chocolate matter.*

"Would you like to sit?" she asked, gesturing to one of the worn but comfortable leather reading chairs.

"I'd rather stand if you don't mind," he told her. "I was in my coach for a number of hours today. Please, sit if you wish."

"I will stand," she agreed. Then she waited. When he said nothing more, but stared at her with interest, she began to feel prickly all over.

"Your Grace?" Maybe he just needed prompting.

The duke sighed. "I am simply happy to see you, Miss Rare-Foure. I've missed you."

She managed to refrain from taking a step backward out of sheer surprise. But barely. That was an entirely improper way to start their conversation. Be that as it may, she could be truthful, as well.

"I enjoyed our meetings over chocolate tastings, too," she confessed, carefully choosing her words.

The duke smiled, and her insides flipped. Such a lovely smile on such a handsome man. *Stop it!* she scolded herself.

"The chocolates!" he suddenly exclaimed. "I haven't had a chance to thank you for the ones you made specially for me."

The ones that had caused all the trouble.

Despite that, she had to ask him. "Did you like them?"

"No," he said quickly. "I loved them! Absolutely adored them. The coffee flavor was brilliant. It was exactly as delicious as anything I could have imagined. How did you do it? I kept expecting to find coffee grounds in the fondant center, but it was smooth and creamy. I thought I was imagining the touch of orange, so subtle. Who would think it would go well with chocolate and coffee? Yet it did. I ate all twelve that night and made myself feel a little ill, but it was worth it. I didn't share a single one. Except for the one Lady Madeleine bit into by mistake."

Amity smiled, unable to contain her joy at making the duke so happy he'd indulged his way to queasiness. After eating chocolates and coffee with him, she'd decided to try incorporating the two flavors into one. First, she'd made regular coffee and stirred it in by the teaspoonful, but the flavor was too bland. It had taken many attempts until she'd figured out the coffee would work best as a liqueur.

"I tried boiling off the coffee to make it thicker, but the flavor was scalded and not pleasant. I knew you wouldn't approve. Next, I brewed very strong coffee, added a sugar syrup and the mildest brandy. It worked perfectly."

"You are brilliant. Will you sell them in the store?"

"I might." She suddenly considered her change in status after she married. She had all but agreed to temporarily giving up chocolate-making, maybe only for a few weeks, while she settled into her new life and set up house with her husband.

The duke frowned. "You don't think it will be popular?"

"I do. Probably more so than a lavender chocolate. Did Lady Madeleine really like it, by the way?"

"She did. I would not lie to you. Everyone did although I could see the men didn't take to it as well as the women."

She nodded. "That might be the case with the *Pelham*, too, with more men than women enjoying the strong coffee flavor. We certainly know Lady Madeleine didn't care for it one whit, especially not with orange, too."

"The *Pelham*?" The duke looked delighted, and she felt her cheeks warm.

Amity shrugged slightly. "In my head, that's what I named your chocolate."

He laughed at that. "I am honored."

"They are a little more difficult to make. I suppose I could teach one of my sisters."

Cocking his head, he asked, "Why wouldn't you make them yourself?"

"I shall be married in a few months," she reminded him.

He made a face, which looked like displeasure. *Why would it matter to him whether she married?*

"So, what of it?" he asked brusquely.

That didn't concern him and was not his business. However, after the long talks they'd had in her workroom and their incredible kiss, it seemed petty not to discuss something slightly personal with him.

"I may take some time off," she confessed, "particularly around my wedding date."

"Naturally," he said gruffly. "No one would expect you in the shop on that particular day."

"And Mr. Cole thinks I might want to do something else with my life," she added with a tilt of her chin, not liking His Grace's assumption she would have exactly a single day off to get married before returning to work, like any good servant.

"What?" the duke exclaimed so loudly Amity feared her family would hear him down the hallway. "That's preposterous!"

She blinked at him. "I don't live in the back room of Rare Confectionery, you know. Soon, I will have the new duties of being a wife, and someday, perhaps, a mother."

Again, he wore an expression of disapproval.

"Do not worry, my . . . Your Grace. I will find time to whip up a batch of *Pelhams*, even if my sisters cannot get the blend right."

He stared at her, with his nostrils flaring and an intensity flickering in his green gaze.

"I don't give a damn about the *Pelhams*!" Again, his voice was a little too loud for their country home.

"I don't understand. What do you mean?"

Stepping closer until she could smell his familiar spicy fragrance, he took her hand. "What I care about, Miss Rare-Foure, is you!"

Amity stared at her hand held firmly in his, then raised her glance to his face, sucking in an awed breath at what she saw. Genuine affection shone from his verdant eyes, plain to see. She shook her head. This could not be happening. *It must not!*

"I am engaged," she said, wishing her voice had held more conviction.

"Pish," the duke said, as if that meant nothing. "I am asking you to marry *me* instead."

The sensitive matter had finally become apparent. She tugged her hand free from his. And with thoughts running wildly in her head, she went to the study door and closed it, leaning against it for support.

"Amity," he began. "Please, may I call you Amity? It is how I think of you in my head."

"You should not be thinking of me at all," she protested, despite the fact that practically all she'd thought about was him since the first time he'd invited her into his coach.

"I stood in front of friends and family," he continued, beginning to pace in the ridiculous slippers, an old pair belonging to her father. "And I could not ask her."

She realized he was talking about his party.

"I simply could not imagine a life without you. When you dashed out of the ballroom, all my happiness went, too. Except for the coffee chocolates, of course. And that joy was also due to you and your thoughtfulness. As soon as I tasted one, knowing you'd crafted something like that solely for me, it gave me hope you felt the way I do."

The duke approached her again, and Amity flattened herself against the door. Her heart was racing, and she desperately wanted to feel his arms around her, hold his face in her hands, and kiss him.

What was wrong with her? It was like a madness, and she fisted her fingers in her skirts to keep from reaching for him. She cared for Jeremy, yet for some reason, she didn't feel this same urgent desire when around him.

"I know we have known each other hardly any time at all," the duke said, mere inches in front of her, his gaze boring into hers, "but we understand one another, do we not? I haven't laughed so much with anyone. And our kiss—"

"*Shh,*" she said, unable to believe she was shushing a duke. Not even an earl or a marquess. *A duke!* Second only to a prince of the realm.

Nevertheless, if her parents heard of her inappropriate behavior in the back room of Rare Confectionery, she wouldn't be able to bear their disappointment. Or worse, if Jeremy caught wind of it—she should have thought of him *before* her parents. He was her fiancé now.

"Please!" she begged. "You must go."

On the contrary, his hands were at her waist drawing her against him.

"Why must I go?" he asked, his glance flickering to her mouth.

In turn, she looked at his. "Because this is outrageously improper. And you know it!"

"Not if we're engaged," he said.

"We are not."

"But we could be," he promised.

"I cannot have two—"

His lips claimed hers, stealing her breath as well as her thoughts. Her hands somehow found their way up his chest and around his neck to clasp behind his head, his intoxicating scent filling her nostrils. He tilted his head until their mouths perfectly fused. She felt the tip of his tongue touch the seam of her lips and opened to him.

He groaned. She moaned. Their tongues slid across one another languidly, and then suddenly, Amity was hit on the back of the head. Twice.

The door! She tried to break free but was trapped. Luckily, the duke realized what was happening and jumped back like a leaping frog in the spring, while Amity turned to open the door wide. It was Beatrice.

"I was about to open the door and you knocked into me with it," Amity said, thinking that might be her first lie to her sister.

"Were you? Did I?" Beatrice asked with a smooth tone, her blue eyes taking in her eldest sister's flushed face.

Amity's mistake was in glancing behind her at the duke, seeing his own guilty expression and feeling her cheeks heat further.

"You two had best cool down a little before you return to the parlor," her sister advised. "By the way, your *fiancé* is asking for you."

With that, and a final knowing smirk, Beatrice turned and left them. Nothing daunted her sister, not even tormenting a peer of the realm.

For her part, Amity could barely look at him. A few moments earlier, she'd been pressing against the length of him while his warm hands were upon her body and his even warmer lips ground against her own.

It was, as she'd thought, a madness! Now, with her head clear . . . frankly, she wanted to do it all again.

"You cannot really want to marry that lawyer and kiss me like that," he said gruffly.

"Shh," she hushed him again. "I would not kiss you like that," she whispered, "if I were to marry Mr. Cole. I mean, *when* I am married to him."

His eyebrows rose. "If you were engaged to me, would you kiss another so ardently?"

"Of course not!" she exclaimed. "Why would I ever–?" Belatedly, she realized he'd trapped her into almost declaring her deeper affection for him than for Jeremy.

"You do feel something for me that you do not for him," the duke confirmed, momentarily satisfied.

"Please," she begged. "We must return to the parlor at once."

He crossed his arms stubbornly. "I have asked you to marry me."

Had he? It seemed he had told her to marry him. Besides, nothing had changed. She could not be his duchess and make chocolate, even if she learned the name and title of every last blasted nobleman in Britain. She shook her head.

"Are you turning me down?" His tone was as astonished as his expression.

How could she not? "I have recently become engaged. And we—you and I—beyond any doubt, do not belong together. *My lord!*" she added, reminding him of her *faux pas* and how they truly were from vastly different worlds.

With that, she followed her sister. If Amity thought she'd had the final word on the matter, though, she was mistaken. After she entered the parlor, the duke—*Henry, as she'd started to think of him*—came in directly behind her. *Too quickly*. When she stopped, he practically bumped into her bustle.

Every eye turned toward them.

Amity didn't know what to say and, thus, said nothing. She should have thought of a chocolate matter but coming up with a lie was an entirely new task with which she was not comfortable.

"We were discussing whether to have lamb or beef for dinner," Felicity Rare-Foure said to break the silence, yet Amity could tell by her mother's sharp look they'd been discussing nothing of the kind.

"Will you stay?" her father asked as the duke came out from behind Amity and casually stood beside her, not the least bit bothered by the air of disapproval coming off some family members and especially from Jeremy.

Amity expected the duke to decline politely and leave. After all, it was a long trip back to London, and she had just turned him down.

Good God! She had turned down the Duke of Pelham, who was a dashing, sought-after bachelor. More than that, he was someone she very much cared for. Feeling ill, she sank into the nearest chair.

"I would love to," she heard him respond, "but I don't know how late I can ask my coachman to take us home. I would hate for him to fall asleep on the road to London. In hindsight, I should have come by train, but it was rather spur of the moment and I didn't know if there would be transport at the station. Or even if there was a station, for that matter."

"Nonsense," her father said, "you must stay the night. You've only just arrived. All this way for an apology no one needed or wanted. You must have dinner with us, and then we shall find you a bed."

Amity hoped Henry refused the offer. Honor demanded he decline for the sake of all that was proper and moral in the world.

"I cannot put you to any trouble," he said, and she relaxed a little. He would leave her in peace.

But to her extreme annoyance, Henry added, "I will certainly take dinner with you, and I am grateful for the invitation. However, if there is an inn nearby, I shall go there after we eat."

Amity was all but glaring at him. He was openly fishing for the offer of a bed to be proffered again.

And her father did exactly that. "Nonsense," Armand Foure declared once more.

Every Rare-Foure female seemed to stare at him simultaneously. He was being welcoming to the point of pushiness. And Jeremy, who'd seemed pleased to shake hands with the duke when he'd first arrived, now wore a pinched expression.

"Perhaps for the duke's comfort, Father," Amity pointed out, "he might prefer the Three Boars Inn."

"I'm positive neither His Grace nor his driver wish to go out again in this dreary weather. Even his horses are probably tucked in the stable munching hay."

"Very well," said Henry jovially as if he were doing them all a favor. "I shall stay and be glad of it. But I insist you put me on a cot somewhere. I would hate for you to turn Mr. Cole out of the guest room if there is none other available."

In fact, it *was* the only one available, the other rooms being her parents' bedroom, Amity's chamber, and her sister's shared room. Amity supposed she could move in with her sisters and give Henry her bed, but even offering to let him rest his body upon her mattress seemed inappropriate.

Henry looked at her father. Her father looked at Jeremy, whose eyebrows rose as he suddenly realized what he must do.

"Your Grace, you must take my room. Besides," he added, rising to his feet so he could go gather up his things, "it's just for one night."

The duke gave a gracious nod of his head, but Amity noticed he did not confirm Jeremy's supposition of the short stay. *What was Henry up to?*

CHAPTER TWENTY-TWO

Amity found out soon enough. His Grace was determined to pander to her parents, charm her sisters, annoy Jeremy, and make moon-eyes at her when no one else was looking. The rain never stopped that day, so the seven of them were stuck together indoors for hours before dinner. What's more, it was an odd number that made everything a little more difficult, whether parlor games or seating arrangements for dinner.

Yet the duke, meandering about in the tartan slippers, acted as if it were no trouble at all, and somehow always made Jeremy the odd man out.

When Amity found herself seated opposite Henry again for a new game of whist, while her fiancé sat brooding nearby, she realized she would have to make a grand gesture.

"Mr. Cole, will you take my place, please, and partner with His Grace. I shall return shortly."

Letting neither man protest, Amity left the room quickly with no destination in mind except to be alone with her thoughts. She wandered down toward the kitchen where their cook, Lydia, was busy with dinner. Delia was seated at the worktable, peeling potatoes, and Amity sat upon the stool beside her.

"How are you both today?" she asked, setting her chin upon her hand.

"How am I?" Lydia asked. "*How am I?* There is a duke awaiting my dinner. I'm thrilled and terrified."

Amity stared at her. "Your cooking is always delicious."

"Thank you, miss. But if something goes wrong on a normal evening, lumpy potatoes or a burnt bit of roast, you and the rest of the family know I'll make it up to you the next night. His Grace has only the one time to taste my cooking. It must all be perfect."

Amity sighed. She had a feeling it would be more than one meal. "How did you know to call him 'His Grace'?"

Lydia and Delia exchanged a look. It was the latter who answered. "We may not have a fancy education, miss, but we are taught a few things, especially about how to call our betters."

"Your *betters*? Delia, I've never heard you use that term before."

"The Rare-Foures are exceptional, miss. Your parents treat us like family, and so do you three girls."

"Why wouldn't we? After all, we live together. Surely, in 1877, you don't believe we are better than you? Nor the Duke of Pelham better than any of us?"

Lydia chuckled. "*Our betters* is just a turn of phrase, dear, but class is class, and that's the way the world works. I'm not going to break bread with a duke any more than I'm going to have an outing with the queen. Bless her!"

Amity nodded. "Just a phrase," she repeated. She certainly didn't think Lady Madeleine was any better than her or her sisters. Undeniably lovelier in a cool and precisely perfect way but not a kinder person. All the same, even Amity had been guilty of thinking an earl's daughter was better for a duke than a shopkeeper's daughter who made chocolates.

Glancing around at all the food these two women were preparing, she realized Henry had already caused changes that an ordinary guest would not have caused. Since her father didn't employ a scullery maid or any other kitchen servants, she offered, "Can I help you with preparations?"

Delia's eyes rounded, and Lydia clucked her tongue in exasperation. "You'd best get out of here, miss. Your place is entertaining that handsome young duke who came all the way here from London simply to see you."

Amity felt her cheeks grow hot. "Do you two know everything?"

As the two women dissolved into laughter, Amity rose to her feet thinking how nice it would be to stay in the warm, cheery kitchen and cut up vegetables. Making her way along the hallway, she straightened her shoulders, put on a smile, and re-entered the parlor.

HENRY COULDN'T GET AMITY alone again that evening. At dinner, he had been seated on one length of the table with Charlotte on his left, Beatrice on his right, and his chocolatier and her fiancé across from him. It had been a delicious country feast, but he wasn't there for the food.

After the meal, they returned to the parlor, but unlike his own sister, none of the Rare-Foure girls played piano or sang.

"They had no interest when they were younger," their father said with a shrug. "But Beatrice can recite all number of literary works, Charlotte is a fair horsewoman, ice skater, and even marksman—I suppose she's a marks-*woman*." He chuckled to himself.

Henry should have held his tongue, but he asked, "And Amity?"

He noticed a few heads turn at his use of her given name, and wished, for her sake, he hadn't said it, but it had slipped out. There was nothing he could do except wait for her father to answer.

"My fiancée has a number of skills," Mr. Cole blurted before anyone else could say a word.

Amity's eyes widened as she turned to the man. Henry had a feeling the lawyer hadn't any more clue than he did what she could do well besides make chocolate. Nor did she need to have any other skills. He continued to wait in silence.

Mr. Cole's face reddened. "She . . . she . . . ," he stammered.

Amity began to look embarrassed, and Henry thought between himself and Mr. Cole, they'd made a right hash of it.

Mrs. Rare-Foure spoke up. "My eldest daughter has two very special talents in addition to making chocolates. For one, she is a consummate storyteller."

Henry nodded. "Yes, I had the pleasure of hearing her tell a tale of an unfortunate chocolate-covered chocolatier in Switzerland. Everyone at the dinner table was delighted to hear her tell it."

"She used to tell her sisters stories in the nursery before any of them could read," Mrs. Rare-Foure added.

"Mother, please," Amity protested. "His Grace doesn't want to hear about me or my so-called talents."

"On the contrary," Henry interrupted her. "I am interested. What is the second, if I may ask?"

Amity shrugged. "I am sure I do not know, except it is *not* ice skating."

Her sisters laughed, as did her father. Mrs. Rare-Foure waited until they'd finished.

"I'm surprised Mr. Cole hasn't come up with it yet. Our Amity has a special way of figuring out what people like. It manifests in her chocolates, but in other ways, too. For instance, she always picks out the perfect present. Sometimes, I believe she knows me as well as I know myself."

"True," Armand Foure added. "Last year's pipe was exactly the one I had my eye on. I'd never said a word, but there it was on Christmas morning."

Henry looked to Amity. "Do they know about the chocolate you made for me?"

Her eyes widened, and she shook her head.

"May I tell them?" he asked, watching Mr. Cole frown. Henry felt a little sorry for the man, but he intended to make him superfluous and return to London triumphant, after securing both Amity's hand and her heart.

When she shrugged delicately, he turned to the rest of the room. "Miss Rare-Foure knew of my deep enjoyment of coffee, and at my party, she brought a tin of chocolates that were, without question, the best thing I've ever tasted, meaning no disrespect to your cook tonight."

"Coffee and chocolate?" her father asked, leaning forward. He nodded thoughtfully and looked at his eldest daughter. "I might like to try that."

"Father," she exclaimed, "you don't even like coffee."

"True, but that's because it tastes to me like something that should be in my pipe not in my cup."

"Ah, your coffee was boiled, I would warrant, and thus, the flavor was scorched," Henry told him. "I can show your cook how to make it perfectly, and you might enjoy it. Regardless, blended with chocolate, it is divine."

"I like coffee," Mr. Cole muttered, and Amity turned to him with a smile.

"I didn't know," she confessed. Henry felt his chest swell. He was winning inch by inch.

After a recitation from the middle sister, the disapproving, scowling one, and an enjoyable few rounds of Happy Families, a card game Henry had never played before but which he found to be jolly good fun, it was time for bed. As customary, even at his own country home, everyone turned in hours earlier than when in London.

"I'll show you to your room, Your Grace," said Mrs. Rare-Foure.

Henry had no choice but to retire along with the family. After saying his good-nights, when he looked back, to his consternation, he noticed the newly engaged couple was being given time alone.

Frowning, he could think of no way to separate them, which put him in a foul mood even though he had succeeded in evicting the lawyer from the comfortable guest room. It was a cheerful chamber, and he could find no fault with the Rare-Foure's hospitality. His overnight bag had been placed at the foot of the bed, and there was a small fire crackling in the fireplace.

Nevertheless, he was out of sorts. Wrenching off the too-tight slippers that had been vexing him all evening, though he would never have shown it, he hurled them at the wall with frustration. Hopefully, someone would have cleaned his boots by morning.

Beginning to undress, he found himself missing his valet. It had been shortsighted of him not to bring the indispensable man, and Henry hoped he wouldn't look too scruffy in the morning.

HENRY GOT UP FRIGHTFULLY early by Town standards, but he hadn't pulled his drapes—or rather, no one had done it for him—and the sun was coming straight in his window to shine upon the pillows and his face.

Rising with a yawn, he stood naked in front of the mirror hanging over the dressing table. A washing area had been set up, with a bowl and pitcher of water, which he poured and used to wash his face and under his arms. Afterward, he dressed in the fresh clothing he'd allowed to wrinkle in his bag all the prior day and night. Tucking in his rumpled shirt, he gave himself a stern inspection in the looking glass.

Normally, his current appearance would not do at all— he looked as if he'd slept in his clothing. All the same, he'd noticed how casually Mr. Foure and the lawyer were clothed the previous day and decided his present state would suffice. In other words, he had no choice.

After shaving at the wash station, belatedly realizing he should have done so *before* dressing, Henry combed his hair and was ready to face another day of winning over Amity Rare-Foure. First, he needed his boots and a cup of coffee. Upon opening his bedroom door, he found the former, clean and shining. He could only hope the cook had some of the latter in her pantry.

She did. They were old beans, which had been stored dry and, thus, without a hint of mold. He let her grind them, and he did the rest. It was quite an interesting adventure, to be in the Rare-Foures' country kitchen with their cook, who'd practically fainted when he strolled into her domain. Again.

The maid who once sat in his drawing room as chaperone for Amity entered next, and her eyes widened to the size of dinner plates. After a few minutes, however, both women got quite used to him. He managed to teach the cook how to prepare coffee properly and to his satisfaction, even while she prepared eggs, bacon, toast, sausages, and potatoes.

"Will Mr. Foure be up and ready to taste this?" Henry asked.

"I believe the whole family is up," the maid said, stirring the porridge, before starting to place full platters onto a tray. "Everyone has gathered in the dining room, Your Grace."

"Good," Henry said, then he eyed what she hefted into her arms. "Allow me," he said, taking it from her as she gasped.

"Oh, no, Your Grace. You mustn't."

"Why mustn't I? I am as strong as you, am I not? If you bring in the coffee service, and Cook carries the porridge, we will have managed everything."

Thus, for the first time in his life, Henry walked into a full dining room with the servants *and* he was being useful.

The reaction was priceless. Mr. Foure jumped to his feet and started laughing wholeheartedly, and Henry knew the man was definitely a good egg.

Mrs. Rare-Foure shook her head as if they were all ruined. Amity jumped to her feet with her father, but seeing Henry was not in any way put out by performing such a duty, she smiled at him. Her sisters laughed with delight. Mr. Cole alone looked sour.

"It's as if the whole world has become topsy-turvy," the lawyer declared, getting up to help himself to the hot breakfast, which was now set upon the sideboard.

Unpleasant fellow, Henry thought. On the other hand, he must be getting under his skin. Maybe the man would leave of his own accord.

"We have made coffee," Henry told them all. "Good coffee. I invite you to add milk and sugar, as you like."

Having worked up an appetite, he filled a plate for himself, piled high with the good country breakfast, and took the seat next to Amity's chair, which Charlotte had been sitting in before she stood up to get her own plate.

When the sisters returned, they both paused. Charlotte took another seat, saying nothing, while Amity shot him a sidelong glance, pursing her lips.

The game was on!

"What a beautiful morning we have awakened to," Henry proclaimed. "What do you normally do on such a day in the country?"

Charlotte spoke first. "I might go for a ride. We have some beautiful views on the property."

Henry nodded, waiting for Amity to declare her intentions.

"I am glad the weather has cleared up for your journey home," she said firmly.

So, she was going to persist in dismissing him along with his suit. That was no matter. No one threw out a duke, not unless the duke wanted to be thrown.

"Since I could see very little yesterday due to the weather, and it looks so promising today, I've decided to stay longer. I have no pressing business in Town. If that's all right with you, Mr. Foure?"

"Yes, of course," her father said almost distractedly as he prepared and stirred his coffee. "First taste," he said, and did so. "Ah! Quite delicious." Looking around to see the others' reactions, he asked, "Mr. Cole, what do you think?"

The lawyer had pointedly eschewed the coffee for a cup of tea. Sighing, Mr. Cole took another cup from the center of the table and poured himself some coffee. He bothered neither with milk nor sugar, sipped, and shrugged.

"Like every cup I've had in a coffeehouse," he said.

Wretched man, Henry thought.

Mr. Foure didn't appreciate the answer either. "You should add the sugar and milk as His Grace instructed. I can even imagine how a spot of cocoa powder might be quite nice stirred in, if not chocolate itself, grated and left to melt."

Henry startled, noticing Amity did, too. They glanced at each other with excitement. She reached for the coffee urn, but Henry beat her to it and poured some into her half-empty cup of hot chocolate. She stirred it, sipped, and smiled.

"It's wonderful. Father, you are a genius."

Apparently without even thinking of the impropriety of sharing a cup, she turned to Henry. "You must taste it. I know you will love it."

Smiling with satisfaction, he took the proffered cup from her delicate fingers and raised it to his mouth, sipping from the place where her lips had touched. He couldn't help sparing a glance for Mr. Cole, who looked positively gray.

Tasting the blended beverage, Henry's tongue was overjoyed. He closed his eyes. When he opened them, he saw everyone was looking at him.

"It's perfect," he declared, taking another sip and returning the cup to Amity's outstretched hand. She was too excited by the new discovery to do anything except snatch it from him and drink from the same cup.

"It is, isn't it? We cannot put coffee grounds into cocoa powder since it won't taste right unless the coffee is already brewed, but we could start to sell our own cocoa with instructions to add it to freshly brewed coffee. What do you think, Mother?"

Unfortunately, Mrs. Rare-Foure frowned and shook her head. "I think people will still buy Cadbury's, Fry's, or one of the hundred other cocoa powders being produced, since they can make it far more cheaply than we can, which is why we've never sold it," she added, looking at Henry. He was pleased to be included in the discussion.

"I think it's best we stick to confectionery," Mrs. Rare-Foure said, "and start selling the coffee-flavored chocolates Amity created. If people love them, we could provide extra value by including a small printed card with instructions on blending the perfect coffee chocolate beverage." She turned to Charlotte. "You can put a card in the bag with the . . . what are they called?"

Amity cleared her throat and glanced at Henry, then her cheeks went a becoming shade of pink. "I call them *Pelhams*. Unsurprisingly."

"Brilliant," Mrs. Rare-Foure said. "Your Grace, you do understand if we call the new chocolate by your name, you will be considered by the public to be a patron of our shop, as well as endorsing the chocolate itself."

"I am honored," he said, trying to sound nonchalant, while being secretly thrilled about the whole connection.

Especially when he looked at Mr. Cole who was decidedly not thrilled!

Tucking into his breakfast with gusto, Henry thought he'd never had a more pleasant morning. And he fully intended to enjoy the rest of his day, too. After putting his fork and knife together on his plate, he leaned back, enjoying another cup of coffee. He liked this family and wanted nothing more than to enjoy breakfast with Amity for the rest of his life and visit with the rest of the Rare-Foures whenever possible.

Out of the blue, Mr. Cole asked, "When did you say you were leaving, Your Grace?"

Henry practically heard the internal gasp of everyone else in the dining room. Mr. Cole, as a visitor, had no say in the matter, nor should he bring any attention to the timeframe of another guest's comings and goings.

Henry paused to see how this delightful family would handle such impertinence.

The sharp middle sister, the one whom Henry had been told brooked no foolishness, was the first to respond. "Mr. Cole, I wonder that you worry over His Grace's departure, unless you need a ride back to London. By the by, when did you say *you* were leaving?"

Time for Henry to step in and secure his position as most gracious guest. "Now, Miss Beatrice. Do not feel affronted on my behalf. If Mr. Cole desires to have your delightful family all to himself, perhaps I should be on my way."

There, Henry thought, having tossed down the gauntlet, waiting for the lawyer to either come to his senses and grovel out an apology or continue along the path of pettiness and insecurity, however justified in this case.

CHAPTER TWENTY-THREE

Mr. Cole flushed an embarrassed ruddy color. "I have been misunderstood. I merely wondered whether I should get a room at the local inn myself, as I had intended to stay and accompany you all back to London." He looked nervously at Henry. "If His Grace wishes to stay until Kingdom Come, I am only too happy for him to have the guest room."

Amity shot Henry a sideways glance. *What was she thinking?* Perhaps his chocolatier was regretting her agreement to marry the ninny.

"As long as no one minds, then," Henry said, "I shall stay a day longer. The bed was so comfortable, and the room so charming. Between that and the fine dinner and delicious breakfast, I must give my sincere compliments to you, Mrs. Rare-Foure for such a well-run household. I wish my own estate near Canterbury was so smoothly managed."

Amity's mother nodded graciously.

"By the way," Henry said, looking at Amity, "Chilham Castle, my country home, has a separate confectionery where they prepare the sweet treats and desserts when my family is in residence. Sadly, it is not for chocolate-making." He paused before adding, "Yet."

Miss Charlotte was the one who let out an ear-splitting whistle of delight. After they all cringed and regained their hearing, she said, "Oh, Your Grace! I had heard country homes had such, but you are the first to confirm it."

"We have a small staff specially for dealing with anything sugar-based, including jellies, cream ice, sweet pastries, frozen mousses, custards, syrups, and naturally, all the patisseries. I suppose I should find out if anyone there is capable of whipping up some chocolate."

He hoped this would duly impress Amity and that she might wish to see his home's confectionery for herself. She wore a thoughtful look upon her face, and Henry felt quite satisfied. Then, without considering his words, he turned to the lawyer.

"Where is *your* country home located, Mr. Cole?"

The man's eyes bugged out of his head, and, against Henry's intentions, Amity rushed to her fiancé's rescue.

"As Your Grace must know, most people who are not of your class, meaning those who haven't inherited wealth and multiple estates, do *not* have country houses."

Her vehemence on behalf of Mr. Cole humbled him. Henry did know that and regretted the mean-spiritedness of his question. His parents had always made him aware how very fortunate the Westbrooks were to have the Dukedom of Pelham, and he'd lived his life being generous and kind to those less so.

When he'd succeeded his father, shedding his title of *marquess* for that of *duke*, he'd vowed he wouldn't lose sight of that humility even as he became more kowtowed and pandered to than ever. That morning, he'd failed spectacularly.

When he said nothing right away, Amity added, "I am sorry if I have offended you, Your Grace."

"You didn't. It is I who spoke out of turn." To Mr. Cole, he said, "My apologies if I sounded like a snout-nose."

This phrase disarmed the lawyer, and for the first time all morning, he smiled.

"Not at all, Your Grace. I was simply caught off guard. I have not chosen a place where Miss Rare-Foure and I shall enjoy our country sojourns because I think it best if we choose a place together *after* she becomes my wife."

The man had finished off sounding entirely recovered from the affront and was back to throwing his engagement into Henry's face. *Touché.*

"Yes, of course," Henry agreed, feeling as if he could spit venom at the notion of Amity and Mr. Cole strolling around country cottages with an agent from Chestertons helping them to pick a suitable one, perhaps letting them inspect the bedchambers and such.

"How considerate of you," Amity said to Mr. Cole, and Henry knew he'd well and truly lost that round.

Mr. Foure spoke up, "That's a grand idea, Mr. Cole. My father, Baron Foure, came over from France with my mother looking for a nice piece of property to please her. We have enjoyed it, haven't we, dear wife?"

Mrs. Rare-Foure nodded in agreement. "It is an excellent respite from the city."

"Nothing could be better than this," Miss Charlotte proclaimed. "Not only our house but the area surrounding."

Refusing to entertain the idea of defeat, Henry had a plan for enjoying the day and getting closer to Amity, despite the prior setback.

"As to the area, Miss Charlotte, are there any sights to see hereabouts? Roman ruins and such?" Between Canterbury and the sea, where his country estate was, there were three Roman ruins, and as a boy, he'd always found them fascinating.

"Oh yes, Your Grace. Right in Colchester, we have a well-preserved Roman gate."

"A gate?" Mr. Cole asked with obvious disdain.

"A gate is nothing to sneer at," Henry said. "A most important means of defense and toll taking, as well."

"Oh, to be sure," Mr. Foure agreed. "And this one was extremely vital, built at the intersection of the Roman road from London and the town of Colchester."

"Or *Camulodunum*, as it was called," Miss Beatrice added. "It's not merely the best preserved of any Roman gateway in the country, I've read it is also the largest at 107 feet wide with two carriageways and two footpaths."

"We must go," Miss Charlotte exclaimed. "It's a perfect day for an outing. It's not too far, and we can eat at that darling tavern. Your Grace, you shall see for yourself how darling it is. Can we, Father?"

Henry was delighted with these two allies but hadn't yet heard from Amity as to whether she would go.

Mr. Foure nodded. "The Hole-in-the-Wall Public House provides a very good meal indeed. As for the ruins, the north tower still stands as well as the arches of the south pedestrian way. What do you say Mrs. Rare-Foure to an outing?"

Amity's mother looked directly at Henry. "I think if our guest has an interest, by all means, we should go."

Mr. Cole cleared his throat, reminding the family he, too, was a guest. Henry almost felt sorry for him. Compared to a duke, the man was now practically an unwanted intruder. Amity clearly remembered his existence, however, and her next words reminded everyone of her fiancé's status.

"If Mr. Cole wishes to go, I shall go along and be glad of it," she said.

Henry immediately felt the lash of jealousy course through him, but he could do nothing, exactly as he had been forced to leave her alone with the lawyer the previous night. All eyes turned to Mr. Cole to see if he was going to be a dispirited wet blanket or a stand-up chap.

Under such scrutiny, what could he do? "Yes, let's have an outing. As long as my betrothed is with me, it doesn't matter where I am."

Well-played, Henry thought, but he would find a way to get Amity to his side. He was confident of that.

First, he offered his comfortable traveling coach for half their party so neither were they cramped nor would some of them need to go on horseback. In case the weather altered, as if often did from morning to afternoon, they would all be covered. If Henry could figure out how to maneuver Amity into his coach, everything would be perfect.

Alas, it was not to be. In fact, it was Amity who, like a traitor, ensured her sisters rode with him.

"If our party is to be split," she said, "I think Beatrice and Charlotte should go with His Grace to tell him all they know of the Colchester gate."

Then she sent Henry a long and knowing look. He returned it with a smile as if he were entirely unbothered. He would use the time alone with the younger Rare-Foures to find out more about Amity. Any information might come in handy as he sought to wrest her away from Mr. Cole, who plainly was not good enough for her.

As soon as they were settled in his coach, he began to ply the sisters with questions although not about the Roman ruins.

"How long have your sister and Mr. Cole been keeping company?"

"About a year and a half," Miss Charlotte volunteered while Miss Beatrice regarded him intently.

"And yet they only recently became engaged. What am I to make of that?"

At this, Miss Beatrice smiled slightly. "Why are you making anything of it at all, Your Grace?"

The middle sister was a tad saucy, no doubt about it. He shrugged. "Idle curiosity. In my experience, people meet, they realize they have affection for one another, and in short succession, they declare an engagement. Otherwise, either party is liable to find him or herself cut out. Either the man finds a woman more eager to be his life partner, or the woman is pursued by a worthier—and quicker—suitor."

"I suppose our sister was fortunate," Miss Beatrice said, "to have ended up with a man moving at exactly the same speed as she."

Or unfortunate, Henry thought. Then to his amazement, she looked him in the eye and said the exact same thing.

"Or unfortunate—if the first suitor was a tepid attachment and their engagement occurred precisely when a more fitting suitor came along."

"What are you on about?" Miss Charlotte asked her sister. "Your Grace, would you like to hear anything more about Colchester?"

"I think I would rather be surprised when we arrive. Tell me, does your sister long for anything in life besides making chocolates?"

Miss Charlotte stared at him, perhaps coming to realize how interested he was in Amity. Still, it was Miss Beatrice who answered.

"Our older sister is funny and smart and lovely and more talented than you could imagine. But in one regard, she is no different than any woman. She wants to be loved for who she is. She doesn't want to have to change or put on airs or affectations."

Henry thought about this. *Would she have to change for him?* She might, more so than if she married Mr. Cole. On the other hand, he already loved her for who she was. That should count for something.

"I think our sister would like a puppy," Miss Charlotte added. "If you really want to know."

He and Miss Beatrice looked at the guileless youngest Rare-Foure sister, and he started to laugh. *A gift of a puppy?* That, he could easily do without upending anyone's apple cart.

"Are you sure it's not you who wants one?" he asked gently.

Miss Charlotte smiled sweetly. "Oh no, Your Grace. I would prefer a cat."

Miss Beatrice sighed and looked out the window.

After a few minutes of companionable silence, Miss Charlotte asked, "Are you fond of painting?"

Henry thought it an odd question. "I do not paint, but I enjoy art."

"I only ask because Constable, a painter I greatly admire, did a lot of his landscapes not too far north of here."

"Ah, yes, they call it 'Constable Country,' do they not?"

"Indeed, Your Grace. Willy Lott's cottage is there from Constable's famed *Hay Wain*. Perhaps tomorrow, if we set out earlier, we could take a day trip to see it."

"Charlotte," her sister warned softly. "We don't know what tomorrow will bring, nor if His Grace will be staying another night."

"True," he confirmed. "Yet it sounds like a good outing, so we shall see."

Not looking the least bit put off, Miss Charlotte suddenly exclaimed, "We're here! And we have plenty of time to look around and work up an appetite."

Soon, both carriages were parked with the coachmen seeing to the horses, and Henry found himself one of a joyful group as long as he ignored Mr. Cole, who stuck so closely to Amity, it was a wonder he wasn't made of tar.

Luckily, Henry found the man easy to ignore. Happy to lay eyes upon Amity once again, he asked, "When you are out in the world, Miss Rare-Foure, do you taste chocolates wherever you go?"

She tilted her pretty head to one side and crinkled her eyes thoughtfully. "I suppose it depends upon the place. In certain cities, I want to see what the confectioners are making, but often, somewhere like this, I don't bother. I'd rather enjoy a good public house lunch and not worry about the sweets."

For the life of him, he couldn't imagine Lady Madeleine uttering words of pleasure about a public house lunch, and again, he felt fortunate not to be engaged to her.

They proceeded along the narrow main street, which was also winding and steeply inclined for much of the way. Mr.

Foure and Mrs. Rare-Foure walked in front, Amity and her fiancé in the middle, and Henry brought up the rear with a sister on either side of him. It was an unusual experience. As a duke, or even when a mere marquess, he usually led the way wherever he was going. At least, from his vantage, he could see that Mr. Cole was not touching Amity.

There was an additional benefit—Henry could watch the gentle sway of her bustle, which was very pleasing and caused his mind to wander wickedly.

Miss Beatrice broke into his thoughts as she said, "The Saxons called the town *Colneceaste*, and it is listed as *Colcestra* in the Domesday Book."

Amity turned to smile at her sister and caught Henry's eye. When he smiled at her, she quickly turned around again.

"It is one of the oldest continually inhabited towns in all of England," Miss Beatrice continued.

They strolled through the Dutch quarter where Flemish weavers traditionally lived and worked. They walked along Trinity Street with the welcoming red brick town hall at the end, its spire the tallest structure they could see. More modern structures were blended in with older ones. They passed Markhams, a busy pawnbroker's shop, with all of them glancing at the treasures in the windows, mostly jewelry.

Henry longed to pop in and purchase the largest bauble for his chocolatier.

"It would take a long time to walk around the entire town and see all the parts of the Roman wall they've discovered," Miss Charlotte told him. "But I was hoping we could stop at the castle on the way out of town after lunch. I think part of it is still being used as a gaol. Is that right, Father?" she called ahead.

"Yes, dear one," he replied.

They arrived at the ruins of the Roman gate, and all seven of them stood silently, perhaps thinking as he was of the great age of the structure. It faced the west, toward

London, and all the traffic going northeast would have come through it.

"The town didn't have a wall at first," Miss Beatrice told them as they dared to place their hands upon the ancient stones. "But Queen Boadicea, according to Roman historians, destroyed the place in 61 AD, and when they rebuilt, the Romans realized the prudence of a good strong wall against the native Britons."

"You are an historian, Miss Beatrice," Henry proclaimed.

While looking pleased, somewhat somberly, she said, "No, I am a toffee-maker, Your Grace."

Peculiar young woman. "They have a number of lovely churches, don't they?" he remarked. They had passed Trinity and St. Daniels already, and he could see more spires.

"Maybe Miss Rare-Foure and I shall marry in one of them," Mr. Cole said, and Henry wanted to clobber him.

"Not if I can help it," he muttered, then startled when Miss Beatrice's head turned in his direction, one pretty eyebrow arched. She had heard him, he feared.

"I'm hungry," Miss Charlotte declared, and they passed under the Roman arch and entered the whitewashed public house with its many windows and shutters. A previous owner had poked a large hole in the ancient Roman stonework of the adjoining wall so his edifice could be seen by those arriving at the train station. Henry thought him a smart business owner and appreciated being able to look outside.

Their group was seated at a large table by a window and were soon tucking into simple fare of thick ham, bread, cheese, and pickled onions. They all drank fruity local ale, and Henry even managed to sit next to Amity although Mr. Cole was on the other side of her. All the same, her warmth seemed to flow more in his direction, and he felt it seeping through his clothing.

Henry couldn't recall ever sitting with family—his own or anyone else's—in a pub and having such a nice meal and discussion. They talked about the amazing Roman domination of Britain, which had, after four hundred years, petered out as quickly as it had occurred. With Amity chatting beside him, occasionally wiping mustard sauce from her lips, it was perfect.

After lunch, they went to the Norman-era Colchester Castle where, for a few pennies, a curator took them around, except for inside the gaol, which was still occupied, as Charlotte had guessed. Between Miss Beatrice telling them how William the Conqueror built the castle as the first Norman keep and the guide explaining how its great size was due to it being built around the podium of the Roman Temple of Claudius, Henry felt as if he were back at Eton in a history lecture.

"With this sacred place already destroyed by Queen Boadicea a thousand years earlier, the Normans wished to show their authority by claiming the spot," the curator added, "precisely because it was of great significance to the English."

It would be of even greater significance, Henry thought, *if he could get Amity alone*. At one point, she lagged behind, speaking with her sisters and examining a tapestry. As the rest of the group rounded a castle corridor, and her sisters preceded her, he simply grabbed her arm and kept her back.

"Your Grace?" she questioned uncertainly.

"This is intolerable," he complained. "Promise me you will give me some time to speak with you alone when we return to your family's home."

"That would be inappropriate." She tugged at her arm.

"So would my kissing you right here in Colchester Castle, but if you don't promise, that's precisely what I will do."

Her mouth fell open before she snapped it closed.

"I may kiss you anyway," he said, getting lost in her soft brown eyes.

AMITY DIDN'T KNOW WHAT to say so she made a joke. "To show your Norman ruling-class authority?"

The duke's handsome mouth started to twitch, and then he laughed. "Yes, exactly." Still, he didn't release her but displayed his dimples until she wanted to melt.

"There is no purpose to our speaking alone," she reminded him. Already, her family would be wondering where she was, and when they noticed the duke's absence as well . . . ."

"That's a lie, and you know it," he protested. "There is our future at stake, and if we are to have children, countless more, as well."

"Countless!" Amity couldn't help her exclamation. "Perhaps three, I would say." Inappropriately, her thoughts flew to being in bed with Henry Westbrook, Duke of Pelham, and creating those children.

"Fine," he continued. "That's at least five lives which our speaking alone will impact—no, six if we include Mr. Cole's, which we must because you won't release the man from this travesty of an engagement."

"It is not a travesty. This—" and she gestured between herself and Henry, "—*this* is a travesty. *We* are not engaged, nor will we ever be."

"Give me a good reason, and I shall leave you alone. And do not again mention your current engagement as that is no impediment at all."

Amity didn't care for his easy dismissal of Jeremy. "All right, the reason you and I cannot marry is because you are a duke, a peer of the realm." That was as plain as she could make it.

He made a sound of sheer exasperation. "Surely, that is a mark in my favor, not a reason for you to remain engaged to your lawyer friend."

"If I must say it even more clearly, Your Grace, you and I do not suit. I am a shopkeeper's daughter. I do not belong with you in the world of the *haut ton*."

"Then we shall remain far from them if they bother you. Regardless, I know with your intelligence, you can learn any trifling social etiquette of which you may be uninformed."

She shook her head. "Even if I could easily catch up with everything Lady Madeleine so *kindly* pointed out she learned while in the nursery, what about my chocolates?"

"What about them?" He frowned, and she wanted to smooth the lines from his forehead, but he would never be hers to touch.

"I could not be a chocolatier as a duchess, therefore, Your Grace, I cannot be your wife."

CHAPTER TWENTY-FOUR

H enry's silence confirmed her worries, especially as he let his hand fall away from her arm, releasing her.

However, when Amity took a few steps in the direction the others had taken, he called to her again, "Miss Rare-Foure."

"Yes, Your Grace."

"Please, give me a few moments of your time tonight, whenever we can slip away from the others. After that, I vow to leave you alone. Tomorrow, I will return to Town unless things have changed."

She could hardly refuse him when he was being so reasonable. "Very well. Somehow tonight, I will meet with you."

AMITY'S STOMACH WAS AFLUTTER all through dinner. Every time she looked at Henry, she thought about talking with him later and what he would say. It might be their final time alone. When she glanced at Jeremy who was keeping a close eye on her after her brief disappearance at the castle earlier, she grew even more anxious. If he found her alone with the duke, she knew he would think less of her, possibly even break off their engagement.

She didn't want that. *Did she?* She could easily see herself married to Jeremy and having a happy life, just as today had been.

Yet when she thought of never seeing Henry again, aching sadness left her deeply troubled and terribly conflicted. In truth, she had enjoyed the day as much due to his presence as Jeremy's.

"Are you well, Amity?" her mother asked.

She looked up from her pottage.

"Yes, why?"

"You sighed heavily as if you had the weight of Ajax upon your shoulders."

"Did I?" Amity glanced guiltily at Jeremy to see him staring at her. She purposefully smiled at him and did *not* look at Henry.

Already feeling as if she had done something wrong, she tried to join in with the conversation during the rest of the meal while her thoughts went around in circles. Even if Jeremy did not exist and she had not already promised herself to him, she would not be the right choice for the duke, nor him for her. Giving up being a chocolate-maker was, frankly, impossible. Amity would be miserable the rest of her life.

On the other hand, if she tried to be a duchess *and* a chocolatier, she would be frowned upon, and Henry would be ridiculed. Together, they would be shunned. Ultimately, she would be forced to give it up.

Then what? She would have to learn to live the life of Lady Madeleine and the rest of the *haut ton*, which Amity only vaguely understood. Charity work, clubs, and lunches during the day. Hosting parties and balls in the evenings. It sounded like a numbing existence. Except there would be Henry to wake up to in the mornings and go to bed with at night. *Henry!*

He made her laugh and made her heart race. And there would be children for her to love and to raise. She could help her sisters to come out in society and find them good matches. Or at least help Charlotte, who was amenable to London's social life. Beatrice would undoubtedly still forego having a Season, but Amity could introduce her to suitable gentlemen anyway.

She wasn't certain she knew what *suitable* meant anymore. Besides, apart from everything else involved with irresponsibly allowing the duke to sweep her away, she had already agreed to marry Jeremy. To go back on her word was not like her. To hurt him was abhorrent.

What a ridiculous conundrum!

The evening passed slowly and also quickly by fits and starts. When it was nearly time to retire, Amity had found no way to meet with the duke alone. She'd even tried excusing herself from a hand of Rubicon Piquet to go to the water-closet, hoping he would find an excuse to follow. Instead, when she exited the small room in the back hall, it was Jeremy who stood close by.

She had the distinct feeling he'd followed her.

"Are you alone?" he asked, his tone filled with dread, and Amity felt a shard of remorse slice through her at giving him even an instant's disquiet.

"Of course. What a question?" she said before adding, "It's all yours," as she gestured to the water-closet behind her.

Jeremy nodded and went in even though she didn't think he really had need of it. Only then did she notice the duke lurking at the end of the passageway. He must have followed her out and raised Jeremy's curiosity.

With a curt shake of her head, she hurried back into the parlor. In another half hour, everyone declared themselves ready to retire. When Henry reached the parlor door, he looked back. With Jeremy's gaze steadily trained on her, she could do nothing except bid the duke goodnight. As had previously occurred, Jeremy stayed behind to have a few minutes alone.

Tonight, she feared the discussion would not be nearly so lighthearted as the previous night when they'd talked of visiting his parents in Scotland or making engagement announcements.

"I do not like the way the Duke of Pelham looks at you," Jeremy began. "He is too familiar, by far."

"It was very kind of you to give up the guest room," she soothed, hoping to take his mind off Henry.

"Well," he seethed, "one of us has to behave like a gentleman. I admit he's the first duke I've ever known, but he seems so . . . regular . . . almost too common."

Amity had to laugh. "Better than him being a snout-nose."

"I suppose." Jeremy took her in his arms, and she tried to relax and set aside the unexpected notion she was betraying Henry. "I, for one, will be glad when he has left."

"I believe he is going back to London tomorrow."

"Truly?" Jeremy's mood lifted. "I thought the man had threatened to stay longer. Didn't your sister mention at dinner about a trip to see Constable Country?"

"Yes, but His Grace did not commit."

"You're right. He didn't." Without any preamble, and completely out of character, Jeremy lowered his mouth to hers and kissed her.

After the shock wore off, Amity tilted her head the way Henry had done, and Jeremy froze, then tilted his in the other direction. Their mouths fit perfectly, but she supposed everyone's did. *What a silly thought!* Every kiss was not the same, and there was nothing wrong with Jeremy's, she reminded herself.

Be that as it may, his fragrance was not making her want to crawl inside his clothing and stroke his bare skin. The touch of his lips didn't cause her stomach to twinge with pleasure, nor her skin to get goosebumps, nor any kind of heat to pool low between her hips. He didn't attempt to slip his tongue into her mouth for her own tongue's caress, and when his hands roamed over her back, she wasn't driven to press her body closer.

Nothing about Jeremy's kiss, except for his mouth upon hers, was like Henry's kiss. Sharp sadness lanced her heart, making her pull away.

On the other hand, when she was with Jeremy, she was placid and usually content. It would be easy to undress in front of him on their wedding night. Their marriage would not be complicated.

After bidding him goodnight, she climbed the stairs to her bedroom, experiencing a pang of regret she hadn't been able to meet with Henry. It was probably for the best. The fates had sealed her destiny, and she'd accepted it.

Delia had lit the lamps in her room and laid a small fire in the hearth, allowing Amity to enter a cozy, cheerful chamber. Closing the door behind her, she sat upon the counterpane and began to remove her boots.

"Don't be alarmed," came Henry's voice as he materialized from behind the curtains like a spirit.

Naturally, she *was* alarmed! Jumping to her feet, Amity didn't know whether to shriek or run to the door. After a moment, however, not feeling particularly threatened, nor in fear of her virtue, she did neither. When the duke crossed the room to stand before her fireplace, he somehow looked the picture of innocence despite being in a single woman's bedroom.

"You agreed we could talk," he reminded her.

"Yes. I tried earlier, as you know."

"Your Mr. Cole is like a hound at the hunt." Henry slipped his hands into his pockets, perhaps to show he wasn't about to snatch hold of her.

"With good reason," she pointed out. "Mr. Cole is wary of you, and you've brought that scrutiny upon yourself with all the staring you've been doing."

The duke grinned, his dimples appeared, and her heartbeat began to race. *Was she so fickle and shallow that his good looks could win her over each time?*

After all, Mr. Cole was handsome, too. *Why didn't his smile melt her insides?* She wished fervently that it did.

"How can I help but stare at the object of my affection?" Henry asked, sounding serious.

He was practically declaring himself. She drew in a long breath. "You said you wished to speak with me and promised to leave tomorrow."

"Did I?" Withdrawing his hands from his pockets, he took a step closer. *So much for the picture of innocence!*

"Yes," she replied emphatically. "I will give you five minutes." She pointed to the clock on her mantle. "Tick tock."

His lovely green eyes widened. "I beg your pardon? You cannot 'tick tock' a duke."

"I can and I did."

He folded his arms across his chest. "All right. I have five minutes, but I need but one. I want you to marry me and not Mr. Cole."

Hearing him say it so frankly made her quite lightheaded.

"I am aware of that, Your Grace. And I am fully aware you usually get what you want. In this case, though, you shall not."

He uncrossed his arms slowly. "Whyever not?"

"I have given Mr. Cole my solemn vow to marry him."

"Literally speaking, Miss Rare-Foure, you have told him yes to his question of marriage, an impertinent one at that since he is blatantly unworthy of you. That is hardly a solemn vow. Vows occur on the wedding day, if I am not mistaken."

"Very well. I gave him my word. I agreed. I said yes. I cannot now say no, even if I wanted to." And a part of her definitely did.

"You do want to, don't you?"

"I didn't say that." But he could probably read it on her face. "I am not breaking my agreement. It would be too . . . hurtful."

He looked incredulous. "You don't want to *hurt* him so you will marry a man and spend the rest of your life with him, all the while having stronger feelings for me. Plainly, you are too chicken-hearted to acknowledge those feelings."

Chicken-hearted? "Are you calling me cowardly?"

"If the feathers fit," he said, still with a teasing tone.

He was sure of himself, that much she could tell. *And why not?* He was every girl's dream, including hers.

"Putting my feathers aside, my main reason remains. A duchess cannot make chocolate."

He sighed. "I don't know of any who do, that's true. I don't know many duchesses at all for that matter. We dukes don't all stand around together at a club, being ducal."

"Don't you?" She couldn't help the mirth in her tone. The image of Henry and a bunch of old men, as most of the current dukes were, standing on the plush oriental rug at whatever club they favored, probably White's, and discussing things only dukes would know or do struck her as immensely funny.

She started to snicker, then to chortle. When he joined in, she grabbed her bedpost and laughed heartily.

"You are making fun of me," he said, "and you've taken up my valuable time, so I am adding another two minutes."

Amity took a few breaths and managed to control herself. "Let us agree neither of us have heard of any duchesses who do anything except sit for portraits, run charities, and become ladies-in-waiting to the queen. Isn't that right?"

He nodded and took a step closer.

"I cannot give up making chocolate, no matter how—" *how very much she loved him*. She feared how empty and lifeless she would become. "No matter how tempting your offer. A chocolatier is who I am." She paused. "And it is unquestionably not the pastime for a duchess."

He had taken another step closer, and by some magic, his hands were upon her waist, drawing her against him.

"I should ask your permission, but I fear you will say no." With that warning, he bent low and claimed her mouth.

Hot sparks of desire shot through her. As Henry's broad hands roamed up her spine, every part of her body sizzled and trembled. Something deep inside seemed to become molten heat at his touch. Her fingers feathered into his hair and held his mouth against hers.

With her heart pounding, Amity let him slide his hands into her hair and dislodge the casual bun she'd created that morning. Pins went everywhere although many stayed put, liable, she feared, to poke one of Henry's eyes out.

"Amity," he murmured against her lips, and she forgot the hairpins.

Moaning slightly, she let his hot tongue slide into her open mouth. Gasping at the sensation drew him in farther. With a wildness she'd never imagined, she sucked on his tongue, making him groan in turn.

She was on fire and began to yank at the buttons on the front of her gown, thinking of nothing except wanting to feel his touch upon her heated skin. Finding it too difficult with shaking fingers, she switched to yanking at his clothing, desperate to touch him.

Contrary to every impulse of her body, she felt Henry freeze. He ceased kissing her and rested his forehead against her own. Then, he grasped hold of her hands to stall their frantic movements.

HENRY WAS AMAZED AT how this proper young woman, who was so determined to honor her engagement, could ignite in his arms with such rapidity. His own body was also in flames, and his manhood was like a flagpole.

He could simply tell her how much he loved her, but that seemed particularly manipulative at this juncture. Either she would feel compelled to return the sentiment—whether she felt it or not—using words she'd probably recently said to her fiancé, or she would *not* say them. Far worse, as far as he was concerned.

If she didn't say them back, he would seem a groveling fool, and if she was determined to marry Mr. Cole, Henry would be exactly that—a fool.

He wanted her to give him some sign she preferred marriage to him over that damned lawyer. Drawing back, he looked at her flushed face. Her eyes were closed, her lips slightly parted, and she was breathing heavily, as was he. He took her pretty chin between his fingers.

"Amity," he commanded.

She shook her head slightly to dislodge his hand.

"Tell me what you're thinking," Henry ordered as she retreated from him.

"That I could not possibly go to the workroom of Rare Confectionery and make chocolates if I were a duchess."

However, when she opened her eyes and quickly looked away from him, he knew other thoughts were flitting in her brain. Thoughts of *him*, perhaps, and not of chocolate.

He sighed. "Can we put that aside for the time being? I cannot imagine chocolate is more important than . . . ," he trailed off. *How pathetic to say he wanted to come before her love of making chocolate!*

He paced the room to give her space to think and, hopefully, to say something more intimate, but he kept his gaze on her. She curled her delicate yet capable hands into fists at her sides. She glanced up at the ceiling and down at the floor. Finally, she looked directly at him.

"Would you give up your seat in Parliament or leave your townhouse to live with me in a middle-class house in the southwest outskirts of London?"

His eyes widened. He hadn't expected that question. Give up the trappings of his inheritance? *Absurd!*

"But there would be no need," he began.

She held up a hand to stop him. "What if marrying me meant giving up your fine house and your valet, as well as membership to your clubs and . . . ?" She hesitated and frowned.

Her lovely face, even when frowning, made his heart ache. He knew this wasn't going the way he had hoped.

"And what if you even had to give up your luxury coach?" she finished and sank her teeth into her lower lip, appearing distraught.

Amity could not see herself as his duchess, and that hurt. If she loved him, she would leave Mr. Cole and enter his world with pleasure and gratitude. She would worry later about being a chocolatier.

With his heart squeezing painfully, all he could do was turn her words into a jest.

"That is unfair. Anything but my luxury coach. Definitely, I would rather have my Italian leather squabs than you for a wife."

They stared at each other, and then she smiled, while tears filled her eyes. He could tell she was not going to acquiesce. She did not love him, or at least, not enough.

"I had best be on my way," he said, feeling suddenly chilled and empty, "before I am discovered in your room and the choice is taken from you."

She nodded, crushing his hopes for a life with this warm and witty woman.

He nearly took her in his arms again. *Who was to stop him?* They both undeniably enjoyed it. But it seemed a shallow, lusty game, and he didn't play those types of games, not with respectable young women.

With a bow of farewell, Henry slipped out of her room and headed back along the hallway to his own. It had never occurred to him that she would choose the lawyer and chocolate over him. *Who wanted to be a regular missus instead of a duchess?*

A part of him admired her for her loyalty. *A very small part!* The rest of him felt annoyed, confused, worried, uncharacteristically insecure, and above all, miserable.

As he undressed, he decided to depart at first light with a note left for the family. He was not one to flog a dead horse, nor to face humiliation at the hands of the victorious Mr. Cole.

CHAPTER TWENTY-FIVE

The next day, Amity knew it would not be easy to tell Jeremy she'd had a change of heart, but at the very least, it would be a relief. Awakening to learn of the Duke of Pelham's departure, her heart felt like solid stone in her chest, and she could think of no remedy. She could not marry Henry and throw away her passion for confectionery, nor give up working with her sisters.

She also could not marry Jeremy, not after experiencing such intense, heady desire in Henry's arms. Jeremy deserved a woman who felt such passion for him, not one who would spend the rest of her life thinking of another man's kiss.

Before breakfast, she invited Jeremy to walk with her. They made it as far as the field of wildflowers behind the house when she turned to him, not wanting to drag it out.

"I'm so sorry," she began.

"But you cannot marry me," Jeremy finished.

She lowered her head, hating to hurt him although she'd made her decision in the long, sleepless hours of the night.

"You are marrying the Duke of Pelham," he concluded, "and I cannot compete with him."

"You do not need to compete with His Grace, nor am I marrying him."

"Then why?" he asked.

"I have searched my heart, and while I have affection for you, I am not in love with you," she said as kindly as she could. She now understood true love, knowing it must be the reason for her ardent emotions whenever she was with Henry. And being with Jeremy was nothing like it.

His expression became perplexed. "The duke hasn't asked you to marry him." He cocked his head. "And yet you're not marrying me . . . because of love?"

She decided not to delve into Henry's proposal or even confess there had been one as that was not Jeremy's business.

"I am not confident you're thinking lucidly," he added. "Whole-hearted love is best reserved for a parent toward a child, don't you think?"

Stunned at his assertion, Amity shook her head. "No, I do not."

How had they never discussed this? She'd assumed and attributed to him a level of sentiment he might not actually have for her. "Surely you feel love for me if you wish to marry me."

"I hold you in the utmost regard," he explained. "I feel tenderness and affection. Your nature, face, and physique, they all please me tremendously. There is very little about you I would change. I also think you would be an excellent mother."

"But you don't love me?" she asked, frankly surprised.

"I suppose I do," he confessed. "As much as any adult loves another."

She stared at him. "Do you ever experience lightheadedness around me? Does your heart race at my approach?"

He opened his mouth, closed it, and finally confessed, "No."

"When we kiss," she persisted, knowing the topic was inappropriate, "do you feel hot inside, as if you were turning to liquid while your skin seems practically scorched?"

"Definitely not," Jeremy said, his face growing a little red. "Whatever can you mean?"

"At my touch, do you feel overcome with wanting?" She laid a hand on his arm, feeling nothing herself.

"Wanting what?" he asked, staring at her as if she were slightly deranged.

"Wanting me, of course!"

"I look forward to sharing our marital bed if that's what you mean."

Amity shook her head, relieved beyond measure to have learned of his tepid nature. "But you don't yearn for me."

Jeremy shrugged.

"Then I am doing you a good service, Mr. Cole, by setting you free of our engagement. I assure you that such intense passion is real, and I do think it represents love, enduring and encompassing. I hope you experience it someday."

With that, she turned from him, walking back toward the house. Over her shoulder, she added, "You're more than welcome to stay for breakfast."

Her step light, she felt almost buoyant at being free, which confirmed marriage to him would have been an egregious error. Her earlier guilt at causing him pain had been replaced by a sense of rightness. Even though upon consideration, Amity couldn't help wondering briefly what it was about her he would change. He'd indicated there was something.

With a sigh of contentment, she accepted that was no longer her concern, and thus, she would never know.

"YOU ARE AS DOUR as . . . as a recently widowed dowager," Charlotte declared to Amity two weeks later after they had returned to London. They were readying Rare Confectionery to reopen, but Amity couldn't find her usual joy as she worked, making enough chocolates to fill the shop's shelves.

"I wonder if that's why they are given such a sad title," Charlotte mused.

"It's not the same *dour*," Beatrice said with a chuckle.

"Either way," Charlotte continued, speaking from the front of the shop where she was dusting every surface, "I miss the old amiable Amity. Isn't that why Mother and Father named you as they did?"

"Are you of the belief our parents noticed I was *amiable* from infancy?" Amity asked. Charlotte's mistaken notion, in fact, did bring a smile to her face.

Beatrice laughed again. She was cleaning the front glass panes with vinegar and newsprint. "Silly goose. They named her Amity after some great aunt and because they wanted her to have a name beginning with *A*."

"*A, B, C*," Charlotte murmured. "I wonder what *D*'s name would have been."

Amity shook her head. *How she loved being with her sisters.* It would have to be enough.

Unfortunately, she next made an absolutely terrible batch of chocolates, doubling the salt and using sour milk by mistake. Wasting good ingredients, namely a block of Menier's chocolate, irritated her no end, and in disgust, she slung them all into the rubbish bin. A shiver raced through her—carrying with it the fear she'd lost her spark, and not because of breaking it off with Jeremy Cole.

That evening, as Amity prepared for bed, a tap on her door turned out to be her mother.

"Where is my happy eldest daughter? What have you done with her?" Felicity Rare-Foure asked, sitting on the edge of the bed.

"I am right here." Amity placed her hairbrush on the dressing table and went over to sit beside her mother.

"But you're not the same as before we went away. No," Felicity caught herself, "I should say, you are not as you were *before* the duke's proposal party. You aren't still smarting over Lady Madeleine's set-down, are you?"

"No." Truthfully, Amity cared not a whit for Lady Madeleine and hadn't spared her a thought in weeks.

"And have you sent Mr. Cole away permanently?" her mother asked. Amity hadn't told her family much more than they'd broken off their extraordinarily short engagement.

"Yes." Amity plucked at the skirt of her gown, feeling out of sorts.

Her mother covered her hand with her own. "So, are you madly in love with the Duke of Pelham?"

"Yes," she said and gasped at her frank admission. "Mother!" She had been lulled by the easier questions into a quick confession.

"And he is obviously madly in love with you, too," Felicity persisted.

"How can you know that?" Amity felt a flicker of joy at the thought.

"Because the man followed you out to the country and toured ruins with you. He bristled every time he looked at Mr. Cole, or you did. He even carried in your breakfast on a tray. Then you hurt the duke's feelings and he ran away. Clearly, a man in love."

Amity shook her head. Apparently, her mother knew everything, so what was the point in speaking.

"How did my amiable daughter make a duke turn tail and run? That is my question. And why?"

"That's two questions," Amity pointed out and felt comforted when her mother put her arms around her. "The duke does care for me, I believe," she began, "and I do love him madly, as you say. But he wants me to be his duchess."

She felt her mother take a deep breath. "Yes, dear. That's usually the way it works. A duke marries, and his wife becomes his duchess."

Amity realized she was wringing her hands upon her lap. "That's precisely it. Don't you see? I cannot be a duchess. I am a chocolatier!"

Her mother paused. "My poor girl. You are not *merely* a chocolatier. You are a woman in love. I believe that takes precedence over nearly everything else. I can't imagine you—or the duke—will let a little thing like chocolate, no matter how delicious, stand in your way."

"A little thing? Mother, how can you say that?"

"Compared to love, Amity, how can I not?"

HENRY WAITED AT THE bottom of the stairs for his mother to descend. He'd promised to escort her to her favorite ballet at Covent Garden. The nights were becoming colder, and the streets were decorated for the upcoming Yuletide Season. To him, it seemed a little early. He might speak to London's mayor about it next time he saw him.

Never had he felt more like a holiday humbug. It had been almost two months since his ill-planned visit to the Rare-Foures' country home, and he hadn't been back to Rare Confectionery to see if they'd reopened. He didn't need to. He'd been served Amity's chocolates at more than one party already and seen a tin of them at a friend's home.

He hadn't been able to eat a single one.

Nor did he examine the papers for engagement announcements. He'd been told by Waverly that most people didn't make as big a fuss if they weren't titled since no one cared who married whom, not unless they were in the upper echelons.

That wasn't always the case. Henry cared very much.

"I'm ready, dear boy. Gracious, don't look as if I'm dragging you to your own hanging. It's the ballet, and we're lucky the theatre is so close. You don't mind being at the ballet with your old mother, do you?"

"First of all, you're not old. I should be escorting you to balls so you can find a new husband. I don't like to think of you alone. Secondly, you know I don't care for the ballet, but I'm happy to suffer through it with you. And there's always the intermission and the well-stocked bar."

His mother patted his cheek fondly. "I am barely out of mourning," she protested. "Although the past two months, you seem to have taken over for me. You are gloomy and cranky." She paused and looked at him, scrutinizing his face. Then she lifted one shoulder in an elegant shrug.

"Regardless, I will not be dancing at a ball alongside the debutantes any time soon. How unseemly. If I am fortunate enough to find another man to love me as your father did, I will be twice blessed."

Henry could only nod at her wisdom and take his dowager mother to the theatre. Amity had been twice blessed to be loved by two men, and it sliced him, leaving him gutted, to have been the one she didn't choose. He wasn't sure he would ever quite recover.

In half an hour, from the Pelham private box, to Henry's consternation—and also keen interest—he saw the entire Rare-Foure family of five walk down the main aisle and take their seats about seven rows back from the orchestra.

His chocolatier wore a plum-colored gown, maybe the one he'd seen her in at the Peabodys' home. That seemed a long time ago. He wished he could invite them up to his box, but that would send all sorts of wrong signals to those who might be watching. Also, it would sting like the devil to be close to Amity.

"What are you staring at?" his mother asked. "Or rather whom?"

She practically hung over the edge to get a better view. "Who has caught your interest? I know only the lady who does not have your attention any longer." She glanced at him again, before training her gaze back on the people still taking their seats. "Tell me, Henry, I command you."

"Mother, please. I was simply watching people entering."

She made an exaggerated gasp. "You have not lied to me since you were a little boy and snuck into the kitchen to eat an entire custard pie. You were sick for a day and tried to pretend you had no idea where that pie went."

"There are no pies here tonight," he said, crossing his arms.

"Don't you want to know how I knew you were lying to me then and now?"

"Apart from my face turning a sublime shade of green and my being dreadfully sick into your needlepoint basket?"

She smiled. "It was the way you lifted your eyebrows while narrowing your eyes at the same time. A strange trick you do when prevaricating and at no other time. I shall have to tell your future wife to be on alert. Is she out there tonight, I wonder?"

He let his glance flit over the Rare-Foures and shook his head. *She unquestionably had been if she hadn't chosen chocolate over him.* Henry wasn't about to tell his mother that.

"Maybe I will let *you* choose the next female I woo. What do you say, Mother? Can you find me a duchess?"

The dowager sat back in her seat and looked at him. She gave him a loving smile that hadn't changed in all the years. "If you're serious, my son, I would be honored to help. Not that I don't think you can find someone for yourself," she added, touching his shoulder. "Nonetheless, perhaps I can discover a female with particular qualities you might be overlooking."

"Which qualities?" he asked.

"Well, Lady Madeleine had but one thing going for her." She wrinkled her nose in the exact likeness of his sister.

Henry frowned. "Not true, Mother. In addition to her obvious beauty, the lady was bred to run a household and to be the wife of a titled lord."

The dowager's face soured. "She was as dry as Brighton beach sand and just as dull. The sole time I ever saw her demonstrate an ounce of spirit was the night she ate the wrong chocolate, and she had a most disgraceful conniption in public over it. Hardly a young woman who would dazzle London as your duchess. You need someone with genuine warmth and capability and with a certain spark." She patted her coiffure. "Rather like your old mother."

He laughed. "I already told you, you are not old. By the way, why aren't Penelope and Randolph joining us tonight? Why aren't they being forced to endure this ballet?" he added teasingly.

"Your sister is married and can set her own schedule. Besides, I think they have more important things to consider than the ballet."

The lights went down, so Henry whispered, "What do you mean?"

"I will tell you more at intermission, but I think you are going to be an uncle."

Henry sat back feeling shocked. *His sister was to be a mother?* Penelope was a year younger than he was. That undoubtedly meant soon after his own wedding, he might be expected to start thinking about producing an heir.

Amity's face instantly came to mind, looking down with love at a wee babe with soft brown hair and her rich mahogany-colored eyes. He would have cherished them both.

Eventually, when he was sure his mother wasn't looking, he leaned over to see if, in the darkness, he could discern Miss Rare-Foure—assuming there had not been a hasty wedding turning her into a *Mrs. Cole*. He thought he could make out her feathered hat by the dim gaslights running along the sides of the theatre.

Warmth and capability, his mother had said. She had both of those things in spades.

"Stop sighing, Henry, I'm trying to enjoy the ballet."

He could hardly wait for intermission and a large glass of wine.

AMITY HADN'T REALIZED SHE was staring, unseeing, at the shelf behind her marble worktable until Beatrice spoke into her ear.

"You are getting nothing accomplished today. Why don't you take a walk? Direct your plum-colored boots to St. James's Place and see if the duke is in. Maybe he needs more *Pelhams.*"

Amity sighed. "He liked them so much, I thought he would come in to buy one or two someday."

Beatrice shook her head. "You ninny. His Grace is not going to come in after you so firmly gave him the mitten."

Amity blinked at the old-fashioned term for turning down a man's offer.

When Mr. Cole had left and never returned, Amity told her sisters—after much cajoling on their part—how Henry had made his proposal.

"Not exactly on bended knee with declarations of undying love," she'd explained, "but a proposal, just the same."

They'd been mightily impressed in any case, and, while understanding her reasons, they couldn't believe she'd turned him down. Since then, they hugged her more and treated her ever so kindly. She hoped they didn't feel a sense of burden from her choosing them and the confectionery over the duke.

In her heart, she wished she could have all three.

"If His Grace wants a chocolate, he can come here," she said softly.

"Men have their pride," Beatrice reminded her. "Besides, it wouldn't change anything, would it?"

Sadly, she shook her head and felt tears prick her eyes. "I am afraid not. I cannot live without being a chocolatier and being with you."

"Nonsense," Beatrice said, as the bell tinkled at the front of the shop. Charlotte was at the counter, so they ignored it. "You are determined to remain here in this back room, day after day, year after year?"

Amity didn't like the way her sister made it sound as if she'd been sentenced to Newgate gaol. Chocolate-making was a joyful affair. On the other hand, she'd felt anything but joy in recent weeks.

"Amity," Charlotte called out, and she got to her feet, glad of the interruption since Beatrice was scowling and looked as if she had more unwelcome words to say on the matter.

Pushing aside the curtain, she entered the front of the shop to see the Dowager Duchess of Pelham and Henry's sister, both of whom she'd met at the ill-fated proposal party.

For a moment, Amity wondered if Her Grace were there to reprimand her for causing trouble. Worse, what if the dowager knew her son wanted to marry a shopkeeper's daughter and was enraged?

"Your Grace," Amity said and curtsied before greeting the young lady with another curtsey, "My lady. How may I help you?"

"Your chocolates were such a success at our last party," Henry's mother said. "I want to order some for the next one."

Amity could scarcely believe the dowager was making mention of the embarrassing disaster of a proposal party as if nothing had occurred out of the ordinary regarding Amity or her chocolates. *How gracious of her!*

"May I ask the occasion? I have some wonderful shapes, perfect for a St. Michaelmas party or a Christmas gathering." Amity wondered if she should give the chocolates for free to make amends.

"An *engagement* party," the dowager said, looking directly at Amity who, at those words, could barely breathe. "Or it will be by the evening's end."

"For the . . . the Duke of Pelham?" she asked, mortified when her voice cracked with tension.

"Indubitably." The dowager glanced at the display case to her left. "So many choices." Then once more, she fixed Amity with the identical green eyes her son had inherited. "However, I believe you already know what my son likes."

Amity swallowed. "Coffee?" she croaked.

The dowager and her daughter laughed. "How good of you to recall!" his mother said. "I believe he also likes chocolate with orange. He said he tasted such a confection here once."

Amity nodded. "Yes, His Grace did, but what of the lady to whom he will become engaged? What does she like?"

The dowager shrugged as if that didn't matter. "May I sample something?"

"My goodness, yes, Your Grace. My apologies." She shot Charlotte a tight-lipped look for not already having put samples on a plate only to realize her youngest sister was holding one out to her. "This is Miss Charlotte," Amity said belatedly.

"Yes, I remember from the party," the dowager said evenly, while stripping off her right glove, without giving away whether Charlotte's memorable presence was good or bad.

"Of course." Amity hoped her sister hadn't said anything in her defense that was too terribly rude in front of the duke's family and all his guests.

Stepping forward, Charlotte seemed entirely at ease. "This one is a milk chocolate with nuts, and this one, also milk, has a soft center of raspberry essence. This one is a plain chocolate truffle with orange liqueur in the center. I believe it is the one the duke would have tasted. Is that right?" Charlotte looked at her.

"Yes, that is the one. Let me get another of each for Lady . . . Lady . . . ." Amity had forgotten Lady Penelope's husband's name and title. She felt her cheeks grow hot with mortification.

Before either the dowager or her daughter could respond, Charlotte said, "She remains *Lady Penelope.*"

Amity stared at her youngest sister in admiration. All the time she spent reading the gossip rags hadn't been for nothing.

"Well done," Lady Penelope said to Charlotte, then turned to Amity, "I married an earl's younger son, you see," as if that explained everything. "Don't worry, it is nearly as confusing to me." She, too, pulled off her glove so she could sample the chocolates.

Amity was glad Henry's sister had not taken offense although the intricacies of her title were still as clear as mud. Using the tongs, she set another orange chocolate on the small white plate, as well as a second of each of the others. "That last one is also plain chocolate with ground dates."

The two women tasted everything, and Amity found herself relaxing as they exclaimed with pleasure. Charlotte brought forth two glasses of water for them to sip between tastings.

"Which is your favorite?" the dowager duchess asked Amity.

Amity's eyes widened. "Honestly, Your Grace, that is like asking me to pick from among my own children—or I imagine it would be." But she reconsidered. "I do favor a confectionery created with both my sisters' help." She returned to the case and picked from the middle shelf, putting two on the plate.

The dowager duchess and her daughter regarded the rectangles covered in marzipan. "What are they?" Lady Penelope asked.

Amity smiled. This was her favorite part of making confectionery—having people taste for the first time and make a discovery. "Please try them and see if you can figure out what they are."

The Pelham mother and daughter each picked up a square and, after the first careful taste, devoured them.

"Gracious," the dowager said. "I could see myself eating an entire tin of those." She looked to her daughter. "I think I know what is in them. Do you?"

"Well, the marzipan has been flavored with . . . vanilla, I think, and it was most delicious. The chocolate was not too sweet but had a hint of some type of brandy. It was perfect. Inside were slivers of something buttery that melted on my tongue. I think it was toffee."

"Treacle toffee," came Beatrice's voice from behind. "And the mysterious flavor in the chocolate is French brandy."

Amity stepped back so her middle sister could come forward, curtsey to the dowager duchess and Lady Penelope, and be introduced. She hoped Beatrice remained on her best behavior, with no outbursts about class unfairness.

"That was utterly delicious." The dowager offered Amity a smile. "Would you tell me why those are your favorites?"

"Because all three of us used our talents to make them. Miss Charlotte makes the marzipan, and it is the creamiest, most delicate ever created." She looked at her youngest sister whose cheeks turned a pretty shade of rose.

"And Miss Beatrice makes the treacle toffee, favored by everyone I know for its perfect texture and taste. Even Queen Victoria loves it."

"Amity is too kind," Beatrice added. "Without her chocolate holding it all together, that confection wouldn't work at all." They smiled at each other, and Amity felt perfect happiness for the first time in weeks.

"Agreed," said the dowager. "Very well. I would like fifty of those—no, better make it two hundred."

Amity gasped at the large order, but before she could say anything, the dowager added, "And two hundred of the coffee chocolates my son favors."

"The *Pelham*," Beatrice supplied helpfully, making Amity's cheeks grow as pink as Charlotte's.

The dowager exchanged a look with her daughter, and they both smiled. "Did you really name it after our family?" Henry's mother asked.

"Actually, it was named for His Grace," Charlotte said, and Amity wanted to wallop her for her frankness.

"The chocolate can honor the *entire* family," Amity said diplomatically, "if you all enjoy coffee and chocolate." Recalling Henry telling her he'd eaten them all himself, she offered, "Would you like to taste a *Pelham*, Your Grace?"

The dowager shook her head. "At the party, I shall. Come along, Penelope."

The two were nearly at the door when Amity remembered her professional duties.

"Your Grace, when is the party, do you want any special shapes for the chocolates, and will a servant come to pick them up?"

The woman blinked her sharp green eyes. "As to when, that is still a little up in the air." She glanced at her daughter conspiratorially. "I hope within two weeks. No special shapes, thank you." She looked at Amity again with her vivid green eyes. "As for the delivery, I hope you will do us the kindness of bringing them yourself. And with four hundred chocolates to carry, you might want to bring your sisters to help you. In fact, I insist."

Leaving the three of them speechless, the dowager duchess and her well-behaved daughter left the shop to the pleasant sound of the tinkling bell.

CHAPTER TWENTY-SIX

The Dowager Duchess of Pelham's party order did two things in quick succession—it gave Amity a reason to get to work in earnest and stop daydreaming, and it also gave her the promise, in the not too distant future, of once more seeing the man who'd irrevocably and entirely captured her heart.

She couldn't wait to lay eyes upon him again, even if she was delivering chocolates. When her mother heard of the occasion, she decided all three girls should have new dresses, even if they were readymade and not *haute couture*.

"But the gowns will cost more than the profit from the confectionery," Amity protested.

Her mother barely batted an eyelid. "We have saved money by neither you nor Beatrice having even a single Season. This will be a celebratory night and you should be dressed appropriately."

And with those words, Amity's delight melted like a chocolate bar on a hot summer pavement. Henry had found a new woman to take as his duchess.

Furthermore, he hadn't come to ask her himself to make the chocolates because he couldn't bear to look at her. He probably hated her for the perceived slight of choosing chocolate over him. If he only knew how many hours she had agonized over the decision. Realizing during her discussion with Jeremy how this heart-palpitating feeling was true love, she had examined the emotion from every angle.

Ultimately, she loved the duke enough to be happy he had found another to share his life. Happy for him and terribly sad, too.

She feared she would never find someone to take Henry's place in her heart. And with that, she started to dread the event even more.

"HENRY," HIS MOTHER CALLED to him as he was passing by the drawing room. Another endless afternoon stretched ahead of him, first a late session in Parliament, and then, if he could drag himself to White's, he would have a meal with Jeffcoat and Waverly. They had nearly forbidden him to go for he had been such bad company of late.

At his mother's bidding, he entered to find her having tea in the late-morning sun.

"It is done," she said without preamble or warning. "I have found you a perfect duchess and invited her to our house to become engaged to you. All you must do is set the date, but the party must be within two weeks, or I shall look a fool."

His mouth had dropped open and hadn't closed.

"Stop looking like you are a frog catching flies," she ordered.

"Mother, I didn't say you could *choose* the woman outright. I said you could help me find a suitable wife. I will—"

"Miss Rare-Foure is my choice for your duchess."

He sighed. His mother was amazing and always had been. "How did you know?"

"I am not blind, nor a ninny. I saw how happy you were when you told me of your visits to her shop. 'Creating the perfect chocolate,'" she mimicked words he had said to her, before rolling her eyes, the very mirror of his own.

"We were doing precisely that," he protested, knowing he sounded like a child.

"I know you were, but you were creating something else, too, something very special for one another. The way you looked at her at our party . . . I tell you, Henry, I could hardly breathe for fear you would go ahead and propose to Lady Madeleine when I could see clearly how you felt for Miss Rare-Foure. I think she is delightful, and so does Penelope. All the sisters are, for that matter. How splendid!"

"It isn't that simple, Mother."

She shook her head. "Young people, complicating things," she muttered. "Of course it is! You love her, she loves you."

"And how does my magician of a mother know this?"

"Easy. I went and spoke to her mother."

"You didn't! That seems rather drastic, not to mention an invasion of Miss Rare-Foure's privacy." He paused but a second later asked, "Her mother said Amity loves me?"

"Amity," the dowager mused. "Such a pretty name, isn't it?" She picked up her teacup. "I shall say no more. As you say, it's private and for Miss Rare-Foure to tell you herself."

"But her fiancé, Mr. Cole?" he asked.

His mother frowned. "That's the first I've heard of such a person. Miss Rare-Foure's delightful mother made no mention of a fiancé at all." She blinked at him over the porcelain cup. "Gather your friends for a wonderful party. There will be four hundred chocolates, too."

"Dear God!" He couldn't imagine what that would look like. In any case, his thoughts were still mulling over the fact

Amity did not have a fiancé anymore. He knew he was grinning like a fool.

His mother grinned right back at him. "I might have gone a little overboard with the number of confections, but I didn't think I could get Miss Rare-Foure to agree to come to the party unless I went very, very big. She will be busy until party time, I believe. And then, it is up to you. Naturally, I invited her sisters, too." His mother sipped her tea again. "Also, her parents, although the young woman is not aware of that."

"Her parents know my intention?"

"They do." His mother looked as smug as a cat with a mouse between its paws.

"And they are keeping it from her?"

"Only for two weeks. They are not a family for secrets any more than we are. As soon as we decide on the exact date of the party, we must send word to the confectionery. Meanwhile, I forbid you to go there and ruin my surprise."

"You are getting entirely too caught up in my life." Nonetheless, Henry bent over and kissed her cheek, feeling nothing but gratitude and love. "I thank you from the bottom of my heart."

AMITY SMOOTHED THE FRONT of her new silk gown for the hundredth time while the Pelham butler and servants took her family's coats and her father's hat, as well as four hundred chocolates. She'd taken it upon herself to change the order so there were two hundred assorted chocolates and one hundred each of the *Pelham* and her own favorite marzipan-chocolate-toffee creation. If it had been the wrong thing to do, the blame would fall squarely upon her own head.

At the last minute, her parents had declared their intent to go, too. It was unlike her parents to do something as rash as attend a party uninvited. Thus, she questioned them in the carriage.

"When the date of the event came by messenger, invitations were extended to your father and to me," Felicity Rare-Foure assured her.

"Why didn't you tell me sooner?" Amity had moaned, squeezed in the seat next to her sisters as they rode toward St. James's Place. "If I'd known, the two of you could have delivered the chocolates with Charlotte and Bea, and I could have stayed home."

Beatrice had shown little enthusiasm in getting into her finery and going to a place where she knew no one. All the same, because the dowager duchess herself had invited her, she had acquiesced. Charlotte, as expected, had been looking forward to her own triumphant return to the Pelham residence all week.

"That is precisely why I didn't tell you," her mother said. "It's good for you to get out and about. Did I tell you how beautiful you look in that gown?"

Indeed, Amity felt like a princess in silver silk with her favorite plum-colored trim around the hem and the sleeves, as well as matching buttons and sash—a princess whose insides were all aflutter with butterflies and hummingbirds.

"Wait until you see the carpeting and chandeliers and the paintings and . . . ," Charlotte went on and on to Beatrice, who was either listening or dozing in her corner of the carriage.

When their quick trip across Mayfair was complete, Amity smoothed her gown again as the butler led them up the stairs.

"Stop fidgeting," her mother said, but her tone was soothing and kind, and next, she smiled as broadly as a crescent moon, something she'd been doing a lot of lately.

At the top of the stairs, precisely as the last time, the Dowager Duchess of Pelham, along with her daughter and son-in-law, stood waiting to receive guests. And as before, there was Henry. He looked, if possible, even more handsome than he ever had, and Amity's heart began hammering in her chest at the sight of him.

She nearly stumbled on the top step, and her mother took her hand to steady her.

"I don't see the future fiancée's family," Amity whispered as Charlotte and Beatrice stepped forward first.

Her mother only smiled again. When it was her turn, Amity greeted the dowager, who gave her a very kind welcome and thanked her for bringing the chocolates. Lady Penelope and Lord Yardley were next. And then . . .

Suddenly, Amity was standing in front of Henry, who took her hand as she curtseyed.

"Your Grace," she said, hardly able to look at him, so tightly strung were her emotions.

"Miss Rare-Foure," he said, and his warm, inviting tone brought her gaze up to his. His green eyes were as friendly as ever, calming her nerves somewhat. "I'm so glad you could come tonight. You look positively ravishing."

Her cheeks heated at his honeyed tone, which seemed most improper for a man about to propose marriage to someone else. Unable to respond, she nodded, curtsied again, and turned away.

How would she make it through this evening?

Unlike the previous occasion, there was no Lady Madeleine in a stunning gold gown. Yet most puzzling, no other young lady appeared either.

As expected, many of the same people were there who had attended the previous proposal party. Amity recognized some faces but doubted she would recall many of their names. Maybe if Henry got engaged three more times, she would be able to remember all his friends.

She wished her private joke cheered her up, but it didn't.

Lord Waverly was there, of course, and Lord Jeffcoat, with whom Charlotte had been previously partnered. Amity went around the room, meeting them all again, as did the rest of her family.

That night, there was no sit-down dinner, but musicians played in the ballroom while food was served in the dining room on small plates, which could be taken either to the drawing room where some sat on the sofas and chairs to nibble on small meat-filled pastries or to the ballroom, where most everyone ate while stand and chatting. Tall tables had been placed around the edges of the room for setting down one's food and glass of wine. The chocolates—all four hundred of them—had been set out without fanfare on a dessert table, dwarfing the other sweetmeats, cakes, and puddings.

"I like this relaxed way of dining," Beatrice said.

"If you'd had a Season," her mother explained, "you would have experienced the like at some of the larger dances when sit-down meals are impossible."

"Will there be dancing tonight?" Charlotte asked, her excitement evident.

"Goodness, I hope not," Amity said. "I can do a poor imitation of a waltz at best."

"Not true," Beatrice said. "We can all manage a fair lancer or polka."

Regardless, it had given Amity another thing to worry about. She looked around, as she'd been doing all evening, to see where Henry was. She expected to spy him with his new ladylove at any instant.

Currently, he stood with Lords Waverly and Jeffcoat, sipping a drink and chatting, looking happier than she'd seen him the entire time he was at her family's country house.

He turned in her direction while she was staring, and to her mortification, he waved.

She spun on her heel away from his gaze. "I think I have to go home."

Her father put a hand under her elbow. "What is wrong? Are you ill?"

"I suspect it's simply nerves," her mother said, and in an uncharacteristically firm tone, she added, "You cannot go home or we shall all be stranded. Why don't you go speak with His Grace?"

"Mother! No. That definitely won't help my nerves."

"He's coming over," her father said cheerfully.

"God help me," Amity said. "I think I'm going to be sick. Where is the closest water-closet?"

Grabbing Beatrice's arm for support, she dashed from the room, even as she could feel the duke behind her, making her skin prickle with awareness.

After a few minutes in the luxurious retiring room with Beatrice applying a damp cloth to the back of her neck, being careful not to get a drop of water on the silk, Amity felt no better.

"I knew I shouldn't have come. I'm liable to melt into a pool of humiliation and sadness on the ballroom floor if the duke so much as smiles at me. Look at my hands."

Beatrice sighed, dropped the cloth on the edge of the sink and took hold of Amity's trembling hands.

"You must stop this nonsense. You are Amity Rare-Foure. You've had a fiancé, you've had a duke ask you to marry him already, you are a wonderful chocolatier. And you are a dear sister. Please, for my sake, because I hate to see you like this, if you cannot wait for him to announce his engagement, please go speak with him. Tell him how you feel before it is too late."

Her sister's intelligent brown eyes staring into hers imparted wisdom. All at once, Amity knew Beatrice was right. She was behaving like a spineless, feather-pated ninny. She straightened her shoulders, examined herself in the mirror, and nodded.

"You are right. Let's go."

Back in the ballroom, she marched straight over to the duke, who was chatting with her parents.

He turned to her . . . and her voice vanished.

Coughing, she gestured for him to draw closer. "Please, Your Grace," she whispered, "may I have a word with you? Alone?"

He cocked his head at her plea, looking downright surprised.

"Always," he answered when he had recovered.

Unexpectedly, instead of speaking discreetly to her parents, he said in a louder voice, encompassing those around them, "If you will excuse us, Miss Rare-Foure and I need to discuss a sensitive chocolate matter."

Amity's eyes widened at his bringing attention to their rather improper private meeting. Nevertheless, he was a duke, and she supposed he could do what he liked at his own party, or anywhere else for that matter.

When her parents nodded, she had to wonder what the civilized world was coming to. The duke gestured for her to precede him out of the ballroom. In the hallway, he paused and considered.

"I believe the drawing room is empty now as everyone has gathered in the ballroom for the grand announcement which I hope to make in due course. That is to say, shortly."

He'd guessed correctly. Amity found herself alone with the duke, who closed the door behind them and waited.

The grand announcement. His words echoed in her brain, making it nearly impossible for her to continue. She hadn't thought about what to say between the ballroom and the drawing room. *Should she declare herself right away?*

When she said nothing, he asked, "To what do I owe the pleasure of a private *tête-a-tête* with London's premiere chocolatier?"

She blinked. Whether to ease her nerves or merely to make a jest, Henry had made reference to their first meeting on the pavement when he'd invited her into his carriage.

In reply, she said the same thing as she had that day. "That is redundant, my lord."

He smiled and showed her his dashing dimples, and she wondered how she could have ever let this man get away.

She could only pray to God and to her queen that it was not too late.

"Not *my lord*, Miss Rare-Foure. Have you learned nothing?"

"I have learned a great deal, in fact," she confessed. "I can but hope I did not learn too late."

He stepped closer, and she let him take her hands in his, feeling a measure of hope and inner fortitude from merely his touch.

Mustering her courage, she said, "First, I must ask outright if you are in love with another woman."

He drew one of her hands to his mouth and kissed her bare knuckles, all their gloves having been removed in order to eat. "I promise you I am not."

She breathed a sigh of relief. "Then I must confess how very much in love with you I am. You intend to become engaged tonight, and now I know you don't even love the woman. Please don't make me watch such a travesty. I couldn't bear it."

He raised her other hand to his mouth and brushed his lips across it, sending shivers down her spine.

"You will never have to watch me pay tribute to or court another woman. I promise you that, too."

"Thank you. I am sorry I turned you away before—*gave you the mitten*, as my sister calls it—but I didn't realize how empty everything would seem when you withdrew from my life. Instead of the happiness I usually feel when making chocolate, now the hours stretch endlessly ahead of me, and my beloved craft has become a chore, all because I do not have you in my life. Without you, it is far too narrow an existence."

"I understand completely," he said, his green gaze flickering over her face. "Everything I usually do to fill my days now seems petty or pointless because my heart wants to have you in my life."

"Are you truly getting engaged tonight?" She could scarce credit him doing so.

"Yes, I believe so." He said, staring down into her eyes through which she could no longer see him as they filled with tears.

"I must leave directly," she said, tugging at her hands to free herself. "You are punishing me for not accepting you the first time. 'Male pride,' my sister said. Yet you just promised I did not have to watch."

"You will be there for this engagement, Miss Rare-Foure." With that, Henry dropped down upon one knee. Still holding her hands, he gave them a gentle squeeze as she realized what he was doing.

"Amity Rare-Foure, you have changed me, making me see the shallowness of my life as a duke. I was missing out on the rich experiences beyond the pampered and the privileged. I didn't think I would find passionate, exciting, real love because I was trying to match up with the notion in my head of a composed and perfect duchess. After I spent precious time with you, I discovered your passion for chocolate and for life to be positively contagious."

She did not want to cry, but blinking caused the tears to fall. Wresting one hand free, Amity brushed them aside before biting her lower lip to stop more from coming.

"I want to eat in public houses and window shop," Henry added, taking her hand again.

She laughed although it sounded more like a sob.

"But only if I can do those things with you," he continued.

She squeezed his hands in return. Then, at last, he asked her, "Will you do me the honor of becoming my duchess?"

CHAPTER TWENTY-SEVEN

Without hesitation, Amity answered, "Yes, Your Grace. I certainly will."

He rose to his feet and enfolded her in his arms. When she looked up at him, he lowered his mouth to crush hers beneath his. The kiss was far too full of desire to be tender, but she didn't mind in the least, pressing close to him, her fingers grasping at his broad shoulders. *He was hers!*

Against her mouth, Henry said, "Thank you."

When he drew back, he added, "And will you stop calling me 'Your Grace.' It sounds like a condemnation every time you say it. My name is Henry Westbrook."

"I know," Amity said, thinking she might be floating for she couldn't feel the floor. "It is very nice to meet you, Henry."

His dimples appeared. "I'm so damned relieved. I couldn't face another day without you as mine."

Amity placed a palm on either side of his face. "I feel the same way."

After another moment, he drew back so they could look into each other's eyes.

"You haven't mentioned chocolate once, and I'm almost fearful of mentioning it now." His hands were tight upon her waist as if he thought she might pull away and change her mind.

"I know chocolate-making is not the proper pastime for a duchess," she told him, feeling him grasp her even tighter as she said it.

"I agree it is not. At least, it never has been . . . until now." He shrugged. "Why not? Who is to gainsay you?"

"Besides you?" she asked, feeling herself start to tremble again, very glad he still held her.

"Yes, besides me," he said. "And, for my part, I say wholeheartedly you should continue. Moreover, you will find no one else has any business saying otherwise. Except the queen, I suppose, and I believe you've already said she adores your confectionery."

Amity was starting to believe she could do it all—be a duchess, a wife, someday a mother, *and* a chocolatier.

"The queen could order me to stop," she pointed out. "Her Majesty might say it is unseemly for a duchess. And the rest of the *haut ton* will have their say, mostly in the newspapers, I imagine."

"After our wedding, Mr. Giles shall burn every newspaper the instant it comes into our house," he teased.

Amity put a hand to his dear cheek. "Once I enter your world, I have a feeling there are more restrictions than I could imagine."

With one of his large hands now splayed against her back, he raised his other so he could stroke his thumb across her chin. She had the insane urge to catch it between her lips but refrained.

"There are rules and restrictions, to be sure," Henry agreed. "Nothing terrible, though, and, quite frankly, nothing that outweighs the freedom of having money and rank. The trick is not to let it go to one's head, but to use what you have to better the lives of others. I do my duty in Parliament, give alms to the poor, support various charities and workhouses, and sponsor an orphanage. I cannot say all my peers behave similarly, but I know many who are extraordinarily generous. Those are the people I count among my friends."

She stared at him. Amity had imagined being a duke was all parties and self-interested amusement and was gratified to hear he had social responsibilities. She would like to be a part of helping people who were less fortunate.

But making chocolate? First, she had to tell him what was in her heart.

"I love you, Henry, and that is more important than anything else. Even chocolate."

He clenched his jaw at her words and his eyes glistened with emotion. "I love you, Amity, and that is more important than anything else, too, even the decorum of a duchess. You shall make your chocolate," he paused, considering. "Perhaps we could give a percentage of the profits to some charity of your choosing. It would be the new Duchess of Pelham's patronage."

"I will make a special chocolate for that very purpose, and we'll donate them to the children to sample."

"I don't want to cause your parents or Rare Confectionery to go bankrupt," he said.

"We shall work it out. If we can create the *Brayson* and the *Pelham*, surely we can create—"

"The *Amity*," he finished.

"Maybe," she said, a little embarrassed at such a tribute.

"Definitely," he promised. "This party has officially changed from a proposal party to an engagement celebration. We'd best go tell everyone our good news. I believe we have about sixty guests and at least four hundred chocolates to consume. We mustn't keep them waiting any longer."

"The guests or the chocolates?" she teased.

"Both." Then he released her, tucked her arm under his and headed for the door. As he touched the handle, however, he groaned. "I need to kiss you again first."

And so, he did.

HENRY DIDN'T CARE ABOUT decorum or being ducal. He instructed his butler to place an engagement announcement in the papers the following day. During the previous evening's celebration with their friends and families, while eating delicious chocolates, he'd secured Amity and her parents' approval for a brief engagement.

Thus, the wedding date was set for a mere three months hence, in the romantic month of February during which Henry was assured of finding both the perfect St. Valentine's card for his beloved, as well as many heart-shaped chocolates.

True, the brevity of their engagement might raise eyebrows, especially among the nobility, but it still afforded plenty of time for the church banns to be read, for her extended family to arrive from France, and for gowns and such frilly female things to be created. Besides, he didn't think he could wait any longer than that to have Amity in his bed.

Further tossing convention aside, Henry spent as much time as he wanted with his fiancée and *her* family, and with his fiancée and *his* family, and, scandalously, with Amity alone.

"I am deliriously happy," he declared to her one evening when they were playing cards in front of the fire in the Rare-Foures' Baker Street parlor, a fully-festooned Christmas tree stationed between the front windows. Her parents were somewhere in the house, her sisters were out, and there was no pesky maid lurking anywhere. *Why?* Because he was an engaged duke and could do what he liked.

And also, because Amity's parents liked and trusted both him and their eldest daughter. Neither of them would do anything to break that trust . . . except, perhaps, for a few kisses.

"Let's sit closer," he suggested.

"What if my mother comes in?" she asked, but her expression said she was going to sit beside him anyway.

"If your mother comes in, we shall make room for her but not between us."

She giggled, the sweetest sound he'd ever heard. She rose from the winged chair on the other side of the card table. He stood, too, and they went to the sofa. At the last second, he pulled her onto his lap.

"Much better!" he said.

Amity lifted her arms and to his surprise, sank her fingers into his hair.

"*Mm,*" she murmured, "such soft silky hair."

"No fair," he said. "I cannot do that to you without that infernally complicated hairstyle coming all undone. If you were seen in such disarray, we would have to hightail it to Gretna Green by morning."

She giggled again. "Kiss me."

"That was my intent. Is this how it will be after we're married, with you messing up my coiffure—which my valet will not be pleased about, by the way—and giving me orders as if I were a servant."

"Probably." She sent him a lopsided grin, and his heart squeezed with love.

"Perfect," he said.

Framing her beloved face with his hands, he kissed her. As her warm lips opened under his, he felt a sense of bliss he'd never experienced in his life. Teasing her tongue, he nibbled her lower lip before he finally pulled away.

"What is that you're wearing?" she asked unexpectedly.

He frowned. "A very fine cotton shirt. Laundered, starched, and pressed. And the best tailored coat on Savile

Row. Why? Is there something amiss beyond the wrinkles you are making?"

"No," she said. "I meant your scent. It is . . . sensual and makes me tingle." Her cheeks turned pleasingly pink.

He grinned at her. "In that case, I shall bathe myself in it daily. It's Penhaligon's *Hammam Bouquet*, sold on Jermyn Street, within walking distance of my home, which is a matter of great convenience. I can send my valet without even having to bother the coachman."

"When I smell it, I want to rub myself against you," Amity confessed and she did, first her cheek against his lapel, and then, moving higher and tugging his cravat aside, she stroked his neck with her nose.

"You will be a very sensual duchess," he said, thinking if she wriggled on his lap much more, he might disgrace himself.

"I am already a sensual chocolatier," Amity reminded him. "Speaking of which, I brought you an engagement present. It cannot match the magnificence of this," she pointed out, holding up her left hand where a large emerald twinkled in its setting of diamonds and gold, "but I think you will enjoy it."

"Is it chocolate?" he asked, as she climbed off his lap.

"Naturally."

He had, in fact, noticed a tin upon the sideboard when he'd arrived hours earlier for dinner. She fetched it and sat beside him on the couch, her face looking wistful.

"I cannot believe this will no longer be my home. What if I get lost in the many rooms of your house at St. James's Place?"

He chuckled. "Our house, and Mother says you may decorate as you wish. She has secured a smaller townhouse two streets away."

Amity froze and blinked at him. "Oh dear! I hate to be the cause of her moving out. You know she is welcome to stay with us forever."

He shrugged. "It is the way of things. I already told her you would feel that way, but she is content. More than that. I believe she's looking forward to setting up a new home that doesn't have the ghost of my father lingering about."

"Understandable," his sensible fiancée said. Then she turned to face him, tucking her legs up under her on the sofa in a most comfortable way, and presented him with the tin. "Open it, Your Grace."

"Stop calling me that."

"Yes, my lord duke."

He couldn't help laughing as he opened the tin. What he saw made his laughter stop, and all at once, his eyes teared up. After a moment, he managed to swallow the lump in his throat.

"You are an absolute sweetheart," he whispered, lifting out a stag-shaped confection. Memories of his father flooded his mind, the best times when they were out hunting together or playing chess or talking about nothing important at all.

"Your mother was right," he said, "about your talent for choosing exactly the right gift."

He watched his bride's eyes sparkle delightfully.

"Now taste," she insisted softly.

Biting into the chocolate, he had to close his eyes as the sweet deliciousness burst upon his tongue, mirroring the new-found sweetness of his life.

"What do you taste?" Amity asked, sounding breathless.

He opened his eyes and looked into her glorious, brown gaze. "I taste love," Henry said. "Pure and lasting love."

EPILOGUE

Birmingham, England, 1878

Henry glanced out of the window as their train left the Birmingham station, taking a last look at the bustling city of factories with its thousands upon thousands of workers.

"The Cadbury brothers are most impressive, don't you think?" Amity asked him, wresting his attention from the smoke stacks and gray buildings. They had just come from George and Richard Cadbury's chocolate factory on Bridge Street in the center of the city.

He looked at his lovely wife of two weeks, wearing her plum-colored traveling clothes. "I think *you* are most impressive."

Her cheeks turned pink, and he leaned forward to kiss her, thrilled when she leaned forward to meet him halfway. His heart thumped as their mouths touched, reminding him of the glorious night of lovemaking just passed as exquisitely as each night since their wedding day, and with the promise of many more to come. He was the luckiest man alive.

When they finally sat back, Amity's sparkling eyes calmed to their usual thoughtful brown gaze.

"Be serious, Henry," she said, although he knew she loved kissing as much as he did. "Imagine how they brought that chocolate business back from the brink of bankruptcy by sheer willpower. Their factory was so clean and . . . happy."

"I'm not sure about the factory, but the workers, all in their tidy aprons, certainly seemed happy."

"The Cadburys give them breakfast if they get there early enough. I don't know many factory owners who would do the same. And now, they are scouting for an entirely new location, somewhere in the country. Mr. Cadbury, the younger one, said they plan to build not only a modern factory but homes for their workers, too. And they're planning on a park and recreational areas for their employees and for the employee's children. It will be an entire town built solely to make sweets. How incredible!"

Henry was equally impressed. "Mr. Cadbury, the older brother, told me they're touring someplace tomorrow that has great potential, about four miles south, near a stream called the Bourn."

Amity opened the bag on the seat beside her, almost absentmindedly, and took out a bar of Cadbury chocolate, tore open the wrapper, broke off a piece, and handed it to him. His wife never tired of eating chocolate, which he found a joy in itself, watching the way she savored every bite.

"Onward to Bristol," Amity said enthusiastically, and he leaned forward to wipe a crumb of chocolate from her pretty lower lip. They were heading to the famed chocolate factory of the Fry family, larger and even more successful than the Cadbury's.

"It's a wonder you didn't want to go all the way up to York and visit the Rowntrees," he teased.

"Another time," she said, entirely serious. He'd learned how she loved to shake hands with the manufacturers and let them know how much she admired them. "That is, if you are amenable, but I am eager to get to the Continent directly after Bristol."

"I cannot wait to stroll the streets of Paris with you," he agreed. A few months back, he'd been facing a life of uncertainty and quite possibly a loveless marriage. Instead, by some miracle, he'd met the sweetest, smartest, warmest, most loving female he could ever have hoped for. In his arms, his bride became a passionate goddess, and to the rest of the world, she was a premier chocolatier.

Giving him her charming lopsided smile, she squirmed in her seat. "I feel positively giddy. We're taking a boat from Bournemouth to France," she declared, breaking off another piece of chocolate.

"Yes, I know." He watched her devour it. It had been fun to arrange the details of their trip together.

"I've never crossed the Channel anywhere except the Dover to Calais route," she added.

"Yes, I know that, too, my love." He grinned at her bubbling enthusiasm.

"I suppose you also know how much I love traveling, especially by train. And by boat. And by coach, even."

Henry absolutely adored her intrepid, adventurous spirit. She would go anywhere with him, whether a day trip to the Royal Botanical Gardens at Kew due west of London, which they'd already done with great amusement, or a long weekend trip to his country estate in Kent, near Canterbury. They'd taken her parents and sisters before their February wedding so all the Rare-Foures could visit Chilham Castle, which already had its own room dedicated to confectionery.

And now, she was equally as excited to take a ferry. Plus, she could swim and had no fear of boats, which would have put a damper on his intentions to travel with her as often as they could, perhaps even to see America someday.

Upon their wedding trip, they were touring chocolate factories because it was one of her favorite things to do, and therefore, it was becoming one of his, as well. And when they got to the Continent, he was going to take her to some of his favorite coffeehouses because she had taken to loving coffee nearly as much as he did, especially when she stirred chocolate into it.

"We definitely should visit the Rowntrees sometime," she considered. "They are still rather small, but you never know what brilliant creation might be made in the most unlikely of places."

"Like the *Pelham*," he quipped, referring to the coffee-infused chocolate confection she'd made for him, "or our union."

"Just so," she agreed, shining her smile at him. "Anyway, I've heard they are very nice people, as the Fry's undoubtedly will be."

"I have been meaning to ask, and I hope this doesn't make me sound too terribly ignorant, but why are all these chocolate-makers Quakers? I would certainly never ask one of them in case I offend. Is making sweets a secret part of their beliefs?"

Her laughter was contagious, and even though he didn't know why they were laughing, he joined in. They amused each other no end, and Henry was certain he felt healthier each and every time they laughed heartily.

"To think," Amity said, sounding utterly amused, "that in their special Quaker *Christian and Brotherly Advices* guide, there would be a page about making confectionery right there next to their rules for austerity." She chuckled again.

He shrugged. "Then why?"

"I will tell you what I know. As to the Cadburys, they started as tea and coffee sellers because the Quakers do not hold with drinking alcohol. Thus, they created a booming business selling products they could consume themselves, which they also considered would promote good health and which wouldn't offend their beliefs about Christian living."

Looking pensive, Amity nodded to herself. "When they heard about the exotic cacao bean arriving in warehouses in

London, particularly its therapeutic claims, they decided to figure out how to sell it. And they certainly have."

She broke off another piece of chocolate and popped it into her mouth before handing him another chunk.

"Mm," she murmured, closing her eyes until she'd enjoyed every last morsel.

The sound of her satisfaction sent a lance of desire through him. If they'd been in the privacy of their own home, he would have taken her into his arms and shown her how much she meant to him. It was Henry's profound honor to make love to her, to worship her body, and to give her the greatest pleasure. Sadly, frustratingly, the train car, not even a sleeper carriage, didn't afford them the opportunity. He ate the chocolate as consolation.

Then her eyelids fluttered open, and her mahogany-colored gaze found his again.

"They've had so many varieties of cocoa, it would make your head spin," she continued as if she hadn't paused to eat chocolate. "But then, so have many others, including the Tukes, friends of the Rowntrees, from whom they bought their cocoa business. Everyone recognized the wholesome nourishment in a cup of chocolate or cocoa. Fry and Sons," she continued, warming to her subject, "is older than the Cadbury business, and the founder, Joseph, started serving his chocolate as a medicinal drink, very popular in nearby Bath."

He watched her tap her cheek thoughtfully. "As fashionable people took the waters in Bath, they also drank the chocolate of Mr. Fry. He found a better blend from another company, Churchman's, which didn't have the oily cocoa flakes Mr. Fry still had in his drink. He took over Churchman's and his superior method of making cocoa, some sort of water-powered machine to make finer powder."

"When was all this?" Henry asked, settling back into the plush seat of their train carriage, happy to listen to his wife while the scenery passed by.

"Oh, my," Amity said, "sometime in the early eighteenth century, I guess. Moving forward one hundred and thirty years, the Cadburys were able to ask fellow Quakers, the Frys, for help due to the close relationships of all of these families. Mr. Francis Fry, who still runs the business, helped Mr. George Cadbury to better his business by introducing him to other cocoa and chocolate manufacturers. I guess the answer to why there are so many successful chocolate-makers who are Quakers is because they are selling something they can believe in and because they help each other."

"Not only in confectionery, either," Henry told her. "Quakers own a multitude of our banks and our railroads, all because of their work ethic and honesty, and their absolute abhorrence to going into debt."

She sighed. "I am so very glad I live in a time when we don't have to drink chocolate that has been blended with coarse corn or even arrowroot." His wife gave a delicate shudder. "Or look into my cup and see greasy oiliness. We are blessed."

Without seeming to notice she was doing so, she broke off another piece and ate it, perfectly content.

AMITY HADN'T REALIZED SHE'D dozed off on the steam ferry until it bumped against the dock in Cherbourg, France. Her wonderful husband upon whose shoulder she leaned—*and had drooled, apparently*—looked down at her with love shining from his vivid green eyes. Wiping her damp cheek with the fingertips of her gloved hand, she knew she would never grow weary of looking into Henry's eyes.

He tucked her arm under his and escorted her off the boat and toward the waiting train to Caen. They would stop there on the way to Paris.

"Very pleasant crossing," she muttered, a little sorry she'd missed an hour or more of it in slumber. "At least the first part, before I drifted off to sleep. What terrible company I was."

"It was calm seas," he agreed. "And it was a joy to watch over you. Are you ready for more adventures, Duchess?"

A thrill shot through her every time he called her that. He knew it, too, which was why he kept saying it, only to watch for her reaction.

She smiled up at him. "I am positively, absolutely ready and entirely willing for adventure, Your Grace."

They'd been treated well in Bristol two days earlier, touring Fry's massive complex of four buildings, before being sent on their way with a bag of sweets, including the delicious flavored cream sticks coated in chocolate.

Upon reaching the southern coast of England, the Duke and Duchess of Pelham had spent the night in Bournemouth at The Royal Bath Hotel, which gaily opened on the queen's coronation day in 1838. Amity thought the hotel had held up well over the course of four decades, delighted by their suite of rooms.

"All this space for us!" she'd exclaimed after the maid and bellboy left them in a large living area off of which was an equally large bedroom, a separate bathing room and water-closet, and even a small tea table and chairs overlooking the sea.

Henry had merely shrugged. "You are nobility now, my love. You shall have to suffer through it and get used to such accommodations."

Amity assumed the regular rooms were just as nice since even the lobby and hallways had been tastefully decorated, and their dinner in the elegant dining room, surrounded by other happy guests, had been as good as either the Rare-Foures' or the Pelhams' cook could provide.

Because the hotel was perched upon Bath Hill, they'd had outstanding views across the bay. Nevertheless, upon the ferry, before she fell asleep, Amity realized she remembered little of her previous night's surroundings, recalling only the delight of being in Henry's strong arms. She had a feeling all sightseeing would forever pale in comparison to the euphoria she experienced with her husband.

Tomorrow, they planned to take the train to Paris after stopping that night in Caen. Henry was practically waltzing with glee when they boarded the train and found their seats in the luxurious carriage.

"I am so happy you are here with me," he crowed, and she sent a silent thank you to his mother and her mother for making their marriage possible. If the two wise women hadn't talked and pushed their offspring together, she and Henry might have continued under the dreadful notion they were not destined for one another.

As the steam train sped along toward Caen, Amity couldn't wait to get to their accommodations, to stretch out beside Henry in the promised feather-soft bed at L'Hotel Saint-Martin, and to show him how supremely happy she was, as well.

Afterward, despite having already endured a long day of travel, they would go to a coffeehouse. As she'd come to expect, Henry knew one in Caen he wished to share with her, and, as long as she was with him, she would willingly go to a thousand coffeehouses if it pleased him.

"A few months ago, you hardly cared for chocolate," she reminded him, "and I had barely tasted coffee, and not a drop of it good."

"You will taste the most splendid coffee in the course of this week," he promised.

"And you will taste the best chocolate," she vowed, as they intended to take a trip to Menier's factory in Noisiel, just east of Paris. She could hardly believe she was going back to one of her favorite places, this time with her husband.

"I can hardly wait until you taste the coffee in Paris," he said.

"I can hardly wait until you see Menier's factory," she returned.

They grinned at each other, both sputtering with excitement.

"I'm sure your Parisian coffeehouses will be a treat," Amity said, "but Menier's! Everyone around it calls the factory *la cathédrale* for its lofty beauty. And the technology! Monsieur Menier produces over twenty-five hundred tons of chocolate each year. The steam turbines that run the process are a modern marvel."

Henry nodded. "I look forward to seeing it although it's hard to believe it can be more impressive than the Fry company's four factories, eight stories each. This chocolate-making is a very serious business."

Amity considered. "That's the beauty of it. It is a large and profitable business, to be sure. Yet it is still chocolate, and so—"

"And so, there is also something whimsical about it."

"Precisely." Amity loved how well Henry understood what she meant.

"Just like my chocolatier," he added, then leaned toward her. He had done this many times on the train trip across the south of England, and each time, she'd felt the added thrill of kissing him in public.

She leaned toward him, and they kissed.

When he drew back, Amity nearly fell forward onto his lap, and he reached out to steady her just in time. He moved across the space between them to sit beside her so they could both face forward. As he took hold of her hand, Amity leaned against his shoulder.

"I cannot believe I nearly missed out on this life with you," she whispered against his ear. "This wedding trip may be a fantastical, extraordinary holiday, and nothing like how our real lives shall be, and we may not have faced any censure as yet—"

He placed a finger upon her mouth, hushing her.

"Please, Duchess, don't start borrowing trouble. Let's enjoy our first of many journeys, and then, we shall go home to London where you will return to the magical back room at Rare Confectionery, and I will return to Parliament. In the evenings, we will discuss each day over dinner and relish one another's company. And I will spend every night of our lives endeavoring to bring you the greatest bliss in our marital bed."

She gasped at him for voicing such a thing out loud—yet how she adored being the recipient of his skilled love making!

Then he added, "If anyone takes issue with your chocolate-making, I will deal with it."

"With your extremely potent dash-fire," she said, nibbling on his earlobe, feeling him shiver before he placed a warm, solid hand on top of her skirts, upon her thigh.

"Precisely," he said, and she noticed he'd closed his eyes, looking content.

"And we shall help the poor with profits from my chocolates," she added in a soothing voice, placing her own hand on his pantleg, freshly pressed by the hotel staff that morning.

"Definitely."

She bit her lip, then, in the same soft tone, said, "And we shall find good and caring husbands for my sisters."

"Yes," he said, sounding mesmerized. Then she felt him startle under her fingers. "Hold on a minute. What did I agree to do?"

However, Amity was already laughing too hard to hear anything else, and to her delight, after a moment, Henry joined in, making them the merriest couple on the train to Caen.

Finis

AUTHOR'S NOTE

Halfway through writing *The Duchess of Chocolate*, while still researching everything chocolate, including the Cadbury family, I found out that in 2002 at St. Mary's Church, Fairford, Gloucestershire, the 13th and 6th Duke of Argyll, Torquhil Ian Campbell, married Eleanor Cadbury. (You read that right—he's a *double* duke!) Eleanor is the great-great-granddaughter of George Cadbury, mentioned in this story along with his brother Richard, and the great-great-great-granddaughter of John Cadbury, the founder of the Cadbury chocolate company. Yes, that tickled me no end—a real-life chocolate duchess!

I learned so much while writing Amity's story, and there were many more chocolate facts I wish I could have worked into this book without it sounding like a treatise on making chocolate or the history of its rise to popularity. If you're interested, an informative, well-written book for chocolate enthusiasts, one which I found immensely helpful, is *Chocolate Wars: The 150-Year Rivalry Between the World's Greatest Chocolate Makers* by Deborah Cadbury (2010).

Also, along the way, I ate some outstanding confectionery (for research purposes, of course!) and drank many, many cups of hot chocolate, preferably dark, often stirring in a dash of coffee, sometimes blended with coconut milk. I hope you enjoyed reading *The Duchess of Chocolate*.

ABOUT THE AUTHOR

USA Today bestselling author Sydney Jane Baily writes historical romance set in Victorian England, late 19th-century America, the Middle Ages, the Georgian era, and the Regency period. She believes in happily-ever-after stories with engaging characters and attention to period detail.

Born and raised in California, she has traveled the world, spending a lot of exceedingly happy time in the U.K. where her extended family resides, eating fish and chips, drinking shandies, and snacking on Maltesers and Cadbury bars. Sydney currently lives in New England with her family—human, canine, and feline.

You can learn more about her books, read her blog, sign up for her newsletter (and get a free book), and contact her via her website at SydneyJaneBaily.com.

www.ingramcontent.com/pod-product-compliance
Lightning Source LLC
Chambersburg PA
CBHW060902190726
48286CB00002B/337